"Take a walk on the weird side."
—**Rob Thurman,** *New York Times* **bestselling author of** *Basilisk*

uncertain allies

"Incredible world-building. There are layers and layers of it, and the political wrangling is incredibly detailed and well thought out." —*Dangerous Romance*

"Outstanding entertainment." —*Romantic Times*

unperfect souls

"Peeling back layers in Del Franco's mystifying Weird series only whets the appetite for more." —*Romantic Times*

"What's not to like? . . . I thoroughly enjoyed reading *Unperfect Souls* and would recommend it to anyone who enjoys contemporary fantasy." —*Fantasy Literature*

"[A] hidden gem." —*Night Owl Reviews*

unfallen dead

"[A] fast-paced ride through the Weird side of town . . . Rob Thurman and John Levitt fans will want to check out this urban fantasy series." —*Monsters and Critics*

"Enthralling urban fantasy . . . Mark Del Franco provides a spectacular paranormal police procedural."
—*Alternative Worlds*

"One of the most compelling aspects of this first-person detective series is the evolutionary track taken by its damaged yet persistent hero . . . a gritty, compelling mystery. In the hands of a talent like Del Franco, murder, revenge, and attempted world conquest add up to urban fantasy at its best." —*Romantic Times*

continued . . .

"Connor is an engaging character with a real heart and a sense of humor that humanizes him to the reader. The world that he lives in is well constructed and easy to sink into. I also find it incredibly refreshing to read [about] a male protagonist when so much paranormal fiction is dominated by female protagonists. Del Franco has created the perfect hero for the modern age." —*BookFetish*

"Damaged druid Connor Grey is back in his third mystery, which ramps up the magical action considerably . . . lots of snarky characters to keep things fun." —*Locus*

unquiet dreams

"A tale filled with magic, mystery, and suspense . . . *Unquiet Dreams* is a well-written story with characters that will charm readers back for another visit to the Weird."
—*Darque Reviews*

"*Unquiet Dreams* is an urban fantasy wrapped around a police procedural, and that makes for a fast-paced, action-packed novel . . . a great new urban fantasy series."
—*SFRevu*

"A solid adventure filled with unique characters and plenty of fast-paced suspense." —*Pulp Fiction Reviews*

"It's back to the Weird for the second chapter in this striking first-person druid-detective series. Del Franco's clear and textured voice ensures that readers [invest] instantly in characters and story. Waiting for the next installment will be tough." —*Romantic Times*

"Readers who like a mystery as the prime plot of an outstanding fantasy (think of Dresden) will thoroughly be entertained and challenged by *Unquiet Dreams*. This is a great new series." —*Genre Go Round Reviews*

"Mark Del Franco is a master at combining modern fantasy with crime detective mystery. Fans of either genre are sure to find a good read in *Unquiet Dreams*." —*BookLoons*

unshapely things

"A richly detailed world . . . It will pull you along a corkscrew of twists and turns to a final cataclysmic battle that could literally remake the world."
—Rob Thurman, *New York Times* bestselling author of *Basilisk*

"An engaging urban fantasy . . . a bravura finale."
—SF Reviews.net

"[An] entertaining contemporary fantasy mystery with a hard-boiled druid detective . . . a promising start to a new series." —*Locus*

"Masterfully blends detective thriller with fantasy . . . a fast-paced thrill ride . . . Del Franco never pauses the action . . . and Connor Grey is a very likable protagonist. The twisting action and engaging lead make *Unshapely Things* hard to put down." —*BookLoons*

"The intriguing cast of characters keeps the readers involved with the mystery wrapped up in the fantasy . . . I look forward to spending more time with Connor in the future and learning more about him and his world."
—*Gumshoe*

"A wonderfully written, richly detailed, and complex fantasy novel with twists and turns that make it unputdownable . . . Mr. Del Franco's take on magic and paranormal elements is fresh and intriguing. Connor Grey's an appealing hero bound to delight fantasy and paranormal romance fans alike." —*The Romance Readers Connection*

"Compelling and fast-paced . . . The world-building is superb . . . Fans of urban fantasy should get a kick out of book one in this new series." —*Romantic Times*

"A very impressive start. The characters were engaging and believable, and the plot was intriguing. I found myself unable to put it down until I had devoured it completely, and I'm eagerly looking forward to the sequel." —*BookFetish*

Ace Books by Mark Del Franco

The Connor Grey Series

UNSHAPELY THINGS
UNQUIET DREAMS
UNFALLEN DEAD
UNPERFECT SOULS
UNCERTAIN ALLIES
UNDONE DEEDS

The Laura Blackstone Series

SKIN DEEP
FACE OFF

undone deeds

mark del franco

ACE BOOKS, NEW YORK

THE BERKLEY PUBLISHING GROUP
Published by the Penguin Group
Penguin Group (USA) Inc.
375 Hudson Street, New York, New York 10014, USA
Penguin Group (Canada), 90 Eglinton Avenue East, Suite 700, Toronto, Ontario M4P 2Y3, Canada
(a division of Pearson Penguin Canada Inc.)
Penguin Books Ltd., 80 Strand, London WC2R 0RL, England
Penguin Group Ireland, 25 St. Stephen's Green, Dublin 2, Ireland (a division of Penguin Books Ltd.)
Penguin Group (Australia), 250 Camberwell Road, Camberwell, Victoria 3124, Australia
(a division of Pearson Australia Group Pty. Ltd.)
Penguin Books India Pvt. Ltd., 11 Community Centre, Panchsheel Park, New Delhi—110 017, India
Penguin Group (NZ), 67 Apollo Drive, Rosedale, Auckland 0632, New Zealand
(a division of Pearson New Zealand Ltd.)
Penguin Books (South Africa) (Pty.) Ltd., 24 Sturdee Avenue, Rosebank, Johannesburg 2196,
South Africa

Penguin Books Ltd., Registered Offices: 80 Strand, London WC2R 0RL, England

This is a work of fiction. Names, characters, places, and incidents either are the product of the author's imagination or are used fictitiously, and any resemblance to actual persons, living or dead, business establishments, events, or locales is entirely coincidental. The publisher does not have any control over and does not assume any responsibility for author or third-party websites or their content.

UNDONE DEEDS

An Ace Book / published by arrangement with the author

PUBLISHING HISTORY
Ace mass-market edition / February 2012

Copyright © 2012 by Mark Del Franco.
Cover art by Craig White.
Cover design by Judith Lagerman.

ISBN: 978-1-937007-25-6

ACE
Ace Books are published by The Berkley Publishing Group,
a division of Penguin Group (USA) Inc.,
375 Hudson Street, New York, New York 10014.
ACE and the "A" design are trademarks of Penguin Group (USA) Inc.

PRINTED IN THE UNITED STATES OF AMERICA

10   9   8   7   6   5   4   3   2   1

For my mom

acknowledgments

Thanks as always to Anne Sowards, my editor, for her input and advice. Sara and Bob Schwager have been copy editors for the Connor Grey series from the beginning, and I am thankful for their knowledge (and recollection!) on each successive book.

My family members have always been among my biggest advocates, and I am deeply appreciative of their continued support.

Finally, a special thank-you to my partner, John Custy, without whom I would have stopped writing long ago.

Please note that a short section of "The Second Coming" by W. B. Yeats makes an uncredited appearance (for stylistic reasons) within the text. The poem, one of my favorites, has had a strong influence on the Connor Grey series—as has Yeats in general. Sharp-eyed readers will notice that the titles of the first two books in the series can be found in, respectively, Yeats's "The Rose in the Deeps of His Heart" and "The Stolen Child," and his ideas about gyres and geometry inspired much of the concept of Connor's world. You cannot go wrong reading his poetry.

1

Detective Lieutenant Leonard Murdock's car was parked out front, so I knew which building had the dead body in it. That was the way of the Weird, my little corner of Boston, where the fey went when they had nothing left. And when they had nothing left, they ended up dead, in a building without an intercom or an elevator or someone to stick around and talk to the police.

Leo and I went back a few years now. I often wondered if he regretted meeting me. I've caused him a lot of pain, none of it intentional, but painful nevertheless. I spent time trying to figure out how to make things up to him, but I worried I might never be able to. Despite that—and the past—we remained friends, and when Leo called asking for help, I showed up. I walked up the stairs that spiraled around the open atrium and led to the sixth floor. The air had the tang of bleach and turpentine and blood. No one opened his door as I passed, caution winning out over curiosity. No interest meant no involvement, and no involvement more often than not was the best course in the Weird.

The last door on the top-floor landing stood open, somber yellow sunlight cutting through the darkness of the apartment interior. I paused on the threshold, sensing Murdock's body signature and that of an elf. Murdock's signature was faint, a touch in the air from his passage. The elf's signature saturated the area, the gradual accumulation of essence from spending time in one place.

"Back here, Connor," Murdock called out.

He did stuff like that now, sensing things he couldn't see, like my presence in another room. When I met Leonard Murdock, he was a detective lieutenant with the Boston Police Department, and he was human. He was still a cop, but not quite human anymore. Recent events had unearthed secrets about his family—and me—that revealed that the Murdock siblings were half-druid, the children of a human father and druid mother. As his druidic abilities appeared, Murdock took them as a matter of course. He had a body shield, which was hardened essence, and increased strength, which was part of the genetics of a druid. As the spell that had hidden his abilities for years faded away, he seemed to be picking up a bit of a sensing ability. His wasn't a refined ability—even full druids didn't always have full use of their abilities—but Murdock was learning how to use what he had.

I moved through the spartan living room—a simple couch with two armchairs, all castoffs from some other time and place. In the corner was a kitchen setup, small studio-style appliances, a drain board with a single plate and mug. Like most living space in the Weird, it was interior decorating via street finds. A fine layer of dust covered everything else, not quite dirty, but untended.

Murdock didn't look up as I entered the bedroom, cool professionalism on his face, dark eyes hiding his thoughts. He wore his standard work outfit of khakis, pressed white shirt, and understated tie. With a small flashlight, he studied the items on the nightstand. He had an analytical mind that served him well in his job, yet he didn't use that same approach with his personal life. He didn't anguish about the day-to-day crud that came his way. That attitude was why we worked so well together. I couldn't stop thinking about crud.

The elf lay on the bed, a sheet pulled to the waist and exposing a naked torso. A quick read of his body signature told me he was the apartment's occupant. He was a man in prime physical condition, skin sculpted with muscle but riddled with old scars. His relaxed face gave the impression that he was asleep, as if oblivious to the black arrow embedded in his chest, a clean shot to the heart. Between the lack of odor and the evident body signature, he hadn't been dead that long.

"Looks like he died in his sleep," I said.

"They say that's the best way to go," Murdock said. With a gloved hand, he picked up a bottle and read the label.

"Where's your team?" I asked.

He replaced the bottle and flicked through scraps of paper. "On the way. Priority delays."

Priority delays were standard op these days. Everyone was short-staffed—the Boston police, the Guild, and the Consortium. Riots and terrorist attacks will do that to a city's administrative functions, and Boston had seen more than its share of both in the past few months. The most immediate cause was the destruction of the Boston Guildhouse, headquarters of the diplomatic arm of the Seelie Court, which ruled over the Celtic fairies. A number of Teutonic elves had died in the building collapse, which tied up personnel from the Teutonic Consortium, the Guild's counterpart and ruling body of the elven people. That left the Boston police to fend for itself, dealing with an anxious human population and not a few fringe elements taking advantage of the disarray. Hence, priority delays.

"Who called it in?" I asked.

"Street worker. She hadn't seen him in a while and wondered if he needed some of her expertise," he said.

"I didn't notice any street worker when I came in," I said.

"She'll call if she remembers anything," he said

"You let her go?"

He picked up a wallet. "Believe it or not, Connor, I have a few longtime sources down here I can trust."

That was a little bit of an ouch. Murdock and I started working together because I could provide a perspective on the fey in the Weird that a human cop might miss. Sometimes I forgot that didn't mean Murdock didn't know how to do his job. "Any signs of entry?" I asked.

"None. Door was unlocked when I arrived," he said.

I leaned over the body for a better look at the wound. Elves used arrows as their weapon of choice. Arrows were hard to trace unless someone was cocky enough to have them made custom. Another advantage was that they could be charged with essence and fired with precision, helpful when one's ability to control essence-fire wasn't fine.

"Notice anything funny about the body position?" Murdock asked.

The arrow in the victim stuck through the heart. A residual trace of essence on the arrow shimmered a faint emerald green. "Sheet's on top of him, so he wasn't standing with it wrapped around him. If the arrow had been elf-shot, it would have packed a punch when it hit. His body wouldn't be this composed. He would have gone flying and not landed comfortably laid out on his bed."

Murdock squatted at the opposite side of the bed to bring his line of sight level with the victim's chest. He lifted the body on one side, then let it fall back. "Arrow goes through into the mattress. He must have been sleeping. He was stabbed, not shot. "

I pointed at the area around the entry wound. "There's another telltale right here. Elf-shot forms with a bowfront of essence around the arrowhead. When it lands, the essence hits first and makes a circular burn mark before the arrow pierces the target. This guy's got some burning, but it's too small. The victim was likely sleeping, stabbed, then hit with a burst of essence down the arrow shaft to make sure he was dead. Janey should be able to confirm with a pathway analysis."

Janey Likesmith was the fey specialist down at the Office of the City Medical Examiner. She was good at her job—great, in fact—though underappreciated. She was the lone fey forensics staff member in an agency that did not hold the fey in the highest esteem. The human staff resented taking care of jobs that the Guild or the Consortium should take, so they perceived fey cases as a drain on limited resources. Janey had helped solve more cases than most examiners, so they grudgingly gave her the space she needed.

"I'll make a note to see her later," Murdock said.

I checked under the bed. "Are you working a lot of cases together?"

He compressed his lips. "Yeah. Mostly routine."

When Murdock stood, I noticed that the windows behind him shimmered with security wards. Wards could be made in all shapes, sizes, and materials to perform pretty much any function. Pump something up with essence, add a little directional spell work, and you had a ward. Glass was a strong essence retardant, but it could still break. The fey—at least those with reason enough to be paranoid—created wards around property entry points. They reflected sight and sound, and even enhanced the properties of glass to prevent essence-fire.

I walked around the bed and examined the window casements. The wood was much newer than the rest of the framing, recently installed. It had been charged with essence to create a barrier shield. "I think our victim was a professional."

"Undercover?" Murdock asked.

I wandered back to the bedroom door. The living-room windows had wards, too. "The apartment's nondescript, not many personal effects, and the security wards on these windows are pretty sophisticated for someone who lives in the Weird."

"Consortium?" Murdock asked.

I pushed my lower lip out as I considered it. "It's a reasonable guess. The Consortium has as many spies down here as the Guild does. The guy could've been freelance, but it won't hurt to ask around."

I stared out the window. A few blocks away, another warehouse rose above its surroundings. A tall tower of wood-and-steel scaffolding stood on the roof, a nest of aged red air-raid sirens clustered together at the top. Murdock and I had found someone hanging from it not long ago. The victim had been someone who had played on too many sides of the game. In the end, no one was on his side.

Whoever the dead elf was, he thought he was doing the right thing for the right reason, even if it might have been for the money. That was the seduction of a life like his. People gave up much in the hope that they would contribute to something so much more. It didn't matter which side of the law they were doing it for, at least not at the end. In the end, they either gave up and walked away, or someone made the decision for them.

A squad car pulled up in the street below. Gerry Murdock got out of the driver's side. No love existed between me and Murdock's brother. He blamed me for the death of their father. I didn't kill the man, but through no intention of my own, the entire Murdock family had gotten messed up.

"Gerry's here. I'm not in the mood for him today. You mind if I skip out the back?" I asked.

Murdock's gaze swept the room. "Yeah, you might as well. The higher-ups are not going to be cutting any consulting checks to you anytime soon. Thanks for the favor."

I knew my consulting days were over. Ever since I lost my abilities, I had been surviving on disability checks from the Guild and the occasional consulting fee from the Boston P.D. The Guild had stopped paying me a few months earlier, and I didn't have the resources to force them to pay me. I figured it was just a matter of time before the police department dumped me, too. It was no surprise.

"Actually, I could use a favor myself. I'm meeting some people at the airport tomorrow and could use a ride," I said.

"Sure." He didn't look up. His tone wasn't enthusiastic. Murdock was having a hard time with my involvement in his life, too. The difference between him and his brothers was that he didn't routinely threaten to beat me up. As much as I would have loved to normalize things with him, dinner would have been asking too much.

A time existed not too long ago when I thought my life was getting back on track. I had given up trying to solve the problem of having no abilities. I had shed my desire to return to the Guild as a top investigator. I even had let go of the anger over the downward turn my life had taken. Yet, here I was again, without many friends or any means of support, with no clear path out of the situation.

"Do you ever feel like your life is going in circles, Leo?" I asked.

He chuckled. "All the time."

"I don't think I have many circles of hell left to go through," I said.

Murdock tilted his head. "You know what people forget about all those circles of hell? They're followed by the spheres of heaven."

I snorted. "And purgatory's in the middle. Heaven's a long way off."

Murdock shrugged. "Patience is a virtue, Connor. It all makes sense in the end."

2

Later that afternoon, I sat amid piles of books and dust deep underground in an old section of the Guildhouse subbasements. I had lost myself in an old book. Its thick, cracked-leather covers showed evidence of poor rebinding, and some of the ink had faded to indecipherable. The pages rubbed dry against my fingertips, as if pulling the oils from them. It might have been. Grimoires were not casual reading. They told histories and parables, but their true value was in the lessons. Manipulating essence was inherent to the fey, different species being proficient in different areas. Becoming a true practitioner required study and practice. Grimoires were the textbooks to the art and science of being fey.

The Boston Guildhouse was gone, destroyed in a terrorist attack by the Elven King. The surviving Guild staff were struggling to get back to business from buildings scattered across the city. They weren't keen about taking on new investigations at the moment.

Several stories above me, the ruins of the Guildhouse pressed down, a shattered heap of stone. Donor Elfenkonig, the Elven King, had destroyed the building by using a talisman known as the faith stone. He broke the bonds that held the building together with essence. I tried to stop him, tried to prevent the disaster, but failed. Donor was one of the most powerful fey in the world. I didn't have much of a chance against him and survived by fate or dumb luck. The building came down anyway. I had killed the Elven King in the process, though I'm not sure if I meant to.

The faith stone survived. The problem was that it was inside my head. A chunk of blue crystal the size of my fist had passed through my skull and embedded itself in my brain. How I survived and why it could happen had brought me to a tiny storeroom of old books that most people had forgotten existed.

It wasn't the first room like it I had been in. The worn, wooden table on thick, rounded legs teetered a fraction of an inch, enough to irritate me every time I leaned forward or shifted a pile of books. Stacks of bound parchment surrounded me in a narrow, vaulted alcove no larger than a monk's cell. Most of the stuff was crap, apocryphal writings on subjects people wished they knew about. Here and there, though, true writings were buried like diamonds in the rough. Or a faith stone in a thick head.

A door slammed off in the distance, followed by the sound of glass breaking, then louder swearing. I hurried into the hall. "Meryl?"

Something heavy slid against a gritty floor. "I'm fine . . . ish."

The hallway curved and dipped, one of the original tunnels beneath the Guildhouse that conformed to earthen energies. Between layers of protection spells and the original foundation, the archives had survived the destruction of the building above mostly intact. It was the not-intact sections that were a problem.

Meryl Dian stood over a fallen box, hands on her hips and annoyance on her face. She wore tight black jeans and old maroon high-top Docs. A dark red lace top set off her black hair as she glared down at the broken glass. "The buffer spell went down. I just lost about a grand worth of crystal inhibitors."

I slipped my arms around her and kissed the top of her head. "It's just stuff. You're working too hard."

She leaned into me, honeysuckle and clove. "Did you find anything today?"

"I've learned how to sicken a flock of sheep from the next town over. It'll come in handy if I ever get my abilities back and need revenge on a wool farmer," I said.

She craned her neck to look at me. "Let's get out of here. I'm hungry and annoyed."

I took her hand as we returned up the hallway. "Great. My two favorite moods of yours."

Meryl gave me a playful shove. "I've been working down here all by myself."

"No one said you had to keep the archives a secret. That was your choice. You have a staff," I said. With all the debris from the collapsed building, wrecking crews were still clearing the street above. The operation had become complicated by the residual essence interacting in the rubble. No one was worried about the basements yet, and Meryl had decided to keep her domain private for a while.

"Yeah, well, you wouldn't be able to move around down here if macGoren found out it was accessible," she said.

Ryan macGoren was Acting Guildmaster, a title he had by default since the actual Guildmaster, Manus ap Eagan, had gone into a coma. MacGoren and I didn't get along at all. I tried to warn him about the Elven King, but he had ignored me. When the Guildhouse fell, he looked like the fool that he was and didn't want me running around telling the truth of the matter.

"I wasn't complaining. You don't have to do all this work by yourself is all I meant. The city's been declared a national disaster area. No one's going to know if you knew the archives were accessible. You deserve a break. I'm a big boy. I can find what I need by myself."

She tugged at my jacket. "Are you saying you don't need me?"

I pulled her close. "You, my love, are hungry and arbitrary. What say I get some food in you?"

She laughed and pushed away. "Okay. Let's do Chinatown. It's about the only neighborhood left that hasn't been trashed."

An hour later, we were sitting on cheap metal chairs at a wobbly table for two. Meryl was digging into a bowl of pho as big as a tureen. "You're awfully slurpy," I said.

"You're supposed to slurp. It's a cultural thing," she said around a mouthful of noodles.

I picked at my tempura. "Yes, tell me more about your Chinese heritage."

"Vietnamese. County Clare," she said. I laughed. Meryl had a comeback for everything. "How's your research going?"

"Boring. I'm not finding anything in the construction files about the faith stone. I know there has to be something there. Eagan knew about the stone and never told anyone. I want to know why," I said.

Eagan had the stone built into the structure of the Guildhouse. Its power was obvious. What was less obvious was why Eagan didn't want it known where it was. I hoped the answer was somewhere in the archives, lost in years of neglect. For a century, Eagan had watched over the dwarf—now dead—who had given or sold him the stone. Meryl had found documents dating back decades that proved Eagan protected the guy. If those records existed, others had to.

"You can question his methods, but Manny always had good reasons," she said.

"Well, he better have had a good one. I've got a rock in my head," I said. At the moment of his death, Donor had lost control of the faith stone. In the resulting explosion, the stone tore through my head and into my mind.

Meryl squirted more hot sauce into her pho. "If it was a real rock, you'd be dead. It would have crushed your skull and smooshed your brain into pulp, although sometimes I do wonder."

"You told me Gillen Yor said it was the stone," I said. Gillen was my healer, my frustrated healer who had no idea how to help me. Meryl had been acting as go-between for us since people had a tendency to take a shot at me whenever I showed my face near any secure facilities.

"The stone is a metaphor for essence that has somehow become bonded to you. It's a stone, and it's not a stone," she said.

"Okay, that hurts my brain more than having the stone in there," I said.

Meryl produced a distinct snicker. It was cute when it was because she was amused. It was embarrassing when it was because she thought you had said something stupid. Sometimes it was hard to tell which was which. "That's what you get for abandoning your druidic training when you did. What we do, Grey, is not just manipulate essence. We interact with the Wheel of the World, and that's a much bigger deal. It's about faith and balance and fate as much as it is knocking someone on his ass with a bolt of essence. Whatever the faith stone is, it is also something tied to the Wheel of the World. That's power on a level we can't understand because it's starting to touch the ineffable, so we try to reduce it to a concept we do understand."

"Like a stone," I said.

"Precisely. The stone is a metaphor for an idea with a purpose wrapped in essence," she said.

"And the dark mass is the opposite," I said. The dark mass had been the bane of my existence for over three years. When I was working for the Guild, I had tried to capture a terrorist named Bergin Vize. I cornered him at a nuclear power plant north of the city. Something went wrong. I woke up weeks later in the hospital with my memory and my abilities gone, and Vize still on the loose. A dark mass had appeared in my brain, preventing me from manipulating essence. I went from being one of the most powerful druids to come along in a long time to a guy living on disability checks.

The dark mass in my head drained essence from anything it touched. When the faith stone hit me in the head, it achieved a coexistence with the darkness. They pulsed against each other in my mind—one hot pain, the other cold. The plus side to the whole thing was my body shield came back. I could form a full one again, thickened essence around my body that slowed physical objects and deflected essence-fire.

"Nothing can be in the World and not be in the World. The dark mass can't be devoid of essence and be in the World. The World, by definition, is essence," she said.

I smiled. "Teacher, teach thyself. It's no different than saying a stone can be a stone and not a stone at the same time."

She twisted her lips in thought. "I'm not buying it. The stone and the idea of faith are things that we can define. You're defining the dark mass as something that can't be defined."

"It has a definition, though. It's the Gap."

Meryl frowned with dismissiveness. "Don't forget who your source was for that idea, Grey. Brokke worked for the Elven King and protected Bergin Vize."

Brokke was a dwarf who had been a high-level advisor to Donor. He was also one of the most powerful seers in the world. The only thing he didn't see coming was his own death when the Guildhouse collapsed. I watched him die. As much as he frustrated me, I took no joy in his death.

He gave me somewhat of an answer to what the black mass in my head was. He called the darkness the Gap, an indescribable force that existed as nonexistence. It devoured the essence that made the World possible. It drained the life out of people. It had the potential to destroy the World, which meant I had that power. Brokke claimed I couldn't control it, that no one could. I didn't believe that—yet. While I lived, I believed I had a choice to let the darkness overwhelm me or to find a way to stop it.

"Brokke understood the darkness, Meryl. He told me he had been studying it for years. That's why I'm down in the archives. If Brokke found answers, I can find them, too."

"If he understood it, why didn't he lift a finger to stop Vize? He knew Vize has the darkness in him, too," she said.

"Just because he didn't understand it doesn't mean he was wrong. I can't dismiss him. I might not agree with his methods and motives, but Brokke told me more about the dark mass than anyone else did," I said.

"And you're still no closer to the answer," she said.

"So what am I supposed to do? Sit around with a dark mass and a stone in my head, and pretend they're not there?"

"Not acting is just as much of a choice as acting," she said. "Maybe you need to take a break. You're stressed. You're tired. You're the target of every law-enforcement agency in the city. Maybe doing nothing for a while is what you need. The dark mass hasn't killed you in over three years. The faith stone has been in there a few weeks. Enjoy not being dead for a while."

"Maybe you're right. If there's one thing I'm good at, it's doing nothing," I said.

She leaned across the table and patted my hand. "Sounds like someone needs some self-esteem sex."

I chuckled. "Yeah, and someone needs I'm-right-again sex."

She grinned with basil in her teeth. "Are we the perfect couple or what?"

3

The next morning, Murdock and I waited inside the doors of the international terminal at Logan Airport as armed security positioned themselves nearby. The plane from Ireland had landed over an hour earlier, and its passengers had not been processed through customs yet. More guards filled the concourse, and the baggage area had been closed to the public. Only people on an approved list had been let inside, and we had been ID-checked several times. With the number of high-level Guild staff and important members of the Seelie Court aboard the plane, the government was not taking any chances.

Before he died, Donor Elfenkonig had been going to great pains to blame the solitary fairies under the leadership of Eorla Elvendottir for the attack on the Boston Guildhouse. He had come to Boston in disguise in order to discredit Eorla. It worked, to an extent, but Eorla was a member of the elven royal house, and many people made no distinction between her and her deceased cousin, the king. The general public didn't know that Donor was dead.

High Queen Maeve fed the paranoia. Anything that made the elven fey look bad made her look good by comparison. The human government had been swayed by what they called credible threats against the Celts. If I knew the way Maeve operated, she had made the threats herself.

Murdock had taken to wearing a black tactical uniform when he was off duty. It intimidated the hell out of people, and they gave us a wide berth. He felt more like a bodyguard than a friend, but I wasn't going to complain if it kept someone from taking a shot at me.

In the roped-off area near the gate, various fey waited for their loved ones and friends to arrive. Body signatures jostled for my attention. I tamped down my sensing ability to ease the noise. Since the faith stone had lodged itself in my head, the pain from the black mass had diminished. It still wanted essence, but with the stone helping out, I didn't need to eat ibuprofen like candy anymore.

When I had lost my major abilities, my sensing ability had become more acute. At first, it was a confusing side effect, a curious piece of the puzzle of what had gone wrong with me. As the black mass had grown and changed inside me, the reason for the acute sensing became clear. The black mass wanted essence. That was how it worked. It absorbed essence from the world around it, around me, seeking out the most intense sources to drain. What had been a nice little investigative tool for me to use had become a means for the black mass to hunt.

The faith stone tempered the hunger of the mass. The stone produced incredible reserves of power, and the black mass fed off it instead of using my sensing ability to feed off others. The two mysteries had formed a kind of alliance, right next to my cerebellum.

Behind me, a strong druid body signature pressed against my sensing field even though I had dampened it. Once a druid met someone, that person's body signature became a recognizable feature, drawing attention like a familiar face in a crowd. There was no mistaking a signature I had known all my life.

"Hey, little bro," Callin said. My brother towered over me. He was a big man, like our father, built to brawl and not one to retreat. From the healing nicks and cuts on his face, he had been in one recently. Behind him lingered Clure—*the* Clure, actually—head of the Cluries clan and Callin's comrade in trouble. The faint odor of alcohol clung to both of them, a not-uncommon condition for either.

"Hey, guys. You remember Murdock," I said. Hands were shaken all around. Since his presence wasn't unexpected, Callin's arrival wasn't suspicious. His showing up on time did surprise me. It wasn't in Cal's nature. I doubted the Clure had anything to do with it either. The only time the Clure kept track of was happy hour.

Cal and I had a complicated history infused with competition, family loyalty, and anger. We had been close as children and into adulthood, but something always managed to drive us apart as we aged. When we were kids, my abilities manifested before his, which he resented. When we hit our twenties and both worked at the Guild, I was promoted faster. No matter what I said, Cal couldn't blunt his aggressive attitude. The more things failed for him, the more alcohol he consumed, with all the attendant fallout. He was drummed out of the Guild and lost friends. He became estranged from me and our parents.

An awkward silence descended as everyone took the opportunity to look elsewhere. Murdock knew about the friction that characterized my relationship with Callin and kept a diplomatic eye, scanning the crowd rather than starting a conversation. The Clure, though, couldn't care less. "Greetings, Connor. You've been missed in the finest swill halls the Weird has to offer."

Despite what I thought of his negative influence on my brother, I could not not like the Clure. With his infectious smile and mop of curly auburn hair, he had a way of making you feel like you were his best friend. "I've been a little distracted, Clure."

He grinned, a rakish slash of teeth that split his face in two. "Ah, distraction needs its own distraction betimes."

"If I remember correctly, all times are betimes around you, Clure," I said.

He chuckled, a warm, smooth sound of unapologetic self-awareness. Callin didn't react. Drinking—his, in particular—was a topic we avoided unless we were alone. Then, the conversation degenerated into argument. The moment was saved by the appearance of the first passengers coming down the escalator. The waiting crowd shifted in place, excited and attentive to the procession of tired people making their way into the baggage-claim area.

The first person I recognized was Keeva macNeve, my old partner at the Guild. I had almost killed her and jeopardized her unborn child when the dark mass had taken me over. She had been at Tara these last few months on bed rest for her pregnancy. Her skintight bodysuit revealed that she had had the baby, but I didn't see a child with her.

Cal whistled low under his breath. "Did you ever tap that, little bro'?"

"No, and I'm glad I didn't," I said.

He chuckled with that edge of derision that he knew got under my skin. "Yeah, there's the difference between you and me. I've never regretted getting laid."

Keeva was smart, hot-looking, and tough as nails. Too tough for my taste and with a side of arrogance I had never liked. That she ended up in a relationship with Ryan mac-Goren proved my point that we wouldn't have made a good couple.

I caught Keeva's eye, but she frowned and looked away. I guess she hadn't gotten over what I did to her even though I wasn't in my right mind at the time. "I don't see a baby. I hope that doesn't mean anything bad."

The Clure cleared his throat. "Not at all. She had a boy. Word is she fostered him out to relatives."

Fostering children out—even babies—was not unusual among the fey, especially among the ruling clans. Keeva was related to the High Queen's family. Not as close as she liked people to think, but enough to make her miserable to be around sometimes.

In the next wave of passengers, I spotted my father and was struck at how much Cal resembled him. They shared the same blunt features that marked them as strong men—the height, the muscle, the swagger—and the same easy smile that could vanish at a moment's notice. A space next him indicated the presence of my mother, shorter than average and lost in a crowd. As they neared the waiting area, I saw—and heard— her. My mother kept a running commentary at all times, and right then, the jingling of massive amounts of jewelry on her neck and arms added a musical accompaniment.

When a gap in the crowd opened and she saw us, her face lit with excitement. She pushed her way forward, leaving my father behind, and ran toward us with outstretched hands. "Callie! Connie!" she shouted, and grabbed me and Cal around the waists in a hug full of bosom and lavender.

She stepped back and rubbed each of us on the side of the face. "What have you boys been doing? Fighting? You've been fighting again, Cal. And, you! Look at you. You're too skinny, Connie."

Callin and I exchanged amused glances over her head, comrades for the moment. Our mother was, well, a mom. We received brief flashes of treatment as adults, but at the end of the day, she was convinced she should have never let us out of the house to fend for ourselves. "I missed you, too, Ma," I said.

My father hugged Callin with a back pat, then me. If I was with my brother, it was always in that order. I often wondered if it was a subtle signal to Callin that he always came first with our father. I didn't take offense. It was one of those things I noticed and could as easily mean my dad hugged in age order.

As I introduced Murdock, both my parents put on their professional smiles. I was sure they didn't know what to make of him, a police officer giving off a druid body signature and wearing an iron weapon.

We wrestled with their bags as my mother pointed out one after another. She pushed back her thick dark hair and cast an appraising eye at us. "Let's have the others sent on."

Murdock, weighed down with two shoulder bags and a suitcase, looked at me. "Others?"

"This is an awful lot of stuff, Mom. How long are you staying?" I asked.

My mother and father exchanged glances as we moved toward the exit. "The High Queen sent us home," she said.

I tried not to stumble. I loved my parents. I did. But I had gotten used to not making the obligatory weekly trips to visit since they had moved to Ireland over a decade ago to work for the Seelie Court. I didn't know everything going on in their lives. The converse was true, but that was for the best. "Is something wrong?"

We piled the suitcases on the curb next to a black car. "Of course, but she didn't say. She sent most of the court away. It's all very mysterious. Is this us? I thought we ordered a limo."

"I have a car," Murdock said.

She smiled up at Murdock. "That's so sweet of you. You can take those bags and meet us at the hotel." She cocked her head up at my father. "Where are we staying, dear?"

"The Bostonian," he said.

Murdock's eyes went a little wider as Callin helped the driver pack bags into the trunk. I covered my smirk by slipping a suitcase into the backseat. "We'll be right along behind you."

My mother hopped into the backseat of the black car. "We'll make room for you, Cal. The Clure can sit up front. See you at the hotel!" She waved as Callin squeezed in next to her and closed the door.

With a thin smile, my father lifted his head. "Got all that?" he asked.

I chuckled as he walked around to the other side of the car. "Got it."

The car pulled away. I turned to smile at Murdock. The bags still dangled from his shoulders. With a flick of the wrist, he flung one at me, and I caught it with a laugh. "I wasn't planning on chauffeuring you to a hotel," he said.

I picked up the lone bag on the curb and walked to

where Murdock had parked his car in the fire lane. "Oh, come on, Leo. It's not like you don't want to see more of this."

He popped the trunk, and we pushed the bags in among his extra police gear, the spare tire, a milk crate filled with cleaning bottles, a pile of books, balled-up blankets, and a closed trash bag I was not going to ask about. It was cleaner than his backseat. "Oh, I think I've seen enough to get the picture," he said.

"You ain't seen nothing yet," I said.

We got in the car, and he pulled into the exit lane. "Connie and Callie, huh?"

I glowered at him. "Oh, shut up."

He giggled.

4

Despite mild pleading and promises of embarrassing family dynamics, Murdock resisted coming into the hotel. He helped unload his car onto a luggage trolley, then slammed the trunk and waved. "I have an appointment."

"But you can eat all the olives in the minibar," I said.

He smirked. "Bribing a police officer will get you a jail cell."

I held out my hands, loosely together at the wrist. "Please?"

"Let me know if you get any leads on the dead elf," he said, and pulled away. I didn't mind. I loved my family, but having an independent ally around when we were all together would have been comforting. I pushed the trolley into the lobby, where a bellhop rushed to take it away from me.

The hotel suite had the hushed eloquence of money crossed with the generic style of hotel glamour. My parents weren't rich, but they were comfortable. My mother appeared from the bedroom. She had removed most of the jewelry from the plane. "Why were you wearing everything you own?" I asked.

She hugged me with a chuckle, then settled onto the couch while the Clure rummaged in the bar. "People run up to you in airports and cut the strap off your carry-on."

"Mother . . ." I said.

"They do! I read about it. I didn't want to take any chances. Your father"—she eyed him dramatically—"thinks I'm alarmist, but here I sit with all my belongings."

My father checked the view out the window. "Except for the diplomatic pouch with fifty thousand dollars you left in the coffee shop."

Callin choked on his drink. "What the hell are you doing with fifty thousand dollars in cash?"

"Your mother was afraid the banks would fail while we were in flight," my father said.

Callin stared at me, another one of our comrade moments, united in the baffling things our parents did. "Please tell me you have the pouch," he said.

My mother tilted her head in thought. "Grey, you had the pouch last. Remember, I told you to tip the porter?" She used a pet name for my father in conversation, but when she used a name, it was Grey.

"You said give him the pouch," he said.

My mother gasped in horror. "I said pound! Give him the pound! You had that change in your hand," she said. When Callin groaned, my mother shot me an impish smile. She was not above playing on her son's perception of her as crazy. She slapped Callin's knee and laughed. Chagrined, he dropped his head back as he realized he had fallen for her act.

My mother and Cal worked like that, joking, chastising, teasing. They connected on a comfort level I never had with her. My parents were always my parents, loved and loving. I knew I could rely on them to fulfill certain needs, sometimes needs I didn't know I had, but our relationships always remained child to parent. We weren't friends in the sense that some parents became friends to their adult children, like Cal and my mother were. I didn't resent it. It was who we were to each other.

Cal didn't have the same relationship with our father that I had, and sometimes I wondered if he felt like I did about him and my mother. Thomas Grey was a man of few words and formidable intellect, someone whom I enjoyed, in the strictest sense of the word, spending an evening with debating politics or history or anything. He absorbed the happenings around him, picking up nuances, making connections that others failed to see. Even then, as Cal and my mother talked, I knew by the tilt of his head he was listening to every word even if he wasn't cracking a smile. If Cal and my mother were friends of personality, my father and I were friends of the mind.

A burst of pink essence heralded the inevitable appearance of Joe to the gathering. He whooped as he circled the room, then plunged to my mother, wrapping his arms and legs around her neck. "Momma Grey!"

My mother took the assault with good nature. She and Joe were a mutual admiration society that served two members. "I was worried you had forgotten about me, dear."

Joe reared back, mugging. "You? Forget you? Why I'd sooner forget to dress in the morning."

My father gave a tired sigh. "Apparently, he did."

Joe never wore more than his loincloth, and even that was a courtesy to nonflit sensibilities. "At least you don't have to deal with his snoring," I said.

My father tilted his head toward me. "And you haven't seen the two of them in the garden after a few drinks."

My mother hopped off the couch, tugging Cal's hand. "Come see what I brought you," she said. Cal let her lead him away. The Clure followed, throwing us an amused smile as they disappeared into the bedroom.

I poured my father a glass of whiskey and joined him by the window. The hotel overlooked Faneuil Hall and Quincy Market. The two buildings had always been major components of Boston commercial businesses, from a sheep auction house to today's restaurants and shops. "She seems in fine form."

He didn't answer right away, caught by some activity in the

street below. An elf in Consortium livery was standing in the plaza. He had a falcon on his hand. "She's had a difficult year."

I hadn't heard about anything wrong from them in the few phone conversations we had had. "What happened?"

He pursed his lips. "No matter how I answer that, it will hurt your feelings."

"Me?"

He smiled into his glass as he sipped. "See?"

I clenched my jaw. "What has Maeve done?"

"Nothing overt, per se. We are members of the Seelie Court, Con. You know that the winds of preference are fickle. You saw what happened to you when the Guild kicked you out. This last year, a chill spread, invitations declined or not offered, whispers behind closed doors, ranks closed. The Seelie Court is all about privilege. I've shielded your mother from the more vile things, but she's no fool. Her receiving room has been quite empty of late, and now we are banished."

The elf removed the bird's hood and released it. The falcon wheeled above an appreciative crowd, swooping back down to the elf's proffered glove.

I gripped my glass to keep from trembling. I had issues with the Guild and the Seelie Court. I had been vocal with my opinions about High Queen Maeve. I stood by everything I had said and done, but, dammit, this was my mom. She had done nothing to deserve being dragged into Maeve's manipulations. "I'm sorry," I said.

My father glanced at my reflection in the window. "You have nothing to be sorry for. Regula's a big girl. No one goes to Court thinking it's all fun and dances. She has never once blamed you. No matter what, you are our son."

"I'm still sorry. If I can figure out a way to get Maeve off my back, I will. I hope she pays for all the damage she's created," I said.

My father finished off his drink. "There are no angels wearing crowns, son. Donor's hands are no cleaner."

"Were," I said.

He narrowed his eyes at me. "Then the rumor is true? The Elven King is dead?"

I nodded. "I tried to stop him from destroying the Guild-house. It would be nice to say I didn't mean to kill him, but I kinda threw a spear at him."

I tried to make light of it, but my father didn't laugh. "I don't know what you faced that day. There is a difference between murder and causing death, and the line between them can be difficult. All deaths have ramifications. All births do, too. It makes me sad that you have to live with that."

My father had killed people. He didn't talk about it often, but he had been a Guild agent himself once upon a time. Pressure bore down on my chest. I had caused the death of another living thing. I had also murdered in my life. Those things could not be waved away as learning experiences, despite what I had learned. The best thing I could do—had been trying to do for years now—was make amends for it. Some people believed that there was no way to atone for the taking of a life. I didn't know if that was true, but I also didn't know it wasn't. Until I did know either way, I was going to do the best I could to achieve forgiveness, if only from myself.

"I hope I stopped him from doing worse than he did," I said.

"We all do," he said.

A crow wheeled against the sallow light of the city night sky. It landed on the weather vane of Faneuil, a giant gold-leafed grasshopper. The bird hunched forward and made a jerking motion with its beak. The thick glass made it impossible to tell if it had called to its fellows for the night, but no others joined it. Instead, the elf's falcon swept up and knocked the crow from its perch. My father gestured with his glass. "Did you see that?"

The falcon settled on the vane while the crow wheeled around it. Below, the elf raised his glove, but the falcon remained perched, indifferent to the call of its falconer. The crow dove, and the falcon leaped to meet it. They rose higher in the sky, diving and dodging until we couldn't see them.

A laugh from the other room drew my attention away.

5

On my way back to the Tangle later in the afternoon, Murdock's reminder about the elf murder prompted me to stop at the Rowes Wharf Hotel. The place had seen better days. Once one of the city's most luxurious hotels, in a few short months, it had become a battered shadow of its former glory. Eorla Elvendottir had taken over the building as the headquarters for her renegade court. Some people called her the Queen of the Unseelie Court because she opposed both High Queen Maeve and Donor Elfenkonig. I liked to call her friend.

I picked my way through the mess in front of the building. Sandbags and sawhorses lined the sidewalk and blocked the street. Every floor had chunks of masonry missing. The fallen brick and cement was piled into hills around the front entrance.

The day the Guildhouse fell, Donor had staged an attack against Eorla. He had wanted to make it seem like she was attacking the Guild, and he had been helping defend it. The ruse worked for the most part. The human government had sent in the National Guard. Together with the Consortium, they had pounded the hotel with elf-shot and mortar fire. Eorla held them off, but the building looked like it belonged in the Weird now instead of the financial district.

Consortium agents across the street took occasional shots at the building. They were careful not to hit anyone but tried to provoke an armed response. Eorla's people restrained themselves. They knew the Consortium was looking for a legitimate excuse to move on them in force. Guards surrounded me as soon as I neared the entrance. My presence tended to invite notice. As if on cue, three or four arrows landed in the masonry over my head, raining dust down on us. Our body shields kept most of it off, but I wasn't going to pretend getting shot at wasn't unnerving.

The lobby of the hotel was a marked contrast to the street. The level of tension dropped as people went about their business regardless of the barricades out front. Despite filling her ranks with a local mix of other estranged Celtic and Teutonic fey, Eorla still ran her business with an elven efficiency.

My escorts took me to the crowded ballroom where Eorla met with administrators and the public. She worked the volume of paperwork on her desk table like an orchestra, noting my entrance with a brief flick of her dark eyes. Her black hair coiled about the back of her head, accentuating her long neck and narrow face. She still wore mourning green for her husband, who had been murdered last year.

To her right, Rand acknowledged me with a nod. He rarely left her side, acting as both bodyguard and confidante. It wouldn't have surprised me if he slept in his red uniform. Despite his formal manner and unreadable elven face, he had let me see flashes of the person inside him. He seemed like a good guy.

After a few moments, Eorla dismissed the other people in the room with a firm gesture to the guards. They ushered everyone out and closed the three of us behind the doors. Eorla stood, took my hands, and kissed my cheek. "You look well."

"I avoided getting shot on the way in," I said.

She gazed up at me. "Ah, you arrived through the front door, then. My apologies for the sniper fire. I do hope someone held the door for you."

I chuckled. "Several, in fact. You treat me too well."

"And how might I treat you today?" she asked.

I pulled out a small snapshot of the dead elf. Murdock had sent it to me with a short note that the apartment had been devoid of any evidence. As expected, his identity didn't match anything in the usual databases. In fact, the victim didn't have any legal history at all, which reinforced my belief that he was a spy. "I'm helping Murdock with another murder. We think the victim might have been an undercover Consortium agent, and I was wondering if you might know him."

Eorla examined the photo. "He does have the look of one of Donor's people, but I don't recognize him." She handed the photograph to Rand. "How did he die?"

"Elf-shot execution-style in his apartment. No disturbances," I said.

Rand narrowed his gaze at the photograph, then arched an eyebrow. "His name was Alfen. He was one of Vize's followers."

Bergin Vize had been a renegade Consortium agent. He had turned terrorist, causing hundreds of deaths, all in the name of returning the fey folk to Faerie. Publicly, the Elven King had repudiated him. Privately, he used Vize to further his own ends and the acquisition of power. Donor might have destroyed the Guildhouse with his own abilities, but Vize had set the whole thing in motion. In the end, Donor discarded him like a tool no longer needed. I watched Vize fall into the collapsing building, his body lost beneath the rubble of the Guildhouse. His followers remained, though, scattered throughout the city.

"The Consortium had spies in Vize's group?" I asked.

"Alfen wasn't a spy for the Consortium. He joined Vize after the Consortium discovered he was a double agent for the Guild," Rand said.

Eorla returned to her desk. "It sounds like this gentleman had issues with loyalty."

"He was a Guild agent?" I asked.

Rand shook his head. "'Agent' is too strong a word. He was an informant for them."

I cocked an eyebrow at him. "And you know this how?"

He hesitated before speaking, glancing at Eorla. "At one time, it was my duty to investigate the loyalty of Her Majesty's officers. The Guild worked to undermine her support."

I snorted. Despite her philanthropic work, Eorla had always been a target of the Guild. Her royal bloodline and elevated diplomatic profile made her motives suspect to Maeve. It came as no surprise that the Guild had tried to place spies on her staff. Back in my early days in New York, my old partner Dylan and I had done our duty and turned our fair share of elven agents. Dylan had been particularly good at it. I learned a lot from him, which was why I had picked up on the dead elf's circumstances.

"Is it asking too much to know who his handler was?" I asked.

Rand shrugged. "That I don't know. I knew Alfren from the old days. He came to Boston because the Guild offered refuge and relocation. Once he left Germany, he wasn't a priority."

Eorla had watched our exchange with quiet interest. "Rand, did you ever use this man for information about Bergin?"

Eorla had raised Bergin Vize, and his descent into terrorism pained her. Vize had tried to leverage her personal feelings for him to gain protection, but she declined, which also pained her. She knew I had wanted Vize captured. While I wasn't sorry he was dead, I had forgotten that she must be feeling differently.

"Never. I kept tabs on a few of Vize's people, but I would have informed you immediately if it became necessary," Rand said, fast and to the point. I liked his "if necessary" caveat, the age-old plausible-deniability defense all heads of state enjoyed. Basically, he was saying he didn't but maybe he did. I didn't care. It didn't matter to me. I wanted to help Murdock out, nothing more.

"I didn't mean for the conversation to go in this direction," I said.

Eorla nodded slowly. "They have not recovered Bergin's body yet. A part of me holds out hope that he escaped death. Even though I know he would continue on his chosen path, I still wish him alive."

"You don't need to apologize for loving him," I said. I startled myself by saying it. I hated Vize. I hoped he had died an excruciating death. Eorla, on the other hand, I cared about. While I didn't share her feelings, I did understand them.

Her eyes glistened, but she didn't cry. I took it as a compliment that this woman—one of the most powerful in the world—felt comfortable showing her vulnerability in front of me. She took a deep breath and moved some papers on her desk. "Have you spoken with Bastian?"

I grunted in amusement. "No. Chatting up the Consortium is not in my best interest at the moment."

She leaned back in her chair. "Bastian is not one to let his pups stray too far even when they've misbehaved. If Rand recognizes this man, Bastian will."

"I'd call him, but there's the little matter of accusing me of killing Aldred Core," I said.

When Donor came to Boston, he disguised himself as his own ambassador. When he died in the Guildhouse collapse, the Consortium was left with several conundrums. It would have to admit not only that the Elven King deceived the Seelie Court and human government by posing as Aldred Core, but that he was dead. The deception would jeopardize every agreement the humans had made with the Teutonic fey. A dead Elven King was even more problematic. Donor had no children, so claimants to his throne would materialize. All of this happening at a delicate point in Celtic and Teutonic relations.

"Yes, well, I have issues with that as well," Eorla said.

I gave her a sharp, confused look. Donor and Eorla had not gotten along. Donor's father stole the crown from Eorla's father. "Not that I don't regret killing someone, but what have I done that you take issue with?"

"Not you. Bastian. He's running the Consortium after the mess that Donor created. He can't do that for long without my support. You don't need to go to him. I can bring him here," she said.

"You do know how to turn the screws," I said.

She grinned. "In this case, Bastian screwed himself."

I don't know what was funnier, what she said or the look of shock on Rand's face.

6

My first surprise the next morning was a frantic call from Murdock, surprise because "frantic" was never a word I associated with Leo. His youngest brother, Kevin, had not shown up at the fire station for his shift, and when Leo checked on him, he was in bed nonresponsive. Leo recognized that whatever was going on with his brother was fey-related, and given his family's less-than-keen approval of the fey, he didn't want to call Avalon Memorial unless he had to.

The second surprise was that he had also called Briallen ab Gwyll. Briallen was one of the foremost fey healers in the world. She was my old mentor and now friend. She had helped both Leo and me on occasion. I took it as a personal compliment that he no longer had reservations about fey healers.

The Murdock home on K Street reminded me of the house I grew up in. Like Leo, I was raised in South Boston. My druid heritage allowed us to look the same age, but I had an easy ten years on him and those years made a difference. When I was a teenager in Southie, it had been the tight-knit community it was still famous for, but back in the day, such closeness was necessary for survival. Boston hadn't always been friendly to the fey, but Southie, with its deep Irish roots, had always included us. As the world grew smaller, divisions that had been tolerated or overlooked became barriers. As time went on, Southie became more insular, less welcoming of the fey, while the rest of Boston opened its arms.

I lingered behind Briallen on the front walk as she rang the bell. I hadn't been in the Murdock house since their father died. I wasn't welcome. "Maybe I should wait in the car."

"Leonard said no one else is home but his sister," she said.

Faith Murdock opened the door. She wore her state police officer uniform. A few months ago, I would have bantered with her, asked if she was coming on or going off shift, whether she was dating. Now, circumstances prevented normal socializing. She glanced at me with professional detachment, a nice change of pace for one of the family, then nodded toward the stairs. "Second floor."

She stepped back to let us pass, a hand on her right hip, a convenient stance that projected a relaxed yet mildly intimidating manner. It meant her hand wasn't too far from her gun. I nodded hello without smiling. I didn't want to push any more buttons than my presence already did.

Leo appeared at the door to one of the bedrooms as we reached the top of the stairs. "He won't wake up."

Briallen entered, but I lingered in the hall. The back bedrooms at the end of the stairwell of Boston town houses were long and narrow, the smallest rooms in the house. The décor in Kevin's room reflected someone whose youth was visible in the rearview mirror—a wrestling poster half-hidden by a woman I vaguely recognized as an actress, Red Sox paraphernalia like any good Boston boy, and a toy ladder truck displayed on a shelf.

Kevin lay on his back on a bed pushed into the corner.

His body shield was active, a thick sheath of gold-tinged bronze. The whiff of essence was in the air, the charged scent of ozone. The Murdock siblings were half-druid, but Kevin had inherited enough ability that he registered as a full druid. I had warned Leo that all his siblings would need training to control their abilities. If they didn't want to use them, that was fine, but they had to learn how to prevent them from activating spontaneously. Abilities reacted to the user's emotions as much as the will, and all the Murdocks could use a little anger management.

"I tried shaking him, but all that did was move the shield a bit. I yelled at him, too, but he won't wake up," Leo said.

Briallen leaned over Kevin, unable to touch him through the shield. She caressed the air over him, her face and hands glowing with faint essence as she examined him. "He's fine, Leonard. No need to worry. He's been playing with his abilities."

"What do you mean?" Leo asked.

Briallen straightened. "He's sleeping it off. Our bodies are stronger than humans; but we're not invincible. He's burned out and needs sleep to recharge himself. He'll be fine when he wakes up."

I tried not to smile too much. "Druid teenagers do this all the time, Leo. They find out they can use essence, and they exhaust themselves playing around with it."

"I didn't," he said.

I nodded toward Kevin. "You're, what, almost fifteen years older than him? Kevin's still a kid in druid terms. And do I have to remind you of someone who liked to run into walls for the hell of it when he discovered it didn't hurt him?"

Leo ducked his head, an embarrassed flush coming to his cheeks. "Okay, I get it. You're sure he's okay?"

Briallen patted Leo on the shoulder. "Positive. What I don't like is his using abilities without supervision. There's a reason druids have formal training. This isn't stuff to fool around with."

The relief on Murdock's face slipped away at the sound

of a door's slamming downstairs. Loud voices carried up the stairwell. "Let's continue this conversation later," Murdock said.

Gerry Murdock stomped onto the landing, anger suffusing his face. I didn't have to guess who had called Gerry. Faith hovered behind him, a slightly guilt-stricken look about her. "Get the hell out of my house," he shouted.

Leo walked onto the landing. "Calm down, Gerry. They were just leaving."

"What the hell were you thinking?" Gerry pushed past him, then shoved me aside. I bumped back against the dresser, cologne bottles and coins rattling, but resisted pushing back.

"Watch it," I said.

Gerry turned from Kevin and leaned in my face. "What did you say?"

I stared down at him. "I said 'watch it.'"

Briallen stepped next to me. "I don't believe we've met, Officer Murdock. My name is . . ."

He glared at her. "I know who the hell you are. You're not welcome here either. Get out."

Briallen showed no fear, not that I expected her to. People like Gerry—even given his possible druid abilities—were child's play for her. "I was asked here."

"Not by me," he said. He jerked his thumb over his shoulder. "Out."

"Gerry, knock it off. Kevin wasn't waking up, so I called for help," Leo said.

"He's fine. He just needs to sleep," Gerry said.

"How do you know that?" Briallen asked.

He frowned at her. "None of your damned business. You people aren't the only ones who know about this stuff."

"What does that mean?" I asked.

He thrust his arm out toward the hall. "Leave. Now."

"I asked them here, Gerry. I don't need your permission to invite people to my home. I live here, too," Leo said.

"Maybe that needs to change," Gerry said.

Leo pushed back into the room. "You got something to say?"

Faith grabbed Leo's arm. "Both of you, stop it." She pointed at me. "Take your friend outside, now."

"Mind your business, Faith," Gerry said.

She stuck her finger in his face. "Shut it. This family is my business. We are not doing this in front of strangers. It's over."

Briallen took my hand and pulled me into the hall. She said nothing as she led the way down the stairs and out the door. Leo came out a moment later. "I'm sorry about that."

Briallen rubbed his arm. "No need. He's in pain, Leonard."

"Yeah, well, it has nothing to do with you," he said.

And everything to do with me. "I shouldn't have come," I said.

Exasperated, Leo glanced up at the house. "I didn't think Faith would rat me out. She usually is the one calming things down."

"I smelled essence on both of your brothers," I said.

Briallen nodded. "I did, too. If I'm not mistaken, it was essence-fire residue."

"Gerry's right about one thing: We're not the only ones who know how to teach about abilities. Have they been training with someone?" I asked.

Leo looked down, then away. "I'm not sure. Kev and Gerry have always been pretty tight. They've been going out a lot together lately."

The look said it all. He was sure but didn't want to think about it. "Maybe you should follow them. If the Guild isn't involved, it could be anyone," I said.

He frowned. "I'm not going to put my own family under surveillance, Connor."

The black car's driver opened the door for Briallen. She paused with one foot inside the car. "You're looking at this as a personal matter. It's not, Leonard. Your abilities are under control, but you have no idea what can happen. I think Kevin, at least, has more abilities. If they're both using essence-fire, they can be putting themselves in danger, if not everyone else. I don't want you feeling guilty if something happens."

"I'll think about it," he said.

The expression on Murdock's face stayed with me the rest of the day, so sad, yet so angry. I knew what it was like to get blindsided by life. It sucked. My problems hadn't destroyed my entire family, but somehow they had destroyed Murdock's. I didn't know what I could do about it, but I hoped I didn't make it any worse.

7

The driver drove us back to Beacon Hill, where Briallen lived in a town house on Louisburg Square. The address was tony, the neighbors aloof, and Briallen was indifferent to both. Back at the house, she made coffee because she knew I needed a constant stream of caffeine before noon.

We wandered up to the top floor of her house so she could show me the results of some spells she had been working on. Rather, some spells that she hadn't had any success with. Briallen faced a sealed stone door on the top landing. Arms crossed, she leaned against the banister. "If I weren't so angry, I'd compliment her on her skills."

"She," of course, was Meryl. I stared at the door, trying to find a break in the stone. Meryl had been in a trance state a few weeks back. Nigel Martin, another old mentor, had devised a spell session to bring her out of it with Briallen's help. I had been dubious. Nigel and I were on less-than-cordial terms these days, and I suspected his motives, with good reason as it turned out. He had attempted to kill Meryl inside Briallen's sanctum sanctorum. Meryl had had other ideas. She turned the tables on him, came out of her trance, and sealed Nigel inside the room. He was still in there.

"Is he alive?" I asked.

"I think so. I'm attuned to some of the crystals inside. They continue to indicate a body signature," she said.

"He probably put himself in a deep-trance mode," I said. Druids can shut their bodies down to a near-death state. From my own training, I knew how to survive several days with minimal sustenance. Several weeks were another matter. On the other hand, Nigel was an archdruid, the highest attainable level of our kind. He had skills only the High Queen's closest advisors could match.

"He can't stay in there forever," she said.

I ran my hand over the surface of the round door. Deep lines were incised in the stone, classic Celtic swirls that represented water and the sun. Here and there, tiny flashes of essence sparkled in the ridges, which meant the tuning spells were still active. Tuning spells helped make the sanctum more conducive to spell work. The stone door met the stone frame in one fused transition. "If anyone can, I'd bet on Nigel."

"That's not helping," she said.

The surface of the door had been bleached white except for the center, which had a dark scorch mark where the focus of Meryl's essence blast had struck. "The tuning spell is not working in the center."

"I tried recalibrating," Briallen said. "The underlying pathways are either damaged, or she left something that is blocking me."

"Under the circumstances, I doubt she had time to set a block," I said.

"You're making excuses because you're biased," she said.

I frowned. "So are you. Just because you're mad at her doesn't make her the bad guy."

"That's easy for you to say. Half the Guild is looking for Nigel, and I've got him illegally imprisoned in my attic."

I scanned the surface one more time, then held my hands up in apology. "I got nothing."

Briallen let out an angry sigh and walked away. I followed her downstairs to the kitchen. She poured herself a mug of coffee, then gestured with the pot to see if I wanted any. I always wanted coffee. "You must have some kind of fail-safe to open the sanctum."

"Of course. It was predicated on, you know, having a door that opens," she said. I chuckled. I couldn't help myself. Briallen glared at me. "I fail to see the humor in this."

"It's nice not to be the subject of your frustration for a change," I said.

She took firm swipes with a dishcloth at the counter. I watched her without speaking. Briallen cleaned when she was angry. Back when I was her student, I was usually the one forced to clean. When the counter was shining, her face softened, and she sat at the island counter with me. "Do you really think that?"

"Well . . ."

"You don't frustrate me, Connor. The world does."

I snorted. "Tell me about it."

She touched my hand. "Through all these years, I've always wanted the best for you. If I could have saved you pain, I would have."

"I know. Half the problem is that neither of us can mind our business," I said.

She laughed. "True. I wish I could give you better answers, but I haven't been able to scry."

Briallen had a talent for perceiving the future. Through chants and spells, she used the surface of calm water to catch glimpses of what might be. Her preferred instrument was the fountain pool in her back garden. The process wasn't exact because so many variables changed from moment to moment. Sometimes, though, outcomes became inevitable, the various potential strands of events converging into a few and sometimes one. Those times were rarely positive and never good.

"Still?" I asked. When major events became so uncertain, no amount of fey ability was able to penetrate the veil of the future. It had happened a few weeks ago when the

Elven King attacked the Guildhouse. Once past the crisis point, the ability returned.

"Not since before the Guildhouse. What about Meryl?" she asked.

Meryl's talent was druidic dreaming. Her ability came on its own, in her sleep. Hers was a True Dreaming. The things she envisioned came to pass. She didn't always understand the details because the images often came in metaphors that she had to interpret. Sometimes she did. Sometimes she failed.

"I haven't thought to ask," I said. Any type of scrying hurt my head enough to cause me to pass out. The reaction came from the dark mass in my mind. It hurt like hell, and I avoided coming in contact with scrying whenever possible. Now that the faith stone was embedded in my skull, I had my full body shield. It kept out the pain as long as I didn't try scrying myself.

"Could you? I've found no one who can scry," she said.

"Sure." She didn't move from the window. "Briallen?" She faced me. "It isn't good, is it? I mean, really not good."

She shook her head. "Something as huge as the death of Donor Elfenkonig should have set everything in motion again. It didn't. Whatever is happening is still happening, Connor. It's not over, and if Donor's death was only the beginning, I'm afraid of what comes next. Truly afraid."

The hair on the back of my neck went up, and I shuddered. Briallen ab Gwyll was not afraid of anything.

"If it's any consolation, I want that door open more than you do. I need answers that I think Nigel has."

"So now you're willing to talk to him?" she asked.

Once I lost my abilities, Nigel abandoned me as a friend. I took it personally. We were no longer on speaking terms. "Question him. He was researching something about me. I want to know what it was."

She tapped her coffee mug. "Maybe you need to talk to someone about opening that door."

"I have. She won't. If I can move past that, I think you can," I said.

"What do you think he was researching?"

I tapped my forehead. "I know he was interested in the darkness in my head, but I think he knew something about the faith stone."

"As far as I know, he shared everything he knew about the darkness with me and Gillen Yor. He didn't have any more answers than we did," she said.

"After everything that's happened, you believe that?" I asked.

She sipped her coffee. "I understand your doubts, Connor, but you have to remember that for a long time, we thought we could cure you. I still believe that. Nigel was fully involved with researching your problem. He might not like my methods, but I don't think either Gillen or I would have missed his hiding something from us. The faith stone is another matter."

"Brokke told me it had the power to instill faith in people," I said.

"Brokke was a master of the obvious," she said.

I shook my head. "Briallen, I'm not interested in competing politics anymore. I just want the truth, whether it comes from the Celts or the Teuts."

She chuckled. "Don't confuse people and principles, Connor. Brokke was an arrogant, irritating ass. He knew things that were better shared and let people die when they could have been saved."

"That's fair—and beside the point. This thing in my head is powerful. The Elven King died over it. What does it mean?" I asked.

She gazed into her coffee mug. I thought she might be trying to scry off the surface of the liquid. I didn't feel any of the usual pressure in my head that happened when someone scryed. The dark mass didn't like my being around the future.

Briallen was considering her response. Based on my experience, she knew something and was trying to decide how little she could get away with sharing—ironic, considering what she had said about Brokke.

She shifted herself on the stool. "Here's what I think: Donor always struggled with persuading allies that the elves were the victims in the war that led to Convergence. No matter his grievances, he ruled in the authoritarian manner of Alfheim, and the modern world never understood or agreed with that method. He wanted something to help him make his case, and he thought the stone would do it.

"Here's what I believe: The stone is exactly what he thought it was. It's the remnant of an older reality, when the righteousness of one's cause could be demonstrated by having the approval of the Wheel of the World. The stone gave credibility to the one who held it."

I smirked. "Well, that part's not working anymore."

"Isn't it? You've been accused of terrorism by both the Guild and the Consortium, yet neither of them has arrested you. How much is that due to politics and how much to the power in your head?"

"You know I don't believe the Wheel of the World cares that much about me, or anyone else, for that matter," I said.

She eyed me with the stern manner of a teacher. "That's a mistake I've tried to correct in you for as long as we've known each other, Connor. You're right. The Wheel of the World doesn't care about individuals, but it does work through individuals to accomplish Its purposes."

"So what do you think Its purpose is with me?" I asked.

She lifted her shoulders in a slow shrug. "Maybe exactly what's happening—the Guild and the Consortium are on the brink of war. If the faith stone is with you instead of someone like Donor and Maeve, maybe that keeps war from breaking out. It creates doubt on both sides about the success of their respective causes."

"Is that why you gave me the dagger?" I asked.

She seemed startled by the question though why I wasn't sure. "I gave you the dagger to protect yourself."

"Really? You didn't give it to me to get it out of the way?" I asked.

She didn't meet my gaze but got up and poured herself more coffee. "You were powerless in a dangerous situation.

I didn't want to see you die, Connor. Why are you making it seem like I did a bad thing?"

I removed the dagger from my boot and placed it between us on the counter. As usual, a few runes reacted to the essence around it—the ambient stuff in the air, a powerful being like Briallen, and, no doubt, the resonant energy given off by the stone in my head. "Because you refuse to talk about it. What is this dagger—this sword. Where did it come from?"

"It's an enchanted blade from Faerie. It has powerful protection wards on in it," she said.

"Stopping dancing around my question," I said.

"I don't know what you're looking for," she said.

"Brokke said he recognized the sword when he saw. He said it was one of the signs in his vision that everything might be destroyed. I don't believe for one friggin' minute that you don't know more than you're saying."

Briallen's eyes went cold, and I remembered why people feared her. I had never spoken to her like that, other than juvenile outbursts when I was a teenager. When I was a kid, I did it to test the bounds of authority. As an adult, I realized I was pushing the bounds of rivalry. "I did it to keep it out of Maeve's hands. She already had the spear. I was afraid if she acquired the sword, it would tip the balance of power between the Seelie Court and the Consortium."

Her words settled on me like an understanding wrapped in an insult. "I didn't matter, so I was perfect."

She scowled. "Don't put words in my mouth. The fact that the sword responded to you means you were meant to have it. That's how the Wheel of the World works. Just because it suited my purpose doesn't mean it's not what the Wheel of the World wants from you."

I pushed the blade toward her. "I don't want it then."

Briallen stared down at the dagger. "You can't give it back. You still need it."

"No, I don't," I said.

She shook her head. "Yes, you do. You know it. You said

you would only give it back when you didn't need it any-more. You bound yourself with that condition. Want and need are two different things, Connor. Put the dagger away."

She was calling my bluff and knew it. I didn't want her to take it back. I wanted answers. "What did you think would happen when you gave it to me, Briallen? Did you think something like this would have no consequences?"

Her eyes became moist. "I didn't think it would harm you. I thought the Wheel of the World would turn without you, and the sword would find its place with someone else. You want me to say you were nobody? Fine, you were no-body. Maeve had never heard of you. I thought the sword was safe. I thought *you* were safe.

"Yeah, well, that brilliant plan didn't work out so well," I said.

Briallen went to the kitchen sink and rinsed her mug. She stared out the window above the sink. "I never in-tended anything bad to happen."

"How do I use this sword?" I asked.

She kept her back to me. "You'll have to figure that out yourself."

I picked up the blade and shoved it back in my boot. "You know what? I was angry at that old man upstairs for ignoring me after my accident. Now, I'm kinda glad he did. Thanks for nothing, Briallen."

8

I left the house pretty steamed. Briallen had dumped the sword on me. I didn't ask for it, and now that I had an ominous warning from a dead dwarf who saw the future, she wanted to let the Wheel of the World decide what I should know.

Despite Meryl's advice to take a break, I couldn't. It was literally impossible when I was carrying around a dark mass and a faith stone in my head. It wasn't like I could turn them off and think about them some other time. They were always there—unavoidable, unignorable, and uninvited.

Brokke said that the appearance of the stone, the spear, and the sword were signs of a coming cataclysm. He hinted that one more element needed to appear but hadn't. It had, but he didn't know about it. It didn't take a rocket scientist to figure out that another stone ward I had hidden—a stone bowl that produced more essence than it absorbed—was part of the package. Somehow, these things had gravitated to me. I needed to understand them.

Back in the Weird, I picked my way over fallen debris on

Calvin Place like a cat walking on a wet floor. Public works trucks couldn't make it through the narrow lane without scraping the walls of the adjacent buildings, and the people who owned the buildings cared little whether the hazardous stretch inconvenienced anyone. It was an old road, one block long, from a time when horse-pulled carts serviced Boston businesses. Only one occupied storefront had held on through years of change. The dilapidated sign across the length of the building was missing letters, and soot obscured the remaining ones. It didn't matter in terms of finding the place. Everyone in the Weird knew BELGOR'S NOTIONS, POTIONS AND THEURGIC DEVICES.

The bell over the door rang with one dull clank. Heat wrapped itself around me, too much heat, the kind an ancient boiler the size of a trailer truck pumped into old building radiators. Why it was still on so late into spring, only the gods and absentee landlords knew. The dampness accentuated the smell of the store: moist dust, old incense, and the burnt-cinnamon tang of Belgor's body odor. A murmur of voices drifted from the rear, where the counter and cash register were.

I lingered in an aisle, listening. Sensing pings touched me as the people in back checked to see who had entered. My essence didn't intimidate or concern them, and they continued their conversational chatter, locals bumping into each other and shooting the shit to delay venturing back to work or whatever passed for work. At the end of the aisle, two brownies and a tall forest elf lounged near the soda case. Belgor sat next to the counter, his bulk threatening to make his stool disappear. He spared me a cursory glance, affecting disinterest, while he listened to the conversation.

I picked up a copy of the *Weird Times*, the neighborhood rag, and leaned against the wall to read about a rise in assaults along Old Northern Avenue. The police had no comment. An editorial implied that the crimes weren't being investigated by the Boston P.D. or the Guild. Nothing new there. When priorities were made at either organization, things like the Weird fell to the bottom of the list.

The brownies griped about the ID lines at the police checkpoints at the Old Northern Avenue bridge into the city. They seemed to be some kind of service staffers for downtown hotels and faced the daily annoyance of starting out for work an hour early to account for security delays.

Belgor nodded and hummed as he listened, filing the trivia in his mental archive of all things Weird like a bloated spider sitting on a vast web of information, to be used for barter and gain. Sometimes he made money, and sometimes he saved his considerable skin. He always survived.

The customers bought lottery tickets and wandered out. Belgor's eyes shifted within fat-folded lids, his long, pointed ears flexing down. We tolerated each other, our association based on needs we wished we could satisfy elsewhere.

"You should clear your sidewalk, Belgor. Someone might get hurt," I said.

He folded thick arms over his ample stomach. "I do not have a sidewalk, Mr. Grey."

He was right, technically. Calvin Place was too narrow to have sidewalks. I dropped the newspaper on the counter. "Kind of interesting."

His eyes scanned the headlines. "Fighting has always been a way of life here."

I turned the newspaper back to face me, pretending to read the article. "True. And death," I said.

Belgor pumped his fleshy lips. "You more than anyone knows that."

I wasn't sure if that was a dig or not. "I have a question for you, Belgor. Actually, it's your expertise I need to consult."

Belgor rolled his wide expanse of shoulders. "I am a simple store merchant, Mr. Grey."

"Can we cut the bullshit for once, Belgor? I need an answer on something, and if you know something, I'll be out of here faster than this conversation is going."

His ears flexed down and back. "And here I thought this was a social call from a dear old friend. What can I do for you?"

I leaned down and withdrew the dagger from my right boot and placed it on the counter. "What can you tell me about this?"

Belgor's face smoothed in surprise, and his ears shot up. "Where did you get it?"

"That's not important. I want to hear what you have to say without any context," I said.

As he reached for the dagger, his hand trembled. A few runes etched in the blade lit with a cool blue light, and Belgor withdrew his hand. "A moment," he said.

He maneuvered his large mass sideways behind the corner and ducked behind the curtain that led to his back room. He returned wearing an antique pair of jeweler's glasses, a wired contraption that hooked around his ears. Thin metal arms jutted from the bridge and ended with polished lenses that hovered several inches from his eyes. He used a thick cloth embedded with glass to pick up the dagger. "It's an old blade out of Faerie. The markings indicate it has passed through several hands."

"Enchanted swords were a dime a dozen in Faerie," I said.

"Not like this. There are ancient magics on this blade from more than one source. I do not recognize some of these runes," Belgor said.

"Does it have a name?" I asked. Swords—important ones anyway—often had names in the deep past. They commemorated great battles or where they were fought, famous people who owned them or died. The dagger was hard to read. While runes covered parts of the blade and pommel, they seemed related to spells. I hadn't been able to tease a name out.

Belgor hummed, tilting his head up and down to adjust his vision through the lenses. "I see many references to chaos and . . ." He frowned. "It is hard to say. The phrasing is old, like Old Elvish or even Gaelic. Break? Notch? Perhaps, a gap between two forces."

"Gap?" I said. That's the word Brokke had used when he spoke of the darkness within me. He called it the Gap that arose in the moment between the end and the beginning of the Wheel of the World.

Belgor shifted the blade and sighted down its length. "Perhaps. How did this come into your possession?"

"It was a gift, a loan of sorts," I said. When Briallen had given it to me, I had sensed its age and value, and thought it was too much to accept. I took it on the condition I could give it back to her when I was done with it. I wasn't sure I regretted that decision now, but it might not have been one of my best. I had no idea at the time that I was binding myself to the blade with a geasa—a form of taboo that would have ruinous consequences if I broke it.

Belgor placed the dagger back on the counter. "Someone did you no favor. I do not know this blade, which, I must say, concerns me. There is something of the Wheel about it, something dire. I do not think it serves the wielder but purposes beyond our ken. How much do you want for it?"

That made me laugh. "Like I said, it's not really mine to give."

"I do not think it is anyone's to give, Mr. Grey. Things like this appear where they need to. It will be difficult to move, but I am sure it will find its next possessor," he said.

"I wanted confirmation that it was as old as I thought it was," I said.

"Older than any I have seen. I would not use it. Such things appear at times of war and chaos, and bode no good thing," he said.

I pushed away from the counter. His words echoed Brokke's too much for comfort. "Thanks, Belgor. Keep your head down. I'd hate to see you get caught in the middle of a war zone."

Belgor nodded. "I have lived a long, long time, Mr. Grey. When you realize war is imminent, it is already too late to stop it."

When I reached the door, he called my name. "It occurs to me that you do not seem yourself."

It would be an overstatement to say that Belgor sounded sincere, but that he was inquiring about me personally surprised the hell out of me. "How do you mean?"

"You seem to be lacking a certain passion in our inter-

action. I am in your debt, as you know. If there is anything
I can do, let me know."

I didn't know what to say. He wasn't smiling, so it
wasn't all warm and fuzzy between us. I had covered up his
involvement in a pretty high-profile crime that would have
sent him to prison. Whatever Belgor's motivations, he saw
that as an obligation to me. If even he thought I wasn't
myself and was concerned that I wasn't, then maybe I
needed to take a step back for some serious reassessment.

"Thanks. I'll keep that in mind."

Outside, the harsh, white sliver of sky between the
buildings cast the street in stark, grim light. Spring was
having a hard time wrenching winter out of the air. I hesitated at the end of the street as nonchalantly as possible
without looking paranoid. Checking my surroundings was
second nature at that point in my life and, given recent
events, was fast becoming my first nature.

Pittsburgh Street stretched in both directions. Not far off
was a door to a basement where I had hidden the stone
bowl that generated essence. The dark mass in my head
yearned for essence, and the bowl had provided enough to
take the edge off my pain. It also filled a deep physical
need, one that had clear addiction issues revolving around
it. When I had first picked the hideout location, it was convenient to my apartment. In a few short blocks, I was able
to sate the urge. Now, my apartment wasn't safe, and the
Tangle was far enough down Old Northern that a quickie
wasn't feasible. It would have been a shame to miss the
opportunity.

On this end of the neighborhood, the streets between
Congress and Old Northern were longer than the average
city block. Warehouses fronted on Stillings and Pittsburgh,
with a long central alley between them. At various points
along the way, access lanes allowed egress to the back. I
ducked down the nearest one, no more than a pedestrian
tunnel four feet wide.

The main alley was a picture of waste and abandonment—dumpsters long gone to rust, wood pallets gone gray,

and businesses just gone. Belgor's was the closest thing to a legitimate business on the block. At night, the darkened warehouses came alive with music and dancing down near Congress. Things people didn't like to think about happened on this end, both day and night. I walked past boarded-up doors and windows, picking up my pace the closer I got to the squat.

A gunshot echoed up the alley, the sound slapping back and forth against the bricks, growing fainter and fainter as it reached me. Gunfire was not unusual in the Weird, during the day it was less common, though.

I hesitated, considering what I was about to do. I'd told myself I wouldn't do it anymore, wouldn't seek out the essence in the stone bowl like some junkie after a fix. I'd told myself that it wasn't me that wanted it, but the dark mass in my head. I'd told myself that giving in to the urge was giving in to the dark mass, giving in to baser wants that I had left behind. I'd told myself all that, yet found myself drawn to the bowl like a moth to flame.

I put my back to the alley, still hesitating. I wasn't going to do it. I wasn't going to give in to the dark mass, give in to its control. I wasn't going to be manipulated like that.

A shot rang out, and this time I jumped at its nearness, the distinct sound of a ricochet off metal close by, then something heavy falling to the ground. I pressed back against the wall, scanning the length of the alley. Row upon row of dark, shattered windows stared back at me. A blaze of essence-fire sliced above the roofline from one side of the alley to the next. Another shot went off farther away, followed by more essence-fire. Whoever was shooting was moving off, the fey pursuer not far behind.

I slipped into the welcome darkness of the next pedestrian alley, a low anger coiling in my chest. I could have been killed in a random shooting all because of a desire that would not go away. I needed to find my focus again, find a purpose for myself other than drifting from one favor to the next.

I wasn't going to find that in the bottom of a stone bowl.

9

After leaving Belgor, I did what I do whenever I'm con-
flicted. I ran. I changed into shorts and a sweatshirt, and
jogged the neighborhood. The good thing about hiding out
in an essence-saturated neighborhood like the Tangle was
that I didn't have to run very far to go very far. I ran the
same loop five times to put some mileage in, but each time
the streets shifted, not always in a dramatic fashion, but
enough to notice that something had changed—different
building façade here, new pavement there, even the way the
sunlight filtered down. It was the same route each time,
only the visual cues had changed.

The dark mass in my mind yearned for essence and
caused me pain without it. When I had found the stone
bowl, I found a way to feed that yearning and lessen the
pain. I didn't like it any better. The desire itself became
consuming. Instead of dealing with pain, I had to deal with
compulsion. The more I gave in to that compulsion, the less
I cared about how I satisfied it.

That road led to death. I had almost killed Keeva

macNeve, my old partner. I was tapping her essence to feed, but I let my mind deny it. My conscience couldn't, though, and I stopped. Because of me, she had to go to Tara to heal.

I didn't need a shot of essence to stem the pain, at least not anymore. Having an unexplained dark mass in my head was bad enough, but now I had a heart-shaped stone nestled against it. The stone and the darkness seemed in their own battle, a stalemate for control of my pain.

Meryl called them metaphors, symbols for things we could not explain. The dark mass, to her thinking, was a manifestation for something we couldn't describe. The faith stone was a manifestation of power that was sometimes tangible—a stone—and sometimes not—a spot of glowing light. The darkness and the stone had found each other or been attracted to each other and ended up having a happy dance in the neighborhood of my hypothalamus.

Even though I had not given in to the urge to take a hit of essence like a junkie, the fact that I almost did made me angry. It made me angry with my situation. With everything else going on in the world, I needed to find an answer to what had happened to me and how to fix it. Time and again, I found myself doing a favor when I thought someone else's situation needed more attention than mine, only to have my life take a backseat to the world. So I ran in circles to work off the stress and frustration, another metaphor for my life.

Since moving into the Tangle, I was amazed at how fast rumors flew. Even given the fey's ability to do sendings, which was a way of sending thoughts wrapped in essence to people, news traveled fast. The Tangle was a cluster of intrigue and danger, the worst the Weird had to offer. People who lived there relied on information to survive, and the network of communication was larger than I had ever suspected.

When a dead body showed up at the edge of the neighborhood, random sendings flew through the air. I caught a general broadcast, meant to be heard by anyone nearby. I had the news about the body before the first emergency vehicle had been dispatched.

I hiked over to the scene, the corner of Summer and Elkins, where the city power plant was located. A dead body meant Murdock would be involved, and I hadn't seen or heard from him since the day I had been at his house.

Police vehicles gathered at the intersection. The power plant looming above bore signs of damage. Soot marks from a fire a few months earlier still streaked down the blank six-story wall, which was painted a strange pink—to mimic brick, I supposed.

The fire had been a false alarm. Bergin Vize had been hiding in the power plant, protected by solitary fey who thought they were helping one of their own. In truth, the solitaries were being used by the Consortium in a proxy war against the Guild. The Guild, in turn, manipulated the Dead of TirNaNog into flushing Vize out of the complex by setting it on fire.

The scheme set off a night of rioting and other fires like nothing Boston had ever seen. The solitaries—always the scapegoats for fey transgressions—fought back against the combined forces of the Guild and the National Guard. The Dead were in it for the bloodbath. Since they were already dead, dying didn't mean much to them. They resurrected with the next day's dawn.

The riots produced profound changes. Eorla brought the solitaries under control and started her own court. Ceridwen, a murdered Danann underQueen, ruled over the Dead in disguise as the King of the Dead. The Guild and Consortium backed down, but not before I lost control of the darkness in my head and almost killed everyone. It was not fun. The entire Weird had become a crime scene that night, so another dead body at the power plant was no more than a coincidence, but an interesting one.

The power plant was a vital component of the local utility grid, and any major crime in the area prompted precautionary measures. Even though there was no fire this time, an alarm had gone out, and a ladder truck idled on standby as a precaution.

As luck would have it, the truck was from Kevin Murdock's station. He sat on one of the running boards, talking and laughing with his coworkers. As Briallen predicted, he was none the worse for wear from his deep sleep, probably better. His body signature glowed a deep bronze among the humans. He stopped laughing when he saw me. His face became a suspicious mask as he tracked my approach to the temporary police barrier.

Kevin, along with his brother Gerry, had decided I was the cause of the tragedies that had struck the Murdock family. I was present when their father—the former police commissioner—was killed. It didn't matter to them that he was a dirty cop who had brought about his own downfall.

They blamed me. They also blamed me for destroying their family by having an affair with their mother. It had happened years ago, when I was young and green, hormone-filled and stupid. I didn't even know the Murdocks then. Leo, who was the oldest, was still in high school then if I had my math right. I had no idea of the trouble the affair caused until years later. But they blamed me for that, too, despite the fact that their mother lied to her husband and initiated the affair. No one wanted to believe their parents were flawed human beings. Scott Murdock and Moira Cashel were as flawed as they come. I survived both of them, so somehow I was the villain.

I ignored Kevin's stare as I waited for a police officer to let me through. Gone were the days when I sauntered past checkpoints, secure in the knowledge I had the authority if not the connections. Too much bad blood existed between me and the Boston P.D. these days. I hadn't killed Scott Murdock, but that didn't stop his son Gerry from encouraging the lie on the force. He wasn't respected like Leo was, but that was what made him a problem. Gerry appealed to the rough edges of the blue, the cops who chafed at the rules. They saw criminality everywhere they looked and acted on it. I didn't want to give them any more reason to pull out a Taser.

Leo waved me over to where the body lay. Not many

other people stood near. The few people who were nearby kept their distance. Jumpers never made for pretty death scenes. The higher they fall from, the less pretty. The dead guy was a Danann fairy, so that mitigated the damage. Dananns have more resilient bodies than humans. He was still dead, though, his wings a tangled and torn mess, a leg bent at an angle legs weren't meant to bend.

"We're going to lose this one fast." Wearing gloves, Murdock held open a small billfold that showed a Guild ID. The Guild might not take cases in the Weird any longer, but it protected its own. The last thing macGoren wanted was his allies on the police force investigating a murder that might expose Guild secrets.

I recognized the name and face of the victim. "He was a low-level administrator."

I crouched by the bloody body. The strong whiff of alcohol wafted upward. Dananns had a propensity for whiskey. Back in Faerie, it wasn't available in quantity, so drunkenness was more an accepted reprieve from the high life than a question of alcoholism. Not so in the post-Convergence world. Whiskey was everywhere, cheap and easy to acquire. More than a few Dananns ended up in the Weird because they had fallen to the bottom of a bottle.

"We're trying to get clearance to check out the power-plant roof," Murdock said.

I glanced up at the wall. The building was high enough to kill a Danann. "He smells pretty drunk. He might've passed out when flying overhead and dropped. You might have an accidental death."

"Yeah, that happens to Guild agents all the time," Murdock said.

Nothing with the Guild was ever simple. "Honestly, I'd call the Guild, Leo. They're going to take over anyway."

Murdock jerked his chin up toward something behind me. "Looks like someone decided to save us the minutes."

Up the block, two dark figures appeared in the sky, telltale silhouettes of Danann security agents. They circled once overhead before landing on the sidewalk. I was surprised to see Keeva macNeve. She strode over and examined the body with a neutral expression.

"Hi, Keev. Nice of you to drop in," I said.

She ignored me as she went through the dead guy's pockets, tossing inconsequential items on the sidewalk—matches, coins, and receipts. Looking at Murdock, she remained crouched, her forearms on her thighs, hands dangling between her knees. "Where is it?"

Without argument, Murdock handed over the billfold.

"You got here awfully fast," I said.

Keeva fanned out some business cards, then tucked them back in the billfold. "You're not the only one with friends on the force, Grey. Mine happen to follow procedure and inform interested legal entities instead of their gym buddies."

"Connor hasn't been to the gym in weeks," Murdock said.

Keeva stood. "You know the drill, Detective. Move along and thank your boys for me."

"I remember this guy, Keeva. He was a Consortium mole. We used him a couple of times for disinformation," I said.

She scanned the surrounding area. "Any other classified information you want to broadcast within earshot of uncleared staff?"

"You get a lot of moles in the Guild?" Murdock asked.

Keeva's glance flashed with dismissiveness. "Why no, Detective. I'm shocked to hear it. How old did you say you were, by the way? I can't tell if you're wearing diapers under those pants."

Murdock narrowed his eyes at me. "Did she imply she's looking at my ass?"

"What's with all the antagonism, Keeva? I mean, more than usual?" I asked.

The corners of her mouth turned down as she stared at the victim. "We've lost a lot of people, Connor. This guy may have been low-level stupid, but he was helping with disaster recovery. Every person lost is more work for everyone."

"Well, maybe the Guild . . ." I began.

Keeva held her hand up. "Connor, I don't want to hear one of your anti-Guild rants. Not today. People who were my friends are dead. People *you* knew are dead, so give it a break."

I wasn't going to go off on the Guild, but that Keeva thought that would be my first reaction under the circumstances was embarrassing. I guessed I had become a one-note ranter in her mind. "I was going to say maybe the Guild should beef up security. Donor Elfenkonig destroyed the Guildhouse, and now someone you need to manage the crisis is dead. That's all I was going to say, to be careful."

She nodded, peering down the street. "Good advice, considering you were there, too, when the Guildhouse came down. Leave, Connor. Now, before I do something we both regret."

I took a deep breath. "How is Ryan?"

I tried to warn macGoren that Vize was up to something. I tried to stop what happened. MacGoren didn't listen. He was arrogant, ambitious, and an ass. He had survived the destruction of the Guildhouse. He had also been injured—seriously, I had been told—but no one would give me any details.

Keeva fired up her hands with essence. "Alive, no thanks to you. Detective Murdock, explain to your friend that if he does not get out of here, I will incinerate him where he stands, and there is not a damned thing you and your badge can do about it."

The police and firefighters nearby were listening. More than a few had smiles on their faces. Murdock tugged at my sleeve. "Come on, Connor. This isn't going anywhere."

I let him pull me away. I was more hurt than angry. Keeva and I had been partners. We might not have been the best of friends, but we got along, at least until she met macGoren. MacGoren's injuries were his own damned fault, no matter what she had been told.

I slumped in the passenger seat of Murdock's car. "That sucked."

He started the engine and pulled away from the scene. "I think she was serious about incinerating you."

"Nah. That's Keeva's way of saying she cares," I said.

Murdock circled around the block and brought us back to Old Northern Avenue. "A lot of people seem to show their affection for you that way."

That was an understatement. After a career as a Guild investigator, I had more than my share of enemies. The funny part was, all those old enemies left me alone now. I wasn't a player anymore, so I didn't factor into their plans. Instead, I seem to be making a career of turning friends against me. Keeva and I had always been competitive, but things had changed since she met Ryan macGoren. I used to think she was being a social climber, that she couldn't possibly see anything in him. I wasn't so sure anymore. She seemed genuinely attached to him and genuinely upset that he had almost died.

When people I considered friends started siding with people who wanted me dead, I had little hope things would get better.

10

After Murdock dropped me off, I returned to my room in the Tangle. I had a bed, a couple of armchairs, a bathroom, and a corner that pretended it was a kitchenette. What it lacked in amenities, it made up for in seclusion and security. I had been offered better accommodations from Ceridwen but turned them down. Accepting a nice, comfortable apartment in the Tangle would have been accepting that I lived in the Tangle. I wanted to pretend it was temporary, like my apartment in the Weird had been temporary, if three years and counting could be considered temporary.

After the fall of the Guildhouse, Ceridwen rescued me and provided me with a safe haven. She didn't have anything to lose by associating with me. For one thing, no one knew she was in the city. For another, she was Dead, murdered by Bergin Vize and barred from TirNaNog when I had destroyed the gate to the fey afterlife. I might have destroyed the whole realm, but no one knew for sure, like no one knew if Faerie still existed.

After taking a quick shower, I joined Ceridwen for what

had become a regular meeting for conversation. Her private rooms were as extravagant as one would expect of a fairy queen. Fine, sleek furniture filled the living room, lush draperies in orange florals hung from the windows, and hand-woven rugs in muted shades of green and blue covered the floors. Everything about them spoke of glamour and money except the view. We sat at a table beneath a brick arch, the top of the frame of a warehouse Palladian window. The Tangle spread below, ramshackle rooftops of water towers and chimneys, odd plumes of essence rising and falling in dark colors. It wasn't beautiful, but it was fascinating to watch.

Ceridwen didn't wear her red leather Hunter getup in her private quarters, but more casual, feminine outfits. Today she wore a light, sleeveless blouse and orange shorts. She tucked her shoeless feet up on the seat as she studied the chessboard between us. If it weren't for her diaphanous wings moving with a languid ripple in the air-conditioning, she could have been mistaken for a young woman passing the time on a hot day. She moved a pawn across the board.

"Your move," she said.

We had taken to playing chess, a game we both loved but rarely played because no one would play us. We were pleasantly surprised to find we were evenly matched. I moved a bishop into position. "I've heard the police aren't coming into the Tangle at all anymore."

Ceridwen's eyes shifted back and forth as she surveyed the board. She took the bishop out with a knight. "Your move."

I pursed my lips. I didn't think she'd expose the knight, but I wasn't going to let it slide. I moved my rook and took the knight off the board. "It's funny, 'cause violent crime has actually gone down."

Without pausing, she moved her bishop to protect her king. "Your move," she said

The board was getting tight, but I saw a scenario that would gain me an advantage. I shifted a pawn one square. "Your move, Your Majesty."

She captured the pawn with one of her own. She had something going, but I couldn't see it. I took out the pawn. "Your move."

She slid her queen along the side of the board, just shy of my men. Something was forming on the board, the lines of conflict crisscrossing.

I saw the opening I wanted and slipped another pawn off the board. "Your move."

She leaned back in her chair. "I don't need the police. Given enough latitude, people fall into acceptable behaviors. I need you to go to Ireland," she said.

"Why me?" I asked.

"I trust you. I'm ready to move my people there, but I need someone on the ground for logistics," she said.

"My passport's probably flagged. I doubt I'd set one foot on the plane," I said.

"Drive to Canada and fly from there. I'd prefer that. I don't want anyone knowing you're there except my contacts. They'll get you what you need," she said.

"Whom have you recruited to your cause against Maeve?" I asked.

"The Seelie Court is made up of many underKings and -Queens who do not love Maeve," she said.

"Enough to commit treason?" I asked.

Ceridwen smiled. "Maeve has violated the most fundamental laws of our Court, Grey. She caused the death of an underQueen. It is not treason to hold her accountable for it."

"You're going to war," I said.

"Maeve has moved her forces onto the Continent. Tara is empty. I cannot let the opportunity pass," she said. She took a pawn out with a rook.

I reached for another pawn, then withdrew when I realized I would lose my other bishop. "Ceridwen, I know she betrayed you, and, well, you ended up dying, but do you really want to start a war over your death? More people will die."

She chuckled. "Wars have been started over lesser things."

"This isn't Faerie," I said.

"No, it's not, but the same rules apply. The threat of war often accomplishes more than war. The Seelie Court never was about one person, but Maeve has made it so. While she wastes time and resources threatening the Teutonic Consortium, the rest of the Celtic fey suffer. It's time for a change, either with Maeve or without her."

"She doesn't sound like the type for compromise," I said.

I moved my remaining knight. Ceridwen glanced down at the board, then at me. "When faced with two courses that will lead to the same result, which would you choose, Connor? The one that causes bloodshed or the one that causes even more?"

"I guess it depends on one's principles," I said.

"I have you in checkmate in six moves. You lost this game two moves ago. Shall we continue?" she asked.

I laughed as a knock sounded from the door. Ceridwen glamoured her face with a haze that masked her features as a servant answered the door. A young dwarf entered, cap in hand, his blunt face giving him the appearance of age. He bowed. "Forgive the intrusion. The Lord of the Dead asked to be informed if any scryers were about, ma'am."

Ceridwen had kept her identity a secret from even her followers. By wearing the glamour, they thought—or feared—that she was the mythical King of the Dead who rode out on a horse of fire bringing death to the unwary. I think she liked the outfit more than the mystery. "What say you?" Ceridwen asked.

"A strange woman has entered the Tangle. She scrys as she walks but speaks not," he said.

"No one can scry any longer," Ceridwen said.

"Indeed. I tremble to err," the dwarf said.

I stood. "You know what? I'll take this. If anyone can tell a true scryer, I can."

Ceridwen faced the chessboard, her expression invisible behind the glamour. "You didn't finish the game."

"Save it. I have six moves to prove you wrong," I said. Her laugh followed me out the door.

11

The dwarf led me through an abandoned floor of an old brownstone. All the walls had been blown out, the support structures replaced with essence barriers to hold up the roof. I didn't like places like it in the Tangle. The barriers often needed to be recharged to keep a building from collapsing, and it was never clear who or why someone maintained the empty buildings. I always worried I was in a building that was about to come down on my head.

The dwarf stopped at an open window and pointed. "She should be coming through any second. You can see her from here."

I looked down into the street, a jagged stretch of a pavement that connected two main avenues. In the middle of the lane, a feminine figure wore a sequined white jumpsuit with red boots. People grouped on the sidewalk, more curious about a large flat package than the strangely dressed figure. The package caught my eye, too—was probably what was catching everyone's eye down there. It blazed with essence. The strange part under the circumstances was that the essence resonated like scrying. Even four flights up, it pulsed against my senses. I kept my body shield activated as a matter of course in the Tangle. Even though the stone suppressed the problems the dark mass gave me, the darkness still reacted to scrying. It pressed against the stone, a heated wave of pain, struggling to shut me down.

"That's a friend of mine. Pull him out of there," I said.

The dwarf snorted. "Are you sure that's a friend?"

"Bring him to the Hunter's hall. I'll meet you there," I said.

He looked me askance. "Is that wise?"

"It'll be fine. It's shielded, so people will lose interest." The hall was Ceridwen's receiving room, where she appeared as the Hunter to her people.

The dwarf crawled out onto the fire escape. I didn't watch him descend but made my way back through the building. The next floor down had a missing wall into the next building, which had a crumbling sky bridge across the alley behind it. From there, I hit the roof and walked the length of the block, then down a stairwell into the basement and into a tunnel. Secret and convoluted paths riddled the Tangle, which made it possible for so much illegal activity to occur. I had been learning the routes, more for expediency than secrecy. People knew I was down here, but I didn't have to make it easy for them to track my movements.

I reached Ceridwen's hall several minutes later. The room held a chair, which only Ceridwen sat in. Essence lanterns hung from the ceiling to throw dim light. Old-fashioned wooden torches soaked in kerosene lined the walls. They were lit for atmosphere when Ceridwen was rallying her troops or intimidating the hell out of someone.

The entrance shimmered open—an opaque essence barrier that was stronger than any door would be. The dwarf leaned in and cocked his eyebrow at me, but I nodded for him to leave. Ceridwen's people were protective of me, but I wasn't worried.

Shay strolled in with his crazy outfit and the package

like he had come from shopping on Newbury Street. The two of us had a complicated and unexpected history. Through some residual arrogance from my Guild days, I had gotten his boyfriend killed during a murder investigation. Shay had almost died a couple of times since then because he had gotten sucked up in my wake.

No matter how hard I tried to leave him alone, something conspired to bring us together, and not in a good way for Shay. He had saved my life, but committed murder to do it. He hid the stone bowl for me, and I had almost killed him in his own apartment. I knew his boyfriend, Robin, was hiding in the city, one of the many Dead, but kept the information from him. He didn't deserve what I had done, and I didn't deserve his friendship.

He flipped his long hair over his shoulder. "That was faster than I thought it would be."

"Are you insane coming into the Tangle dressed like that?" I asked.

Shay held his hands out dramatically from the waist. "Exactly, Connor. Anyone who shows up in the Tangle looking like this is either too crazy to deal with or too powerful to screw over. I made more people nervous than the other way around."

"How did you know how to find me?" I asked.

He leaned the package against the chair. Essence radiated off it—the paper was insufficient to block it. I didn't look directly at it. It shifted and swirled and made my head hurt. "Process of elimination. Your apartment's being watched. I didn't think you'd abandon the bowl, so I figured you were still somewhere in the Weird. The end of Oh No is too close to the police and stuff, and you don't strike me as the type to hide out in a burned-out building. The Tangle was the only thing left."

Shay was too smart for his own good sometimes. "What's in the package?"

Shay ripped the brown paper to reveal a painting canvas. "It's your friend Meryl's painting."

He flipped it around to show me the plain white surface,

but plain only in the visible sense. "That doesn't look like much of a painting to me, Shay."

He pursed his lips in appraisal. "Color blocking is a bit passé, although she did use some interesting fingerwork."

Essence swirled and danced across the surface. Multi-colored shapes bent and twisted, dancing like clouds on the wind. They reacted as I approached, and the dark mass in my head threw little pain spikes down my neck. "It's infused with Meryl's essence."

Shay stepped back, still staring as if he could see what I was talking about. Shay was human, though, with no fey abilities. Sometimes he seemed to exhibit a fey sensitivity, but it appeared more intuition than talent. "I thought something was up. It won't take paint. Every time I painted on it, the paint ran off onto the floor. Uno wouldn't stay in the same room with it. It's been taking up room in the studio, and I figured you would want it."

Uno was a dog, of sorts, a big black dog whose eyes glowed red in the dark. He was the Cu Sith, the hunter of souls, demon dog of TirNaNog. After he died, Robin sent the dog to protect Shay, but Uno spent an uncomfortable amount of time watching me. In history and legends, the Cu Sith was a harbinger of death. For Shay and me, he was an overgrown puppy that drooled a lot and occasionally protected us from getting killed. At least the drool vanished on its own by the next day.

"I need to get Meryl to take a look at this. I keep hearing no one can scry, but I'm getting a scrying buzz off it," I said.

Shay turned his attention to me with the same appraising eye he had trained on the painting. "You look like hell."

"Thanks."

"Seriously. Are you all right? Your eyes look funny."

"It happened at the Guildhouse," I said. My irises were crystallized like stained glass. With the faith stone emanating its energies in my head, I had the look of an Old One out of Faerie. It made me feel ancient.

Shay licked his lips and turned away. "I knew some people who died. Not a lot."

"One's enough, isn't it?" I asked.

He played with the sequins on his sleeve. Shay wasn't one to dwell on sadness or misery. "Well, you could use some sun anyway."

I walked him to the door. "Will do. You keeping out of trouble?"

He slipped a strand of hair around his ear and smiled. "Actually, yes. My life is quite boring at the moment. I could use a little excitement," he said.

The essence barrier faded open to reveal a bustling alley camp outside. "Well, please don't find it here. I'm trying to keep a low profile."

He paused at the door. "If you keep leaving important stuff at my apartment"—he leaned in and tapped his finger on my lips for the next words—"people will talk."

I tweaked him on the nose. Shay had flirted with me since the moment we met. It flattered and amused me, but it was all good-natured. "Get going. Don't stop until you're well into the Weird. I don't want to hear that you caused a riot."

He laughed and walked into the alley. Uno faded into view, his dark form slipping in behind Shay. People pulled away, uncertain. Not everyone could see Uno, but they could feel him. It wasn't a good feeling. Shay and I didn't have the same reaction to him as everyone else. It always made me worry. About the both of us.

12

After Shay left, I had the painting brought up to Ceridwen's rooms. I didn't know what to make of it, but leaving it around unattended was not an option. Ceridwen was subdued as she stared at the whirling essence but didn't say why. She agreed to put dampening wards on the canvas so that whatever scrying was operating wouldn't split my head open with pain.

Afterward, I decided to pretend my life was normal. The Tangle was living in a stew of essence. People who remembered claimed the atmosphere reminded them of Faerie, but with urban buildings and no positive relief. After weeks in the neighborhood, I understood what they meant. Essence saturated everything in the World but intensified in the Tangle. Part of that was the high concentration of fey, but it also was what those fey did.

Essence in the Tangle was activated in all its forms—spells, wards, incantations, shields, glamours, barriers. To my mind, the difference between the Tangle and Faerie was in kind. The Tangle was about warped uses of defense and offense, of catering to baser impulses and exploiting the weak or unsuspecting. I didn't doubt that Faerie had all those things, but they wouldn't define it so narrowly. It had been a place where people lived, good people and bad, but not a place that was inherently exhausting. Wearing a body shield all day in the Tangle was not unusual. Wearing one in Faerie to plow a field was probably unnecessary.

As a here-born, someone who had never lived in Faerie, I had the added difference of being attuned to the modern world. I had lived in places where essence was ambient, not a regular tool for the locals. I had friends who were not fey, who didn't resonate with body signatures after standing in the sun too long. I noticed the difference between life in the city and life in the Weird. I liked the relief of the city sometimes.

I went for a nice long run in a stocking cap and sunglasses in the cool evening air, unnoticed and unrecognized. For a half hour, I was a guy in running shoes, not a suspected murderer. I did my favorite route down the waterside of the Weird, hopping over gaps between docks and balancing up and down old planking. I left the Weird and made for the loop down at Castle Island, feeling the harbor wind on my face.

During the day, Castle Island was a favorite public park for nearby Southie. It was devoid of people at night, not a safe place for anyone. It wasn't crime-ridden, per se, but sometimes an opportunistic mugger took advantage of the abandonment.

I slowed as I approached the parking lot. The land sloped up to an old fort from the 1800s, when the park was an actual island not connected to the mainland by fill.

A thin haze floated over the fort like a mist, not unusual since it was on the harbor, but the mist seemed only above the fort. My sensing ability picked up ambient essence stronger than usual, too.

Castle Island was where things first fell apart last year, where Shay and Keeva had almost died, and Murdock's family history started to crack open. A madman under

Vize's control had almost destroyed a dimensional barrier and released a race of beings called Fomorians, or what might politely be called monsters. The impact of those events lingered—much as nasty things lingered in the Weird and the Tangle—and took a long time to fade.

I jogged in place, searching the air. Other than the mist, nothing seemed wrong. I shrugged off the feeling as paranoia. A bunch of fairies could have been doing aerials up there before I arrived. They liked playing around in the conflicting air currents.

I circled around the parking lot and back up the access road. Before turning for the Weird, I made a detour into the edge of Southie. The Tangle wasn't known for its coffee shops, and a place around the corner made some excellent mud.

I came around the corner and almost barreled into Murdock and Janey Likesmith. Janey held a coffee-to-go cup away from her, checking to see if any had spilled on her while Murdock stared at the half of scone on the sidewalk that I had knocked out of his hand. "Can I expense that?" I asked.

"Please tell me you're not being chased by a marauding horde of something," Murdock said.

I stretched my hamstrings against the side of the building. "Nah. Went for a run. What's up? You guys get a call over here?"

Awkward looks flashed between them, then Janey sipped her coffee. Murdock picked up the fallen scone and tossed it in a bin. "No. We . . . uh . . . met for coffee."

I pulled my foot up behind me to finish the stretch. "Oh, are you going over the elf case?"

Janey started laughing and threw Murdock a wide-eyed expression. "Yeah, that's it. Tell him about the case, Leo."

Murdock blushed, and I finally got it. Janey and Murdock, together, having a coffee in a part of the neighborhood neither of them lived. Murdock was wearing jeans and a long-sleeved T-shirt. Janey was wearing a long casual dress with a sweater over her shoulders. In other words, neither of them was working, and I was an idiot for not see-ing it. "Oh . . . um . . . oh," I said.

Murdock focused on wiping crumbs off his hands. "Yeah, um, Janey says there's something up with that ar-row."

"Did you get a signature off it?" I asked. I cringed at the overly polite tone in my voice, like I had just met them.

Janey kept the wide smile on her face. "Several actually, mostly residual, but the odd part was that it wasn't elf-shot. The charge sent through the arrow had some kind of soli-tary essence on it. Isn't that right, Leo?"

Murdock smiled uncomfortably. "Yep. That's what the report said."

"The one I wrote. Right? Was there something about coffee in there?" asked Jane, then laughed.

"I don't remember," he mumbled.

"Did you get that ID I sent?" I asked.

Janey tilted her head, waiting for Murdock to respond. He slipped his hands in his pockets. "It's unofficial, but I was able to confirm that Alfren was working for the Guild. Mostly, he passed information about the Tangle and move-ments of Eorla's people."

"Has the Guild taken over the case?" I asked.

He shook his head. "He's still in the morgue. No one wants him."

"That sounds like political dodgeball. I guess we wait and see who picks him up. That'll tell us who has more to hide," I said. I wanted to bite back my words, but they were out.

Janey could not keep the smile off her face. She was loving Murdock's discomfort. "Maybe everyone should go out for coffee."

Clearly defeated, Murdock eyed her with amusement. "Coffee is good for a lot of things."

I decided to let them off the hook. "Speaking of which, I could use a cup. You guys want anything?"

"No, thanks. I'm meeting someone for dinner," Janey said.

"Yeah, me, too," Murdock said.

I rubbed my hands together. "Okay, then. I guess I'll check in with you later. Let me know if something comes up."

Janey lost it. She backed away, laughing. Murdock glared at me in a way that told me I would pay for that. Amused, I watched them walk away. When they reached the corner, Murdock held Janey's arm above the elbow as they crossed the street.

I sighed and went into the coffee shop. It never crossed my mind that they had any interest in each other. I guessed I wasn't good about predicting the future.

13

Late the next morning, a knock at the door startled me out of sleep. I was expecting Meryl for lunch, but it was too early, which meant that Ceridwen's messengers might be rousting me out of bed for something. I had been avoiding Ceridwen since yesterday because I didn't want to give her the answer she didn't want to hear. I didn't want to go to Ireland, at least not now. As she lay dying, I had promised to help her get revenge against Maeve, but that didn't mean I had to do it her way.

I opened the door and cringed as my mother grabbed me in a full body hug. "Still an early riser, I see."

"How did you find me, Ma?" I asked.

She entered the room, eyeing it with suspicious appraisal. "I asked."

I closed the door behind her. "Mother, I'm in hiding. You didn't just ask for directions to my apartment."

She peered down at the seat cushion on the armchair. "Actually, I did. I asked Amos the Apothecary, whom I have known for years. He gave me the general direction and a contact on Ceridwen's staff, who referred me to that rather disheveled dwarf who keeps the lookout on the water tower next door. He told me."

I pulled my jeans on and sat on the bed. "And why would he tell you where I lived?"

With a deep breath, she sat in the chair. "I told him I was your mother."

"And he believed you?" I asked.

She put on an innocent face. "I knew his mother. We played cribbage years ago. She stank at it."

"You shouldn't have come down here. It's dangerous," I said.

She pulled her chin in. "Is it? It looked rather shabby as I came through. Not like the old days. Do those trolls still live under the channel? They kept things lively down here."

"There's only one troll. He pretends to live under the bridge but has a nice underground apartment nearby," I said.

She clicked her tongue against her teeth. "Only one left? No wonder there are so many feral cats around. Do you have any tea?"

I glanced at my empty kitchen. "I haven't been shopping. Why don't you give me a sec to wash up, and we can grab lunch?"

She waved her hand. "No need. I have a luncheon date already. I wanted to see you."

"Is everything all right?" I asked.

She pursed her lips. "Hmm. Yes, of course, everything's all right. I have spent half an hour sitting on top of a water tower talking to a lonely dwarf because everything's all right."

I sighed. It was going to be one of those conversations. "What's wrong?"

"I'm worried about your father. This business with the Seelie Court has taken the wind out of his sails," she said.

I was getting more lost by the second. "I thought the entire court was sent home."

She brushed her handkerchief on the arm of the chair,

draped it over, and rested her hand on it. "Yes, that was after he was shut out. Oh, he didn't think I knew, but I'm no fool. He's had a hard year. It started with him being dropped from the missions to the Continent. Then Maeve put him on desk work entirely. You know your father loves travel."

I couldn't believe I was hearing this. "So, um, what exactly do you want me to do?"

She waved her hand in the air. "I don't know. Guy stuff. Get Callin to join you. He'd like that. All you boys together."

I stared at my stocking feet. "Mother, I am never, ever going camping with Callin and Da again."

"Well, what about bowling? You used to be quite good," she said.

I hid my disbelief beneath an amused smile. Sometimes mothers forget that their children outgrow their childhoods. "I'll see if I can find Cal. Maybe he might have some ideas," I said.

"Oh, I already went to see him. He said he would love to do something. Now that you mention it, he did say to suggest camping to you. He said he has fond memories of the two of you in the woods."

He would. He spent all our camping trips making my life miserable as only older brothers can do. I have had enough of bugs in my bedroll to last a lifetime. "You went to see Callin? Where?"

"His apartment. He's not much better at decorating than you, but the view is lovely," she said.

I had no idea where my brother lived. No one ever seemed to know. "Mother, have you been walking around the Weird looking for us? Do you have any idea how bad an idea that is right now?"

She huffed and fell back in the armchair, then bolted forward, eyeing the cushions for dirt. "I'm desperate, Connie. If I don't get your father out of that hotel, I'm going to scream. He needs something to do."

I didn't laugh, but I did smile. My parents loved each other but tended to get on each other's nerves. "Okay. I'll think of something."

In a bright flash of pink, Joe burst into the air. He held a take-out cup half as tall as he was. A tag on a string dangled from the lid. He held the cup out to my mother. "I thought you might be here and like some tea, Momma Grey."

My mother popped the lid on the cup and inhaled. "You are such a dear, Joey. Earl Grey is my favorite."

Joe threw me a smug look over her head. "Is it? I had no idea. Great minds drink alike."

My mother giggled. "You are so naughty. Where were you last night? I thought you might drop by."

Joe fluttered over by the window. "I was helping some children with their lessons."

I shook my head. "Children? Really, Joe? You were with children?"

Joe shrugged. "Everyone is someone's child. I didn't say how old they were."

My mother bubbled with laughter.

"Suddenly, I remember something I didn't miss when you moved to Ireland, Ma," I said.

She drank her tea, the amusement fading from her eyes. "Speaking of Ireland, I've been trying to contact Nigel. You wouldn't happen to know where he is, would you?"

I feigned nonchalance. "I haven't seen him. We're not on the best of terms anymore."

She hummed. "I heard. I'm not going to interfere in whatever is going on between you, but I'd like to speak to him."

"Why?"

"Because Nigel has insight into Maeve's thinking. She is rushing headlong into war, and that's never a good thing. If there's a way to avert it, Nigel will know."

"I don't know, Ma. I don't think Nigel would be interested in stopping Maeve. He's always done her dirty work," I said.

She gestured with her mug. "Exactly. If he's around, she doesn't have to do it herself. Nigel has a way of making things happen behind the scenes. We don't need war. Maeve needs her advisor."

I was impressed. I never talked politics with my mother. I had no idea she had that much interest. "That's . . . shrewd," I said.

"I am not a diplomat's wife for nothing, dear. The trick to avoiding war is to find something more enticing. Maeve might be a bit of a hothead, but she's still a ruler. She wants something more than defeating the Consortium. If we can understand that, we might be able to end this nonsense."

I loved the way my mother referred to war as nonsense. I might not have thought of her as a politician, but she always was sensible. Half her silliness was contrived, I knew, but now I saw her in a different light.

Another knock came at the door, and my glance shot to the clock over the kitchen sink. I groaned inwardly as I answered the door. When I opened it, Meryl kissed me, then stopped short when she saw I had company. "Oh! Am I early?" she asked.

Meryl was wearing a black bustier with a short jacket and jeans that might have been painted on. Oh, and she wore her knee-high boots with all the buckles. My mother put on her most diplomatic smile. "Not at all, dear. We were just discussing lunch."

Meryl turned a confused smile toward me. "I didn't realize it was a group lunch. My bad."

"Meryl, I'd like to introduce you to Regula Grey. Mom, this is Meryl Dian," I said.

Meryl batted her eyes in stunned silence. My mother held out her hand. "Pleased to meet you."

Meryl shook hands, staring at me over her shoulder. "You're his mother."

"And your his . . . ?" My mother said.

Joe swooped closer to my mother's ear. "That's his hootchie."

Meryl held her hand in the air. "Connor, can you hand me the fly swatter?"

My mother smiled. "It's okay, dear. I was someone's hootchie once."

"Mother!" I said.

She stood up. "I must be going. I'd love to have you for dinner, Meryl. You can meet Mr. Grey."

"Um . . . sure," Meryl said.

"This isn't happening to me," I muttered.

My mother hugged me and kissed my cheek. "Get some food in you, Con. Call me later."

"I will," I said.

She paused on the threshold and looked at Meryl. "Oh, by the way, you look lovely, and I understand the desire not to feel constricted, but, trust me, in a pinch, a bra makes a great sling weapon."

"I did not hear that," I said.

Meryl tugged at the bottom of her jacket. It didn't cover anything. "I'll keep that in mind."

She patted my chest. "Just girl talk. See you soon."

I closed the door behind her and turned toward Meryl. "Do not say a word," I said.

She grinned like I'd never seen her do. "What? I liked her."

14

Meryl and Joe pretended to talk to each other while I jumped in the shower. They tolerated each other at best, suspected each other's motives at worst. Flits had a history of innocent spying, which no one liked, and Meryl had a history of strict privacy, which she made no exceptions for. Joe had a habit of annoying whomever I dated. I thought of it as hazing the new person in my social life, but my dates tended to think he was a pain in the ass. He was, but he was part of the package when someone hung out with me.

I came out of the bathroom, towel-drying my hair and wondering if I had clean socks. For such an empty room, I had a hard time keeping track of stuff. I opened the top drawer of the small dresser and found Joe sleeping in my underwear. Without waking him, I managed to find two socks that looked the same color. Joe looked comfortable, so I closed the drawer again.

I overlooked Joe's less-than-mature antics—didn't even notice them most of the time. I grew up with him. Joe was who he was. His bad side was irritating, but at least that was the extent of it. Lots of people had bad sides that were worse, Meryl among them. She was grumpy, quick to anger, and an intellectual snob. I wouldn't have either of them any other way because when they flew, they soared.

Across the room, Meryl stood in front of the blank canvas, intense concentration on her face. I had pulled it out of the closet and shown her the protection wards Ceridwen had placed. Meryl had stripped them off and let the scrying essence free again. I activated my body shield to keep the more intense radiations from bothering the dark mass.

The visible surface of the canvas remained white, the dried paint lumped and swirled in random directions. Meryl had slopped the paint on with her hands, evidenced by furrows with obvious finger marks. With sensing ability, though, the canvas came alive, a kaleidoscopic array of moving colored essence that separated and re-formed into shapes and images. It made my head hurt, the darkness pulse in the same way it reacted when someone was scrying.

"I did this," Meryl said.

"Yep."

When I first found the stone ward bowl, I asked Shay to take it for safekeeping. He had hidden it at his place, which no one but I knew. A few months earlier, I thought someone was hunting for the bowl, so I went to warn Shay that it was time to hide it somewhere else. I wanted him to move it to the abandoned squat—which he did—but that didn't happen until after. I had taken Meryl with me to Shay's studio that day. She was in a mindless trance, then. The next thing I knew, the stone bowl was reacting to her presence and shooting essence into her body. Meryl had grabbed at Shay's paints and attacked the canvas as if possessed. The result was the scrying-infused artwork in the middle of my room.

Meryl held her hand close to the surface of the canvas. The essence reacted, the images sharpening into more recognizable shapes. A sword danced into view, then something like flames. "Did I say anything?"

"No." She had painted in a trance, fueled by the energies of the stone bowl.

Meryl stepped back with her hands on her hips. "It's my dream. I painted my dream from the trance."

I pulled on a black T-shirt and tucked it into my jeans. The living room had no mirror, so I fumbled fingers through my hair. It's what I would have done in the bathroom mirror anyway, to worse results. "The one you couldn't remember?" I asked.

She withdrew her hand, and the essence shapes disintegrated and swirled again. "You know how when you're trying to remember something and you have this vague idea of what it is and then it comes to you and you're, like, yeah, that's it? That's what looking at this is like. It's like a blurry memory coming into focus."

I came up behind her and leaned my chin on her head. "You said you didn't remember doing this. Do you know how you did it now?"

She walked to one side of the canvas, then the other. "The paint's infused with essence. Can you feel it?"

"I can see it," I said.

She whipped her head toward me. "You can see it? My dream?"

I gestured at the canvas. "Well, I don't know if it's your dream, but, yeah, I can see the essence with my sensing ability. That's why I brought you up here."

She moved away again. "Huh. What do you see?"

"Right now? Mostly nothing but smears of essence light."

She pointed at a space near the center. "What about here?"

"A patch of silvery essence," I said.

She pursed her lips. "I see a war helm."

I moved closer. The silvery essence changed and sharpened. "I see a pair of eyes."

"And now I see a silvery patch," she said. She put her hand against my chest and pushed me away gently. "And now, the helm's back."

Banging sounded from inside the dresser, followed by creative swearing in Gaelic. Joe flashed in over our heads. "What's all the freakin' noise out here?"

Meryl and I exchanged glances. "We weren't making noise, Joe."

He shook his head like a dog coming out water. "There's shouting and screaming and banging and booming."

I craned my neck up, as Joe became more agitated. "I don't know what you're talking about, Joe. Calm down."

Meryl tugged at my sleeve. "Hold on a sec. Joe, take a look at this painting, and tell me what you see."

Joe swept up to the canvas, tilting his head back and forth. From where I stood, the essence swirled and shifted in shades of blue and white, but nothing resolved into focus. "I see beer and tiny breasts," he said.

"What do you see in the painting, Joe, not wherever you were last night," I said.

His spun his head toward me in surprise. "Yggy's serves quail?"

"What?"

He pointed. "There's a lovely quail on a plate next to a pint of beer. Who painted this? It looks delicious."

"I did, sort of," Meryl said.

He crossed his arms and nodded, impressed. "I had no idea. Very good."

"That's it? You see food?" I asked.

Joe went back to the canvas. "Well, there's a few few burning buildings and something that looks like a tornado. Oh! And roasted potatoes!"

Meryl glowered at me. I shrugged. "You asked him, not me," I said.

Joe frowned. "She doesn't like potatoes?"

Meryl ignored him. "We're all seeing something different."

"Our own futures?" I asked.

"That would seem logical," she said.

Joe whirled in a circle. "Oh, good. I hope it's tonight. That blueberry sauce looks amazing." He hovered closer to the canvas. "Or are they currants?"

"Can we focus on the fire-and-disaster images, Joe?" I asked.

He sighed heavily. "Fine. But you shouldn't let them get in the way of a fine meal. I mean, the world ends all the time, but it's a terrible thing to waste a good quail."

"Glad he has his priorities straight," Meryl muttered.

Joe turned his back to her and faced me. He crossed his eyes and stuck out his tongue as he pointed at Meryl. "Someone woke up on the wrong side of the coma."

Meryl glared but didn't respond. I moved closer. A line of silver bled down the center, sprouted two branches, and became a sword. "So, it seems to be working like some kind of mirror, a future for whoever stands in front of it."

Meryl paced behind me. "And I haven't had a dream or vision since I woke up."

"Maybe you still haven't recovered fully."

She watched from a distance as the essence continued to morph. "It's bigger than that. No one is seeing the future. It's like the visions have been turned off . . . except for that thing."

The sword that had appeared reconfigured itself into a crescent, then a heart. "The Guildhouse's falling wasn't the blockage."

"That's what I was thinking," she said.

Over the last year, one disaster after another had struck Boston. I had been a focal point. I almost died. Meryl almost died. And Eorla and Joe and Murdock. Lots of people did die. Each time, scryers and dreamers in the city had lost their ability to see the future. That happened when cataclysmic events were unfolding and the outcome was uncertain. The future became so muddied on such a grand scale, no one could predict it.

"Well, nobody's admitting that the Elven King is dead. Maybe that's it," I said.

Meryl moved to the same distance from the painting as I was. My vision hazed back to kaleidoscope swirls. "Now I'm seeing Joe's tornado. I don't get it."

"We all have our own metaphors in the visions. Someone told me that once," I said.

She backed away. "Yeah, but I know my metaphors, and this isn't one of them."

The essence shifted and changed again when she stepped away. It cycled in a slow circle, the colors stretching into streamers of red, blue, and yellow. They coiled thinner and thinner, ribbons merging into purples, oranges, and greens. The colors pulled tighter, the main mass of essence in the center fading to pastel, then white. The colors tightened, darkening to gray. The circle spun faster, and the essence intensified around a black center.

Heat flared in my head with intense, pulsing pain. My vision went red, then white as my skin prickled with the jabs of a thousand needles. A maelstrom churned in front of me, a cyclone of white and black. The pain built until I felt nothing but the pain, the sting of it becoming one with my body. The vortex filled my sight, filled the room, filled the world. Nothing else existed but a stunning burn of white and black. The black center blossomed like an angry blot of ink in water, and I trembled.

"Stop," Meryl shouted.

My sight went black, the sudden shutting down of light as the vibrant essence vanished. I staggered back as the room reasserted itself around me. Meryl stood a few feet away, holding the canvas away from me so I couldn't see it. "What happened?"

"Your face turned white with essence. Black flames shot around your head," she said.

I rubbed my eyes. Red and yellow spots danced behind my eyelids. "Sounds kinda cool."

"It was a negative image of the painting," she said.

I pressed the heels of my hands into my temples to counteract the pounding. "You saw the same thing? You saw the flamy, whirly thing?"

"Bright and clear, and so were you. I thought something was going to explode," she said.

"Me, too. It was pretty for a while, but then, it always is," Joe said.

"What always is?" I asked.

"The Wheel of the World," he said.

Meryl placed the painting faceup on the floor and pulled the cheap plastic tablecloth off the table. "I'm taking this home. I don't think you should be around it."

I wasn't going to argue. Even if Meryl reactivated Ceridwen's wards to keep the scrying from hurting, there was little she could do to stop the temptation to look at it. Right then, looking at it was the last thing on my list, but I knew me. I had never been one to resist temptation well. I slumped onto the bed. "When will this be over?"

Joe hovered above the painting, staring at it as Meryl wrapped it. "Looks like Tuesday next, after dinner."

15

Lunch had to be postponed while Meryl took the canvas back to her place. She refused to let me tag along because she never let me go to her place, but this time she had a point. If I knew where the painting was, knowing me, I'd want to check it out. She wasn't interested in pretending she wasn't home while I leaned on the doorbell. Instead, I went to the Guildhouse, which had been our postlunch plan anyway. We both had work to do there, so she met me afterward. We spent most of the day apart, though, me working in various library stacks while Meryl tended to mysterious chores on another floor.

Meryl's office was a mess. Boxes filled with salvaged items from damaged storage rooms competed for space with her usual stacks and stacks of ephemera. Some things stayed for a few hours while Meryl found a better place for them, but I suspected a good chunk of it was going to hang around for a long time. I wasn't helping by leaving books on her desk, reference titles I had found in the library section. Under normal circumstances, Meryl would scream at

me for unshelving so many items at once, but I was digging
in the older sections of the archives that she hadn't cata-
loged. No catalog number technically meant no proper
place.

I moved some files on the desk to place a stack of histories that I was going to take home. I was about to leave and
resume my search when a piece of parchment on Meryl's
chair caught my eye. Hand-painted illuminations weaved
up the side margins. At the top of the sheet was a blue heart
pierced by a sword with white flames surrounding it. The
stone in my head was blue beryl, at least when it had a
physical form, and shaped liked a heart to some people's
eyes.

I picked up the sheet and skimmed the text. It was Old
Elvish, dense and hard to decipher. The best I could make
out was that it was a list of names, a lineage of some kind.
Other sheets on the chair seemed to be from the same
source. The illustrations and writing looked the same, but
my translation skills of the language were rusty.

"You ruined my surprise," Meryl said.

Startling at the sound of her voice, I held up the parchment. "What is this?"

She dropped some files on the floor. "I found it this
morning. It refers to a faith stone."

"Why didn't you show me when I got here?" I asked.

She held her hand out. "I was looking for the rest. Pages
are missing."

I passed the first few sheets to her and picked up the rest.
"My Old Elvish is rusty."

Meryl hummed. "There's not much here. The illuminations caught my eye. It starts with a recounting of an old
German clan's victories over its rivals. A war breaks out,
and the clan chief finds a talisman that stirs the hearts of his
followers. Sound familiar?"

"Does it talk about rituals or spells?" I asked.

She dropped the pages on her desk. "Not in this stuff.
Maybe in the missing parts. I found them in a hallway upstairs, outside one of the temperature-controlled storage

rooms. The ventilation system wasn't warded inside. It looks like a tornado went through the room when the building came down."

"Show me," I said.

She slipped her hands on my chest and tugged at my jacket. "No. I warded the area until I can get someone to straighten it up."

"I'll do it," I said.

"No, you won't. I've seen you do research. You'll start on it, then get focused on looking for the pages and tossing stuff aside until you make more of mess."

"Meryl, this could be the answer I'm looking for. I need to know what do about this thing in my head," I said.

She used the jacket to shake me from side to side. "Could, could, could. We have a few floors of stuff that could answer your questions. This is my playground, not yours. I've been pointing you to likely areas first," she said.

I held up the papers. "This seems likely."

She glowered at me from under her bangs. "Do not question the Chief Archivist. The Chief Archivist knows all. She will smite you if you ignore her."

I wrapped my arms around her waist and pulled her close. "I love when you talk tough."

"Crotch-grinding will not change my mind. Unlike you, my thinking parts are above the neck," she said.

"Maybe it will change *my* mind," I said.

She laughed. "Really? Maybe?"

I pouted in the best innocent expression I could muster. It wasn't very good, which occasionally made it cute. "Wouldn't hurt to try," I said.

She slipped out of my arms and neatened the parchments on the chair. "No, thanks. That's taking 'love among the ruins' a little too literally. Wanna see a dead body instead?"

I leaned against the doorway. "Now there's a sexy segue."

Meryl straightened up and destroyed my view. "I've been working upstairs. Druse is up there," she said.

Meryl knew how to redirect a conversation better than I did. Druse was a *leanansidhe*, one of the most dangerous fey alive. Fortunately, few existed—and one less did since the night Shay saved my life and accidentally killed Druse. Her body had disappeared until Meryl found it in the ruins of the Guildhouse. Apparently, Nigel Martin had found the corpse and brought it to the Guildhouse.

I had complicated feelings about Druse. Her ability had accessed the same darkness as the one in my head. She used it to survive by draining essence from living beings. I thought I could learn something from her, that she could show me how to use the darkness without being overwhelmed by it. The darkness was seductive, though, and draining essence was addictive. I found myself acting like a drug addict—not caring how I went about getting my essence fix. That road led me to almost killing Keeva macNeve and too many other people. Meryl knew I wouldn't be able to resist seeing Druse's body, if only to discover answers from her death that I didn't get from her in life. "Okay," I said.

Meryl's office was in one of the lower subbasements of the Guildhouse. Between its depth and her security shielding, it had sustained little damage when the building came down. The levels above were another matter. The next floor up had survived the collapse with mixed results, mainly because Meryl hadn't had control of the entire area. The floor was devoted to research and investigations—some of it academic, some the Guild equivalent of the police medical examiner's morgue. We passed a series of rooms that looked all too familiar.

"When did they put holding cells up here?" I asked.

Meryl glanced at me with a sly grin. "Oh, something about discovering the dungeon had secret trapdoors and passages."

Last year, a prisoner had escaped through one of the secret tunnels. Meryl knew more about the Guildhouse than almost anyone, and no one had bothered to ask her about security then. "Was anyone in here when the building collapsed?"

Meryl led me through a hallway strewn with debris. "They were evacuated in time. Some prisoners escaped. I double-checked anyway but didn't find anyone."

We entered a section that had not held up as well as the rest of the floor. Cracks had formed in the ceiling and walls. Stone had fallen in places, and walls had collapsed. As I passed a crumbled holding cell, a body signature snagged at my senses. I paused at the remains of a door and scanned the room. "That's odd. Rand was in here."

"Eorla's Rand?" Meryl asked.

I stepped inside the room, which was furnished with a bed, chair, and small table. Deactivated dampening wards were anchored in each corner. Rand's body signature registered the strongest, as if he had spent time there or expended some essence. "His body signature is all over this room. Do you have any records of who was held here?"

Meryl watched me scan the room. "I haven't found any. When they closed off this section, they separated the security. Nigel seemed to be running the joint."

I restrained myself from looking at her. The easy answer would be to ask Nigel, but Meryl had made it clear that she wasn't going to let him out of Briallen's sanctum anytime soon. My curiosity was trumped by Meryl's revenge. I understood where she was coming from on the issue. I wasn't going to force her to make any more choices because of me.

The room revealed nothing about what had happened in it or who had occupied the cell. Rand's signature and faint whispers of others told me that people had been in the room, but not why. "I'll see if Rand will tell me anything."

We continued down the debris-strewn hallway to the back of the building. The force of the building collapse had shifted the wall and popped a door from its frame, leaving it hanging askew on its hinges. Meryl pushed the door aside to let me by.

Inside, a makeshift examining room had been set up. A small table occupied the center, the better to access the body from all sides. Druse lay on her back, a plain white sheet covering her nude body. The *leanansidhe* were small of stature, and she looked like a battered child. People always seemed smaller in death than they did in life, which was somehow sadder.

Shay had hit Druse with the stone ward bowl, leaving an indentation on the side of her skull like the dent in a deflated ball. The *leanansidhe* had lived deep underground, hidden from the people and the light. Nigel had cleaned up the body—even the years of dirt and grime. Her skin was bone white, with dark gray shadows. Her whiteless eyes were half-closed, as was her mouth. I had pitied her when she was alive, even though I found her revolting. Death did little to change my feelings.

Her body hadn't decomposed. Square stone blocks on each corner of the table had a preservation spell running. I sensed Nigel's body signature everywhere. "Did you recharge the wards?" I asked.

Meryl opened and closed drawers in a nearby cabinet. "Yeah. I have to figure out how to get the Guild to take her without their figuring out I'm down here. I'm not in the mood for midnight digging."

I lifted the sheet. Old scars riddled the body, but nothing more recent like the head injury. Whatever Nigel was doing, he hadn't performed an autopsy. "Why did Nigel have her here?"

Meryl crossed her arms and leaned against a counter. "Most of the stuff in here is for body-signature examination. He was probably trying to figure out what made her tick."

"And me, by extension," I said.

Meryl sighed with exasperation. "Ah, yes, it comes back to you."

I frowned. "It's not ego. One of the conditions the Guild had for dropping charges against me was that I submit to an exam by Nigel. I refused, but I bet Nigel wanted to investigate his theories."

Meryl gazed down at the *leanansidhe*. "I'm teasing. You're right. Nigel might not have said much to you after you lost your abilities, but he was interested in what happened to you."

I pulled the cloth over Druse and smoothed it out. "For whatever his latest project was, you mean. It wasn't me he was interested in but my condition."

Meryl rubbed my arm with affection. "Can I say something? I know Nigel hurt you, and you guys will probably never be friends again . . ."

"Especially since you locked him up in Briallen's attic and won't let him out," I said.

She grinned. "Well, yeah, that, but don't forget, whatever his motivations, Nigel isn't inherently evil."

"I didn't say he was," I said.

"Yeah, you kinda do. Don't mistake his sociopathic tendencies for malice," she said.

I smiled down at her. "I didn't think you were that forgiving. He tried to kill both of us."

She nudged me. "And don't mistake my position with forgiveness. He can only hurt you if you let him. That doesn't mean you can't lock the freak up and throw away the key."

I hugged her. "I love your brand of tough love."

As we stood holding each other, I gazed down at Druse. I didn't know if a *leanansidhe* could be rehabilitated, but I did know she didn't have anyone in her life who cared. I was lucky. I did. If I didn't, I was positive I would end up on a slab like her.

My sensing ability picked up the ghost of her body signature. Nigel's wards had maintained the residual energies as they were when he found her. It didn't mean she was alive. Like all fey, her signature was unique to her, but the darkness produced a complicating effect. Her signature was riddled with tiny dark pits. Like the larger disruption in my head, they were entry points for the darkness to come out. I realized I had seen a signature like it before.

Guildmaster Manus ap Eagan was dying. His health had been failing for years, his essence fading away. When Murdock's father tried to kill me, Eagan had used the last of his energy to defend me. As a result, he had been near death for weeks. I had attended his bedside. My presence provoked a reaction from his body signature. What had been a faint haze erupted into pinpoints of the dark mass. Eagan had had the darkness in him the entire time. It was what was killing him.

As I stood over Druse, I saw the same pattern of darkness. She had spent her life siphoning essence from others to keep the darkness at bay. When she couldn't get essence from living beings, she sustained herself by using the stone bowl.

"Danu's blood, Meryl, I think I've figured out a way to wake up Manus ap Eagan."

16

By the time I reached the subway station through Meryl's secret access tunnel, I had formulated a plan. If Eagan recovered, macGoren would be knocked off his perch at the Guildhouse. Eagan had always gone his own way within the Seelie Court. He had been among the strongest under-Kings, standing up to Maeve as far as possible without risking treason. His voice held tremendous sway within the Court, and his recovery would derail Maeve's plans, at least temporarily.

It was a nice plan, except I hadn't had much success against Maeve. I'd slipped her noose a few times, but I hadn't seriously challenged whatever arcane strategy she had.

Sirens were blaring as I emerged from Boylston Street station. In the weeks since the Guildhouse collapse, sirens were sounded whenever a body was found in the wreckage. Search-and-rescue workers stopped their work to honor the dead. This time, a stream of black cars rushed through the streets, followed by the wailing of police cars. Curiosity got the best of me, and I hurried up to Park Square.

The square had become a staging area for debris removal. Construction and fire equipment sat amid the rubble. Stocky, hard-faced workers stood by the idle machinery. The salvage crews were mostly human. The recovered bodies were mostly fey. Even in a disaster, divisions between us were apparent.

When the Guildhouse had come down, it took surrounding buildings with it. Several small shops and restaurants were buried, with no way of knowing who was in them. The Park Plaza Hotel had escaped relatively unscathed except for blown-out windows. Since only the morbidly curious would want a view of the destruction, the hotel had suspended its regular business and become a de facto Guildhouse, housing administrative offices for the Guild as well as the recovery effort. The sidewalk around the hotel was the closest public access to the Guildhouse, and people gathered along the barriers to watch the spectacle of a body's being carried through the debris.

With sunglasses and a baseball cap as simple camouflage, I went unnoticed in the crowd. In the press, macGoren had made a lot of noise about what a threat I was, but so far he hadn't made a serious public move against me.

Joe popped in. Flits don't like crowds—especially human crowds—so he came in low and quiet in order not to attract attention. "Word's out they found someone important," he said.

That wasn't a surprise. Watching rescue operations was much like watching a movie shoot—nothing happening for long periods of time, people standing around doing nothing, then a brief flurry of activity. In this case, the rescue workers were obviously waiting for news camera crews to set up closer to the action. There was no rush. The star of the show was dead. Delays wouldn't cause any harm, but live news shots brought attention. A local on-scene reporter was more attentive to fixing her hair than the scene behind her.

"I can think of two people who might generate this much interest," I said.

Joe settled on my shoulder, the better to avoid attention. "Shall we wager?"

I glanced around the square. There were more Consortium agents than Guild staff, and a number of them were military as opposed to standard security. When a situation involved terrorists, you called security forces. When it was a high-level diplomat, you called an honor guard. "It's Donor. He was higher in the building when it came down. Vize is under a few more layers," I said.

Joe grabbed my collar to secure himself. "I wouldn't know about that, being sucked into a spear and all."

When the spear was active, it retained its shape and heft, but became a thing of pure essence. When I fought the Elven King, Joe was caught in the cross fire. The spear somehow destabilized his essence and sucked him inside it. I thought it had killed him, but a few days later, the spear returned him. "What was it like, Joe?"

"Bright. Dreamlike. White. It was like a nap, only awake," he said.

"Did it hurt?" I asked.

He didn't answer right away. "Only to leave."

Police and fire vehicles had pulled up into a cleared stretch of the main intersection. The heap of the building sloped up from the street, the recognizable remains of turrets, windows, and walls loomed in the chronic cloud of dust that hung over the site, a forlorn, ghostly image of war and destruction that evoked a sense of futility.

Firefighters and paramedics appeared near the top of a stone pile. Between them, they carried a body strapped to a gurney. Behind them, the tall figure of Bastian Frye appeared, confirming not only that the dead man was not from the Guild but that he was a highly placed individual. The group turned around a pile of granite, allowing me a clear line of sight to the dead body.

To all appearances, the man on the gurney was dressed in the diplomatic robes of Aldred Core, the Elven King's ambassador. Core was, in fact, a member of the extended royal family and an important figure in Consortium politics. The dead man was not Aldred Core.

When Eorla Elvendottir established her court in exile, Donor decided to show up in person to convince her to return to the fold. Not wanting to give the appearance of a king begging a subject—even a royal subject—Donor wore a glamour that changed his appearance to Core's. He showed his true face only in secrecy while in Boston.

When I fought Donor at the Guildhouse, he had dropped the glamour by withdrawing his essence from the amulet around his neck. Since he had intended to destroy the Guildhouse all along, he didn't think there'd be any witnesses. He had been almost right. Everyone who did see him was dead, except me and Joe. Unfortunately, we didn't have the credibility of macGoren, so no one was going to listen to us.

When the fey died, their body essences faded away. Depending on the intensity, it happened in moments, like with flits, or days, like with an Elven King. Enough of Donor's body essence lingered to activate the Aldred Core glamour. Even dead, he was able to maintain his subterfuge.

An honor guard of elven warriors marched into the square. A saddled horse was led behind them and behind it, a woman with an empty quiver and a man with an empty scabbard. The procession usually happened at elven funerals, but the destroyed Guildhouse was prompting more immediate ceremonial displays of grief.

It irritated me. The banners the warriors carried were of the Teutonic Consortium and the Core clan. Aldred Core wasn't dead. He was in hiding while the Consortium sorted how to handle the political crisis of a dead king with no heir—a dead king who was also engaged in his own espionage. The display of mourning wasn't right. No matter what I thought of Aldred Core, someone somewhere cared about him and thought he was dead. They were *seeing* him dead. The level of callousness in service to political ends was sickening. Besides, if I was going to be accused of being a terrorist, the least they could do was blame me for the right deaths.

"Joe, how'd you like to cause an international incident?" I asked.

He chuckled in my ear. "Is it Tuesday already?"

"Think you can get in there and remove that glamour stone without being seen?"

He narrowed his eyes as he stared at the rescue workers. They were repositioning for maximum exposure to the television cameras. "Now?"

"Now."

He winked out. He was fast. I barely noticed the flash of pink over Donor's chest, and I knew to look for it. I didn't think anyone else saw him. One moment, what appeared to be Aldred Core was getting the full military honor, in the next, the body blurred and changed to reveal the battered corpse of the Elven King. Donor was recognizable, but having a few tons of building fall on him had not left him with the most attractive appearance.

Horrified shouts and screams rose from the crowd. News cameramen scurried around the gurney for better angles as they realized whom they were seeing. Another cluster of shouting came from people near a news van. The local female reporter had transformed into a tall, slender version of Aldred Core. Confused, she spun in place, waving her microphone toward the crowd. Chaos was breaking out, absolute, glorious chaos.

Joe reappeared and dove onto my shoulder as the crowd surged toward the staging area. I backed against the hotel and let people pass. "You had me worried there, buddy. Where'd you go?"

He giggled. "I thought someone might sense the glamour gem if I came right back here, so I hid it."

"Yeah, no one will suspect that the news reporter has it. I'd say that was a great idea," I said.

He shook his head vigorously. "Well, I've always been the one with great ideas."

Sendings fluttered through the air as fey folk relayed news of the event. Bastian remained calm amid the whirl of activity. He wasn't watching the emergency personnel hustling Donor's body into an ambulance. He leaned on his staff and scanned the crowd. A cool touch passed across my face, then returned. Bastian was too far for me to see his face, but I sensed his attention.

Your doing, Mr. Grey? he sent.

I shrugged, and Joe grabbed my ear to keep from falling.

Passions are high. You should have waited. No good will come of this. You were already a target when people thought Aldred was dead. You make things worse for yourself, Bastian sent. He strode down the slope and climbed into the back of the ambulance. It backed slowly through the bystanders, then followed a police escort toward the consulate. The ceremonial warriors milled about the scene with confusion on their faces as the rest of the crowd dispersed.

Bastian's comment rankled, like I was participating with him in a shared scheme. The Elven King would have been exposed eventually. The Consortium couldn't hide his death forever, and I doubted that Aldred Core—the real Aldred Core—would be willing to go into hiding for the rest of his immortal life.

The truth would come out. If I made a couple of failing monarchies uncomfortable about that, so much the better.

17

It didn't take long for the various players in the city to react to what I'd done. People were angry when they thought I was responsible for killing Aldred Core and the people who died in the Guildhouse collapse. By nightfall, they became outraged when they realized it was the Elven King who had died and not Core. Bastian was right. Death threats flew fast and furious—even from people considered responsible members of society. Ceridwen made me move my quarters—which wasn't that difficult—and against my wishes, she had people shadowing me if I so much as stuck my nose out the door.

In the predawn mist, I walked a twisted lane of a cobbled street with no sidewalks. On the edges of my vision, the blue-black buildings to either side shifted in place. The soft whirr of wings in the shadows overhead revealed I wasn't alone. Ceridwen insisted on the escorts. I told her it wasn't necessary. She said she didn't care.

Through a strange series of events, I counted a Dead fairy queen as an ally, if not a friend. Ceridwen had died in service to the High Queen, an event that did not sit well with her. She had plans for power and plans for revenge. Where I fit into those plans, I wasn't sure yet, but I knew she considered me a factor. I did promise to help her when she died. Now that she had become the leader of the Wild Hunt, it was going to be hard to say no to her—like accepting bodyguards I didn't think I needed.

I turned down a lane that led to the loading docks by the harbor. The sea informed everything about life in Boston, from the way the streets were laid out and named, to the establishment of particular neighborhoods, to the smell of the air. The city's seafaring heyday lay in the past, but it was still a port with dank buildings on crumbling pilings, brownish green water lapping against skeletal barnacles, and the ever-present tang of rotting fish.

The Weird sat in isolation from the rest of the city, bounded by the interstate to the west, the working area of the port to the south, and the channel to the north. Old Northern Avenue ran through it like a fetid artery feeding into a series of subneighborhoods—dwarf and elf gang turfs, the bar strip, the squatter warehouses—and ended in the Tangle, a chaotic mishmash of the worst the Weird had to offer.

People down in the Tangle didn't bother anyone as long as no one bothered them. The people who made eye contact with strangers were either looking to kick ass or get theirs kicked. Etiquette dictated that entering the Tangle meant you were not visible. Wanted criminals walked its streets and byways, and no one said a word. Law enforcement feared the place and left it alone. That I was safer among the most dangerous people in the city than I was in my apartment up the street said a lot about my life.

The lane ended on a broken wharf, ancient planks of wood thicker than my arm running parallel to the shore. The occasional boat docked, but its business was more likely to be unregistered with the harbormaster's office. I turned south toward the working port area, acres of wind-swept land piled with discarded shipping containers.

Strange things happened so close to the Tangle. Mechanical devices didn't work well. The landscape seemed subject to random change. People disappeared. The city had ceased operations along that section long ago. "Abandoned the place" was a more accurate description.

Something scurried in the deep shadows of the containers. Its stealth would escape the notice of most people, but I sensed its body signature. Druids had the ability to sense essence, the powerful energy that ran through all living things. My ability was more acute than most. In addition to the Dead fairy in the air, two *vitniri* tailed me. The lupine men kept out of sight, marking a perimeter around me. More bodyguards I didn't ask for.

Coming out of a narrow gap between stacked containers, I paused to watch the gantry cranes across the Reserve Channel. The giant steel towers stood several stories high like skeletal beasts grazing on the tanker ships below them. The stark brightness of phosphorus lights illuminated their movements, dockworkers moving like ants beneath their massive supports.

On my side of the channel, different lights flickered, the blue and red of emergency vehicles. Police officers and EMTs wandered along the wharf or leaned against their cars. No one seemed anxious or concerned except a lone figure standing on the edge of the wharf, hands on his hips as he stared down at the water.

"Hey, Leo," I said.

Murdock cocked his head at me, the annoyance on his face slipping toward relief. "After this afternoon, I wasn't sure you'd come out of your secret lair, Connor."

"It was a tad quiet in the Batcave."

He gestured at the water. "Well, riddle me this. I have no idea what's going on or what they're saying, but that's a dead body if I ever saw one."

Several feet below us, a Coast Guard skiff was pulled up to a decrepit floating dock. Two cadets lifted a naked woman onto a tarp on the dock, her skin bone white and mottled with gray spots, eyes a milky glaze that stared unseeing at the lightening sky. Three pale-skinned women treaded water near the skiff, thick cascades of their deep green hair floating around them. They shot angry stares at Murdock and me as they swam back and forth in the water.

"Those are merrows. They're sea fey," I said.

Nonplussed, Leo cocked an eyebrow at me. "Yeah, I got the sea part. I'm more interested in why they've got a dead body and almost drowned anyone who came near them."

I crouched near a piling. The merrows chattered among themselves, arguing, maybe. Their language was hard to decipher. Their soft voices rose and fell in clicks and whistles I didn't understand. "They're reclusive. They tend to spend most of their lives out at sea and don't trust outsiders. They haven't had a lot of good experiences with humans. I'm not sure what they're doing with the body."

I swung my leg over the side of the wharf and held my breath as I stepped onto an ancient wooden ladder. It held my weight. Murdock followed me down, waiting a judicious few seconds so that we weren't on the ladder at the same time.

Bodies in the water were one of the most unpleasant crime victims to deal with. Water did strange things to bodies, turning them into macabre versions of their former selves. With a body on land, insects were the primary living creature to deal with. With a drowning, just about anything in the sea might have something to contribute to the disintegration of a dead body.

Beyond signs of early bloating, the woman didn't appear to have any major injuries. "How does a sea fairy drown?" Murdock asked.

I crouched, taking a deep breath. The body gave off a rancid odor of rot mixed with the sea. "They're not fish, Leo. They're mammals like you and me. They hold their breath when they dive."

Murdock pressed his hand against his nose. "Her hands are pretty mangled."

I held out my hand. "I need a glove."

Murdock handed me a latex glove from his coat pocket.

I pulled the glove on and lifted the woman's arm. The hand bent at the wrist. The flexibility coupled with the smell told me she had gone beyond rigor mortis, which meant she had been in the water a while. The ends of her fingers were torn and ragged. "Could have been something nibbling at her," I said.

Murdock leaned in closer. "The damage looks uniform on all her fingers. She was scratching at something."

I lowered the arm. "Maybe she got trapped under something."

Murdock swayed from side to side over the body to get a better view. The motion caused the dock to rock, something that my inner ears did not care for at all. "I'm not seeing any bruising. If she were trapped, whatever held her would have left a mark."

At her stage of decomposition, bruises would have shown up as dark gray blotches. "And also would make me ask why she stopped being trapped."

Murdock eyed the merrows treading water near the dock. "Maybe they know."

The merrows circled and thrashed but kept their distance. I stepped to the edge of the dock. It dipped below the surface of the water, and my shoes got wet. I moved back a little. "My name is Connor Grey. Can you tell us what happened?"

The merrows exchanged more angry glances and chattered in their own language.

"Do you speak English? Gaelic?" I asked.

One of the women peered up at me. "Whom do you speak for?" she asked in Gaelic.

"No one. I'm helping out the police," I answered.

She made a guttural sound deep in her throat. "Need Guild."

I translated for Murdock. "That's going to be a problem. Since your stunt in Park Square, the Guild has pulled most of its investigators out of the Weird," he said.

"The Guild cannot come," I said to the woman.

She slapped the water, sending a spray that landed on my legs. "Guild must come. Guild matter."

"Ask her to come with us, and we'll see what we can do," Murdock said.

I translated his suggestion into Gaelic, but she wasn't having it. She spoke to her companions, and all three began whistling and slapping at the water. I smiled up at Murdock. "I think she said no."

Frustrated, Murdock stepped forward. With the weight of both of us, the dock sank beneath the water. I lost my balance and grabbed Murdock's arm. The water dragged at our feet, and I slipped onto my knees. Murdock lost his balance, tripped over me, and we went over the edge.

I came up for air, spitting water and wanting to vomit. I did not want to think about what was in the harbor water, especially that close to the Tangle. I didn't know how the merrows survived in the polluted stew. Murdock came up swearing like I had never heard him do.

"That was not my fault!" I shouted.

He grabbed the edge of the dock. I waited as one of the laughing cadets helped him out. When he was far enough back to keep the dock from submerging again, I swam closer, and they pulled me out.

Anger etched his face. "I'm sorry," he said.

I wiped at my forehead, trying not to laugh. "Don't worry about it. Unless I get plague or something."

"They're gone," he said.

I faced the water. Bubbles spiraled and trailed along the surface, but there was no other sign of the merrows. "We probably scared them."

"How long can they stay under?" he asked.

I shook my arms to shed some water. "An hour or so."

He slicked his hair back and held his hands against the back of his neck. "Do you know anyone who speaks their language?"

"There are a couple of people I can ask," I said.

I climbed the ladder back to the wharf. A light breeze made me shiver in my wet clothes. Murdock swung over the pilings next to me. "You doing okay?" he asked.

"I'll dry," I said.

"That's not what I meant," he said.

I gazed toward the lightening haze in the east. I had been in hiding for months. I was being hunted by angry elves and crazy fairies. A Dead fairy queen wanted my help, and a live one wanted me dead. My girlfriend could read the future, and it didn't look good, and my mother thought I should go bowling with my uncommunicative dad and alcoholic brother. "I'm not dead. How are you holding up?"

He chuckled. "This, too, shall pass, you know?"

We didn't speak for several long moments. Murdock and I had gone through a lot together. I didn't know what I would have done without him the past few months. It was a measure of his friendship that I had caused him pain, but he'd stuck by me. I couldn't ask for more than that in a friend.

"How's Janey?" I asked.

"Be careful going back." I didn't take offense at the abruptness or the lack of an answer. Murdock didn't like to talk about his feelings. He turned away. Murdock didn't like saying good-bye either.

18

Later that day, I waited for Murdock at the end of Tide Street. Mechanical devices malfunctioned in and around the Tangle, and the street was the closest parking that wouldn't screw up his engine. The western sky burned a brilliant orange behind the buildings opposite me, making them seem on fire, an unwelcome reminder that they had been. Most stood gutted and dark, too structurally unsound for even persistent squatters.

Murdock pulled his old heap up to the curb and parked it behind the burned-out shell of a taxi. A parking ticket fluttered on the shattered windshield of the taxi. At least someone did his job in the Weird.

"You're looking a bit world-weary," he said. He was wearing what I liked to call his urban tactical uniform, black jeans, black ankle boots, black militaryesque shirt. Over time, Murdock had gotten more comfortable blending into the scenery of the Weird. His outfits didn't scream "cop" anymore with khakis, white shirt, and tie. Of course, for Murdock, that didn't mean his clothes weren't impeccably clean and ironed. Meryl still liked to tease him about his wardrobe.

"I had a bad day," I said.

He glanced at me, circumspect. "That's not a good thing where you're concerned."

I grinned over at him as we walked down Tide. "No interdimensional meltdowns. It was more personal."

"This time," he said.

"This time," I said.

We turned into an unnamed street, one that didn't exist on any maps or maybe didn't exist at all. The Tangle was filled with illusions. Streets existed, to be sure, but the illusion of streets did, too.

"What happened?" he asked.

"Nothing particular. I spent most of my time avoiding people. Apparently, even in the Tangle, some people supported the Elven King. I was at a bookseller's stand, and someone threw a brick at me."

"Did it hit you?" he asked.

"I had my shield up," I said.

Murdock paused, then resumed walking. An ornate building shimmered beneath the image of a plain brick-front warehouse. "I'm having some kind of double vision."

"You're seeing through the glamours. Not many humans venture this deep in the Tangle. The glamours are more tuned to fey sensibilities," I said.

I left it unsaid that Murdock was fey now. Technically, he always had been, but a suppression spell kept him as clueless as everyone else. He avoided talking about it, but I thought if I kept bringing fey matters up, eventually he'd relax. He didn't relax. If anything, his face became closed, and he watched the ground as he walked.

"I'm concerned about Gerry and Kevin. When they came home last night, Gerry had essence burns on his hands. He said it happened by accident, but I think he's been playing around," Murdock said.

Gerry Murdock's using essence was a concern. He had a short temper and a chip on his shoulder. He, like his brothers, was also starting to exhibit more aspects of fey ability inherited from his druid mother. "They need to be trained, Leo. Dru-kids have seriously hurt themselves because they didn't have training. Just because they're adults doesn't mean your brothers are immune to accidents."

"They won't talk about it," he said.

I feigned surprise. "Really? I'm shocked. The Murdocks don't talk about their fey abilities?"

"Oh, shut up," he said.

"Seriously, Leo, I'd think suddenly having fey abilities would be a major conversation. Why are they avoiding it?"

"You and this conversation. I think they do talk about it, just not in front of me. They don't want your knowing anything about them," he said.

"Oh." Yeah, the Murdocks hated me. I understood their feelings. It didn't matter that I didn't kill their father. It didn't matter that I had been young and their mother initiated our relationship. From the outside, my actions appeared intentional. Despite my innocence, their parents were dead, and I was an easy scapegoat.

We stopped in front of a building with three arches capped with large granite blocks. Warm blue neon glowed from inside a bar called Fathom, and the faint sound of a bass line thumped at my ears. "They need to be trained, Leo. You don't need me to tell you that."

He nodded. "Anything I recommend is assumed to be coming from you. If you can think of a way around that, let me know."

I opened the door, and the music became louder, with a lush, low energy. Down the center of the main room, a long pool of water was lit from below. The effect threw undulating shadows across the ceiling. Merrow women lounged in the water in small groups or leaned against the sides to talk to other customers. They weren't a floor show.

Water fey preferred little to no clothing, which invited trouble for them, even in the Weird. The Tangle provided a refuge from stares and hassle. Outside, in the real world, they had to rely on police or the Guild or the Consortium for protection. In the Tangle, if someone bothered them, they could use their full strength to fight, and no law enforcement was around to stop them.

The air hung thick with the tang of the ocean. We endured hard stares as we lingered at the door to adjust to the dimmer light. Getting checked out was standard op whenever you trod on a subculture's turf. The stares gave notice that any games would be met with resistance. If you came to laugh or gawk or get your kink on, you'd be shown the door faster than a fist could fly.

We made our way around the pool to a low table surrounded by plants and curtains. Melusine Blanc reclined on a pillowed lounge. She wore a loose robe of soft blue cotton and nothing on her bare feet. Her long, thick hair draped in intricate knots behind her. She smiled up at us as we took seats opposite, her sharp teeth dull in the dim light.

Melusine wasn't a merrow. Some say she came from Germany or France, but that didn't mean she had any inclination toward the Consortium. One could be Teutonic and not be aligned. She was a solitary water fey, her skin like translucent porcelain, her legs longer in proportion to her body than a human's were. She had a compelling attraction, her features exaggerated and narrow, offset by deep, blue eyes. I could imagine a sailor or two crashing against the rocks for her.

Decades ago, she had gained respect among the solitaries of Boston with her tough nature, and her selection as the representative of the solitaries on the Guild board had become routine. Her independence from both the Guild and the Consortium gave her power over both groups at times, but more often she struggled to defend her positions alone.

When Eorla set up her independent court and invited the solitaries to join, everyone expected Melusine to resist. She didn't. Instead, she welcomed Eorla and deferred to her at almost every turn. In fact, when she learned of the dead merrow in the harbor, Melusine sent word that she would help in any way she could.

She extended a languid hand. "Connor Grey. At last, we meet."

"My pleasure. This is Leonard Murdock. He's a detective lieutenant with the Boston police." We took seats opposite her, low divans that prevented us from sitting up. Murdock perched on the edge of the cushion, intent on not falling back in a sprawl.

Melusine rolled onto her side and gestured at the table. Serving trays loaded with oysters, clams, and shellfish crowded the table. "It's a terrible cliché in merfolk restaurants, but the raw bar here is quite amazing."

"No, thanks. We were wondering if you could help us with something," I said.

She slurped a raw oyster. "Of course. The dead merrow's name was Wessa, from a pod off the coast of Norway. She migrated south to the English Channel with some of her sisters about a decade ago and worked for the Consortium on and off since then. Sea surveillance, if that wasn't obvious."

Murdock and I exchanged surprised looks. "How did you know why we were here?"

Amused, Melusine pursed her lips as she picked through the shrimp. "Is it that surprising? You were both seen when the body was recovered. You and I, Connor Grey, have never spoken, and I get word from Eorla that it might be wise for us to meet."

"Why didn't you go to the police with the information?" Murdock asked.

Melusine leaned back among the cushions. "Why would I? Wessa was a Consortium agent. As soon as that became known, any local investigation would have been suspended."

"What was she doing for the Consortium?" I asked.

She toyed with her hair. "Could be anything. I haven't been inclined to find out."

"Why not?" I asked.

"Because it doesn't concern me as far as I can see. Look, Connor—may I call you, Connor?—solitaries work for the Consortium and the Guild. They all have their reasons, and I'm sure Wessa had good ones, for her anyway. How someone chooses to navigate between the Guild and the Consortium is their business. It's a difficult strategy to play in the best of times, and these are not the best of times."

"I thought you were a Guild director," said Murdock. "It doesn't bother you that one of your people was working for the other side and was murdered?"

Melusine swiveled on the lounge in order to lean closer to Murdock. "You mistake my role, Detective. A Guild director attempts to safeguard the people she's chosen to represent. I do not answer to Maeve any more than Eorla Elvendottir does. The side I concern myself with is that of the solitaries. Whom they chose to ally themselves with is their own affair. I try to ensure that neither monarchy takes advantage in the process."

"A woman's dead. That feels like an extreme form of being taking advantage of to me," Murdock said.

His annoyance didn't bother her. She reached over and collected more shellfish. "Don't mistake my pragmatism with callousness, Detective. I'm not indifferent. An investigation will be done. The difference is that neither of us will be privy to it. Now, that might bother you, but it does not bother me. Who does the job is irrelevant to me. You sure you won't have something to eat? These oysters are from Wellfleet."

At that point, I couldn't resist. Wellfleet oysters were among the best in the world. Living near the clam beds on the cape was one of the advantages of life in Boston. I put a dash of hot sauce on the nearest shucked one and ate it. I held the bottle out to Murdock, but he shook his head.

I tossed the empty shell into a bowl provided for discards. "Does Eorla have anything to do with your lack of interest?"

"Why would she?" she asked.

"Well, she's moved into your territory. Solitaries are looking to her for leadership," I said.

Melusine watched the other patrons splashing in the pool. "Anyone who protects us is an ally, Connor. I do my part, and Eorla does hers. We're not competitors."

I wiped my hands on a cloth napkin. "Sorry. I had to ask."

She smiled as we stood. "No offense taken. Say hello to Bastian for me."

I laughed and shook her hand. "I'm glad we met."

Outside, full dark had come down on the Tangle. Murdock and I didn't speak until we were a block away. "That is one smart lady," I said.

"Well, talking to Bastian Frye is our next logical step," he said.

"'Our'?" I asked.

"It's my case until it's not," he said. He withdrew his phone from his pocket and read the screen. Smiling, he put it away. "That didn't take long. Janey texted me that the Consortium picked up the merrow's body."

"And that makes you smile?" I couldn't resist.

"She made a joke," he said.

"So . . . you and Janey," I said.

"Yep," he said.

"You didn't say anything," I said.

We reached his car, and he opened the door. "Nope."

"Aaand, I'm not going to get anything out of you now," I said.

"Nope."

I let it pass. It wasn't any of my business, but it did surprise me, considering Janey was as fey as they come. I wasn't sure how well received she was going to be at Sunday dinner in Southie.

"I'm still curious about the merrow. You?" he asked.

"I have a few other questions for Bastian myself," I said.

"I can't believe you ate that oyster," he said.

"Come on, Leo. She gave us information. I was being polite," I said.

He shuddered and grimaced. "No, I mean ick, man. Raw ick."

19

The boat sliced through the water without a sound. I wasn't fond of water travel, but visiting Eorla had become complicated. Old Northern Avenue had become a shooting gallery, and I had become the big prize. A little nausea was better than a lot of bullets. Melusine had offered the services of a merrow to tow me across the channel. He kept underwater, his white skin a ripple beneath the surface. As bodyguards went, I couldn't ask for someone tougher and scarier.

In the bow, a kobold hunched, his flat, suspicious face intent on the dock behind the Rowes Wharf Hotel. Apparently, everybody thought I needed some bad-ass protection. Kobolds were another species of fey it wasn't a good idea to get on the wrong side of. Prone to anger and poor impulse control, they liked to make their points physically more often than verbally. The kobold didn't offer his name. I'd probably never see him again.

I couldn't walk across the Old Northern Avenue bridge without official sanction at the moment. Too much hysteria—a

lot of it promoted through the Guild by Ryan macGoren—
made anything as controversial as walking the street difficult for me. When Eorla sent word that she needed to see
me, she made the clandestine arrangements.

I clutched the gunwales. Boats were not my favorite
mode of transportation. I crouched on the little seat and
stared into the damp bottom of the boat. I kept my hood
pulled far down over my eyes, as much to avoid seeing the
bobbing dock ahead as to hide my face.

Midway through the channel, my stomach calmed
enough for me to lift my head. The inner harbor was quiet
at that time of night, ships rising and falling in place like
they were dozing. A few smaller boats moved among them,
but nothing like the frenzied activity of daytime.

Toward the middle of the harbor, a thick, muddy haze
wavered, green with essence. It resonated like a druid fog,
a protection barrier meant to confuse and subdue anyone
who ventured near. I suspected it was intended to keep
Eorla hemmed in—the National Guard and the Consortium
holding the front of the hotel while the Guild controlled
harbor access. As far as I knew, Eorla didn't have enough
water fey to consider a naval force, so the barrier seemed a
bit of overkill. But then, Maeve liked to use the threat of
overwhelming force to intimidate her enemies.

We reached the dock. The merrow rose far enough out
of the water to reveal the top half of his head. Dark eyes
peered from either side of a hatchetlike nose, his black hair
plastered to his bulbous gray forehead. As I stepped onto
the dock, he slipped beneath the surface, a faint swirling
wake trailing away through the pilings.

"Use the service entrance beyond the gazebo like you
do it all the time. Someone will meet you inside," the kobold said. Gazebo was an understatement. The hotel's most
popular function room stood like a giant cupcake detached
from the main building on the dock overlooking the marina.

The kobold secured the boat, then busied himself among
some crates on the dock, keeping his back to me and head

down. His business with me was done, though I assumed he would jump in and help if anything happened to me. I hoped.

I understood my role. We all were acting out a scene designed to look inconsequential, another boat pulling up with supplies or workers. No one shot me as I walked away, so that was nice. Rand waited for me inside the door.

"You look a little green around the gills," he said as he led me down an empty corridor.

"Yeah, boats," I said.

We waited for a service elevator. "We might not have that option left for long," he said.

"I noticed some kind of barrier going up in the harbor," I said.

"We're looking into it. So far, no one's claiming it as their own, but it's probably the Guild," he said.

The elevator opened on a residential floor. Rand led me through more empty corridors to a private suite. "I'll be waiting outside."

Inside the modest suite, Eorla stared out the window, thick protection shields blurring the view of the harbor to random smears of red and gold lights. She held her hands out at the waist as she crossed the room. We clasped hands, and I kissed her offered cheek. Her skin glowed a pale green. "How fares my fellow fugitive?" she asked.

"I don't mind using the back entrance, but I prefer walking,"

"The channel has been the safest way for people to come and go. I've been thinking of moving operations into the Weird to ease things," she said.

"I can't picture you living in the Weird," I said.

She tilted her head, amused and proud. "No? Would it surprise you to know I lived in a forest camp for years?"

I helped myself to bottled water from the minibar. "Nothing about you surprises me. Why the change in location?"

"The National Guard has guns and tanks out front. The Guild has snipers on nearby buildings, and the Consortium has set up a command center on the elevated highway outside the conference-room level," she said.

I slouched into a chair. "And that's a problem because?"

"I don't like the view." Few knew that in private, Eorla Elvendottir had a sense of humor. She wasn't going to be doing stand-up anytime soon, but she appreciated sarcasm and a good joke.

"Rand hinted at something. What's going on?"

Eorla settled onto the couch and lifted a glass of wine from the coffee table. Circumspect, she sipped. "I've received a communiqué from Maeve. She said she will not interfere with me if I do not interfere with her. I am assuming it's a stalling tactic."

I grunted. "Maeve doesn't make equal alliances. She's asking you to accept a truce until she can eliminate the Consortium. Then it will be your turn."

Eorla rolled her glass, watching the light color the wine. "I agree. She's massing her forces as we speak."

"I've heard rumors," I said. From my parents, I knew she had emptied Tara and closed the shield wall around it. No one was allowed in. Across Europe, Celtic fairy warriors were appearing in greater numbers.

"Civilians have been evacuated from the demilitarized zone around Consortium territory in Germany. She's on the move," Eorla said.

"Sounds like war," I said.

Eorla nodded. "Without Donor, the Elven Court will tear itself apart in a fight over succession."

"Giving Maeve the perfect moment to strike," I said.

Eorla had struck out on her own as a means to force Donor and Maeve to negotiate. In the months since she founded what had become known as the Unseelie Court, unaligned fey the world over had committed to her cause and her leadership. The threat of aligning with one court or the other had kept Maeve and Donor at bay for a brief period.

"While Donor lived, the Seelie Court and the Consortium were at equilibrium. A destroyed elven court is not to anyone's advantage," she said.

"Except Maeve's," I said.

"Precisely. Thus, my dilemma," she said.

"Are you going to remain neutral?" I asked.

"I do not think I can accept her offer, but I cannot allow the Elven Court to fail for lack of an uncontested monarch," she said.

Eorla walked a fine line between supporting monarchy and the will of the ruled. More than any other royal I had met, she recognized that Convergence had changed the way of life for those born in Faerie. Absolute monarchies were a thing of the past, for good or ill, and adjustments had to be made for the modern world. While Donor and Maeve clung to their old ways, Eorla saw that new paths needed to be considered. At the same time, she saw the need for transition, that a people conditioned to accept royal rule needed something familiar to guide them to something new. That was the primary motivator for establishing her new court.

"Support for the elven monarchy seems strange coming from you," I said.

"Not if the alternative is accepting a foreign monarchy. That's what's at stake, Connor. Civil war among the elves will mean nothing if the end result is fealty to Tara," she said.

"Who's officially in line for Donor's crown?" I asked.

"A few cousins with competing claims. No one everyone will agree on. I have a stronger claim and a larger following than any of them," she said.

Eorla's father had been king. Donor's father usurped the throne. When he died, Elven Court rules refused the crown to a woman, and the court passed to Donor. "You're going to claim the crown? You were denied the throne before," I said.

"Over a century ago, in another time and place. I think my people have changed enough that they will favor survival over legal niceties."

"You'll need support," I said.

"I've already reached out to Bastian," she said.

Bastian Frye had been Donor's chief advisor, spy, and assassin. "Strange bedfellows."

She chuckled. "But very elven."

"Are you going to make a formal reply to Maeve?"

"Not yet. There are other considerations, which is why I asked to see you. I cannot lead the Consortium unless I am in Germany. I will have to leave Boston," she said.

I stared at my water bottle. Eorla was the only thing standing in the way of the Guild steamrolling over the Weird. "What about the people who rely on you?"

"They don't rely on me, Connor. They rely on the idea that someone cares. I'm not going to abandon them," she said.

I tilted my head. "Who can replace you? Rand?"

A cryptic look came over her though with a touch of evasion. "Rand would not be . . . suitable. I have someone else in mind."

"Who?"

She stared into my eyes. "You."

I laughed and swigged water from the bottle. "That's crazy talk."

She couldn't be serious. Eorla's amused expression made me wonder if she was teasing me. "Not at all. You know the people and the city. You know how it works and, more importantly, how it doesn't. And you know how to work with anyone."

"A lot of those people think I caused the destruction of their homes," I said.

She crossed to her desk and arranged some folders. "Not true. Guild and Consortium agents spread those rumors, but the people down here are suspicious of anything they hear from those quarters. You have more allies and supporters than you think, Connor."

"Eorla, I appreciate what you're saying, but the fact remains, I have no abilities. How can I lead fey folk with no abilities?"

She arched an eyebrow. "Donor Elfenkonig was an extremely powerful man with many abilities, yet here I stand in opposition to what he stood for. Having abilities didn't enable him to stop me."

"That's different. You could hold your own against him in the power department if you needed to," I said.

"Connor, you stood in the room when I unmasked Donor's disguise and revealed that he wasn't Aldred Core. A physical altercation did not ensue. Donor asked for my co-operation, not my submission."

"You make a lot of sense, but ruling a court isn't something I've ever wanted. You know I don't like monarchies," I said.

She shrugged off the comment. "No one said you have to. Don't call it a court. Make it a transition to something else. I don't care what you do with it. I didn't ask to be here. I serve at the will of these people. You would, too. The point is, the old ways are over. We have to create the new ways. They won't be handed to us."

"I don't know what to say."

"Say you will think about it," she said.

I laughed. "That I can do. In fact, I doubt I'll be able to think about anything else for a while."

"Good. Events are speeding up, but we have some time before a decision needs to be made. Shall I call Bastian in now?" she said.

"He's here?"

She gave me a sly smile. "Of course. You said you wanted to ask him some questions about these murders. He agreed to wait until we were finished."

20

Bastian Frye moved with a formal bearing, methodical and deliberate, as if the act of walking into the suite was a practiced art. Despite his reputation as an assassin for the Elven King, I had never been in a physical confrontation with him. It was hard to imagine the frail old man in a fight. Of course, he had spent a lifetime learning shamanic rituals, honing his body in ways known only to the initiate, and as an Alfheim elf, his ability to manipulate essence rivaled that of the most powerful people in the world. He probably didn't need to lift more than an eyebrow to defeat an opponent.

"You've brought war upon us, Mr. Grey," he said.

"I think that's a bit of an exaggeration, Bastian. How are the funeral preparations coming along?" I asked.

"Exaggeration? I think not. Intelligence reports indicate massive numbers of Celtic warriors moving on Germany," he said.

"Not that part. The 'it's Connor Grey's fault' part. Donor brought this on all of us," I said.

"But you killed him," he said.

"I'm not going to lie, Bastian. Yeah, I killed him, but in point of fact, I was already dead anyway. It was pure luck I hit him with the spear. I'm not going to shed any tears for Donor," I said.

"What do you mean you were dead?" he asked.

"He threw me off the damned building. I was falling to my death when I hit him with the spear," I said.

Bastian relaxed, if going from very stiff to plain stiff was relaxed. "If you were dead, how did you survive?"

"That's a tale for another time," I said.

Bastian didn't participate in conversations. He processed them, one line at a time. His deep eyes, dark wells of iris pinpointed with a rich blue light, stared as if he could read my thoughts. "I shall look forward to hearing it then."

"I was hoping you could save the Boston P.D. some time and answer a few questions," I said.

"The Boston Police Department and the Consortium are not on particularly good terms at the moment," he said.

"All the more reason to earn a little goodwill, don't you think?" I asked.

"Ask," he said.

"An elven agent named Alfren was found dead in the Weird last week. Was he one of yours?" I asked.

"At one time. He was no longer in my employ though he did provide occasional information in exchange for funds," he said.

"He worked for Vize. You had a plant on your own agent?"

"It is no longer a secret between us that I was often in contact with Bergin. Anything I needed to know, he told me," Bastian said.

"So what information was Alfren providing you that was worth anything?"

"Alfren had connections in Park Square," he said.

"The Guild? How does a former Consortium agent working for Vize connect to the Guild?" I asked.

"He was quite good, despite his flawed history. Unfortunately, his contact was not as careful," he said.

"Dead?"

"A fall," he said.

"The Danann at the power plant?"

"The same," he said.

Talking with Bastian was an exercise in feints and jabs, admitting to something, then undermining its meaning. Done over beers about politics or religion, it was fun. When it was about murder and espionage, it was dangerous. People died if you misunderstood, and sometimes that was the intent.

"So they were both feeding you information," I said.

Bastian's long face cracked a thin smile. "That is the nature of double agents, Mr. Grey."

And the risk, I thought. Going undercover was a delicate dance. You had to be smart enough to get close to valuable information, which meant you have to provide valuable information. But you had to be careful enough not to expose too much information and make someone suspicious about how you knew so much. If you went deep enough and long enough, you had to pay attention to the line between whom you worked for and whom you worked against. Some people lost sight of it. Those people usually ended up dead.

"You think the Guild had them killed?" I asked.

"Do you want answers or guesses? In coming to me, you have been thrown off the trail by Melusine's suspicions. Do you prefer I send you down another false trail?" he asked.

In the world of undercover, it wasn't a coincidence when two people who knew each other were killed within days of each other. "But you don't know if the Guild was responsible."

"I am saying that they provided valuable information on Maeve's troop movements. Now they do not," he said.

I nodded as if I agreed and understood. Now I had to decide what he was really telling me. Implicating the Guild but claiming he didn't know might mean he wanted me to go after the Guild. On the other hand, he merely might be helping me sort through the evidence.

"What about the merrow that died? Was she involved with the other two?" I asked.

"That one is a puzzle. She was someone who worked for Melusine, then joined Eorla's cause," he said.

"Melusine is the reason I'm asking you," I said.

He chuckled. "She has always enjoyed stirring the pot between the Guild and the Consortium."

"All the solitaries do," I said.

"Indeed. While I do not agree with what Eorla has done, she has given the solitaries hope that someone stands with them instead of relying on the whims of foreign kings and queens," he said.

"That's the fey in a nutshell. Today's friend is tomorrow's enemy," I said.

"Yes. What concerns me more is that someone in our operations is a traitor. Undercover agents are understandable. Killing those agents is unacceptable. It is often difficult knowing whom to trust and whom to believe," he said.

A small prickle went up my spine. When the dwarf Brokke knew he was dying, he told me to believe Bastian. Coming from someone who saw the future, it was hard advice to ignore. Sometimes you had to trust people who lied to you. Sometimes you had to believe people who didn't act in your best interest. The hard part was knowing when to do which.

Bastian gave me the tiniest smile. "Are we done, Mr. Grey?"

I sighed. "Are we ever?"

21

I paced a warehouse roof in the northern edge of the Tangle as evening settled in. A harbor breeze blew over the desolate remains of buildings that had gone down in a firestorm. The heat had been so intense that the bricks crumbled to dust. From the Tangle to the center of the Weird, entire city blocks had become a wasteland of shattered concrete and brownstone. That was the legacy of a war, a prelude to the conflict Maeve wanted between the Celts and Teuts. Maeve's war wouldn't be restricted to a few blocks in a lost neighborhood. She wanted to take countries. She would leave them in worse shape than the soot-stained debris scattering in the wind below my feet.

Gillen Yor had been intrigued over the phone when I pitched him my idea about Manus ap Eagan and the stone bowl. Even Gillen—who stayed out of politics—knew that Eagan was needed in the face of the coming crisis. He arranged for someone to pick me up and bring me out to Brookline, where Eagan lay dying in his own bed.

The exposure of Donor's death and his espionage tore

through the media like its own raging fire. No longer content to let her public-relations people make accusations, Maeve had come out of her compound to accuse the Consortium of an act of war. Technically, she was right—Donor did target and destroy a Guildhouse. He also planned to step it up afterward and go after Maeve more directly. All that said, Maeve was now using the actions of a dead man to justify her own start of a war.

She had moved her troops across the English Channel. Great mist walls of essence hiding her forces had sprung up on sea and land. She had informed Washington that she was sending troops to the U.S. as a precautionary measure. The president agreed, and the American people were distracted by a new argument with Congress over foreign troops on American soil. Meanwhile, the mist wall grew in Boston harbor.

Maeve must have been beyond elated. The Consortium was in chaos, so she had no true opposition there—yet. The human government was rolling over for her, content to let her be the harbinger of war against an enemy they already feared. All of it was in service to her plans. She had moved too quickly for her strategy to be anything but planned. She had wanted this war for a long time.

I understood why Eorla was considering going to Germany. Even if she didn't take the throne, the Teuts were her people. She had defended them for over a century, lived among them even longer. No one wanted to watch their heritage disappear on the point of a sword. But if she did go, Boston—and the U.S.—would lose a strong opposition voice.

For all her flattery, I didn't think I could be that voice. I understood her logic—everyone hated me anyway except the people I cared most about. She hadn't put it that way, but that was the crux of it. Boston needed someone respected—and powerful—to oppose Maeve, if not as an enemy, at least as the friendly opposition. Briallen wouldn't do it. MacGoren wouldn't even think of it. The one person that would be able to stand up to Maeve was in a coma.

Manus ap Eagan had been Guildmaster of Boston my

entire life. He was also a respected underKing of the Seelie Court. Unfortunately, he had been dying for three years. His illness started as a wasting disease, the fat melting off his frame, then the muscle. The tremendous reserve of essence that his kind enjoyed seeped away day by day.

In one night, the situation accelerated. Scott Murdock, Leo's father, shot at me. Eagan blasted him with essence, and Scott Murdock died. The effort almost killed Eagan. He collapsed and had been in a coma ever since, his disease accelerating. It was a miracle he was alive, but it was only a matter of time before he died.

Eagan's condition baffled Gillen Yor, the foremost druid healer in the world. The night Scott Murdock died, Gillen found a partial answer, which led to a deeper puzzle. Eagan was suffering from the same thing I was—a darkness inside that devoured essence. His version seemed more diffused, speckled throughout his body. If he hadn't been a Danann, the darkness probably would have consumed him, but his powerful innate body essence kept it at bay. When he fired an essence blast at Scott Murdock, he depleted his natural reserve beyond the point of no return.

When I examined Druse's body at the Guildhouse, I realized that Eagan's condition mirrored hers. The *leanansidhe* resisted the darkness by feeding it essence. When she didn't have living essence available, she used the stone bowl. I had used the bowl, so I knew it suppressed the darkness. It didn't eliminate the problem—the thing in my head was much bigger than what I had seen in either Eagan or the *leanansidhe*—but it helped me function. With Eagan's more powerful body signature, I hoped the bowl would burn the darkness out of him.

My senses picked up a thin streak of Danann essence against the night sky. My ride had arrived. He took his time coming in—too fast, and he would attract attention—and kept his body essence reined in so that it wouldn't flare. I spotted him because I was looking for him. He rode the wind currents, his translucent wings shifting around him. The wings didn't provide lift. They weren't strong enough.

They acted like airfoils, shunting essence away from the body to power a fairy's flight.

Satisfied that he wasn't followed, he shut down his essence and plunged toward me. In one smooth motion, he grabbed me by the straps on my jumpsuit and lifted me in the air. Now that he had his passenger, he fired up his essence and shot south at full speed. My body shield tempered the force of the motion, but some wind leaked through and made my eyes tear.

Several streaks of essence burst from the surrounding buildings as other fairies investigated our odd movements. The Danann lost most of them with small effort but dove to street level a few times to shake off the fastest of the pursuers. Several miles later, he slowed to a more comfortable speed and banked northwest toward Brookline. Without further incident, he dropped me off on the front steps of Eagan's mansion and disappeared into the night.

Tibbet opened the door as I stepped up, a smile failing to hide her worry. She was Eagan's everywoman—assistant, attorney, administrator, and defender. She was also one hot brownie, tall for her species, with a tawny complexion that set off her warm eyes. Tibs and I were old friends and shared the intimacy of old lovers who had parted on good terms. She hugged me, her long, tiny braids tickling my nose. "Hey, handsome," she said.

"Hello, gorgeous," I said.

She took my hand and led me inside. I slipped my arm around her. She rested her head against my shoulder. "It's hard to see him like this."

"Has there been any change?" I asked.

"None of it good. Did Gillen tell you what happened?"

"No. He just said to come," I said.

"I was dozing in the chair last night, and he sent your name to me. It was faint but clear," she said.

"Just my name?" I asked.

"Yes. I contacted Gillen because it was the only sign of life from him in months. He's still in there, Connor. He's not gone," she said.

I hugged her close. Tibbet had been with Eagan for longer than I had been alive. She kept his life running, and he kept her life interesting. If I couldn't imagine either of them without the other, I couldn't imagine what Tibs thought. "He's a tough old crow, Tibs. Anyone else would have given in by now."

She nodded into my shoulder. "I tell myself that every day since he fell ill. I almost lost you both that night, and when it happened again, I feared the worst."

We swayed back and forth as I caressed her hair. The night Scott Murdock died, Tibs had been amazing. She took immediate control of the situation, dealing with the police, taking care of Eagan, and protecting me. She had stood up to the angry Murdock brothers, the governor, and the acting police commissioner, and coordinated medical care, all in the space of hours. As I reflected back on that night, I paused. "Tibs, what do you mean 'again'?"

She pulled away, wiping tears from her face. "The Solstice Party. I thought I was going to lose the two of you."

I stared down at her. "You said 'again,' Tibs. What do you mean 'again'?"

She brushed hair back from my forehead. "The night you fought Bergin Vize at the nuclear plant."

"Eagan fell ill that same night?" I asked.

Her eyebrows drew down together. "Yes. It was chaos. I was getting sendings about your being in critical condition. People from the Guildhouse couldn't reach Manus. I thought he was ignoring everyone because he was concerned about you, but when I went to check in with him, I found him collapsed here in the grand hall."

"What did he say?"

She shrugged. "Nothing. Refused to talk about it."

"How come I didn't know this?" I asked.

She gave me a wry smile. "You were in the hospital for weeks. We had to deal with the state authorities because of the power grid going down. Time . . . I don't know . . . passed. I guess by the time you woke up, it didn't seem important when things happened. Keeva never mentioned it?"

"She knew?"

"Sure. She was here that night—complaining about you, as a matter of fact. She said you weren't supposed to be there. Is that true?"

"Yes. I'd forgotten," I said. Keeva was supposed to take the lead on the next Vize appearance. When we were partners, we used to argue about who was leading an investigation, so we agreed that we would take turns. When we had word Vize might be in the Boston area, I couldn't resist. He had gotten away from me before, then he was on my home turf. I held back information from Keeva and went to the nuclear power plant alone. I didn't remember thinking that was stupid then.

Tibbet frowned. "You sound so suspicious, Connor. What's going on?"

"Think about it, Tibs. Whatever happened to me that night gave me the dark mass in my head, and Eagan went down with it the same night. Don't you think that's more than coincidence?"

"Sure, now that you point it out. I never made the connection."

I looked at the bed. "The bigger question is why didn't Eagan?"

She glanced up at the balcony above the main hall. "I don't know. I miss the old grouch complaining about everything. I'd even pour him a drink if he opened his eyes."

Eagan had a thing for whiskey that was more than a thing. It didn't appear to be debilitating, but I often wondered if his Danann constitution saved him from alcoholism even as it was a cause. "And I'd join you," I said.

"Gillen and Briallen are already here. Your friend should be along shortly."

I kissed her hand. "Thanks, Tibs. Let's hope this works."

"Go on up. I'll join you shortly," she said.

I climbed the stairs in the great hall, curving around a stuffed Asian elephant until I came level with the John Singer Sargent portrait of Maeve on the opposite wall. I always looked at it. It was impossible not to—larger-than-life, her commanding stare daring you to look away. If everything went well upstairs, she'd soon have a new thorn in her side, and it would please me to no end that I helped put it there.

In his bedroom off the second-floor corridor, Manus ap Eagan lay against soft white sheets surrounded by brocade pillows in shades of silver and blue. He was on his side, his knees drawn up to his waist. His long wings had gone stiff, curling forward around his body like a shroud, a sign of death among fairies. I had seen something like it before though not in someone as powerful as a Danann.

Essence hovered over the silent figure in hazy layers of gold and white. Briallen and Gillen tended Eagan from opposite sides of the bed. The layers dipped and swirled, flashing and fading along his wings. At brief intervals, his body signature would flare, then dim again as the essence leached away.

"Grey," Gillen barked. Despite—and often because of—his gruff manner, people deferred to Gillen. He treated everyone the same, though, both as a healer and an acquaintance. Even Maeve had been subjected to his temper and let it pass. Whatever his personality flaws, Gillen cared about what he did and had little patience for other people's dramas.

I moved forward with reluctance and stopped at the foot of the bed. The last time I was near Eagan, the darkness in my head had fed the darkness in him. It had intensified in both of us, shooting pain into my brain and almost killing Eagan. I worried that my presence might push him beyond the brink.

Gillen peered down at the patient. "Come on this side."

I did as he ordered. The essence Briallen generated swirled and shifted away. "Now back slowly away."

I took one step back at a time until I was against the wall. Gillen tilted his head from side to side, essence light scattering through the halo of gray hair around his bald spot. "That's enough, Briallen."

She leaned back in her chair. The essence stream from her dissipated like smoke and evaporated as she withdrew. Eagan hadn't moved.

"How long have you been doing this?" I asked.

With a tired smile, Briallen rolled her head against the crook of the chair to see me better. "We've been taking shifts for a while."

Gillen grunted as he checked a series of stone wards on the bedside table. "He took a turn for the worse when the Guildhouse came down."

"He was bound to the building," I said.

Briallen nodded. "A Guildmaster is bound to his place. A Guildhouse rises and falls on the strength of the Guild-master."

"I was hoping proximity to the faith stone would have some effect. It didn't," Gillen said.

"What about the darkness? Last time I went near him, it made him worse," I said.

Gillen shifted stones around on the tray next to the bed. Essence dimmed on some, grew brighter on others. "The faith stone is dampening the effect. I didn't see any change at all this time."

"Did you know the faith stone was in the Guildhouse?" I asked.

He frowned. "Why would I? Do I look like a mason?"

Briallen looked up at me. "I don't think he told anyone about it. If he didn't mention it to me, I doubt he told Nigel or Maeve."

I pursed my lips. "That sounds plausible. I'm sure Eagan had no personal agenda he didn't wish to share."

Briallen glared at the sarcasm in my voice. "Yes, I'm sure one Guildmaster would have told another Guildmaster, unlike, say, a reckless student who oversteps himself."

"I'm not a student," I said.

"And I'm not listening to this," Gillen said. "If you two need to argue about something, do it somewhere else."

Briallen and I stared at each other. The silence was broken by a knock on the door, and Tibbet entered. "He's almost here," she said.

22

Tibbet and I waited in the dark outside the greenhouse. The grounds lights had been dimmed or extinguished to reduce visibility in case anyone was watching. At the edge of the lawn, shadows darker than their surroundings moved with a glint of light reflecting off chrome helmets. Out of sight, brownie guards roamed the perimeter of the property. Two of them maintained their normal watch in front of the house and another two on the rear patio. Danann security agents patrolled the air, pale traces of essence marking their passage like subtle shooting stars.

"Things seemed a little tense upstairs. Everything all right?" Tibbet asked.

"Yeah. Well, no. Briallen and I are having a disagreement about information-sharing," I said.

She sighed and leaned against me. "Sometimes all the knowledge in the World can't change a thing."

I slipped my hand in hers. "This is going to work, Tibs. I can feel it."

She shifted on her feet. "They're here."

A buzzing sound tickled my ear, the whirr of fairy wings moving at speed. With a gust of wind, two Danann agents appeared above us, holding Shay between them, and lowered him to the ground.

Shay wore black jeans, a long black leather coat, a thick black woolen hat with a rolled brim, and silver goggles. The strap of a messenger bag crossed his chest. With gloved hands, he lifted the goggles and settled them on his forehead. "That . . . was . . . awesome."

"I take it there was no trouble?" I asked.

We walked across the lawn toward the house. "They wouldn't take me over the Hancock Tower, though. That would have been cool."

Mildly confused, Tibbet glanced at me over Shay's head. "Secrecy was the point of the trip. There is security all over that area of the city."

Shay eyeballed me. "She sounds like loads of fun."

I gave Tibbet an affectionate smile. "I can vouch for her, Shay."

We entered the house through the side entrance by the library. Shay could not hide his awe, his head swiveling from one side to the other as he took in the expensive furnishings and artwork. "I think you can fit my studio in that fireplace."

"Old money buys a lot, doesn't it?" I said, as we climbed the back stairs.

Shay stopped short when we entered the bedroom and he saw the frail body on the bed. He patted the messenger bag. "Except health."

Gillen waited at the bedside, his face intent as he monitored the wards. "It's about time. We haven't got all night."

Briallen held her hand out. "You must be Shay."

Shooting me looks of amazement, he took her hand. "Pleased to meet you, Lady Briallen."

I had traveled among the rich and powerful for so long, I didn't think about it anymore. It was easy to forget that other people held them in awe. Once you got to know them, though, you realized they were no different than anyone else, luckier than most, their negative character traits exaggerated as much as their positive. Money let them be that way. It didn't make them nicer people. It just made them rich. People like Eorla and Briallen were exceptions, but I knew that even they used their privileges to get what they wanted in ways the average person never could.

Shay lifted the strap from his chest and placed the bag on the floor. Ripping open the Velcro, he retrieved the stone ward. In the subdued light, the bloodstone bowl shimmered, its green surface rich with the red spots that gave the stone its name. Without any release in the past weeks, a substantial charge had built up on it.

"Put it on the nightstand, boy," Gillen said.

For once, Shay seemed nervous. He played tough down in the Weird, but in a mansion surrounded by powerful fey—truly powerful—he was out of his element. He did as asked, then stared down at Eagan. "He looks terrible."

Gillen scowled, then lifted his eyebrows. "Thanks, kid. Now get out of the way."

Shay stepped back as Gillen leaned over the bowl. He pulled his reading glasses farther down his nose, tilting his head up and down. His hand lit with essence as he caressed the air above the ward. "Does it require direct contact?"

"I've seen it . . . used it . . . with both touch and proximity," I said.

"Chants? Commands?" he asked.

I shook my head. "It's ambient."

Stone wards worked like electrical components—inductors, capacitors, resistors, and the like. Most wards require some catalyst to work—an interaction with an essence field, a spell, or something as simple as sound. A few worked by what druids called ambience, becoming activated by its surroundings or something in its surroundings. The stone bowl worked with whatever essence was at hand, making it ambient.

Whoever created it had been a master of stonework. Not only did the bowl store essence, it reproduced it in exponential amounts. It shouldn't have been possible. Even with essence, energy was a closed system. It didn't burst into existence out of nothing. The stone had to be tapping into an essence reserve somewhere on a level I didn't understand, maybe even an aspect of the Wheel of the World. Before Convergence, the Ways opened onto many realms. I didn't think anyone ever knew how many and what lay there.

Gillen touched the edge of the bowl. Essence light flared, a spark of gold from his hand that swirled into the stone. He grunted and withdrew his hand. "Never seen the like. How do you use it if you can't move it?" he asked.

"I touched it, and the essence flowed into me. With Meryl, it seemed to jump into her on its own," I said.

Annoyed, Briallen crossed her arms. "Why didn't you tell us that the bowl caused the mysterious essence burst you said revived her?"

"I don't know. Maybe I didn't feel like explaining the properties of a mysterious essence instrument to you," I said.

I couldn't help the dig. I accepted that Briallen treated me like her student long after I had left her charge. I couldn't help wanting to remind her I didn't answer to her anymore and that sometimes she overstepped as much as I did. She didn't tell me about the sword. I didn't tell her about the bowl. It was quid pro quo even if I didn't intend it to be. My words had the effect I intended. Upset, Briallen straightened her back but didn't say anything.

Gillen glanced at Shay. "What do you feel when you touch it?"

"It feels kinda odd, warm and soft instead of hard and cold," he said.

"No burns or shocks, young lady?" Gillen asked.

"No. I'm a guy, by the way," Shay said.

Gillen grunted. He cleared his throat and pushed at the bowl. It didn't move. Since the bowl could be moved only by a virgin, that told me more about Gillen than I needed to know.

"What are you thinking?" I asked him.

He tilted his head up and down, still examining the bowl. "I'm gassy. I shouldn't have had the broccoli with dinner. Come here and stick your hand in it."

Despite being made a fool of on other occasions when he told me to do things, I always did as Gillen asked. A prickling sensation ran up my arm, and the stone in my head beat a warm pulse. A veil lifted inside me, connections leaped together and burst with energy. My hand flared with essence, power shooting down into the bowl, and I felt that I could do anything with a simple thought. I had not felt that sensation for over three years. I stumbled back with a gasp and stared at Gillen.

"What happened?" he asked.

"My abilities. It felt like my abilities came back," I said. The sensation faded as quickly as it had risen, the stone in my head and the darkness resuming the tired dance that blocked my abilities.

Gillen tapped the edge of the stone. "Handy little gizmo. Are you ready, Briallen?" She joined him by the bed and placed her hand on the bowl. "Begin," Gillen said.

Briallen's body shield swirled around her, and the bowl reacted with a spark of clear white essence in the depression. With measured bursts, Briallen fired essence at the stone. It absorbed each infusion, glowing whiter and brighter. Static arcs jumped from one edge to the other, from inside the bowl to Briallen's hand. She closed her eyes in concentration, pulling more essence into her and directing it out again.

Gillen took Eagan's hand with a gentleness that belied his usual nature, stretched the Guildmaster's arm toward the bowl. As the skeletal hand neared the ward, essence sparked between them, and Eagan's fingers twitched. Gillen lowered the hand onto the stone.

White fog swirled around the hand. Dark spots formed on the skin, and the essence gathered over them, tiny funnels of light pouring into the spots. Briallen maintained her stream, adding more essence from her fingers with each pulse.

A bolt of essence shot into the air, froze, then bent back

over the bed. It splintered and plunged into Eagan's body. Pain lanced through my head, like a fist hitting my brain. Eagan convulsed, his brittle wings unfurling with a sharp snap as he rolled onto his back. He arched when another surge hit, his mouth straining open in pain. Beside him, Briallen stood transfixed, her hand locked onto the bowl.

More pressure built inside my head. I moved back, the essence pounding against my brain, the yearning of the darkness inescapable. It shifted inside my mind, the familiar burning sensation of its unquenchable thirst. The faith stone burned, too, cold and heat oscillating between it and the darkness, fighting for dominance. I closed my eyes against the infinite loop of pain.

Essence coursed into Eagan, splintering and splintering again. Burning white lines fed into the pinholes of darkness that speckled his body signature. The essence overwhelmed the darkness, stitching together his body essence with flashes of light.

With a last burst, the essence from the stone bowl faded. Spots danced in front of my eyes. I fell back against the door. Briallen swayed as Gillen helped her to the armchair. She slumped on the seat, worn and exhausted, her own body signature a smoldering ember of its normal brilliance.

Tibbet came to my side and lifted my head by the chin. "Are you okay?"

I took her hand and stood. "Yeah. Stunned a little."

Eagan lay on his back, his wings spread across the sheets. They rippled with the air currents, essence dancing among the veining. The flesh on his face had filled out. He didn't look well, but he didn't look dead anymore. I scanned him with my sensing ability. "He's regenerating on his own," I said.

Gillen touched the wards on the nightstand. "I'm not sensing any of the darkness."

"Me either," I said.

Gillen turned with a pensive look. "I don't know how that thing works, but if he's cured, there's hope for you yet."

Excitement surged through me. To be free of the darkness was unfathomable, to be whole again, to be cured. "Gillen, can we . . ."

He held up his hand. "One step at a time, Grey. Eagan didn't have nearly the amount of darkness in him as you do, and it's drained Briallen to her core."

"I'm fine," she said.

"Spent is what you are," he said. "You need to sleep. We all do. Tibbet, please call the car. I'm taking Briallen home. I'll be back by daylight."

23

Rest, Gillen had suggested. As if the idea that Manus ap Eagan might be healed or that I might have a chance at getting rid of the darkness were rest-inducing. I tossed and turned in a bedroom on the second floor, the deep silence in the house not helping me to relax. The Tangle was full of noise that became a soothing backdrop to fall asleep to. Eagan's house was out in the suburbs and removed enough from the main road that a police siren was a faint echo.

Intruders.

I was out of bed with my daggers in hand before Tibbet's sending faded from my mind. In silence, I moved behind the door, keeping out of the moonlight. I didn't have the ability to respond to Tibbet and didn't know where the intruders were. I crept along the wall, keeping my eye on the door as I approached the window. Nothing moved on the lawn outside. At the foot of the front steps, a brownie guard lay on the ground, unmoving.

Third floor clear. Meet me in the back stairwell.

Without hesitation, I entered the corridor. Toward the

main staircase, a dim light flickered from the grand hall. It was too far off and opposite Tibbet's direction. Tibbet knew her territory, and if she told me to jump off a bridge, I would. I went the other way, slipping into the next door to retrieve Shay.

Shay's bedroom was black as pitch. I closed my eyes to focus with my sensing ability. Faint purple wisps showed where Shay had crossed the room to the dresser, the open windows, and the bed. A thicker buildup on the bed indicated he had been asleep. I checked on the opposite side and under the bed, but the floor was empty. He wasn't in the room.

At the open window, essence splayed along the floor and over the sill. Two flights below, Shay's hat sat on the lawn. I peered into the darkness, trying to figure which way he had run.

"Dammit, Shay, you could have killed yourself," I said under my breath. I quick-stepped back to the door and listened for sound in the hall.

"I'm here, Connor," Shay whispered.

I spun on my heel, daggers wide and low. Shay, fully dressed, stood by the windows. "Where the hell did you come from?"

He crossed the room on silent feet, avoiding light from outside. "Behind the curtain."

"I thought you'd jumped," I said.

In the dim light, his faint body essence illuminated his face. "The fey always assume that because humans can't manipulate essence, we can't use it. It's an old trick in the Weird to hide in your own shadow. You looked where I made you look."

"Well, it worked. Nice move," I said.

He grinned. "Thank you."

"Why did you hide?"

"I heard essence-fire. It was faint, but when you live around it and have no defense against it, you kinda get sensitive hearing. What's going on? The guards are gone."

"Security breach. We have to meet Tibbet. Stay behind me and do exactly as I say," I said.

I opened the door. The light from the grand hall seemed brighter, and I heard muffled voices. We slipped out and hustled in the opposite direction to the back stairwell. Someone moved on the landing below us, then Tibbet's essence tickled at my senses. We descended to the first floor.

Tibbet didn't look at us when we turned the corner. She leaned against the wall, trying to see something out the window. She had a headset on. Her face was not something you want to see in a brownie. Her cheekbones and eye ridges had become more prominent. The hand that rested on the windowsill had elongated fingers tipped with nascent claws. She was not far from going boggie.

"What's the status?" I asked.

She held up a hand as the headset whispered. "Aerial support is gone. Front gate and lawn perimeter down."

"What about Eagan?" I asked.

"His bedroom is sealed. Not even Maeve can get in there. The front of the house is breached. Let's move." She led us back up the second-floor corridor. A brownie in a house uniform waited outside Eagan's bedroom. She wasn't regular security, but her calm manner despite the boggart signs of long claws and teeth told me that Tibbet hired multi-skilled cleaning staff. At the far end, a brownie in full boggart mode guarded access from the staircase.

Inside Eagan's bedroom, Tibbet hurried to the window. "We've been co-opted, but the silent alarms triggered."

"What the hell is going on?"

She did look at me then. "I don't know. Sendings are being jammed. They're either after that stone ward or you. Those are the two main variables here."

"Gee, thanks," said Shay.

Tibbet glanced at him. "Since you're the only one who can carry the ward, I wouldn't be too disappointed."

"Pack the bowl, Shay. We're getting out of here," I said.

Tibbet moved to the opposite window. "That might not be possible. The Danann security agents have vanished. They were on a regular rotation through the Guildhouse. The house guards are our staff. Except for the two outside,

they're either nonresponsive or dead. It will be at least fifteen minutes before major backup support responds to the
failed system. Get Shay to the greenhouse. I can cover you
from here."

Shay adjusted the straps on his messenger bag. "Are you
kidding? That place looks like I can kick it over."

"Glass and iron. It'll screw up whatever's coming
down," Tibbet said.

"We're not leaving you alone," I said.

Shadows accentuated the changes in her face. She was
not the concerned brownie anymore but the cold boggart.
"This is major opposition, Connor. We need to separate the
potential targets. I can hold the house for a while. There's a
bunker under the greenhouse. The door is under the rug."

"You have a greenhouse with a bunker?" Shay said.

Tibbet smiled. "And a tunnel and a few booby traps.
There's a car at the end of it."

"That's preparation," he said.

She leaned over Eagan's sleeping body, placing a hand
on his forehead. "I throw a mean party, too. Get moving."

I grabbed her. "Tibs."

I stared into eyes tinged with a feral red light. "Go.
Now," she rasped.

I kissed her. Grabbing Shay by the arm, I hustled him
out of the room. The brownie guard outside the door was
gone. Sounds of a struggle echoed up the back stairs. We
ran for the grand staircase on the opposite end of the house.
The brownie that waited there had gone full boggie, but
had not lost his senses. Tibs had some amazing staff. He
growled as we approached and scampered down the stairs
ahead of us.

"Don't leave my side for a second," I said to Shay.

We waited in the gloom. The boggart moved through the
great hall at an astonishing speed. He returned to the base
of the stairs and waved us down.

"There are French doors at the back of the hall, Shay.
The greenhouse is a straight shot across the lawn from
there. Keep low and do not stop," I said.

He clutched the stone ward against his chest. "They can't take the bowl, right? Why don't we leave it somewhere and get out?"

"Because they'll find it and figure the geasa out eventually, and we'll never see it again. I don't want to think about something that powerful being in the hands of whoever is out there. Get going before we can't get out," I said.

A muffled explosion shook the house as the attackers dropped any pretense of stealth. We ran around the stuffed elephant and into the back alcove. Through the windows in the doors, the greenhouse loomed in the darkness, its skeletal frame a dull white against the backdrop of tall cedars.

I activated my body shield, enveloping Shay in its protection. Another explosion from the right shivered against the glass doors. Shredded essence floated across the back lawn, the remains of barrier shields that had been disabled. Without the wards anchoring them, their energy dissipated in the night air. Here and there at the far end of the property, pools of essence indicated the passage of Danann fairies and brownie security. From that distance, I couldn't identify specific signatures.

Something moved across the grass, a dark shadow pierced by glowing red eyes. The shadow resolved into the shape of Uno. He had grown enormous, his legs almost three feet long and his muzzle as wide. He trotted toward the greenhouse and stopped next to the door, settling on his haunches.

Frightened, Shay leaned back against me. "Why is he here, Connor?"

"Uno has never hurt us, Shay," I said.

"It's not him I'm worried about," he said.

"He's waiting for us. Fifty yards, tops. Are you ready?"

He moved to my side. "You've got longer legs than I do. Don't leave me behind."

"I won't," I said.

I took his arm to reassure him. We moved out the door, crouching across the pavers and onto the grass. Essence-fire flashed and burned, more warning shots than directed blasts. We started to run, closing the distance to the greenhouse.

Gunfire erupted from the back lawn. I wasn't expecting guns, a rookie mistake. The fey came at each other with essence, not bullets. My body shield shifted and folded as bullets grazed it, the force of impact knocking us apart. I shoved Shay to the ground among low shrubbery.

Shay's messenger bag flew free as he tumbled, its contents spilling out. The stone bowl rolled onto the grass. Instinctively, I grabbed it, surprised that it moved at my touch, my fingers slipping across wet stone. I lifted my hand. Blood covered the palm. I was sore from my shield contracting, but I wasn't bleeding. I cradled the bowl against my side and crawled toward Shay.

More shots fired, turf spitting into the air around us. Shay kept his head down, not reacting. I shook his shoulder. "Are you hit, Shay?"

He didn't move. I pushed against his side, rolling him onto his back. His eyes fluttered open. "Connor," he whispered. Blood oozed from his lips.

My hands came away with more blood as I searched his chest and stomach. "Dammit. Where are you hit, Shay?"

Uno howled, an unearthly wail that shot fear up my spine. He lumbered toward us, howling louder—and growing bigger.

"He looks so beautiful." Shay's voice echoed with moisture.

"Hang on, Shay. I'll get you out of here," I said.

As I leaned over him, placing the bowl against his chest, I gathered him in my arms. Uno barreled into me, pinning me on my back, his muzzle looming over me, huge and foul. Snarling, he backed away, then shifted his bulk over Shay. He opened his mouth—and opened it and opened it—a huge maw of shadow spreading over Shay. Lowering his head, Uno wrapped his jaws around him, knocking the stone ward bowl to the ground.

I scrambled to my feet. "No!"

I leaped, slamming into Uno's flank. I flopped away like

I had hit a brick wall. Uno lifted his head, Shay dangling from either side of his jaws. The massive animal arched his back and stretched his neck out. Shay rolled inward, curling into a fetal ball, then vanished into the shadowed gullet.

Uno threw his head back and yowled with a song of sorrow. Tears burst from my eyes at the sound, a keening that reached deep into my soul. I fell to my knees as grief shocked through me. Uno lowered his head, staring at me with his eyes ablaze. With a soft bark, he turned and lumbered off, vanishing into the night.

I jumped to my feet, roaring with rage at the darkness, when someone tackled me.

24

Tibbet's body signature registered, and I stopped struggling. She eased off me, crouching in the grass and facing the back lawn. Light glinted off metal there as faint human body signatures moved against the dark.

Tibbet's face contorted, with an extended jaw bristling with teeth. She clutched the grass with sharp claws on her hands and feet, a feral gleam in her eye. Unlike her brethren, Tibbet was able to retain her sanity when she was boggie. The skill came from years of practice and a strong will. *Get to the greenhouse now,* she sent.

"I can't leave you, Tibs," I said. Not then. Not after what happened with Shay.

No time. We are defenseless, she sent.

"Tibs . . ." I said.

She bared jagged teeth, gripping my arm with sharp claws. "Please," she rasped. Her eyes showed a determination I couldn't argue with. She spun in place, then leaped into the darkness, the shape of her lost in a blur of preternatural speed. Someone screamed out there, a man's harsh cry. Gunfire sprayed the grass, then more screaming rent the air. Tibbet was not going to let the mansion go down without a fight.

I scooped up the stone bowl from where it had fallen and ran the remaining yards to the greenhouse. The door let me into an air lock. After closing the outer door behind me, I opened the inner door and left it open. The outer door wouldn't open if the inner was open. It would slow down pursuit until someone decided to smash through the glass walls.

Inside, the humid air stank of rot. Eagan had spent a lot of time in the greenhouse, the heavy moisture easing the brittleness in his wings. The vegetation had been lush and thick once. The plants had been allowed to wither. The room seemed bigger as result, and the windowpanes along the walls were more visible. The muzzle flash from gunfire lit the air like lightning, and glass shattered overhead.

I knocked aside two armchairs on the oriental carpet in the center of the room. Yanking back the carpet, I exposed the trapdoor. Tucking the stone bowl in my jacket, I heaved the door open with both hands and clambered down a short flight of stairs. The door slammed shut behind me, and I slid a large dead bolt across it.

Motion detectors brought the lights up. The bunker was a narrow room with a simple table and chairs and shelves filled with boxes. An open door led to a bedroom/office that could have been photographed for a design magazine. I skipped it and made for the door on the far end. More lights flickered on to reveal a long, narrow corridor. I locked the door behind me. The lights flashed on and off as I followed the long line of bare bulbs down the corridor and off the estate.

After I had run about a mile, another door appeared ahead. Beyond it, a staircase led up to a garage, empty except for a small black sedan. I jumped in and fished keys from under the seat. The glove compartment and the console held nothing but a few rolls of quarters and the insurance and registration papers. People who could do sendings didn't think of storing a throwaway cell phone. I hit a remote on the dashboard. As the garage door opened, I put the car in gear, then shifted back into park.

I reached in my jacket and withdrew the stone bowl, cradling it in my hands, hands stained with Shay's blood. The bowl was stained, too, Shay's blood seeping into the grain of the stone. Shay might have been worldly beyond his years, more a man than most, a quirk of fate that made him a virgin in the eyes of old Faerie. His blood broke the geasa; a young man, barely past boyhood, was dead because he had been pulled into the craziness of my life.

From the day I laid eyes on him, I wanted to see him safe. He had fire and spirit that deserved more than the lot he had been given in life. I wanted him to have the chance to become all he wanted to be, but he'd had the misfortune of meeting me. He never expected me to protect him, but I tried anyway. And I failed. Of everything that had happened to me, to the people around me, I didn't know what I could ever do to atone for his loss, but I would try. That was all I ever wanted to do for him. Try.

I settled the bowl in my lap and put the car in gear. I pulled out into a quiet neighborhood, modest by Brookline standards, which meant the multimillion-dollar homes were within spitting distance of each other. I saw no one as I followed the GPS map out of the area.

Unless someone from the Guild responded to reports of the shooting, the Brookline police would be the first responders. They shared resources with Boston, but they weren't likely to call them until they knew they needed help. I tuned the radio to local news stations. No one was reporting gunfire. I had some room to maneuver before a call went out looking for me, and the more distance I put between me and Eagan's house, the more at ease I was.

I drove Route 9 back into the city, considering my options. The Tangle was being watched. Briallen's town house had to be under surveillance. Murdock's house was out of the question. I considered hiding in the Guildhouse archives, but only one way in existed that I knew about. If I was discovered, I'd be trapped.

Aimless, I circled Boston Common. Each time I made the loop, I stared at the great stone pillar on the hill. The night that I sealed the Way into TirNaNog, the trees surrounding the pillar had been destroyed in the blast. Over the last few months, the city had removed the debris, exposing the hill. The pillar radiated with powerful essence and attracted gargoyles from everywhere. The 'goyles faced the pillar, covering the hill in a field of tortured stone as they bathed in the radiant flow.

The high levels of essence gave me an idea. I pulled the car into a semilegal space, the rear bumper edging into a bus stop. By the time a cop noticed and a tow truck was called, I'd be gone. I tucked the bowl inside my jacket and entered the Common through the Joy Street gate.

The hill had been cordoned off. With the power emanating from the pillar, the city had declared the hill a disaster site and turned security over to the Guild. A few brownies guarded the fences, but they didn't have much to contend with. The place gave everyone the creeps, so the guards only needed to chase away curiosity-seekers and the occasional drunk goth kid. I watched them as I strolled down the path, timing their patrols. Two of them ran an overlapping pattern that brought them back-to-back briefly as they meandered among the gargoyles. It was enough time for what I needed to do.

I waited for my moment, then jogged between a twisted angel and a giant green-man head. As my feet touched the hill, a buzz built in my ears, the grating hum of gargoyles talking. Not everyone could hear them, but one had decided to speak to me long ago. I thought of it as a privilege, having access to some kind of secret knowledge. I had relied on the words of one of the gargoyles whom I had named Virgil, and it had saved my life. I discovered recently from Joe that all the gargoyles repeated the same things to whoever listened, that my survival had to have been luck. It was disappointing to learn that, but at least I was alive.

I scrambled through a cluster of smaller 'goyles, mis-shapen animals worn with age—lolling-tongued dogs with human arms for legs, cat-headed birds, and human-headed snakes. The essence from the pillar beat against my senses, a powerful thrumming that reverberated in my chest.

I spotted a small child with long sheep horns curling around its ears, its palms lifted in supplication. I slipped the bowl out of my jacket and placed it on the hands. I liked the way the red-splattered green bloodstone of the bowl blended with the red marbling of the 'goyle. To the casual eye, it belonged there, and its essence was lost in the in-tense background field the pillar generated. It was risky to leave it, but now that Shay's blood had broken the geasa, anyone could move it. Until I understood what was going on, I didn't want to have it on me if someone detained me. I didn't have a choice but to hide it.

A brownie guard shouted. Instead of running, I waved at him with a smile. He thrust his arm away from the hill and shouted again, coming nearer. I hurried down the slope, smiling and waving, doing my best to appear properly scolded. I reached a break in the storm fence and walked onto the empty concrete pond basin. The brownie kept his distance as I returned to the steps that led to the gate. As I settled in the car, I was astounded to see a parking ticket. I left it on the windshield.

The sun was coming up, saturated pink-and-orange light coloring the downtown buildings. I drove down to the har-bor and left the car, pumping quarters into a meter and tear-ing up the ticket. It would be a few hours before anyone noticed it.

I walked back toward Faneuil Hall. When all else failed, I went home, or, in this case, my parents' hotel. I hoped no one would think I would go there. At the back end of Quincy Market, Joe flashed into sight in front of me. "Oh, good, you're not dead," he said.

I walked with my head down. "Shay is. He got shot."

Joe's face fell, embarrassment at his poor choice of words showing. "I am truly sorry, Connor. He was rather sweet."

"And didn't deserve my coming into his life," I said.

Joe didn't argue with me like he usually did when I said stuff like that. He settled on my shoulder and wrapped his arm around my neck. I knew he didn't agree with my sentiment, but he comforted me without words anyway.

I slowed my step when I reached Cambridge Street. The Bostonian Hotel was across the street, but I spotted Kevin Murdock at the end of the block. What he was doing there at that hour couldn't mean anything good, especially since he had his body shield up. It was an impressive demonstration of control on his part so soon after gaining essence abilities.

"What do you make of that, Joe?" I asked.

He leaned forward to see around my nose. "All the Murdocks like to wake up early?"

If there was one thing I had learned from putting people under surveillance, it was what people looked like when they were doing surveillance. Kevin was watching the street, the approach from downtown, waiting for someone or something. "I don't like it. Let's get inside before he sees us."

The entrance to the hotel was a series of flat arches along the sidewalk. As I reached the curb, Gerry Murdock stepped from behind a pillar. He was dressed in black like Kevin, not his uniform, but he did have his gun belt on. He glanced at Joe, then back to me. "Funny running into you," he said.

"I'm not laughing, though," I said.

"Your mother's staying here, isn't she?" he said.

I froze. "Meaning what?"

He shrugged. "Nothing. It's not very safe down here at night. I'd tell her to be careful."

With two long strides, I was in his face. "If anything happens to my mother, Gerry. I am coming after you."

He gave me a cocky grin. "Whoa, whoa, whoa, there, big fella. I believe you are threatening a police officer. You're under arrest."

"You stink of gunpowder, Gerry. Where were you tonight?"

"Picking off scum. Think I got a tranny," he said.

That did it. I grabbed him by shirt and shoved him against the wall. "You killed a kid, Gerry."

He surprised me by activating a body shield, not a strong one, but enough to force my hands to slip off him. He grabbed his gun. "Surprised, Grey? Playing field's level now."

With an abrupt thrust of my hand, I slammed my body shield against his without touching his body. His arm jerked up, hitting the wall, and the gun dropped out of his hand. "Call me when you think you can take me," I said.

I had passed under the arch into the driveway when I heard the gun. "Stop right there," he said.

I put my hands out and pivoted. Joe flashed into the air next to me. I hadn't noticed him vanish. He hadn't said a word during the entire exchange. "What, Gerry? You going to shoot me? Go ahead, I dare you. I'll have that gun out of your hand and up your ass so fast, you'll be choking on the bullets."

"Is there a problem?" Dread clenched my gut when I heard my mother's voice.

"Get back inside, Ma," I said over my shoulder.

In her dressing gown, she came up next to me, her hands folded in front of her. "I asked if there is a problem here?"

Gerry kept his gun aimed at me. "Do what he said, ma'am. This is a police matter."

My mother moved forward. "My name is Regula Grey. I am a member of the Seelie Court. I have diplomatic immunity from local matters and, through me, so does my son. Now I ask you, sir, what is the problem here? Do I need to contact the Guild for advice?"

Kevin joined Gerry as he relaxed his stance and lowered the gun. The two of them stared at us for a long moment of failed intimidation. "A misunderstanding, ma'am," Gerry said.

My mother nodded once sharply. "I see. Well, then, good day."

She turned and entered the hotel.

"This isn't over," Gerry said.

"Stay away from my family, Gerry," I said.

I followed my mother. Joe flew backwards in front of me, watching the Murdocks. "Did you call her?"

"Your father wasn't there," he said.

My mother waited by the elevator. She pressed the UP button. "Honestly, Connor, you need to be more careful. You know I worry."

The elevator arrived, and I punched the button for my parents' floor. "That was foolish, Mother. You could have been hurt."

She waved her hand. "Oh, I would have flattened him in another moment if he hadn't dropped his weapon. You know how impatient I can be when I haven't had my morning tea. Who was he?"

"Gerry Murdock. Leo's brother," I said.

"That nice man who delivered our bags?" she asked.

"Yeah. It's a complicated family," I said.

"Well, at least you can join us for breakfast. Your father should be back from his exercise shortly," she said.

We got off on our floor. "Have I really had diplomatic immunity all this time?"

She opened the door to the suite. "Oh, no, of course not, dear. You were stripped of it a year ago or so. Although, I'm not sure your father and I qualify anymore either since Maeve sent us away."

I allowed myself a tired smile. "You lied?"

"Well, not really. It didn't seem the time to speculate on the matter. Shall we order tea?"

I dropped onto the couch. "Yes. Tea would be nice, but first I need to make a phone call."

She waved at the handset on the table as she went into bedroom. "I'm going to finish dressing. I won't be long."

I called Eagan's house, but no one picked up. I wasn't sure whether to be surprised or not. I dialed Briallen.

She picked up on the first ring. "Are you all right?"

"Yes. Did you hear what happened?" I asked.

"Manus and Tibbet are fine. The attackers were human

with a few Dananns who are being billed as rogue agents. A few were captured, but they have no identification, and they're not talking, of course."

Tibbet was fine. That's all I heard that I cared about. She hadn't gotten killed because of me. "Thanks, Briallen. I'm with my parents, but I'm not staying long. I don't want them in the middle of this."

"That's probably wise," she said.

"Still don't want to tell me what I need to know?" I asked.

"Connor, it's not like that," she said.

"Sure it is," I said.

"Someday you will understand," she said.

"Maybe. Until then, I don't." I hung up. Her refusal to explain the sword infuriated me.

Joe danced a sun ritual in the window. I watched his aerial display, the loops and turns that coaxed the sunlight into energizing his body essence. I was too tired to join him. Besides, standing naked in front of an unprotected window was not the best course of action for me right then.

"I'm going to leave before my mother comes back, Joe. Tell her I'll call her later," I said.

He finished the ritual and dropped to his feet. "But what about the tea?"

"I'll have to take a rain check. Tell Ma I'll call her later. And tell her thank you," I said.

25

After retrieving the car again, I drove to Albany Street in the South End. This early in the morning, the traffic consisted of ambulances and staff from Boston City Hospital. I reached the Office of the City Medical Examiner and parked across the street. A police car drove toward me, siren lights off, and I waited a tense minute until it passed. I got out and hustled across the street.

The back door to the OCME was guarded by a retired police officer. He sat reading the newspaper and drinking coffee. I wore my sunglasses even though it wasn't light out yet, but I didn't want him to see my eyes. Janey Likesmith had told me enough stories about the animosity for the fey in her office. Since druids didn't look fey, the officer was more likely to think I was a drug addict.

"Is Janey Likesmith here?" I asked him.

He took a slow sip off his coffee and reached for the phone without looking at me and jabbed an extension line. "Name?"

I hesitated. "Connor."

I held my breath, worried that my common Irish name would set off alarms. Instead, the guard repeated it into the phone, pressed a buzzer that released the door lock, and I was in. I made way to the stairs and went down to the basement. Coming out of the stairwell, I was surprised to see Murdock waiting with Janey in the pool of light from her office.

"What are you doing here?" I asked, then wanted to kick myself for asking.

Murdock didn't show any annoyance, though. "Keeping Janey company. What's wrong?"

Granted I was showing up at a daybreak, but it rankled that people assumed something was wrong when they saw me. "Eagan's house was attacked. I got out, but Shay was shot and killed."

"Damn," he said.

Janey put a hand on his sleeve. "Who was it?"

"Street kid. Always in the wrong place at the wrong time," he said. His voice was flat, which meant he was upset. Murdock had introduced me to Shay. He had encouraged him to get off the street. Shay did, but that didn't stop him from getting messed up with me.

"I needed someplace to lie low while I figure out where to go," I said.

"And you picked the morgue," Murdock said.

"I was actually going to call you for a ride back to the Tangle. I thought whoever attacked me wouldn't expect me hiding out in a law-enforcement building," I said.

"You were the focus of the attack?" he asked.

I started to answer, then closed my mouth. After what happened on the lawn, I had assumed the attack was against me. "I don't know. There were bullets flying everywhere. It might have been Eagan. His guards were killed, and his Guild security agents were missing. That had to be mac-Goren's doing."

Murdock pursed his lips and looked at Janey. "Maybe you need to see something."

I didn't move. "There's something else, Leo. Gerry was

involved. He threatened me in front of my parents' hotel less than thirty minutes ago. He admitted to killing Shay."

Janey let out a small gasp. In the uncomfortable silence, Leo stared at the floor. A muscle along his jaw jumped.

"Let's look at the evidence, Janey," he said.

"Leo . . ." I said.

He gave me a cold hard stare. "I will deal with it, Connor."

He walked into the office. Janey and I exchanged concerned glances before following him in. Her office had always been cramped, but now it looked like a storage room. Files and boxes were piled everywhere with little room for more than the three of us. While bodies were being recovered from the Guildhouse site, everything went through the OCME until the victims were identified. There were a lot of victims.

Janey handed Murdock a folder. He turned it toward me, flipping it open to the report on the elf with the arrow in his chest. He pointed to Keeva's signature as the Guild liaison. Closing that report, he opened another, the dead Danann. The body hadn't even gone to the OCME since he had been a Guild agent. Though it wasn't any surprise since she had been on the scene, Keeva had authorized the transfer of the body.

Janey gave me a single sheet of paper, a request from the Guild for the body of the merrow, signed by Keeva. "This came in last night. The body hasn't been processed out yet."

I handed the sheet back. "I see what you're getting at, but Keeva's the Community Liaison Director. Sign-offs like that are routine."

"She's signed off on only those cases since she returned," said Janey.

"And unmarked vans have picked up the bodies. They won't say where they're taking them, and any follow-up has to go directly through Keeva," Murdock said.

"Do you think she killed these people?" I asked.

Murdock made a curious face. "Either that, or she's part of a cover-up. What do you think?"

Keeva and I had been partners for almost a decade. In that time, I had come to understand she could be efficient, ruthless, and single-minded in getting what she wanted. "I never saw her kill someone in cold blood. I'd be surprised."

"She also spent several months at Tara," Janey said.

I leaned back against the boxes. "I talked to Bastian. He says the victims were all agents working for him who were leaking information from the Guild. He basically said the Consortium didn't kill them."

"For undercover agents, things leak in both directions. Maybe they leaked too much in one direction," Murdock said.

"Then it's something about the waterfront. That's where the bodies were. Since this mist wall went up, maybe that's not a coincidence," I said.

Murdock tapped the folder, straightening the papers inside. "Well, it's out of my jurisdiction now. If what happened at Eagan's was about you, you need bigger firepower than I can give you."

"Bastian said the elf victim told him Eorla had a spy. Maybe because I'm close to her, they think I might know who it is," I said.

"Sounds like Eorla's your best bet then," Murdock said.

Janey held out a small plastic envelope. "Any idea what this is?"

I held the envelope toward the light. Inside was what looked like a broken guitar chip, pale gray and translucent. "Is this from the merrow?"

Janey nodded. "I found it under one of her fingernails. It's not a merrow scale that I've ever seen."

"Eorla has a lot of tree fairies working for her. Can it be a skin cell?" I asked.

"That's possible, but the color is so strange. My database isn't that extensive for this type of thing, though. I was hoping you might have seen someone with skin like that," she said.

I handed it back. "Doesn't ring any bells. What about the Danann? Any trace evidence on him?"

She shook her head. "No, but he didn't die in a fall. The organ damage isn't consistent with a fall. He was crushed under something."

"That would explain the alcohol. Dananns are strong. It wouldn't be the first time someone thought to get a Danann drunk before killing one."

Murdock gave me a significant look. The first major case we worked on together had had Danann fairy victims. The first few had been drunk when they died. Gethin mac-Loren, the murderer, had been captured and executed. "He's dead, Leo."

"He wouldn't be the first Dead person I've met," he said.

I shook my head. "No, this is something else. Ceridwen would know if macLoren came back. She has the Dead under control."

"Which brings us back to someone who does know: Keeva," he said.

A cool fluttering touched my mind, then a sending from my mother hit me like a ton of bricks. "I need to get to AvMem."

"What happened?" Murdock asked.

"My brother Cal's in the hospital."

26

The previous twenty-four hours didn't feel tethered to reality anymore. The nonstop bombardment of events left me with nothing but the need to react, with no time to think or feel or consider. I was running on adrenaline. My body slipped into automatic, running down the hall, going out the door, rushing to the hospital.

I strode into the emergency room at AvMem without any recollection of the trip. Arriving had been my only focus. I left the car in the drop-off lane with the keys in it. At that point, I didn't care what happened to it.

In the waiting room, news cycled on a crooked flat screen TV, the volume turned to a whisper. An aerial shot of Eagan's house appeared. Smoke trickled from the side of the house, but it didn't look serious. The greenhouse windows were shattered. Dark uniformed figures were scattered about the lawn in an obvious police search grid.

As I approached the desk, Keeva came out the door that led to the treatment bays. She hesitated, surprised to see me. *Don't talk,* she sent.

She spoke to the desk nurse and flashed her badge. The woman looked from the badge to Keeva, then nodded. She glanced at me, curious, yet with an attitude of not wanting to draw attention. Keeva waved me around the desk to the door

The emergency room at Avalon Memorial was much like one in any other hospital—professional staff moving quickly, people moaning, bad odors, and blood. An injured fey person brought an extra layer of free-flowing essence that needed to be contained. I peered into the bays as we passed, hoping and dreading to see Callin.

"What was that about?" I asked, as she led me in back.

"Your name is flagged for security. I told the desk you were with me, so you didn't have to identify yourself," she said.

"Wow. Thanks," I said.

"Don't mention it," she said.

"Now tell me why you did it," I said.

She frowned. "You always have to push, don't you? Callin's your brother. While it would please me to see you in handcuffs, you shouldn't get arrested for visiting your brother in the hospital."

We walked through the unit to a door at the back. Away from the doctors and patients, I caught the faint scent of ozone coming off Keeva, the telltale trace of essence-fire. "You're in the field?"

She glanced at me with impatience. "In case you haven't heard, Connor, the Guild lost hundreds of agents. Everyone's in the field."

I took her gently by the arm, and, as usual, she pulled away in anger. "I was going to ask you about the baby," I said.

Her expression didn't change. "He's fine. Thank you for asking."

"And you?"

She sighed and opened the door. "Take the back elevator to the seventh floor. Callin's in ICU. Go. Now. Before I change my mind."

She walked away. Keeva and I had always had a prickly

relationship. Since she returned from Tara, she had avoided me like the plague. I wanted to talk to her about what had happened between us, about the night in the *leanansidhe*'s cave. I wasn't sure if she had been aware of everything that had happened that night. I had almost killed her. I had drained her life essence. The guilt weighed on me enough that I needed to confess it to her. I needed her to know how sorry I was.

I wondered if hanging around with Murdock and his Catholicism was starting to rub off. I didn't know if confession was good for the soul so much, but it definitely would have put my mind at ease. Keeva would probably hate me. Hell, she barely spoke to me as it was. She might already know, which would explain her attitude. At the same time, I was bothered by Murdock's suspicions about her role in the deaths of the double agents. Now my brother turned up in the hospital, and she was there to meet me. Her presence could mean more than compassion about a bad day for the Grey family.

The elevator doors opened onto the seventh floor. Keeva would have to wait. I walked down the hall, peering into rooms. Hospital staff eyed me. Intensive Care Units were not welcoming to visitors. I passed a waiting room and heard my mother call my name.

We met in a hug at the door. She pulled back, touching my cheek, her face pale with worry. "Clure is in with him. He's allowed one visitor at a time."

Behind her, Gillen stood watching a nurse lean over my father, who sat in a chair. Blood drained through a tube in his arm to a bag next to the chair. I hurried to his side. "Da, what's wrong?" I asked.

He gazed at the blood flowing out his arm, wiggling his fingers. "It's a blood donation. Nothing to worry about."

My mother came up behind me and slipped her arm around my waist. "Callin lost a lot of blood."

I unrolled my sleeve. "Hook me up. I'm the same type, too."

Gillen glanced at my father, then away. "Callin was

fighting when he was injured. His blood is saturated with essence. It's not a normal transfusion. We need a close essence match, too."

I frowned. "Then all the more reason I should do it. Sibling essence factors are more similar than a parent's."

"In this case, Thomas is a better match," said Gillen.

"I don't understand," I said.

My father flexed his fingers. "Connor, let's get through this crisis without argument. If Gillen says I am a better match, then let's defer to his judgment."

I frowned, confused. "You were a field agent, Da. You know this stuff. We stockpiled our own blood, and Callin was my backup."

"Did you ever need his blood?" Gillen asked.

In my career, I had had two serious injuries that required emergency surgery, one of them serious enough to use the blood on hand. "No. We had enough of my own."

My mother twined her arm in mine. "Connor, sweetheart, you're upsetting me. Let Gillen do his job."

I pulled away from her. "What? No! He isn't making sense. I don't understand why I'm not a better match."

"The dark mass . . ." Gillen said.

I cut him off. "In three years, Gillen, you haven't said a word about the dark mass affecting my blood."

Angry light glinted in Gillen's eye. I was pushing his patience, but I didn't care. "Look, Grey. I will do what I think is best for my own damned patients. Is that clear?"

"No, I want . . ." I said.

"Connor," my father said, low and sharp. It was that tone, that particular parental tone, that reminded me that I was once ten years old and my father knew how to stop me dead in my tracks with the mere mention of my name. I didn't shudder, but the memory of shuddering crossed my mind. I composed myself. "Da . . ." I said.

"Let Gillen do his job. We have complete faith in him," he said.

My father stared at me with his implacable gaze, while my mother hovered between us. She had spent a lifetime—my lifetime, anyway—breaking up arguments. With my father and Gillen in agreement, it was futile to argue. "What happened to him?" I asked.

"He was in a fight, of course," my father said.

"Where?"

"We don't have the details yet," he said.

"What was Keeva macNeve doing here?" I asked.

My father tilted his head toward Gillen. "I didn't know she was here."

Gillen shrugged. "It's a big hospital, Grey. Your brother's not the only one prone to getting beat up."

"Can I see him?" I asked.

"Send the Clure out. One maniac in the room at a time," Gillen said.

Controlling my anger, I left them in the waiting room. I didn't understand, but I wasn't a healer, and now was not the time to argue. My brother was injured.

In Callin's room, the blue-green glow of monitors and a small spotlight near the bed provided dim illumination. The humid air was heavy with lavender and dill and bitter green herbs. Callin lay in a stone crèche, an oblong slab of quartz charged with essence. Bandages wrapped his chest and left shoulder, and a thin layer of essence hovered over his body like a mist.

The Clure had pulled a chair close to the crèche and slumped over its edge. With his face somber beneath his mop of curls, he traced his fingers along Callin's brow. I cleared my throat. The Clure stood and wrapped his arms around me, burying his face into the side of my neck. He smelled of whiskey and tears.

"I wasn't there," he said.

"It doesn't matter. You're here now," I said.

He pulled away, his eyes watery. "It can't happen like this. It can't end like this."

I rubbed his shoulder. "Callin's tough. You know that. It's not over."

We spent a few moments staring at my brother, the

Clure hugging himself against the hurt. I slid into the chair, staring at the bandages, trying to guess at the injuries.

"I'll be outside," said the Clure.

Tubes ran into Callin's nose and mouth. His battered face showed signs that he had been in a fight that had turned up-close and physical. One eye was swollen shut, and the bridge of his nose was broken. Typical. Cal got himself in over his head and got knocked on his ass for it.

"What the hell did you do this time, Cal?" I asked.

I held his hand. I couldn't remember the last time I had touched him like that. We never were all that affectionate, but holding his hand reminded that we were brothers, that family mattered. I might not like a lot of the things Cal did with his life or to himself, but I cared.

He hadn't come to the hospital when our roles had been reversed. I woke up alone, with no family except Joe and Briallen. My parents had visited after my accident, but after weeks of no change in my condition, they were called away to a diplomatic mission. Cal had been nowhere in sight.

He's down. Is he okay?

It had been so long since Cal and I had exchanged sendings, I almost didn't recognize his voice in my head. "Clure's fine, Cal. He'll be right back."

I didn't know if he could hear me. I was surprised he was aware enough under the sedation to talk. *Too many. Clure's on the way.*

Irritated, I checked to see if the Clure was coming back to boot me out already, but the hallway was empty. "It's okay, Cal. They're letting only one of us in at a time," I said.

Dammit, Keeva.

The force of the sending startled me, the equivalent of shouting in my head. Cal knew Keeva through me. She had been my Guild partner for ten years. We occasionally bumped into Cal, but not often. In those days, I didn't care much about the Weird other than as a place to party, and I never did that with Keeva. Why she would be on his mind now puzzled me.

My memory flashed to the essence-fire residue I smelled on Keeva. She had more than once saved my butt in the nick of time. As much as we bickered, she had a sense for being in the right place at the right time, and I wasn't going to complain if she had intervened with Cal somehow.

Cal wasn't talking to me. He was sending in a delirium state. "Everything's fine, Cal. You need to rest."

Connor.

"Yeah, it's me, Cal. We're all here. Don't worry about anything," I said.

Too many. Clure's on the way.

I didn't understand my brother in the best of times, never mind delirious from pain and medication. We had spent the better part of our adult life arguing, mostly about his drinking. We had drifted apart the last decade, and he fell in with a rough-and-tumble crowd I wanted no part of. Despite the Clure's propensity for chaos, hooking up with him was probably the most stable thing Callin had done. Now he lay in a crèche, and I wasn't able to do a damned thing about all that. I wanted the chance to fix things between us.

Gillen entered with his surgical team. His cranky manner had disappeared behind the focus on what was to come. Almost as an afterthought, he dismissed me. "We're ready in the operating room. I'll have someone keep you updated."

Back in the waiting room, Joe had arrived. He sat on the arm of a sofa, talking with my mother. They stopped when I entered, guilt-stricken looks on their faces. "What's going on?" I asked.

"Has he gone into surgery?" Joe asked.

"Yes, and that's not what I'm talking about," I said.

"Connor, our focus should be on your brother right now," my father said.

I took a seat opposite my father. He looked tired. "I'm not letting this drop, Da. I should be the best candidate for an essence blood match. What are you not telling me?"

He unrolled his sleeve. "It's not important."

"My brother's on the verge of death, and I'm not being allowed to help. I deserve an explanation," I said.

He kept his attention on readjusting his clothing. "Watch your tone."

"I'll take whatever tone I want," I said.

He glared. I knew that look. I was about to be put in my place. My mother stood. "Enough, Thomas. We knew this day would come."

A thick silence filled the room. "Okay, now I'm more worried," I said.

Joe fluttered around my mother, his expression fluctuating between confusion and boredom. "I don't understand why it's a big deal, Mama Grey. Flits foster everyone."

"Joe!" my mother said. His eyes gone wide, Joe slapped his hands over his lips.

I heard the word. I stared at my parents, searching their faces, looking for, well, me. Cal resembled my father enough to be his clone—red hair, stocky muscle, and blunt features. I always assumed I took after my mother's side of the family. We had the same dark hair and similar features, but no particular characteristics marked us as mother and son. She looked Irish. I looked Irish. I assumed my blue eyes were a genetic throwback to an ancestor no one recalled. "I was fostered," I said.

My mother dropped her gaze and took my hand. "We always meant to tell you."

It wasn't sinking in, at least not on an emotional level. I heard what she said, but I felt a distinct objectivity, as if we were discussing the weather. I was fostered. Thomas and Regula Gray were not my biological parents. As Joe said, it wasn't unheard of in the fey world. What made it different was that I hadn't known. Everyone always knew. It was an old tradition, without controversy. "Why didn't you tell me?"

My mother squeezed my hands. "Nigel asked us not to."

"Nigel? What does . . ." I closed my eyes, dread slicing across my gut. "Danu's blood, please don't tell me Nigel Martin is my father."

"He's not," my father said.

Utter relief swept over me. With everything that had gone sour between me and Nigel, the last thing I wanted to hear was that he was my father. I steeled myself for the next logical question. "Who are my parents?" I asked.

"We don't know," Thomas said.

Not telling me I was fostered was at least plausible. Human parents kept the knowledge of adoption secret all the time, but fostering didn't work like that. Someone had a child and placed it with another family to raise for a variety of reasons—all of them open knowledge. "How can you not know?" I asked.

My mother squeezed my hand. "Nigel said he didn't know. You were a foundling."

I couldn't help the derision in my voice, but it was directed toward the absent Nigel. "Foundling? Not likely. Nigel didn't find a baby and hand it over to the nearest couple. He knew more than he was telling."

"Indeed. I pressed him on the issue repeatedly. I did my own discreet investigation but found no one with a missing child," my father said. "In the end, I accepted his word."

My mother sat in silence, staring off to the side. I moved off the chair and sat beside her. "I didn't want it to come out this way," she said.

I put my arm around her and kissed her temple. "You didn't do anything wrong."

"We wanted another child so badly. I had just lost one when Nigel came to us," she said.

I kissed her again. "It's okay. You're my mom. Nothing will ever change that."

I stood. "I need a moment. I'll be right back."

I passed Callin's room. The Clure stood at the window. I don't know if he saw me, but I continued down the hall to another waiting room that was empty. I leaned my hands against the windowsill and breathed deeply. I had no idea what this meant to me. I had spent my entire life thinking one thing, taking it for granted actually, to find it was untrue. The people I thought I knew were not the people I thought they were. I was not the person I thought I was.

Joe appeared behind me, his essence flashing pink in the window. He fluttered up, trying to see through his reflection. He hovered close to the glass, intent on a smudge.

"You never said anything," I said.

He licked the window and frowned in disgust. Unlike him, I wasn't surprised. "Your mum asked me not to," he said.

Joe had been around my family for generations. He was an Old One, one of the few confirmed people I knew who had come from Faerie. He didn't remember much, mostly people he had known, but larger events escaped him. Not that memory loss bothered him. Flits remembered what they cared about, and what they cared about didn't always make sense. He was around when Nigel showed up with a mysterious baby. He knew my mother hadn't been pregnant with me. He had been my companion, from birth I thought.

"Did you know Nigel was involved?" I asked.

He settled on the windowsill. "He visited a lot when you were a baby."

"Did he ever say anything about my parents?"

"He trusted them to raise you," Joe said.

"No, I meant my biological parents."

"Oh. Not that I remember. Connor, you seem upset."

"I just found out my parents aren't my parents. It changes things, doesn't it?"

He shrugged. "I don't see how. Tom and Mom are bestest parents. You could have got stuck with mine."

"They did name you Stinkwort," I said.

He tilted his head at me. "Exactly. Really, who cares, Connor. We end up who we are for a lot of reasons."

"What if it turns out that Meryl and I are brother and sister?" I asked.

"What if you are?" he asked.

I glanced down at him, wondering if he were that indifferent to the ramifications. He smirked at me. "Okay, fine, I'm overthinking the situation," I said.

"Again," he said.

"Well, I'd like to do a little of that alone. Can you give me some space?" I asked.

"I'd say you have enough space between your ears, but I know how crowded it is in there."

"Thanks. Come get me if I'm not back when the surgery's over," I said.

He winked at me and popped out. I stretched out on a couch and stared at the ceiling. People walked by the door, their body signatures growing and fading as they went about their business. Someone entered the room, a Danann fairy with a strong signature. I shifted on the couch to see who it was. From behind, the man's wings obscured his features. The wings were huge, multilayered, and vibrant with essence. Even without his fey aspect, he was physically imposing, tall, and muscular. He seemed to be waiting for someone. I settled back and closed my eyes.

I snapped them back open when I sensed the shot of essence. As I sat up, the Danann put the finishing touches on an essence barrier across the door. When he faced me, a shiver went over me, one part surprise, one part fear.

"Brion Mal," I said.

An assured, maybe smug, smile crossed his face. "I'm flattered you recognize me," he said.

Flattered, as if he couldn't possibly know his fame among the fey. Brion Mal was leader of the High Queen's Fianna, the greatest fighting force in the world. When people talked about elite fairy warriors, they spoke of Danann security agents with their menacing black outfits and blank silver helmets that hid their identities. They spoke about ability levels they could only dream of having. They spoke in tones either hushed in awe and fear or raised in anger and bitterness. When Danann security agents talked about elite fairy warriors, they spoke of the High Queen's Fianna.

The Fianna served the Seelie Court, regardless of High Queen or King. They came from ancient clan lines, the sons and daughters of powerful leaders and warriors. Their reputations preceded them, They didn't hide their faces behind masks. They wanted people to know who they were. The mention of their names instilled fear and dread in whomever the Fianna targeted.

"Somehow, I don't think you're here for my brother," I said.

"Your brother concerns me even less than you do," he said.

Whatever his intention, he was going to succeed. I didn't think I was a match for Brion Mal even at the peak of my abilities. I didn't bother activating my body shield. He would break through it with ease and leave me bruised in the process. That didn't mean I was going to go down without a fight. I rubbed my calf, using the nervous gesture to bring my hand near my dagger.

"Don't struggle," he said.

I never touched my dagger. Essence leaped from his fingers, a fine mesh that spiraled through the air and settled over me. The binding immobilized me without pain. Mal didn't need pain to control me. He blew a deep breath at me, the binding shivered, and my mind clouded. I was asleep before I finished falling off the couch.

27

I woke up in a room about ten feet square that was sheathed in glass and steel. Stretching, I dropped my feet from the bed to the floor in the empty surroundings. From the small size and low ceiling, I guessed I was in a safe house, one of many the Guild had scattered around Boston and its suburbs. Safe houses were two-edged swords. Good to be in when someone was hunting you down. Bad to be in when the Guild didn't want anyone to know what it was doing to you. Under the circumstances, the latter was more likely, so not so good for me. At least, I had gotten some sleep, and I wasn't dead.

From the inside, holding cells looked the same, so I had no idea where I was. Unlike the police, the Guild needed safe havens with the added level of glass-and-steel sheathing, which slow down someone with essence ability and give the guards time to defend the room. Cost wasn't an issue, but secrecy was. It wasn't easy building one without the neighbors' noticing. The Guild didn't like abandoning them unless they had good reason.

I didn't have to wait long to find out what I was doing there. The door opened, and Ryan macGoren entered without ceremony. He raised an essence barrier between us, dividing the room in half. He wasn't taking any chances. I didn't blame him after our last encounter, but the barrier said more about macGoren's paranoia than about the threat I posed. He was a Danann at the height of his ability. I had a stone in my head.

MacGoren had been injured in the catalyzing event of the Guildhouse destruction. He bore scars from a blast of pure essence that had hit him. His once-handsome face, which had turned heads on the fey social scene, had been scorched smooth. The bones of his cheeks stood out, hard-edged and bleached. His hairline had been burned back, the hair that he had prided himself on was now an odd sweep of blond that hung lank from the top of his head. The most dramatic change, though, was that his eyes had crystallized. The same thing had happened to me, but only my irises had been affected. With macGoren, the eyes had vanished beneath an almost insectlike faceted layer of glittering membrane over the entire surfaces.

Beyond his previous good looks, I never understood what Keeva saw in him. His power was obvious, but Keeva had the looks and brains to attract anyone. Yet she chose macGoren.

MacGoren managed to retain his smug arrogance. "I hope you're not comfortable."

I faced him through the barrier. "What do you intend to do, macGoren? Word's going to get out that I'm missing. There will be fallout."

He snorted. "Fallout? You staged a major terrorist act on the Guildhouse. Do you think the public is going to rally to your pathetic cries of innocence?"

"The State Department might have a problem with Brion Mal kidnapping an American citizen," I said.

His smile made stippled lines in his cheeks. "Do you think we would have used someone as high-profile as Mal if we were worried about the human government?"

MacGoren had brought Vize into the Guildhouse despite my warnings. He didn't listen to me then. He wasn't going to now. "I tried to stop you from making a fool of yourself. Enough witnesses survived that know you were the one who let Vize in and I was the one who tried to stop you."

His eyes shifted, a disconcerting movement that left me with nothing to focus on. He could be staring at me or the wall behind me. "No one cares, Grey. The Elven King is dead. Maeve has won. No one will criticize anything she does. We attacked that traitor Eagan in his own home with human support without any repercussions. You don't matter. You're a clean-up detail."

While we talked, I scanned the barrier. A good punch with a full body shield sometimes collapsed a barrier, but macGoren knew what he was doing. The barrier was stable, without any flaws. "If I don't matter, then why am I here?"

He chuckled. "Ah, but that's thing, Grey. You're not here. You're not anywhere. You went into hiding by your own choice."

"You're going to keep me locked up? As usual, mac-Goren, your plans are pointless. Stop the games and let me out. If what you or Maeve says is true, prove it in public," I said.

If possible, his stiff face became more unreadable. "You think I am pointless, that I am a fool. Do you have any idea who you are looking at, Grey? I am one of the most powerful fey in the Seelie Court now. Brion Mal does my bidding. I have exposed the Teutonic Consortium in an act of war. No human government will ally with them now. I have given my queen her greatest victory since Convergence. She is well pleased."

"You know the problem with making a queen happy, macGoren? It's only a matter of time before you make her unhappy. Maeve's used you."

He laughed. "You think I don't know that? That is what loyal subjects do, Grey. We exist to serve our liege. That's something you seem to have forgotten."

"Oh, I haven't forgotten. I was never her subject, mac-Goren. I have better-things to do than lick someone's boots."

"It's that perspective that makes you a failure, Grey, why you have always been a failure. When you garner as much favor as I have, you acquire power. The trick, which you have never learned, is to earn enough power to become untouchable. I have Maeve's favor. With the Elven King gone, nothing stands in her way. She needs me more than ever, and I will not fail her."

"This isn't Faerie. It isn't even Ireland," I said. "Even if the humans side with her against the Consortium, they might have a problem with a queen using a U.S. city as her playground."

His eyes glittered with a yellow light. "You misunderstand, Grey. Maeve is done with you. The Elven King has been exposed. She no longer needs to lay blame at your feet. You have outlived your usefulness."

"Great. It's nice to know she's moved on. Now what do you want?" I asked.

MacGoren lifted his arm to show me a dagger—my dagger, the one Briallen had given me. "Justice. Revenge. Call it what you like."

"Are you kidding me? You're threatening me?"

MacGoren held the dagger up, focusing his strange eyes on it. "Not at all. I'm stating the facts of the situation," he said.

With the speed that comes with the nature of a Danann, he swiped the dagger through the protection barrier, then back. I flinched, the slice of the blade leaving a stinging sensation on my cheek. I touched my face, and my hand came away with blood. Belatedly, my body shield activated.

"That was childish," I said.

"This blade is quite interesting, Grey. Ancient, if I'm not mistaken." He jabbed forward. It pierced my shield and nicked my ear. I backed away, putting as much distance as possible between myself and the barrier.

MacGoren returned his attention to the dagger. "It may appear that my vision is damaged, Grey, and in some sense it is. They say when one sense is deadened, the others compensate. Take now. I see strange essence on this blade that I am sure is not visible to others. Notice the way it slices through the essence barrier as if it weren't there."

He swept his arm in front of me. My shield creased and crackled with white light. He stepped back. "I was under the impression from Nigel that you no longer had a body shield."

"There's a lot about me you don't know," I said.

He pursed his lips. "True, but here's something I can guess." He held his free hand up and pressed against the barrier. His palm glowed with pale fire, and the barrier shimmered toward me. MacGoren stepped forward. "I'm willing to wager that your offensive abilities remain ineffective."

I steadied my gaze at him. "Drop the barrier and find out."

I didn't see him move. Beneath my open jacket, the fabric of my T-shirt split with another swipe of the blade. MacGoren kept up that annoying chuckle of his like he was a cat playing with a mouse. "I'm sure you think you can best me in a physical contest, Grey, but I am not interested in a test of strength. I am interested in watching you suffer."

He stabbed again. I gasped and clutched at my arm. The swipe had cut through the leather to hit skin. "Coward," I said.

The door opened behind him. Keeva paused on the threshold, her expression alert and assessing. MacGoren cocked his head without turning. "Hello, love. I did not expect you for another hour or so."

"Obviously," she said.

Her manner indicated that Keeva didn't know what was going on. She wasn't in on his plan. He covered his discomfort with a feigned pleasantness that I saw through easily. I knew Keeva had to see it, too. "How did you know I was here?" he asked.

She held up my old steel dagger. "This looked a little lonely. I was curious."

"I'm settling some old scores with our guest," he said.

Several emotions crossed her face—annoyance, anger, and, oddly, I thought I sensed fear. "I have a few myself," she said.

A sending fluttered through the room. MacGoren gave her a curious look, and, for several moments, sendings fluttered back and forth between them. MacGoren nodded with an understanding smile. "As you wish, my love. I've made my point, but you deserve the honor more than I."

With a flip of his wrist, he presented the handle of the dagger to her. Keeva stared at it, turning the weapon in her hand as if she had never seen a dagger before. She lifted her gaze and met my eyes. "It comes to this."

"This isn't your thing, Keeva. You don't work like this. Let me out of here," I said.

"You almost killed my child, Connor. How can I forgive that?" she asked.

"It was out of my control, Keeva. I didn't know what I was doing. When I realized what I was doing, I stopped," I said.

She moved within striking range, a step in front of mac-Goren. His faceted eyes glittered with a hungry anticipation. "How does it feel, Grey, to finally face the consequences of your actions?" he asked.

"Keeva, listen to me," I said.

She shook her head, tears brimming in her eyes. "It has to be done."

I fell back in shock as she whirled and plunged the dagger into macGoren's chest. Essence flashed off him, and the barrier went static with feedback. MacGoren staggered back; his jaw dropped in shock. He hit the wall and held himself there for a moment, hand held out to Keeva. She raised her own hand and shot essence into the dagger protruding from his chest. MacGoren convulsed and slid to the floor. She stood over him, her back to me, shots of red spiraling in her agitated wings. I struggled to find my voice. "Keeva?"

She silenced me with a cutting gesture. We watched as macGoren's body signature pulsed and faded, cycling darker until it became a dull haze. Keeva reached down and withdrew the dagger. She deactivated the barrier between us. "Keeva, why? What the hell are you involved in?"

She leaned down again and slid my steel blade into macGoren's wound. "Don't talk, Connor. Don't say a word," she said.

"But, you could have . . ."

She slammed me against the wall, her eyes blazing. She pressed my other dagger against my chest. "I said don't talk. I did what needed doing. Now take this and get out of here."

I took the dagger, and she shoved me aside. "What should I say about this?"

She turned away, gathering essence into her hands. "Since I was the only one who knew you were here, I suggest you say nothing."

"Keeva, you killed him in cold blood, and now you're planting evidence using my dagger. I'm not going to take the fall without an explanation."

She released an essence burst to cleanse her body signature from the room, leaving behind a sterile ozone odor. She stepped up to me again. "You want an explanation? You were seconds away from your own death, and no one knows you were here. I saved your life. That's the only explanation you're going to get from me. Don't make me regret my decision any more than I do. Now get out."

"But . . ."

"Go!" she screamed.

28

Outside the holding cell was a short hall, a door open to another cell, and a staircase. I ran up the stairs into a typical suburban kitchen, barren of any signs of someone's living there. My cell phone and keys lay on the table, a subtle hint of Keeva's body signature on them. It was almost three in the morning by the clock on the stove. I turned off the lights when I saw my reflection in the window. The backyard became visible, a small square of grass surrounded by a weathered stockade fence. Neighboring houses crowded near, triple-deckers and old wooden hovels with Victorian details. The yard had no exit.

Down the hall, I peered through the sidelight windows of the front door and recognized the general area. I was somewhere in Dorchester, the large neighborhood south of Boston proper. Nothing moved on the dark street, and the surrounding houses showed no lights. I slipped out as quietly as possible.

Despite my racing heart, I forced myself to a nonchalant walk. I didn't want a casual observer becoming suspicious.

I pulled my jacket closed to hide the torn and bloody T-shirt. A block later, I took out my cell and called Meryl. "Can you pick me up?"

"I don't pick people up. I make them desire me, then reject them for being needy," she said.

"I'm in a bind here," I said.

"Really? You mean you aren't disturbing me at work because you went grocery shopping?" she asked.

"You're at work? It's 3 A.M.," I said.

"Shoot. I forgot to eat my lunch," she said.

"Can we get back to my apparently unimportant desperation?" I asked.

"Where are you?" she asked.

A few cars passed the large cross street ahead. I recognized a deli on the corner. "You know where Georgie's is on Dot Ave? Oh, and I could use a shirt."

"Be there in ten."

I made myself inconspicuous near a silver electrical box on Dorchester Avenue. Dot Ave was to Dorchester what Oh No was to the Weird, only longer. It stretched through eight or nine subneighborhoods, old villages that became home turf to various waves of immigrants. At any given time in its history, two or three gangs controlled the street, making it, depending on perspective, safe or dangerous. It was like that before and after Convergence. No matter the time period, urban cycles of prosperity and poverty repeated. It didn't need the fey to do it. It made me realize that all the crap I stressed about, the empty promises of the governing powers, the endless grind of lives unfulfilled, were as much simply the nature of life as they were symptoms of social decay.

I leaned against the building next to the box and realized that somewhere else in the city, other people were probably in similar predicaments to mine. Maybe they didn't leave a dead body behind, but they'd fled a situation out of control, something that would lead to more problems in time. Shit happened. Sometimes a little, sometimes a lot, but always and often, and sometimes there was nothing to be done about it. The thought didn't make me any happier, but it gave me a little perspective as I waited alone on the desolate street. I bet myself that no one else had an intangible stone in their head or a gaping dark hole that sucked the life of everything around it. Those were my special treats.

Meryl pulled up in her MINI Cooper, and I hopped in. Without a word, she handed me a black T-shirt, pursing her lips as she eyed my bloody clothes. I leaned across the console and kissed her as she knocked me in the leg shifting gears. "Thanks," I said.

She pulled a perfect U-turn and headed back toward the Weird. "Gods, I haven't been down here in ages. Were you at the safe house over on Dewey?"

That Meryl knew about the house didn't surprise me. I struggled out of my jacket and pulled off the sliced-up T-shirt. "It wasn't very safe," I said.

Meryl glanced at me. "So I notice. What were you doing? Your mom said you left the waiting room and never came back," she said.

I pulled on the clean shirt. "If I told you I was kidnapped by Brion Mal and macGoren tried to kill me but Keeva showed up and killed him and let me go so I called my girlfriend to come pick me up, would you believe me?" I asked.

"You never told me you had a girlfriend," she said.

"I'll take that as a yes. First, tell me about Cal," I said.

"He came out of surgery fine. The recovery is expected to take a while because of some essence and blood issue," she said.

"A full recovery?" I asked.

She gave me a brief tilt of the head. "I'm not privy to everything, you know. I'm not family."

"Right. Sorry."

Meryl downshifted and turned off Dot Ave. "Why did she kill him?"

"She refused to talk and threw me out."

"Did you call Leo?"

"I can't do that."

She made another turn, glancing in the rearview mirror. "Why not?"

"I don't think Leo needs any more to deal with right now. Gerry Murdock was involved at Eagan's. He killed Shay," I said.

Shocked, Meryl slammed on the brakes. "Tell me that didn't happen."

I looked out the window. "We were trying to escape. Shay was shot, and Uno . . . ate him, I guess."

"That poor kid," she said. Meryl liked people to think she was a mean hard-ass, but she had a soft spot for kids who got mixed up in the Weird.

"Gerry basically confessed to it when he tried to arrest me," I said.

"Whoa! When the hell did that happen?" she asked.

According to my cell phone, I had been under the sleep spell for over a day. "Day before yesterday, before I got the call about Cal," I said.

She started driving again. "Danu's blood, Grey. This is a freakin' mess. So, no police and no Guild for help. Can Eorla protect you?"

"She's my best bet at this point, unless I go to Bastian," I said.

"That might be the plan—force you to publicly align with the Consortium," Meryl said.

"Keeva's using me for something. She didn't have to kill macGoren to save my life. She planted evidence right in front of me to make it look like I killed him," I said.

"Then you need to keep a low profile until you see what she does." She turned again, making it the fourth unnecessary turn since I got in the car.

I twisted in my seat and checked the rear window. "Are we being followed?"

Meryl pulled back onto Dot Ave. "Yeah. He's being pretty obvious about it. Picked him up about a block after you."

She stopped at a red light and revved the engine. A block behind, a small dark car idled in the middle of the street. "Why is he sitting there?"

The light turned green. Meryl hesitated, but the car behind us didn't move. She drove on. "He's pulling our chain. Someone wants you to know you're being watched."

I slouched in the seat. "Yeah, big news flash."

We entered the Weird, driving down the back end of Summer Street over the Reserve Channel. In the odd way nighttime neighborhoods worked, we were safer in the industrial zone in the middle of the night than a few blocks away, where people lived. Muggers hung out where they expected to find people, which wasn't warehouses closed up for the night. The people on the streets around the channel were people you didn't want to mess with, and people who were not likely to help if you needed them.

Meryl glanced at her mirrors. "Tail's gone."

"Guess he either got his message across or he was too chicken-shit to come into the Weird," I said.

Meryl cut across Drydock Avenue and pulled up near the edge of the Tangle. She patted the dashboard. "Poor baby takes a nap if I drive in any closer. You going to be all right from here?"

"Yeah. Want to come spend the night?" I asked.

She leaned over and kissed me. "We already played man-on-the-run-meets-hot-chick-for-sex this week."

"Yeah, but this time I have wounds and bloody clothes," I said.

"Here," she said. She placed her hand on my chest and built up essence. A warm layer of light spread across my skin. A burning sensation ran across the slash on my chest. Short pops of pain shot in my cheek and ear. The warmth slid away, and Meryl withdrew her hand.

I kissed her again. The healing spell didn't wipe away the injuries, but it pushed them past the pain and discomfort phase of healing. My druid nature would speed up the rest, and within a day the cuts would be gone. She put her hand on my neck and rubbed her thumb along my cheek. "Are you going to be okay?"

I debated bringing up the whole fostering thing but decided not to, not tonight. I was tired and had a lot to think about. "Cal's going to be okay now. That's all that matters. I do want to talk to you about it, though. I learned some family history. It's kinda world-altering."

She stared out the windshield. "Families usually are. Go get some sleep."

29

The white noise echo of the city faded as I entered the Tangle, the sound of my footsteps becoming louder in the narrow space between buildings. The Tangle exaggerated everything, like a focusing lens for our baser instincts. What was commonplace to me—even before I ended up in the Tangle—outsiders saw with fear and wonder. The illicit tryst in a darkened doorway heightened the passion of the moment. The shimmer of essence in an eye held the promise of love or danger, maybe both. The swagger of a step promised confidence and menace. The bones of old buildings were at once beautiful and foreboding, flickering candlelight hinting of both refuge and danger. A stranger was as likely to hurt as help.

Even my feelings about the place existed in a nervous tension. I didn't like the pain the Tangle produced, nor the sorrow. Blood and hate flowed in the gutters as often as rain. Yet I couldn't deny the rush of life that permeated the air, of dramas and fates unfolding in unexpected directions.

People lived in the Weird, but they resonated with life in the Tangle. A lifetime could be lived in a single night.

My thoughts played along those lines, musing on the last twenty-four hours that began with the fear of a hospital room and ended with death in a cell. I saw no irony that places that others found safe—a hospital, a residential neighborhood—were places of pain for me, and the Tangle, where dead bodies were statistics instead of events, had become a place of comfort. Until, of course, a blaze of essence nearly took my head off, and I remembered that I wasn't safe anywhere anymore.

My body shield flickered on the moment I sensed the attack, and I bounced against a brick wall as I ducked. The shot struck high, hitting a row of second-story windows. The essence raced in lightning streaks around the metal frames, ricocheting back on themselves before the glass dissipated them.

The narrow pedestrian alley was empty, a common shortcut people used to get through condemned warehouses, a lane of bricked-over doors and worn advertising posters. That didn't make it a busy place to be even in the late night of the Tangle. I pressed myself into a doorway of a former garage as another blaze of essence split the air.

I craned my neck to get a handle on the source. The trajectories were angled down, so the shots were coming from above. My sensing ability picked up hints of druid essence, but deadened, as if it were weak or muffled.

Near the entrance to the alley, a couple paused, their attention attracted by the electric sizzle of essence-fire. They stood under a vapor lamp, curiosity on their stark faces. Their body language didn't convey any threat or aggression, so the shots didn't come from behind them.

I leaned back into the doorway and tried to call Meryl. Static crackled from the receiver, the weave of metal fire escapes and tendency of the Tangle to screw up tech. Annoyed, I closed the phone.

A woman entered the lane from the opposite end. Another essence-bolt shot down, fracturing the pavement at her feet. Panicked, she backpedaled, running when she reached the corner. No one seemed to be interested in helping a trapped druid, a classic reaction in the Tangle.

I dodged across the alley into the next doorway. An essence-bolt from ahead of me struck the wall. Shots from two different directions meant I had a tag team. Random essence strikes showered. Neither attacker seemed skilled at what they were doing. At such close range, they should have been able to sense my body shield and pick up that it was from a high-level druid.

I was caught in a standard Tangle jack-up: target someone, gauge the response, move in on the weak, and collect any valuables. I was wearing nondescript clothing, so maybe it was a case of mistaken identity. My options were to fight, which I couldn't because I had no offense abilities, or reason with them, which was pointless when dealing with a street mind-set prone to random violence. That left running. Running was always good.

The pauses between strikes were similar in length, which meant the attackers needed to give their bodies a chance to recharge. Higher-powered fey didn't need any recovery time. I gauged the timing of the shots and the distance to the next doorway, and made a dash for it. Wild essence struck the walls around me. I had taken them off guard, and their already poor skills couldn't cope with the surprise. I relaxed, confident I'd be able to outwit them now that I had their measure. It wasn't the fastest way to get home, but I would get out of the alley without much more trouble

Two essence-bolts streaked toward me. I dove behind a dumpster, my shield flashing with sparks as I was grazed. The first attacker had moved in closer behind me, which helped improve his aim.

I pulled my daggers from my boots. The gold dagger warmed in my hand, then shifted and stretched, becoming a sword. That wasn't good. I hadn't been able to figure out how to turn the dagger into a sword, but every time the thing grew on its own, I was in trouble—as in near-death trouble.

To add a new complication, the stone in my head pulsed with heat, not painful like the darkness but a wave that cascaded through my body. My body shield reacted to it and hardened, golden-faceted planes refracting the ambient light.

I huddled between the dumpster and a wall. The sword was nice to have—if a bad omen—but without abilities, surprise was what I had to work with. I darted from the dumpster and ran back the way I had come. As I hoped, the one who had been blocking my exit mistook my direction, and his shots fell short. The other fired from a second-story window, the strike warping off course around the metal of the dumpster. The mistake gave me a twenty-second clear run to the end of the alley before they recharged, and I took the chance.

A man in black stepped into the street ahead, a ski mask hiding his face and a weak body shield shimmering on him. He fired a jagged burst of essence at me. My sword hummed and leaped to the side, deflecting the bolt of its own accord, dissipating it into the air. Things like that would have been nice to know, but Briallen didn't see it that way.

Unharmed, I came up from a crouch, preparing for his next move. I stepped from the wall and marched toward the figure in black. He fired again, but I shunted the essence away with the blade. He wasn't that powerful, yet he seemed surprised that I had more than a shield to protect myself. He wasn't going to like it when I reached him.

The sword pulled in my hand, like a ship yawing with the wind. I followed my instinct and let it be, spinning in the direction of the stroke. The blade knocked down another essence strike—my second attacker was still in play. I had twenty or so seconds before the next strike. I pivoted back to the man in black, then froze. He had pulled a gun—a druid with a gun—aiming down the sight even as I registered the situation. He fired.

The bullet struck my shield as streaks of green fire lanced over my head. I ignored a scream behind me, focusing on the bullet sizzling into my shield. The shield dimpled as the bullet funneled through the hardened essence. I twisted, torquing the bullet's path, my own shield acting against me as it pulled the bullet in. More green fire flashed above as I forced myself to the pavement, trying to bend the bullet's trajectory away. The disintegrating edge of the shield prickled against my cheek. Flat on my back, I twisted my neck as I watched the relentless approach of the bullet. It seared across my scalp. I flinched as it hit the pavement next to my face, shards of asphalt digging into my skin.

Someone leaped over me firing elf-shot, the source of the green essence flashes. An elf, red-uniformed, landed at my feet. He thrust his arms apart, pointing to either end of the alley and fired simultaneously from both hands. Silence settled over the alley. The elf relaxed his stance and turned. Rand leaned a concerned face over mine. "Are you hit?"

I pulled myself up with his outstretched hand. "Grazed. I'm okay. Nice timing."

His hands glimmered as he scanned the windows behind me. "You were fortunate I was nearby."

The black-clad figure lay still near the entrance to the alley. Beyond him, people peered from the far side of the street. Most pretended not to see anything and continued on their way. I held my sword and dagger at the ready as Rand and I approached the body. He gestured me back as he squatted by the still form, keeping a handful of essence charge at the ready in case of an ambush. Rand relaxed his hand, the line of tension across his shoulders easing. He pulled off the ski mask. "He's dead."

Stunned, I dropped my arms to my sides. "Shit." I turned and walked away, then stopped. "Shit. This isn't happening." I turned again and walked back to Rand. "Danu's blood, Rand. Tell me this didn't happen."

The dead man was Gerry Murdock.

30

I leaned my head back against a brick wall. A block away, police lights flashed up the alley from dozens of cars parked far enough away to avoid the mechanical dead zone of the Tangle. About twenty feet away, a wrinkled sheet covered Gerry Murdock, the stillness of his body a stark counterpoint to the activity around him. A stalled paramedic van had been pushed down the alley. Uniformed police officers and administrative police staff crowded near the crime scene. Whenever an officer was killed, the brotherhood turned out. It was understandable. They put their lives on the line every day. Until the dust settled, it didn't matter whether the cop was doing the right thing or the wrong thing. Respect was paid.

Rand stood guard over me, and I kept my body shield hardened. My presence brought an added knee-jerk reaction to the situation. A number of people remained suspicious of my involvement in Commissioner Scott Murdock's death. That investigation remained stalled until—if— Manus ap Eagan recovered. Now I was involved in another cop's death and another Murdock—one who was convinced I was to blame for his father's death. I wasn't going to get any objectivity while Gerry's blood was on the ground.

Leo stared at his brother's body. Grief etched his face, a confused shock of denial and anger. When he had arrived on the scene, he hadn't come near me. I didn't approach him either. A ring of police officers surrounded me and Rand, and I was getting enough angry glares without giving someone an excuse to pull a weapon.

Meryl stood next to Leo, her arm around his waist. I had asked Rand to do a sending to her, and she had been among the first to arrive. Leo wasn't reacting to her presence, but she talked to him, shutting out the scene around her and focusing her words on him alone. They were too far away for me to hear.

"I need you to tell me there was no other choice," I said.

Rand watched the officers, his face intent and alert. "There was. He could have not fired his gun."

I grunted but did not laugh. The last thing I needed was to be seen smiling. I knew where he was coming from. Regardless of what the public preferred, policing authorities did not shoot to incapacitate. The risk of missing far outweighed the risk of getting killed by the bad guys. Gerry pulled his weapon. Gerry fired his weapon. Gerry paid the price for his decision.

I bowed my head, staring into the space between my feet, shifting my gaze between one boot and the other. The sword had resumed its dagger size when Gerry died. I had returned both daggers to their sheaths before the authorities arrived. The first responder had demanded I turn them over, but I had refused. I had a right to carry them, especially in that end of town, and hadn't used them for anything other than defense. Rand took my side, asking the officer if he would like Rand's hands, since those had been used to kill Gerry.

Rand had made no attempt to hide the fact that he had fired the elf-shot that killed Gerry. In the same breath, he asserted his diplomatic immunity. Despite the break with the Consortium, Donor had not revoked the status of Eorla and her people as envoys of the court. Doing so would have validated her own court, and that wasn't something Donor wanted to give a hint of legitimacy. Of course, diplomatic immunity was also the reason Manus ap Eagan wasn't in a prison hospital. Two police officers, a father and son yet, were dead by known assailants who could not be arrested for their crimes. The excuse did not sit well with present company.

The faith stone was feeding my body shield, but I was reaching the point of exhaustion holding it together anyway. Despite my more resilient constitution, using essence took effort. Maintaining a body shield was a constant drain. I was at my breaking point.

"What are you going to do?" I asked.

Rand monitored everything and everyone around us, scanning, assessing. I realized that this was how Eorla saw him, his back always to her, facing her only when they were alone and in direct conversation. I had never had a full-time bodyguard and never thought about how much trust existed between protector and protected who didn't look each other in the eye.

"I will answer their questions until they start to repeat, then I will excuse myself and return to Eorla," he said.

Eorla. Not Her Majesty. I wondered if that was because she wasn't present or if she allowed him to use her personal name in private. "Well, give me a heads-up because I'm not comfortable staying here without you."

"Ceridwen's people have set a perimeter for you. Once you leave this alley, they will not allow anyone with guns to enter the Tangle," he said.

I didn't need another debt to Ceridwen. She was going to hold me to my promise to help her get revenge against Maeve. I didn't mind that so much. It was her subtle manipulations that bound me tighter every time we interacted that worried me. Promises made had a tendency to look very different from promises fulfilled.

I stood but remained near the wall. People nearby cast looks at me that ranged from anxious to angry. Janey Likesmith had arrived, but she didn't tend to the body. She hugged Leo and remained with her arms around him. Meryl stepped back, still talking. Leo nodded over Janey's shoulder.

Someone from the OCME—a human, I noticed—was breaking out crime-scene equipment. Clearly, no fey was going to touch this case. I wondered if news had gotten out in the force about the Murdocks, if people knew they were, in fact, fey folk. I wondered if it would matter now.

The officers out on the sidewalk shifted, shuffling to make room for someone. As a gap opened among them, Kevin Murdock strode through. His hair was disheveled from a hat, and red colored his cheeks. He stopped beside Gerry, his jaw set, hands clenched. Leo reached out a hand and said something, but Kevin shrugged him off. He raised his gaze, and we made eye contact.

His pale blue eyes shone with anger—and more. Essence flickered there, the telltale reaction of angry fey. In a flash, a body shield blossomed around him, pushing Leo and Meryl back. He stalked toward me. With a snap of his wrist, his hand burned incandescent white with essence. In reflex, I tapped my own body essence and shuddered as the darkness squeezed my mind. Kevin let the essence fly. The strike lanced toward us, shearing through Rand's shield and throwing him off his feet. My head burned with heat as the stone pulsed and my shield—exploded was the only word I could grasp. It wrapped itself around both Rand and me, a solidified barrier. Kevin's bolt hit with a splash of fire that washed over and away from us.

More essence launched through the air as Rand and Meryl recovered, ribbons of binding spells dropping over Kevin. They spun around him, cinching his arms to his sides, and he staggered to a halt. He remained calm, yet defiant. His gaze bored into me, his pale blue eyes burning with essence. Cops flooded the space between us, pushing Kevin back and pulling their guns on me and Rand.

This isn't over. You're a dead man, Grey.

My jaw dropped at the sound of his voice in my mind. The shield, the essence fire, and the sending were all high-level work. Regardless of where he was training, Kevin didn't have the level of experience to achieve such ability. It was all raw talent.

Leo pressed into the crowd. "Hold fire! Hold fire!" he shouted.

"Leo . . ." I said.

He glared, his eyes tired and red-rimmed, and held his hand up to my face. I snapped my mouth shut. He pointed at Rand. "Get him out of here. Tell your boss she better take my call, or there will be hell to pay."

Rand extinguished his essence and bowed. He took my arm and escorted me through the officers. As we passed Kevin, Rand removed his binding spell with a druidic hand gesture.

I'll stay with Leo, Meryl sent. I gave her a barely detectable nod, letting my eyes tell her I understood.

At the mouth of the alley, a tree fairy, her face rough and stern, waited in a black car on the sidewalk. Rand guided me into the back like I was under arrest, then slid into the seat next to me. The tree fairy edged the car through the officers. The interior of the car rang with the sound of batons hitting the fenders. The tree fairy remained calm, though, and took us to Old Northern Avenue without further incident.

"That went better than expected," Rand said.

31

Rand ushered me through heightened security at the Rowes Wharf Hotel. The death of a police officer at the hands of one of her people had brought protesters to the street out front. The National Guard had increased its presence, claiming it was about crowd control, but they didn't seem much interested in calming anyone.

Eorla, on the other hand, acted as if it was another day in the life of the Unseelie queen. We arrived in her private office to find her calmly fielding phone calls. She gestured me to the guest chair. Rand waited at attention by the window. "No, I'm not concerned," she said into the phone. "I will make a public announcement when I make my final decision . . . I have guns pointed at my front door, sir. I apologize if I seem a bit distracted . . . It is my understanding that the man was disguised, did not identify himself, and was firing on a civilian . . . Fine. I will let you know."

She ended the call and leaned back in her chair. "How are you holding up?"

"I've had better days," I said.

"You look exhausted. I've had a room prepared for you," she said.

"I shouldn't stay here, Eorla. It complicates things for you. My place in the Tangle will be secure once the news cameras go away," I said.

Eorla pursed her lips. "What do you plan to do?"

"I need to get some sleep before I can process all this," I said.

"Publicly, I'm putting you on restricted duty, Rand. We need to deflect attention," she said.

"Understood, Your Majesty," he said.

I peered at him. For weeks, I had been noticing curious things about Rand, small things, things that didn't add up to my understanding of an elven warrior in general and him in particular. In front of Eorla, he was all business—the picture of a high-level elven operative. When we had been alone together, though, his façade slipped, letting some of the man behind the image show through. I assumed it was because we had become friendly. Contrary to popular belief, elves were not dour and taciturn at all times. They were reserved in public, but among their own, they were like anybody else, high-spirited or low, with every personality between.

"What were you doing down in the Tangle anyway?" I asked. I kept my voice nonchalant and conversational. I didn't want him to think I was accusing him of anything.

Rand glanced at Eorla with a mild flutter of a sending. "I was checking Ceridwen's defenses."

"Is there a problem?" I asked, couching the question to seem concerned about me rather than him.

"I think that would be obvious after what happened. Many approaches are unguarded," he said.

"That's true. Security is difficult because there are no clear boundaries in the Tangle. But I wasn't attacked by someone from the Tangle. Someone has been training Kevin and Gerry Murdock to use their abilities."

"You must have noticed their strategies and execution. I suspect they've found training from the Guild," Rand said.

"MacGoren did say Maeve was behind the attack at Eagan's, and I know Gerry Murdock was there," I said.

"It would rehabilitate their image with the family after their involvement with their father's death," Eorla said.

"Kevin and Gerry hate the Guild," I said.

He glanced at Eorla again with another sending. The pause made me wonder which one of them didn't like the direction the conversation had taken. "I confirmed their Guild training. I saw it as necessary and neutral," Rand said. "Regardless of who trained them, I was more concerned about the individuals' being safely trained than who their trainers were."

"Yeah, that didn't work out so well tonight, did it?" I asked.

Rand stared down his nose at me. "You are alive. I'll make no judgment whether that is for good or ill."

I had to appreciate a rebuttal wrapped in a subtle insult. "So what went wrong?"

He considered before responding. "I was more concerned about Kevin Murdock. He appears inordinately powerful. I had full surveillance on him, but only daytime watchers on Gerald. With macGoren dead, it remains to be seen what they do next," Rand said.

Keeva didn't seem like she was going to be broadcasting macGoren's death anytime soon. The events in the safe house happened less than twelve hours ago. Another reason to be curious about Rand. "How do you know macGoren's dead?" I asked.

"My contacts at the Guild are high level, Connor. An extraction for you was in process when Keeva macNeve intervened," he said.

"Have you ever been in the research labs at the Guild-house?" I asked.

The question threw him, as it was meant to. "Excuse me?" Rand asked.

"The research labs on the second-level subbasement. Ever been there?" I asked.

His face became neutral, hiding whatever emotions he was feeling. "May I inquire the point of the question?"

I smiled to hide the fact that I was going to bait him with a lie. "Oh. Sorry. My mind was leaping around. The Guild was working on body-signature tracking. They've been trying to develop a method for tracking someone by body-signature markers. Pretty sophisticated stuff."

"I'm not aware of this," he said.

"Really? I would have thought you heard about it when you went down there. The guys working on it tell everybody," I said.

"I have never been in those labs."

Eorla smiled. "The Guild wouldn't let Rand have clearance. Believe me. I tried."

I leaned forward. "Eorla, can you lock down this room? No one in, no one out?"

With an intrigued look, she muttered under her breath. Essence swirled across the doors and windows. "Well?" she asked.

I looked up at Rand. "Who are you working for?"

He didn't take it as an accusation, although this time I made it sound like one. "Her Majesty," he said.

"Were you in the subbasement level of the Guildhouse where the research labs are?" I asked.

Rand clenched his jaw. "Your Majesty, I take issue with what is apparently an interrogation."

Eorla tilted her head. "What is wrong, Connor?"

"I think Rand is a Guild spy," I said.

No one said a word. Eorla looked down at her desktop while Rand looked at her. "Why do you believe he was in that subbasement?" she asked.

"Because I was there and his essence is there. It was as recent as the day the Guildhouse collapsed," I said.

"Did it occur to you that he might have been doing something on my orders?" Eorla asked.

Rand relaxed when she said that. That was enough for me to know I was right. "Of course, it did. And if he was, his lying to me right now would make perfect sense. What I can't dismiss, though, is how he used a druid spell tonight to bind Kevin Murdock."

"I am adept at many modes of essence ability, Mr. Grey," Rand said.

"I buy that. I'm sure most people would. But part of the issue with what's going on in my head is that I am highly sensitive to essence, more than anyone I know. You killed Gerry with elf-shot, but it was laced with druid essence. The binding spell had more of it."

I tensed, ready to react to whatever happened next. If Rand was going to make a break for it, that would be the time. Instead, he remained relaxed but alert. "With all due respect, Mr. Grey, I believe it has been well established that your faculties are impaired. You are mistaken."

"And you happened to be in the Tangle tonight for something a midlevel agent could have handled," I said.

The tension in the room hummed. I focused my attention on Rand, but I wanted to know what Eorla was thinking. "Connor, I cannot have you undermining Rand, especially after what happened tonight. We need unity."

I jerked my head toward her. "None of this bothers you?"

She licked her lips and glanced up at Rand. "I am aware of Rand's, shall we say, conflict of interest."

Rand reacted predictably. "Your Majesty, I have ever been . . ."

Eorla held her hand up and a sending fluttered through the air. "Let's not dance any longer. There are larger issues involved. Connor has seen through your subterfuge. Now I am concerned that he might not be the only one who has noticed these things."

A sending fluttered from Eorla, then a soft knock sounded from the door behind her desk. The door opened, and I jumped to my feet. Standing in the doorway was an elven warrior, the exact image of Rand. Eorla cocked her head toward him. "Gentlemen, allow me to introduce my first officer and confidante. Rand, this is Connor Grey and"—she smiled at the man in front of her desk—"your name, sir?"

I looked from one man to the other. The one in the red

uniform whom I had known as Rand looked exactly like the man in a plain green house uniform standing behind Eorla.

"How long have you known, ma'am?" the imposter asked.

"Rand escaped from his cell when the Guildhouse was destroyed, but I have known your deception from the beginning," Eorla said. "The Elven King himself could not create a glamour to deceive me.

The imposter glanced at Rand. "I will reveal myself in private."

Eorla sat for a long moment. "Please excuse us, Rand."

He bowed and closed the door. The imposter bowed his head in thought. Essence shimmered over him, twisting and smearing his image. The tight elven hair loosened into a head of curls as the ears shrank and rounded. His skin lightened, and a subtle shift in height—still tall, but a more slender build. The essence fell away from his face, and I started laughing.

"Surprised to see me, Con?" he asked.

"Danu's blood, Dylan, I can't believe I blew your cover," I said.

32

Seeing my old partner Dylan macBain dressed as an elven officer was strange. Stranger still was realizing he had been undercover for months, and I had no idea. Dylan and I stood alone on the roof of the hotel. When we reached the open air, he dropped the Rand glamour. The muffled sound of protesters echoed through the financial district.

"Why didn't you tell me?" I asked.

True regret showed on his face. "It's complicated."

I leaned on the parapet, staring out over the harbor. The entire inner harbor was now cordoned off by the mist, the essence barrier rising from the sea like a wall of fog. "Uncomplicate it."

"I don't know if I can. There was concern you would expose me," he said.

"Whose concern? MacGoren's?"

He pressed his lips together, glancing down. "I don't work for macGoren."

I faced him. "Maeve? You're working for her?"

He inhaled deeply and rubbed his face. "We're not going to play a guessing game. I'm not going to tell you."

Anger burned in my chest. Dylan and I had been Guild partners. Beyond that, we had been more than friends. "Did you kill those undercover agents?"

"No," he said. He wasn't upset. He knew it was a fair question under the circumstances.

"If you don't work for Maeve, who do you work for?" I said.

He nodded. "An explanation wouldn't help. Suffice it to say this was the highest-placed agent we've ever accomplished, Connor. You have to appreciate the delicacy of my position."

"I would if I understood the purpose," I said.

It was his turn to be angry. "That's just it, Con. You don't have to understand."

"You killed my friend's brother, Dylan. I think that entitles me to something. You're not the one who has to face Leo," I said.

"What I said before stands true. Gerry made his decision. You would have done the same thing in my position," he said.

I would have. If Dylan were being attacked, I would have done the same thing. I did do it. I killed fourteen people when I thought he had been killed. "You don't seem remorseful," I said.

"I'll deal with it in my own time. I'm not like you," he said.

"Damn right you're not," I muttered.

I didn't know what to make of him. We had been so close, and now this wall was between us. Maybe it was inevitable. Dylan had remained the good Guildsman. I had gone my own way. Maybe two people can't always be what they once were to each other. I grunted in amusement. Maybe that wasn't always such a bad thing.

"What's so funny?" Dylan asked.

"Meryl and I used to hate each other. It's funny how things change," I said.

"The Wheel of the World turns as It will. Sometimes that's good," he said.

Sometimes it wasn't. Sometimes life put you in a corner and dared you to come out. Briallen taught me that I had to change to meet new challenges and accept it when I couldn't. Nigel taught me that I didn't have to accept anything I didn't want to and that I could push life in the direction I wanted. Somehow, they were both right and both wrong.

From the top of the hotel, I could see destroyed buildings. I could imagine the destroyed lives. I had helped stop some of that, keeping it from being worse than it was. I couldn't shake the feeling, though, that a lot of it happened because of me.

"What's Eorla going to do?" I asked.

"She said it didn't matter if I stayed or left. She's going to handle things the same either way," he said.

"So your lying was pointless," I said.

"I don't think so. I learned a lot," he said.

"Like not lying?" I asked.

He chuckled. "No. If I hadn't done this, Con, if I hadn't fooled everyone, I wouldn't have met Eorla. Regardless of everything else, I learned from her that sometimes doing the wrong thing can be in the service of doing the right thing."

"Is she in danger?" I asked.

He leaned both hands against the parapet. "Of course she is. She's the Unseelie Queen."

"Have you compromised her, Dyl? I want to know if something you said or did is going to hurt her," I said.

He didn't answer, so I glanced at him. He was pensive, a bit bemused. Then he smiled. "I'll tell you this, Con. I stopped reporting on Eorla weeks ago. I've seen what she wants, and it's not terrible. I've been helping her."

"Sounds like you have a need to lie to someone all the time," I said.

He flicked his eyebrows. "That's the business, I guess."

"That sounds cold."

He shook his head. "I saved your life. I didn't have to."

And I had saved his. He had had a knife in his heart. I had saved his life because he was dying for trying to help people. More than that, I saved his life because I couldn't imagine a world without Dylan macBain, the guy that made me laugh, the guy that made me feel like I could do no wrong. He was in love with me then, maybe still was, but I was the one who didn't want to change what we had. "You know what, Dyl? I think I figured out why I left New York. You said you saved my life but didn't have to. You know what? When the situation was reversed, I saved your life because I did have to."

His face went tight. "Ouch."

I nodded, staring at the mist wall. The level of essence in it was higher than that of any druid fog I had ever encountered. No good would come of it. When it did whatever it was going to do, I wanted to be someplace good. "Yeah. I think I'm going to go home now."

"You're going back to your apartment?"

I shook my head. "No. I said home. I'm going to Meryl. She's home now. Thanks for saving my life."

I left him alone on the roof.

33

I waited for Meryl in the lobby. Eorla didn't want me to go out the front, but I was tired of feeling like a fugitive or like I had done something wrong. All I wanted was to sleep in a warm bed and not worry about getting shot at or kidnapped. It wasn't much to ask. People went to bed every night with that expectation.

Meryl's MINI Cooper zipped up on the sidewalk and under the grand arch of the hotel. An escort of brownies followed me outside. Across the street, people shouted about death and murder. My name was mixed in there. A flurry of bottles and cans flew through the air, but they bounced uselessly against the barrier shield.

Meryl shifted into gear, then rubbed my thigh. "How're you doing?"

I dropped my head back against the seat. "Tired—no—exhausted. My brain has turned to mush. How's Leo?"

"I think he's in shock. He can barely speak. What the hell happened?" she asked.

I gave her the brief version of Gerry's attack. "I was on

the ground at that point. If he had fired again, I would have been dead if Dylan hadn't shown up."

She turned onto the Oh No bridge. Normal-sized cars had to creep over the twisted surface, but Meryl bounced the MINI across without any fear. "*Dylan macBain?* As in, dead Dylan macBain whose funeral I went to?"

"Yeah. It was all a setup for him to go undercover. He's been impersonating Rand for months," I said.

It said something about the world I lived in that Meryl wasn't shocked Dylan was alive and wasn't furious I didn't tell her. "Huh. Now I know where all that intel was coming from," she said with an understanding look.

"You knew Eorla had a spy?" I asked.

She flicked me her trademark of-course look. "Come on, Connor. Everyone spies on everyone. Stop acting surprised."

"You could have told me," I said. Suddenly, I felt like I was having the same conversation as with Dylan.

"And what? Eorla would have increased security? Double-checked her advisors? She was doing that anyway. That's how things operate normally. Saying it out loud doesn't change it."

"Still . . ." I said.

"Oh, please. You're looking for an argument. How's this: The Guild has spies in the Consortium, the police department, the statehouse, and, yeah, Eorla's hotel. By the way, Eorla and Bastian both have spies at the Guild. I don't know the names of every single mole, but, yes, occasionally I do see reports. Now, what are you going to do about it, and how will it change anything except that I told you what you already know?"

I crossed my arms. "It would be nice to decide on my own whether I would try."

She slammed the clutch into a downshift. "Really? Tell me more about your little magic bowl, Mr. Transparency. I don't seem to remember that coming up in conversation. Or how about using it on Manny? I heard about that from Gillen Yor, for Danu's sake. You want to go down this road, you better be damned ready to answer some questions, too."

The car rocked as she swerved around a pothole. "I'm sorry."

"Yeah, me, too," she said.

"No, really, I am sorry. I've been bombarded the last few days, and I don't even know what I'm saying anymore. Let's start over. Does Leo hate me?"

"I don't think he hates you, Grey. Does he associate major hurt with you? Yeah, I think so," she said.

"How do I fix this?" I asked.

She pulled into a dark alley near the Tangle and parked, not something that would be most people's first choice. "I don't think this is something that gets fixed. It's something that you have to get past. His brother was killed. It doesn't matter what Gerry was doing when it happened, and it doesn't matter that it was you it was being done to. Let him grieve."

We got out of the car. "What are we doing here?"

"We walk the last few blocks. I washed my car, and I don't want it getting shot at. Ceridwen has the harborfront guarded," she said. She dropped the strap of her giant bag over her head and wore it across her chest.

I wrapped my arm around her, and we walked amid the burned wreckage of the neighborhood. "Maybe it's time I left Boston."

"Yeah, I was thinking I'd dye my hair," she said.

"Okay, I'll bite. Meaning?"

We sidestepped a crater in the ground. "Meaning it will reflect my mood, but it won't change who I am."

"People don't die when you're around," I said.

"Exactly. People can die as easily somewhere else," she said.

"You're not helping my mood," I said.

We turned the corner into the Tangle. Dead essence rose around us, a haze of blue that lined the streets. Shadows moved among the shadows, and furtive figures appeared in windows and doors. Ceridwen's people were out in force.

Meryl looked toward the harbor, then up at me. "You see that mist wall out there? That's Maeve's doing. Why? Because of something Donor did. Why? Because of something Maeve did. Why? Because of something Donor did. It's the Wheel of the World, Grey. They play the music, and we dance. I think wherever we are, we'll hear that music. It might as well be here as anywhere else."

"You forget. I don't dance," I said.

She stopped in front of an old building, its once-beautiful front door scratched and pitted with time, a carved garland of oak leaves chipped and worn. "This is it."

I could feel the Dead around us, scent the *vitniri* manwolves and a variety of solitary body signatures. Ceridwen was taking no chances for me. "Things can't go on like this, Meryl. I can't run and hide for the rest of my life. Something's got to give. I have to find the answers to why this is all happening to me."

She tugged at my belt loop as she opened the door. "I know, but not tonight. Let's go upstairs and close the door on the world for a while. Maybe I'll teach you how to dance."

I closed the door and followed her up the stairs inside. "Go slow," I said.

"Not likely," she said over her shoulder.

34

I didn't know what woke me. Maybe Meryl made a noise. Maybe the stone in my head reacted to what was happening. Maybe I sensed the dagger. How didn't make a difference. What mattered was that I awoke to find Meryl standing beside the bed, the rune dagger clutched in both her hands, ready to plunge it into my head. We stared at each other for a long moment. Her arms trembled, her hands white-knuckled with strain.

In the dark, with the pale silver light of the moon coming through the window, she looked mythic, like a wild goddess intent on a sacrifice. Oddly, I didn't feel fear. Something told me either she wasn't going to do it or maybe I was going to let her. In the moment, though, I thought one of us was having a break with reality. The scary part was I didn't know which.

"Did I leave the seat up again?" I asked.

Meryl dropped her arms, tears welling up in her eyes as she let the dagger fall to the floor. Sobbing, she did a slow pivot and sank to the edge of the bed. I sat up as she covered her face with her hands. Uncertain, I pulled her toward me, hugging her close. She let me but didn't hold me. I caressed her hair as she cried into my chest. "This is awkward. I appear to be comforting someone who I'm pretty sure was about to stab me to death."

"That's not funny," she said, her voice a strained whisper.

"Am I laughing? I don't think I'm laughing."

"I don't know what to say. Maybe I was sleepwalking?" Meryl said between sobs.

"Well, that would explain the standing-up part, but not the dagger-to-the-head part," I said.

She pulled away, running her hands through her hair, trying to collect herself. "I don't know where to begin."

I slipped off the bed and put my pants on. I didn't think it was going to be a conversation that made any sense naked or clothed, but given the choice, clothes made more sense. "Were you going to kill me?"

"I think so," she said.

I checked the windows. Plumes of essence rose from the rooftops. No one moved nearby though I sensed people, guards keeping discreet watch over me. The body signatures were normal, no one powering up essence, no one ready to fight. They assumed an attack would come from outside. "Why?"

She exhaled, the sound of tears and anguish. "It was like a compulsion. I saw myself doing it, and I realized what I was doing, but I couldn't stop myself. If you hadn't woken up, I don't know what would have happened. Does that make any sense?" she asked.

I stared out the window. I remembered back to the night in the *leanansidhe*'s lair. I had become aware that I was draining Keeva's life essence, but I didn't stop right away. I almost killed her. "Yeah, I can understand how that happens."

"You're going to do something. Something terrible," she said.

I pulled my shirt over my head. "Is this something you dreamed?"

She shook her head. "I saw it in the painting. I saw a circle of light with a spot of darkness. The darkness spread until it covered everything, then it faded away, and the canvas went blank. There's no essence on it at all anymore."

"Seems a bit cryptic to be killing me over," I said.

An edge of anger crept into her voice. "I didn't say that's why I did what I did. It was a compulsion. The painting is something greater than itself. There's a connection. I think you're the darkness, Connor. I think you're going to do something that spreads the darkness until it covers everything."

"Let's talk about this compulsion. Where did it come from?"

"I don't know. It has to do with you. I've been combing the archives looking for references to the stone and reading them over and . . ." She stopped talking.

I whipped my head toward her. "What did you say?"

She held her hand up as she stared at the floor. "Give me a sec."

I grabbed her by the shoulders. "What documents are you talking about?"

She pushed me away, her body shield shimmering into place. "I know what you're thinking. I just realized the same thing."

"You never told me you found more documents," I said.

"I . . . I know. I think that's part of what's wrong," she said.

"I want those documents," I said.

"Of course. But why did I keep them from you? And why don't I care if you see them now?"

I walked away from her again. "I don't know what game you're playing, Meryl, but I don't like it."

She came up behind me and touched my shoulder. I shrugged her off. "Don't touch me."

"I'm sorry," she said.

"How long has this been going on?"

She narrowed her eyes as she gazed out the window. "I

found the first document my first day back in the Guild-house. The one you found on my desk."

"I wasn't even looking for them then," I said.

Meryl frowned. "It was the first thing on my mind when I went back. I checked on the *leanansidhe*, then went and pulled the doc."

That seemed strange. "You checked on the *leanan-sidhe*?"

She looked baffled, as if trying to make sense of her memories. "I remember thinking I needed to secure the room in case anyone found it."

"You knew she was there?"

"Yes—I mean, no. Before I returned to the archives, I did not know she was there. I'm sure I didn't."

"You said you found her when you were securing the archives," I said.

Meryl sat on the bed, her face contorted with concentration. She was using her druidic recall, reviewing her memories with a precise clarity. "I did. I"—her eyebrows arched—"lied. I lied about it. I started to tell you but changed the details. The same thing happened when you were in my office. I started to tell you, but I didn't."

"You're not making any sense" I said.

She stood. "Don't you see the pattern? It's all about you."

"And?"

"There's only one person who could have done this to me, Connor. Nigel must have known I might beat him at his own game. He made me his fail-safe. He put a compulsion in my mind," she said.

Angry, tired, I leaned against the sill. "Convenient it was Nigel. Shall we ask him?"

"This wasn't my doing, Connor," she said.

"Where are the documents?"

"They're all in my office," she said.

"Go get them," I said.

She hesitated, then started dressing. "I didn't want this to happen."

"It has," I said.

She opened the door, her face stained with tears. "I stood over you for ten minutes fighting the urge to stab you in the head. I didn't do it. If I meant to kill you . . . if I didn't love you, Connor . . . you would be dead."

I had nothing to say to that, so I gave her my back. The door closed, and I listened to her footsteps fade off down the hall. I stared across the rooftops, across the city at night, watching the essence play in swirls through the air.

I was alone.

35

Meryl sent the documents by courier first thing in the morning. Inside a sealed box, several dozen parchments were tied with a ribbon. She had attached a note: "Believe me." I didn't. Not when I got out of bed after having not slept much. Not after the box arrived. Not even after struggling through translations that weren't telling me much. But as the day wore on, I calmed down and thought more about it.

Gods knew that I understood uncontrollable compulsions. I had seen myself do and say things I didn't mean, didn't want to do, and still did them. I also knew Nigel Martin. Nigel always had a backup plan. He knew it was risky doing what he did in front of Briallen. He knew it had a chance of failing—or worse, that he would get caught. He would have had a backup plan. Burying a compulsion in Meryl's mind would qualify. Why that included an impulse to kill me was the part I couldn't understand.

I spent the day reading through the documents, trying to

decipher the arcane language with little success. I was fluent in modern fey languages, but Early Elvish and Saxon were tough without a dictionary—or a Saxon elf.

I had been trapped inside all day, venturing out only for food. My involvement with Gerry's death had triggered an elevated military presence around the Rowes Wharf Hotel. Apparently, because I had left with Rand, people assumed I was at the hotel. When I showed up at a vendor stall for some lunch, I got anxious looks and sent more than a few people running. Some of that was fear, of course, but I knew well enough that some of that was informants.

The sending from Melusine couldn't have come at a better time. She had updated information she wanted to share about the dead merrow. The police weren't interested, and Eorla wouldn't respond. I had less chance of getting the police to investigate anything at the moment, but at least I could pass information to Murdock. He might not be on the cases anymore, but he liked closure.

As night fell, I made my way unseen down to the waterfront. With all the law-enforcement focus on the Rowes Wharf Hotel and the Tangle, Melusine and I agreed to meet behind the Fish Pier. The sex trade down there held little interest for anybody under the present circumstances, which meant we could talk unobserved. I slipped through the police checkpoints around the Tangle easily enough—skirted the falling pilings on the harbor and cut across the destroyed buildings behind the World Trade Center through one of the many neighborhood exits. Just like Ceridwen's people couldn't cover them all to protect me when Gerry attacked, the police didn't have a hope of containing anyone in the Tangle determined to leave it.

I gave the darkened cars along the back of the pier a wide berth. Business was going on in those cars, the oldest business in the world. They didn't need to think I was checking them out. The police had long ago given up rousting people from the place at night. Fey folk knew how to cover their tracks, didn't fall prey to sting operations, and cleaned up after themselves. As long as the local street workers didn't cause problems for the daytime fishing operations, the two businesses coexisted.

No one would bother Melusine and me—either the police or the locals—in the middle of the night. The tide rode high as I walked along the concrete head of the pier. In the near distance, the mist wall shimmered in the harbor, a cloud of soft light that shifted in shades of blue and gray. Helicopters circled above it, their searchlights scanning for a glimpse of what lay beneath. All sea traffic had been routed out of the inner harbor until someone could figure out whether the mist itself was dangerous or what it hid.

No one had taken credit for the mist, but given that similar oddities had appeared off the coast of Germany, everyone knew it was some kind of defensive measure by Maeve. Another two were in New York and Washington, but the Seelie Court had not responded to inquiries. Maeve liked to operate in secret, and keeping people off-balance—even her theoretical allies—was normal for her.

Down here, Melusine sent.

A ramp led off the pier to a floating dock in much better condition than the one Murdock and I had had to deal with the other night. Two large fishing boats were tied up, their rise and fall in the slack tide barely perceptible. I checked over my shoulder. The floating docks were considered off-limits. Crossing the owner of a working boat happened once. They were not people to anger. I hopped over the thin chain barring the way. I liked it better down by the boats. I wasn't visible from the pier, and unless either of the boats had guards, Melusine and I would have privacy.

"Melusine?"

End of the dock, she sent.

"What's with the sendings?" I asked.

From what I understand, something about the configuration of my vocal cords in the water only allows the sounds of my native language, she sent.

I stopped short. If Melusine was in the water, she wasn't

in human form. I had never seen her in her natural state. "I'm not a big fan of boats."

A sound like laughter rippled across my mind. *Neither am I. We will need no boat.*

I edged toward the water and peered into the darkness. Something moved beneath the surface, wellings of silvery flesh sliding by—and sliding by and sliding by. Melusine wasn't a merrow. In polite conversation, she was referred to as a mermaid. In reality, in her natural form, she was a huge serpent with a bad temper.

A set of fins coasted by. Despite asking me to meet her, she was using her form to intimidate me. At least, that was what I thought, so maybe I was intimidated. Her silvered length sank deeper beneath the surface, and I lost track of her.

"Melusine?"

The soft slap of water against the boats answered me. A ripple trailed across the water, and Melusine's head broke the surface. Her face hadn't changed though it had grown in proportion to her body. At first, she appeared to be a nude woman rising from the water, straight into the air, her pale skin glittering with moisture in the darkness, deep gray aureoles marking almost vestigial breasts. Her hair shivered out in thick dark strands that stood out from her head and flowed down her back. She rose a few feet higher than her waist, revealing a thick swell of dark gray scales. She agitated the water around her, several yards of her tail writhing to keep her afloat.

I have made contact with someone within the mist wall, she sent.

"How? No one can get in from what I've been told," I said.

Look at me, Connor Grey. I am not "no one." The wall does not recognize me, she sent.

Essence barriers were keyed to prevent specific types of essence from passing through. Their level of sophistication depended on the skill and ability of the creator. If someone had never encountered a specific body signature, it wasn't possible to defend against it. Melusine took her name from the progenitor of her race. It was within the realm of possibility that she was the original Melusine, which would make her centuries old. In either case, it wasn't likely that whoever created the mist wall had ever encountered someone like her.

"What does this have to do with the merrow's death?"

Redemption. I made a mistake thinking Bastian was responsible for the murders. Eorla no longer trusts me, and I would find her trust again.

"It was a pretty big mistake," I said.

I agree. I strove to uncover the truth, and I found something more. Someone in the mist wall is willing to trade information for gain, she sent.

"So why tell me?" I asked.

She shifted in the water, her torso sinking so that we were eye to eye. *Eorla will listen to you. Will you help me?*

I stared at her face, strangely beautiful in the midst of her ropy hair. I had believed her when she pointed me toward the Consortium because the conclusion had been plausible. Bastian would have killed his own men to save an operation. I moved to the edge of the dock. "Who's out there, Melusine? I know that mist wall is the work of the Seelie Court. Who would betray Maeve at this late date?"

She leaned closer. *He does not want his name known until you speak. If you do not go, he fears you will reveal him,* she sent.

I knew how these things went. Espionage and counterespionage were delicate games of feints and promises built more on trust than hope. Someone highly placed couldn't let it be known that he had decided to betray his queen. He would operate through a chain, each link in that chain depending on the strength of the next, risking all yet protecting the whole.

Connor? Time grows short, Melusine sent.

I nodded. "He's out there in the mist?"

Melusine leaned down, the scent of the sea washing over me. *He will show you what Maeve is planning.*

I didn't like it. Melusine had been wrong about Bastian. Regaining Eorla's favor was in her interest, but helping her didn't seem to be in mine. Going into the mist wall was like entering the lair of the lion, but this lion wouldn't be sleeping.

"I said I don't like boats."

She reached out her hand, the fingers long and tipped with sharp gray talons. *I will bring you personally. My essence will mask your passage.*

I decided to believe her. The tides of war always turned on fortune. Maeve had enough enemies in the States. It wasn't beyond comprehension that she had enemies at Tara—maybe even Ceridwen's underground opposition.

I took Melusine's moist hand, hard muscle like wet marble beneath the skin pressing against my palm. Melusine twisted, presenting her back to me. I coiled her hair in my other hand, its texture like bulbous seaweed. Something splashed out in the water, and I paused. "What was that?"

Melusine turned, her head winding on her neck farther than natural. *We must hurry before we are discovered.*

I loved her eyes, the glitter in their depths like a promise of home. Their phosphorescent glow assured me that she understood the water like no one else. "I thought I heard something."

I pulled myself onto her back, my feet finding loose purchase among the strands of hair and fins.

Use your knees to steady yourself, she sent.

Another noise caught my attention as I adjusted my position. My sensing ability kicked in, and the area glowed with essence, the silky pale green of the water, the blue-white of barnacles and crustaceans embedded in the pilings and dock, and deep emerald streaks coursing under the water—the large streaks of several body signatures. Startled, my grip slipped, my hand slick on her skin. "Melusine!" I said.

She drifted from the dock as my legs lost their purchase. *They are my protectors. Remain calm.*

As the gap of water between us and the pier grew, panic

and fear of the water overcame me. I flung myself off her and caught the edge of the floating dock, my fingers clawing at the rough wood as my feet kicked water. The splashing of Melusine recoiling her body filled the air. I was soaked as I pulled myself onto the dock. Down at the other end, a merrow hauled himself half-out of the water, propping himself up with massive hands, his hatchet-shaped face arcing over the dock. I spun back to Melusine. "We've got trouble."

She undulated forward, settling part of her bulk on the dock, her arms held out in supplication. *'Tis nothing, m'love, but the sea and me. Come now, the hour grows late.*

My head grew heavy and clouded with a feeling like sleepiness. Melusine smiled down at me, gesturing me forward with her hands. She was so beautiful in the light, her eyes so deep, her voice so sweet. Her fingers curled with a mesmerizing slowness, beckoning me with longing and desire. Her essence wafted over me, a sweet mix of salt and water. I wanted to hold her, wanted her to hold me. Her essence slipped into mine, touching my body essence, and I shivered.

The stone in my mind flared like a punch inside my skull. I hunched forward in pain, falling out of Melusine's embrace. I stumbled to the dock. It rocked beneath me as Melusine shifted closer. *What's wrong, m'love? Come to me. I will soothe your cares.*

Nausea rippled through me, and I wretched as her true scent reached my nose in a pungent stew of decay. As I lifted my head, I saw another merrow had joined the first, their wild black hair lank around their shoulders. I shook my head, trying to make sense of things. The stone flared again, flushing Melusine's essence away. Confused, I rolled on my back.

Melusine towered over me, her serpentine body sliding across the deck. "What the hell are you doing?" I asked.

She didn't answer but swiped at me with a taloned hand. My body shield activated as I scrambled to my feet. A wave of her essence enveloped me. *Come, m'love, I will love you forever.*

My shield shimmered, deadening the effect of her spell. "Stop it."

Please, m'love. The conflict to come has one conclusion, she sent.

"What have you done, Melusine? Who's out there?" I asked.

She swayed in the water, her undulating motions mesmerizing. *Strength always wins in the end, m'love. Save yourself and come with me.*

As she shifted farther onto the dock, shards of her skin flaked off and fluttered to the surface of the water, floating like thin translucent petals. My memory sparked, my druidic recall flashing with the image of Janey Likesmith holding a small plastic bag to the light. She hadn't recognized the skin cell from beneath the dead merrow's fingernail. None of us had. We had never seen Melusine in her serpent form. Realization dawned. "You're working for Maeve."

I work for my people, m'love. I work for my life. Come, save yourself, m'love. The High Queen can have a forgiving nature for those who lose their way.

Desire welled up within me, desire to make Melusine happy. I wanted to hold her in my arms, feel her lips against mine. I pushed more body essence into my shield, and the desire faded away. "Give it up, Melusine. I'm not buying."

She must have sensed the collapse of her spell. With a feral screech, she lunged forward. I swung over the railing to the gangway. The metal walkway shuddered and rattled beneath my feet as Melusine grabbed the lower end. She tore it from its moorings as I reached the top and leaped onto the pier.

Cars started up and raced away at the commotion. Melusine was breaking the local noise rules. I waved my arms for the last car, but the driver reversed, squealing its tires against the pavement before it spun in a tight turn and drove off. The parking area was empty.

Melusine screeched again, her head lifting over the edge of the pier. She was too large for the foot ramp and was pulling herself up the pilings. On the opposite end, three merrows climbed over the pier, their pale blue-gray bodies writhing as they fell to the ground. Their heavy tails whipped and coiled, then split. Before their legs had fully formed, they were standing. I didn't stay to watch the final transition.

I ran for the pier's processing building. I needed witnesses—lots of them. On the other side, streetwalkers huddled on the long stretch of loading docks. They weren't likely to help. I made for Old Northern Avenue, the slap of wet feet coming up behind me. I hesitated on the sidewalk. I wasn't picky about where I would find protection. The Rowes Wharf Hotel and the Tangle were equally distant.

A loud hissing drew my attention. Melusine, in her full serpentine glory, slithered down the Fish Pier. The hotel was less than a mile away. I could do a five-minute mile, faster if I put a burst of essence into it. The last place I wanted to be with a mad fey beast was in the desolate stretch of road between me and the Tangle.

I ran the center line of Old Northern Avenue, cars wailing their horns at me. I tapped my body essence, pushing myself harder. My head sang with pain, the darkness resisting the use of my ability. A glance over my shoulder revealed Melusine gaining on me. I was halfway to the bridge. I wasn't going to make it.

I ducked down an alley. Yggy's bar had been a safe haven for the fey for over a century. Heydan, who ran the place, had one main rule of the place: leave animosities and conflicts outside. I doubted a crazed shape-changing serpent would respect the rules under the circumstances, but I hoped at least to find help. I reached the old steel door, dented and scratched with a large Y painted on it. I grabbed the handle and pulled so hard I almost yanked my arm from its socket. The door didn't budge.

I stared, amazed. Yggy's was never closed. Ever. Day or night, people knew that one place existed where they could go and take a break from the world. And now it was closed.

I banged on the door. "Heydan!"

A shiver ran over me, like a blanket of cool air. A deep and subtle essence filled the air, and Heydan appeared beside me as if he had been there all along. I didn't understand how he did that. He was a giant of a man, a unique fey with no peers that I knew of. Bony ridges beneath his skin curled from his temples and around his ears to the back of his bald head. A light glimmered in his deep-set eyes.

"I need help, Heydan. Melusine's gone crazy," I said.

"I am Heydan. I watch and wait," he said.

I had no idea what that meant. "Listen to me, Heydan, Melusine . . ."

The rip of metal filled the air, and a car tumbled across the end of the alley. People ran screaming along the street.

"The Watch is over. The Wait begins," Heydan said.

He was gone. One moment he was there, the next I was alone. I ran out of the alley, intent on reaching the hotel. Melusine slithered down the pavement, her arms cast wide as if to embrace me.

I rolled into a dive between parked cars and pulled out the rune dagger. As I came up on my feet, the blade stretched to its full length, burning with cold white light. Melusine swerved to meet me, elation on her face. She dodged the blade with ease.

I needed space to maneuver, so I slid over the hood of a car and cut back into the street. Melusine swayed, her essence pouring over me. *Stop this, Connor, and come with me.*

If nothing else, she was persistent. Now that the faith stone had given me the heads-up, it was easy to reject her attempts to seduce me. "It's over, Melusine. It didn't work. I'm not going with you," I said.

She reared up higher. *Pity that, little man. I do not accept rejection. Maeve will be displeased.*

She darted forward, swinging her arm. I underestimated her speed, and she swept my feet out from under me. I rolled and jabbed at her exposed side. She shrieked as the blade sliced skin, but it was a superficial cut. Translucent scales fluttered to the ground.

I was not told of your sharp little tooth. I will have a word with Maeve about that when we are done, she sent.

"Tell her I said hi," I said. I lunged forward, thrusting toward her chest. She slid backwards, her body rolling across the pavement. Her tail came around. I ducked as it slammed the ground. I jabbed, and Melusine screamed. She yanked her tail away, wrenching the blade from my hand.

Melusine hit me from behind. My shield absorbed the blow, but the force of it pitched me hard against a car. I pulled myself up. Melusine slithered forward, stretching her body in a wide loop to cut off escape. Down the street, her merrow companions were catching up, five of them now. Things were going to get worse.

A resounding roar filled the air, a guttural animal sound that reverberated in my chest. Melusine hissed and reared as a wild wave of primal essence rolled over us. I grabbed my sword from the ground. Something knocked me aside, something huge and dark and rank.

I stumbled backwards, blade out, as an enormous beast leaped at Melusine. She held her arms out as if to embrace it. It fell on her like a mountain, a beast flickering with indigo essence. They rolled in a tangle of fur and scales. Enormous pawlike hands battered Melusine from side to side as she screamed and clawed.

The beast bunched its neck like a great bear and bellowed as Melusine constricted her coils. Its powerful roar shivered across my skin. The monstrous bear bared its teeth, thick and long canines dripping with saliva, and bit into Melusine's neck. Her scream went from a high-pitched note to a strangled screech as the beast shook its head. Melusine's arms flailed across its back, clawing for purchase. The bear swung her around, slamming her down against a car.

Her arms went slack with the blow. The beast found its feet, backing out of the nest of coils with Melusine's limp torso in its mouth. When it was free of her scales, it tore out her neck and threw her body to the ground.

Rearing onto its hind legs, the beast stood over a dozen feet high and roared in victory. It dropped to all fours and lumbered toward the merrows, thrusting its huge round head forward with a snarl. They fled without a fight. The beast growled and retreated, maneuvering its bulk around toward me.

I held my sword out as it approached. As it closed on me, it became smaller, its bulk shifting and contracting. The fur receded and the bearish muzzle flowed inward, exposing thick rolls of skin. When it was a few feet away, long, pointed ears slid through greasy hair, and a thick sagging gut grazed the ground.

I stared slack-jawed as Belgor stared up at me. He leaned on the car, struggling to bring his girth off the ground. He leaned heavily against the fender, his chin and bare chest smeared with black viscous blood. "I do not care for snakes," he said.

"I had no idea you could do that," I said.

Still catching his breath, he shrugged. "I have not lasted these many years on my wits alone, Mr. Grey. I trust this settles my debt to you?"

Dumbfounded, I nodded. "Yeah, I think that covers it."

Belgor waddled off like he had stopped by to chat and had to be going.

36

I didn't stick around for the police after-party. Leaving the scene of a crime was a crime, but I wasn't worried about it. Being attacked by a giant snake-woman and four or five of her semiaquatic friends was probably justification in most people's eyes to go into hiding for a bit. Enough witnesses were available to report that a crazy guy with a sword was the victim. Some people might even consider it a typical night down in the Weird. Besides, I wasn't about to discuss Belgor, not after what he did. He might be an underhanded slimebag who would sell his own mother to keep himself out of jail, but the man had saved my life.

When I reached the Old Northern Avenue bridge, *vitniri* swarmed down the steel struts and surrounded me. The man-wolves huddled close, snapping at anyone who showed the least curiosity in me. They escorted me all the way to Rowes Wharf Hotel, pacing along the building's shield barrier until they were sure that Eorla's people detached another bodyguard for me.

Elven warriors from the Kruge clan, their bows notched

with glowing elf-shot, ushered me inside and up to a suite overlooking the harbor. Eorla arrived after, and, for the first time, she let herself show uncertain upset, grabbing me by the arms when she entered. "Are you all right?"

"A little banged-up, and my boots got wet, but not bad considering," I said.

She relaxed though her worry remained. "Why did she attack you?"

I filled her in on the conversation, such as it was. "I think Melusine was doing what she's always done: playing both ends against the middle. She thought she would have better luck allying with Maeve in the long run."

Eorla pursed her lips. "My main concern now is that she was aware of several defense strategies I have in place. I wonder how much of that has reached Maeve?"

I shrugged. "She managed to cut off information on Maeve's troop movements by assassinating your spies. I'd worry about any strategic vulnerabilities you know about."

Eorla wandered to the window. Down in the harbor, the mist wall shimmered with complex swirls of essence. Threads of blue and orange coiled through and around each other as they moved in a flowing course across the face of the wall. "Your relationship with Ceridwen and me made you a target, Connor. I think it's time you went underground. I have places to offer you in Germany. Ceridwen has hinted she's offered you a similar proposal."

"That sounds a lot like giving up," I said.

She smiled and turned slightly to look at me. "Caution isn't giving up, Connor. Choosing your moment is always to your advantage. It took me a hundred years to get to this point."

Amused, I flexed an eyebrow. "You have a slight advantage over me in the time department."

She released an exasperated sigh. "I know you see my point."

I moved behind her. "I do. I honestly do. But after everything that's happened, I can't walk away. I've lost so much, Eorla. I don't want to lose my home, too."

Eorla held her hand up, her brow furrowed. "Something's happening."

Outside the window, the mist wall had become agitated, streaks of white and red slicing through the other colors. The streaks surged across the face of the wall like storm patterns, cyclones forming and breaking apart, thick bands of color marching through everything in their paths. The essence brightened, the colors muting as the surrounding areas became white with heat. "It's building in strength. Has someone attacked it?"

"I'm not getting any reports," Eorla said.

The army helicopters danced in the energy currents and pulled higher to stabilize themselves. I directed Eorla's attention to the airport. The army units stationed near the end of the tarmac were scrambling into trucks and more helicopters. "That doesn't look good."

Someone knocked and opened the door. Rand—Dylan, actually—joined us by the window. "The facility is on full alert, Your Majesty."

"Brion Mal is head of Maeve's forces. Get him online and explain our stance in case this isn't the Guild's doing, Rand," she said.

Dylan peered at the mist wall. Now that I knew he wore a glamour, I couldn't look at him and call him Rand. At the same time, it was odd calling him Dylan when he looked like an elf. "Our calls to the Guild are unanswered."

"I guess that answers its own question," I said.

"Where's Bastian? He's not answering my sendings," she said.

"Our reports indicate he is en route to the airport," Dylan said.

"Something about rats and ships is tickling at my memory," I said.

"No, if Bastian knew something, he would not have waited this long. I'll wager he's as confused by this as we are," Eorla said.

The mist wall had lost all color, becoming a sheet of

solid white light. The top rose and shredded, great spires of essence spewing upward. "I don't like this. We should . . ."

The wall exploded. Essence billowed across the water in a towering white wall of heat twenty stories high. Dylan and I dragged Eorla away from the window as she gathered essence in her hands. We grappled, trying to see out the window and get out of each other's way until we tumbled to the floor. The building trembled as the essence surge hit. Glass shattered with a concussive roar, shards flying everywhere, sparkling against our body shields as they slid away. Ceiling tiles scattered with the wind as cabling pulled free.

It was over in a cloud of dust. Dylan sat up coughing, a fine film of white grit covering his red uniform. Eorla was on her feet already, staring out the gaping hole that had been the window. I pushed ceiling tiles off me and joined her. The mist wall was gone.

"Danu's blood," I said.

Ships filled the inner harbor, hundreds of fey ships, low-hulled and shining with amber, their masts a forest across the water. The air rippled and glimmered with the light of Celtic warriors, rank upon rank of fairy clans spread across the sky in an uncountable host. Across their leading edge, a dozen Danann fairies hovered, their body signatures burning with an intensity that outshone everything. Brion Mal had not come to the U.S. alone. The entire Queen's Fianna was with him.

A deep rumble echoed through the air and the building shuddered. "That's artillery fire," I said.

"The National Guard is firing on the front of the building," Dylan said.

Eorla crossed her arms. "So they have thrown in with Maeve at last. I shouldn't be surprised. Donor played his hand wrong from the beginning."

The building shuddered again. Over the harbor, the army helicopters had turned and faced the city. I took Eorla by the elbow. "We need to get out of here."

"The evacuation is already in progress. Show Connor to

the tunnel. I will join you at the bunker in thirty minutes," she said.

"What are you going to do?" I asked.

She smiled. "This is not an unforeseen contingency. Follow our friend, please. I do not have time for you right now."

She gave me her back, scanning the skies with her dark eyes. So many sendings rippled in the air that someone with the slightest ability would sense them. I stared, struck once again at the steel in Eorla. She knew how to commit to her goals. "Good luck, Eorla," I said.

She acknowledged me with a slight nod but didn't turn. "Be well, Connor."

37

The building shook with multiple hits of artillery fire. Thick dust filled the air as Dylan led me down a back stairwell. "What is she going to do, Dyl?"

"Retaliate," he said.

"Yeah, I figured that part out," I said.

We reached the lobby level and kept going down. "It is not my place to discuss it if Her Majesty did not."

"Suddenly, you've decided who you're loyal to? At least tell me where we are going," I said.

Dylan popped the door to a basement hallway. He pointed toward another flight of stairs. "You are going down there. Turn right and continue through the access tunnel until you reach the exit."

I hesitated. I trusted Dylan macBain with my life. He trusted me with his. "Come on, Dyl. War's breaking out up there. Clue me in."

Even beneath the glamour that made him look so different from the man I knew, I could see a crack in his resolve. "I know you, Connor. I know you want to know why and how and where and all that. But we've made different choices here. I promise you this: I will never hurt you."

"Then tell me what's going on," I said.

He shook his head. "We have no time. I will tell you this because I know enough about you to say it: Human suffering will be avoided at all costs. Now go. Someone will meet you at the other end."

He winked at me and hustled back up the stairs. I debated following him but went down the stairs instead. Dylan was right. Wanting to know was more curiosity than need. Eorla would have told me anything I needed to know. She knew how to take care of herself, but it went against my nature to leave a friend alone facing an attack fleet of fairy warriors. It's a thing I have.

Thick utility conduits two feet in diameter lined the tunnel, feeding gas, electricity, and steam into the building. I ducked pipes as I ran down the center, the sound of explosions fading into the background. The tunnel ended, but the pipes continued through the wall above a battered steel plate. My heart skipped a beat at the fleeting thought that I had been trapped, then I noticed that the plate was leaning against the wall. I worked my fingers under the top edge and pulled, jumping back as it fell. The reverberation echoed like a cannon shot.

A plain, featureless arch had been shaped through the concrete wall behind the plate. Under other circumstances, finding myself underground with the heavy scent of troll-worked essence would have made me nervous. I stepped over the threshold and started jogging through another tunnel molded out of the earth. The walls wept with moisture that pooled on the floor. It would have annoyed me more if my boots weren't already wet. A wooden ladder at the end led up to a trapdoor.

I listened for movement. The sound of artillery fire was louder than it had been in the hotel, but I didn't hear anything like the movement of people. I pushed at the door and poked my head up.

Dim light filtered through decayed wood. Old army-issue metal desks were pushed against a wall. Brown paper, torn and water-stained, covered the windows. I climbed out of the tunnel and smiled as I peered through a broken window. In better days, the Old Northern Avenue bridge pivoted on its moorings to allow ships up the channel. I was in the bridge's abandoned wheelhouse, with a view of my old apartment.

I pushed through the exit door onto the sagging porch that hung over the channel. The end of the wheelhouse had been hit, its wall had splintered and slumped. I glimpsed tufts of a red fabric amid the wreckage—a house uniform of one of Eorla's people. Whoever he was, he'd had an unfortunate posting that put him in the wrong place at the wrong time.

Fairies filled the air over the hotel as their ships surged toward the dock. Essence-fire streaked down, hitting the building façade as defenders along the marina fought back from under a shield barrier. Oddly, no return fire came from the hotel. I didn't understand what Eorla's plan was—either for her own defense or my escape. The dead guard wasn't able to clear matters up for me. I was on my own.

I climbed over the railing to the walkway connector for the bridge. Fey folk streamed from the financial district—solitaries who had joined Eorla's cause, renegade elves from her Consortium troops, and unaligned Celtic fey. I saw the ruse—they were fighters masquerading as refugees, overwhelming the police checkpoint and flooding into the Weird. I jumped to the sidewalk and lost myself in the crowd.

As I reached the Weird side of the bridge, the first fairy ships landed behind the hotel. The defenders on the dock scrambled back, firing intermittent elf-shot. Still no return fire came from the hotel.

The attackers showered essence-fire onto the docks, violent streams of energy that splintered across the face of the building. The hotel shuddered under the onslaught, burning an intense white and orange. The pent-up energy rippled the air as the stone façade absorbed essence like a sponge. Now I understood Eorla's lack of return fire. She had turned the building itself into a massive ward. It was absorbing the energy from the attacks and had become an incandescent fuel cell, bristling with power.

The channel waters rippled as vibrations spread out from the hotel. The remaining defenders fled the dock in a move that seemed too calculated to be panic. Their attackers landed, confident in their numbers and firepower advantage.

The façade exploded. Stone shattered outward on a wave of essence, leaving behind a honeycomb of empty rooms gaping open to the elements. The stone showered down, tearing into the docking ships with concussive force. The ships burst into flames as fairies launched airborne, swirling in confusion. Shipbound fey dove into the water to escape the smoke and heat. With one spectacular move, Eorla had turned the element of surprise against them.

Smoke drifted down the channel. People milled about on the bridge and along the seawall, mesmerized by the destruction, watching Maeve's forces dive in and out of the haze. Several ranks of fairies filled the sky with glowing wings above the burning hotel. They split and re-formed into tighter units, spreading toward the city in several directions.

As I debated my next move, a sharp sliver of essence blazed in my mind, and I tripped to a stop. The spear had reappeared—or rather, my access to it. It was a thing of the Wheel and, like the Wheel, it had an arbitrary aspect that was impossible to anticipate. I reached out with my mind and tapped the spear with my body essence. With a burst of ozone, it materialized in my hand, six feet of honed applewood crackling with pure essence. Startled, people around me pulled away, cautious of a dramatic essence display in what was quickly becoming a mob.

I activated my body shield, the golden-tinged ripple of essence swirling around me like a cape. Closing my eyes, I conjured an image of the Boston Common, envisioning the hill and the gargoyles and the distinct essence signatures that comprised them. A tunnel spiraled open in my mind, cascading white and red lights that swirled to a point in the distance. The spear bucked in my hand, and I poured its essence into the image.

I soared through the tunnel, a strange, weightless sensation of movement yet not-movement. Raw essence bombarded me, trying to tear at my flesh and mind. My body shield shunted the energies around me through the nothingness, protecting me from the pain and hemorrhages I had experienced in the past. The tunnel collapsed at its end point, and I landed with a solid thump on Beacon Street. I released the shield, relieved at the lack of pain or fatigue.

Pink light burst in the air, and Joe whirled around me in agitation, his sword in his hand. He spun in place, his face set with concentration that melted to confusion. He sheathed his sword. "Great. All I get for my concern is finding you fondling your spear in public."

"It's a very nice spear," I said.

He cocked an eyebrow at me. "I'll admit it's rather long, but I doubt you know how to handle it."

I cradled the spear in the crook of my elbow, assessing the layout on the Common. The brownie guards huddled in confusion up near the glowing pillar. "I thought you'd be down in the Weird having the time of your life."

Joe picked up a discarded lottery ticket and sniffed it. "I was, but when a giant dead lady snake appears in the road and a fleet of fairy ships shows up out of nowhere and a hotel explodes all in the time it takes me to finish a pint, I figured you were probably having a bad day."

I leaned back from the curb as a police car raced by. "Oh, please. You could have finished at least three beers in that time."

He grinned. "You flatter me, you do. The spear lit up in my head like a candle. Now *that*, I am sure, don't mean no good thing."

Joe flew at my shoulder as I crossed the street. "You felt the spear?"

"Aye. Indeed."

"Can you call it?" I asked.

Joe looked at me as if I were crazy. "Why ever would I do that?"

While the guards were distracted by the fairies in the air, I hurried across the pond basin and jumped the storm fence. More gargoyles had shown up since I had been there earlier, changing the layout somewhat. It took me a moment to get my bearings before I spotted the small child with the horns. I dodged from gargoyle to gargoyle to get closer, keeping watch on the guards and the sky.

Joe gasped with excitement when he saw the bowl and swarmed around it like a bee after nectar. He darted down and licked the stone, then shuddered. "Oh, my."

I grimaced. "That's gross, Joe. Have you any idea where this has been?"

He licked his lips. "A ship, a cave, and a mountain."

Impressed, I looked down at the bowl. "Really?"

Joe shrugged. "Well, at least the side I licked."

I pushed the bowl into the front pocket of my jeans. It was a tight fit and made an uncomfortable bulge. I shifted it back and forth. "Remember when you used to do something like that with a roll of quarters?" Joe asked.

"I was ten, Joe," I said.

"And this will be as successful if memory serves," he said.

He was right. It looked embarrassing. I took it out and wedged it into the inside pocket of my jacket. Joe let out an impressed whistle. I thought he was breaking my balls again, but he was looking up in the sky. Three people descended, a man and two women, their white robes fluttered in the wind. Silver light flickered from long swords in their hands. "Check it out, Connor. The High Queen's Archdruids! I haven't partied with those guys since—" His thrilled expression fell when he saw my face. "Oh. It's not good they're here, is it?"

"Yeah, I'm not having a good day," I said.

38

"Find Ceridwen for me, Joe. Tell her . . ." I paused. An image fluttered across my mind.

Joe snapped his fingers. "Hello?"

The image sharpened, and I saw Ceridwen, dressed in her Hunter garb, the red leather armor and antlered helm. "Never mind; I see her."

Joe sighed toward the skies. "They grow up so fast, don't they? First they're waving their spears around, then they're figuring out how to use them."

"Follow me if you can keep up," I said. I tapped the essence in the spear, and a tunnel spiraled open in my mind. Joe stuck his tongue out at me as I let the tunnel pull me in, essence swirling around me with a streak of pink that I knew was Joe.

As I appeared on the street in the Tangle, Ceridwen spun, sword at the ready. She relaxed when she recognized me, turning her attention back to the scene behind her. "Well met, macGrey. I sensed the spear was in play but did not call it until I knew why."

A thickened essence barrier stretched across the street. On the other side, three Danann fairies were letting loose a field of essence-fire. The barrier sizzled and burned like a fireworks display. "We've got the Queen's Fianna and Archdruids in the city," I said.

She surprised me by smiling. "Maeve knows how to bring a good battle. I look forward to her defeat."

"They took out the Rowes Wharf Hotel," I said.

Ceridwen sent a burst of essence into the barrier. "We anticipated that."

"We? You coordinated a response with Eorla?" I asked.

She moved closer to the barrier. With the Hunter glamour hiding her face, it was impossible to tell what she was thinking. "The hotel was an obvious target, as is the Tangle. I am protecting access to several evacuation routes."

"Like the tunnel under the hotel," I said.

The antlered helm turned toward me. I didn't need to see her face to feel the confident amusement in Ceridwen's voice. "One of many. The Dananns are trained to fight the Consortium in the open air." She clenched her fist. The buildings to either side shuddered, their façades curling into the street, closing off access. The sounds of essence-fire became muffled as the barrier merged with the masonry. Ceridwen walked away. "They also have never encountered a place like the Tangle."

"But what the hell is going on?" I asked.

"Maeve and the U.S. president made a joint statement as the attacks began. They are fighting the Consortium terrorists and their allies who destroyed the Guildhouse and endangered human lives," she said.

She paused at the next intersection. "We are about to be cut off from my main force three blocks over. The Dananns are shifting in this direction."

I lifted the spear. "Where to?"

She held out her hand. "Tide and Summer Street."

I closed my eyes and visualized the street corner. A transport tunnel opened in my mind, a crisp image of the location at the opposite end. I took Ceridwen's hand. We jumped and landed in the middle of a firefight.

An essence barrier had been erected across a side street as a bulwark along Old Northern. The barrier bowed outward, shielding solitaries and the Dead. Opposite them, Danann fairies ranged along the street, throwing an effortless stream of essence-fire at the barrier. A few hovered in the air, testing the limits of the barrier. None of them seemed particularly aggressive. "They're not fighting very hard," I said.

Ceridwen stalked behind her line of defenders. "I noticed that as well. More are coming down from the hotel."

"That's got to be a feint. Eorla is a primary target," I said.

Ceridwen nodded with a satisfied gleam in her eye. "They've lost her. We never intended to hold the hotel, and now the Dananns are confused."

"What the hell is this plan? Eorla wouldn't tell me," I said.

She swung the great helm toward me. "You should not be here. I am trying to draw the Fianna here so that they will leave Brion Mal's headquarters with weak defenses. It will mean nothing if you are captured here."

"Where is Eorla?" I asked.

"We don't have time for this, Grey," she said.

"Tell me," I said.

Ceridwen ignored me, moving closer to the barrier. Sparks cascaded across the barrier, forming a curtain that rippled and bucked. Sections thinned under the stress, random streaks of fire breaking through. "We can hold these Dananns off, but they have numbers on their side. Where are the Fianna? I want the Fianna."

The barrier was threatening to collapse. Despite the skill of the solitary defenders, the Dananns had firepower to match. All my abilities were defensive at this point, except the darkness, and I didn't want to think about unleashing it again. Already, I could feel its pressure against the inside of my skull as it sensed the intense body signatures beyond the wall. I stood helpless with my sword. It was an offensive weapon and not long-range. I clutched the spear to my chest. We needed help.

I turned my thoughts inward, focusing on Eorla's body signature. A tunnel spiraled open, the preternatural green glow of Eorla's body signature dancing in the ether. The vision sharpened, and I saw her face. She lifted her head, staring at me through the tunnel. With a cutting gesture, she held out her hand. Essence flashed, and the tunnel collapsed.

I opened my eyes in surprise. I hadn't considered that it was possible for someone to shut down the spear. Given what I had seen the spear do, I doubted many fey could. I got the message. Eorla didn't want me wherever she was.

The barrier collapsed on one end, fairies pressing forward to exploit the advantage. A company of Dead surged into the gap, throwing themselves against lethal essence bolts. A ripple of essence burned along the pavement, and the street undulated as the asphalt and concrete heaved upward.

My skin shivered as a wall of stone and tar rose. It was troll work, and I recognized the body signature. I had the same essence, a residue from a troll named Moke, who had saved my life once. I sensed him beneath my feet, like a leviathan in the deep as his passage created the wall. I doubted it would hold long, but it was buying time.

Ceridwen rode the wave of stone. As the wall peaked, she let out a burst of essence, a spray of fire that pressed the Dananns back. They scrambled to reassemble, intent on taking her from her perch. Despite their abilities, they were facing an underQueen of the Seelie Court. In the past, I had watched Ceridwen take on ten times their number. She died only because Bergin Vize used the spear against her.

As the Dananns focused their attention on the barrier, solitary fey threw ineffective bolts of their own. It was obvious the Dananns were not concerned. The solitaries were chaotic and disorganized. The Dananns were a trained fighting unit. They needed their overconfidence poked.

I raised the spear and opened a short jump to the opposite side of the barrier. Landing near two Dananns, I swept their feet out from under them with the spear and jumped back. Joe danced in the air around me. "That's flit fighting if I ever saw it. Not bad for someone so tall."

The Dananns shifted away from Ceridwen's barrier and toward me. I hesitated. My shield would protect me from the brunt of an attack, but I had to get close in for the spear to be any use. Time slowed as I took in the scene, the flashing of the essence-fire, the burnt-ozone odor in the air. I already had a sheen of sweat under my jacket, and my heart was beating with adrenaline. It felt good, like a long run after a night of drinking, the stink of alcohol oozing out of my pores. I felt alive like I hadn't in a long time. I grinned at Joe. "Care to join me?"

He saluted me with his sword, and we jumped through a weak spot in the essence barrier. Flashing back into sight, Joe batted his sword on the top of a Danann's head and blinked out before she saw him. She whirled in place, angry but confused, as I was too far away to have hit her. She raised her hand to strike. I ducked under the bolt, using the move to hit another fighter behind me. This time, I didn't play nice, and jabbed him in the hamstring with the point of the spear. I jumped back.

The other Dananns moved in. One remained behind at the breach, drawing off Ceridwen's forces while the rest concentrated their attack on a single point of the barrier. It crumbled, giving in to the weight of the strikes. Even Ceridwen couldn't defend so many positions. One by one, the Dananns slipped the barrier, faster as the ones preceding them provided coverage.

"Watch and learn," Joe said, and blipped out. In quick succession, he flashed in and out of sight behind the Dananns, hitting and stabbing. He reappeared by my shoulder, his face glowing with excitement. "Ready?"

I jumped. We crisscrossed our way through the attackers, hitting and swinging swords. They fought back hard, their deep training showing in the instant reactions to my appearance beside them. My head rang with sound, the clash of sword blades, the deflection of essence, and the whirring of jumping. I wasn't Joe. I was tiring, my body no match for the constant jumps even with a shield protecting me from exposure. At least I wasn't bleeding to death this time.

The dark mass in my head struggled against the faith stone as essence heightened around us. Pain flashed on and off, blotches of red and black appearing in my vision. The dark mass sensed the intense living essence. The stone bowl in my jacket flushed heat against my chest as it amplified the energies. It was becoming too much. The combined sensory input was overwhelming—the faith stone, the dark mass, the stone bowl, and the spear all activating at the same time. A balance existed—I could sense that—but the middle of a fight was not the time to learn. I jumped away and landed alone farther up Tide Street.

Joe popped in next to me. "You okay?"

I nodded. "Taking a breather. I don't know what the hell I'm doing."

He hovered toward the fighting. "Kicking ass is what you're doing. Nice moves for a glow bee."

Several Dananns swooped through the air along the street, keeping low on the roofline. They were setting up some kind of formation but didn't seem to be advancing. "I don't get what they're doing. What do they care about the Tangle?"

Joe swiveled in place, watching as they alighted on the buildings. They weren't firing. "Purging, m'friend, oldest game in the book. Don't like the neighbors? Purge 'em. Don't like the next town? Purge it. Don't like the next county? Purge it. Damned Dananns never did know how to make friends with anybody."

"But why the Tangle? I can see the beef Maeve has with the Consortium, but the Tangle? It doesn't care about international crap," I said.

Joe glanced at me slyly. "Well, it does tend to hide rogues and thieves that do."

The Dananns lined the sides of the street. I had a few more jumps in me before I gave up to exhaustion, but that moment was getting close. "But Maeve doesn't know about Ceridwen."

"Speakin' of, here she comes," said Joe.

Ceridwen reached the end of Tide. *Get out of here, Grey. It's you they want. If you leave, I can delay them.*

I didn't understand what she was talking about. I wasn't a favorite of Maeve's, but taking down an entire neighborhood to get at me didn't make much sense.

The spear shuddered in my hand. Annoyed, I frowned. Now wasn't the time for Ceridwen to try her hand with it. I pulled back, clamped my mind on the spear's essence, and held it in place. It shook away from me, pulling my arm up. I struggled as the spear dragged and pulled away from me. "Knock it off, Ceridwen," I shouted to her.

Dananns dropped into the street and faced Ceridwen. If she heard me, she ignored me. The spear bounced and leaped in my hand like an animal on a leash. I decided to give in and do what she wanted and leave. I visualized Meryl's office, tapped the spear—and was knocked on my ass. A surge of essence flashed back at me, shutting down the jump. The spear burned hot in my hand and vanished.

Furious, I faced Ceridwen. She didn't have the spear. As one, the remaining Dananns dropped onto the street. I circled with my sword, keeping an eye on Ceridwen. She wasn't as close as I'd like. The Dananns didn't fire. They faced me on all sides, cutting off any escape. "That was a stupid mistake," I muttered.

Joe hovered in close behind me. "What happened? Where's the spear?"

The Dananns raised their hands in unison, golden essence sparkling across their palms.

"It's gone. It had to be Bergen Vize. He's the only other person I know who can use the spear like that. He's alive. The bastard's alive," I said.

Joe's wings brushed against the back of my head. "Well, that's rude."

I had no hope of fighting off dozens of Dananns. I shrugged off my jacket and held it out. "Get this out of here, Joe. There's no way I'm letting them get it."

He swooped in front of me. "Geez, Connor, we can get you another jacket. Let it go."

"It's what's inside," I said.

He took the jacket as the Dananns released their essence. Streaks of burning light arced through the air. They tangled into each other, weaving in and out.

"Where should I take it?" he asked.

I swept my sword at the forming net. Strands broke and frayed, but more took their place. "Anywhere but here."

He flew level with my face. "You're asking me to leave you again."

"They're not going to kill me, Joe. They would have by now. Go, before it's too late," I said.

He hovered up. "I'll be back with reinforcements."

With a shout, he swept in a circle around me, brandishing his sword into the faces of the Dananns. He popped out as the net fell. Essence bindings draped over me, searing my flesh. I fought against them with the sword, but there were too many. The net brought me to my knees. I cut a swath through, managing to free my head and my sword arm. The Dananns moved closer, replacing the destroyed strands. The bindings became heavier, forcing me to the ground.

Three dark figures appeared in the air over me, and I recognized the archdruids from the Common. They dropped with the slow precision of levitation spells. I swore under my breath as they held their right palms out and, as one, shouted, *"Codlah."*

My eyelids drooped as the command to sleep fell over me.

39

The sleep spell lingered like a fog. Awareness tickled at me as it faded. The dark mass pulsed in my head, a mild warmth against the cool light of the faith stone. My eyelids lifted with gritty slowness. Essence bindings held my arms and legs to a chair, immobilizing tethers that didn't constrict but had no give. I sensed someone in the room. I stared at an empty chair facing me. My vision blurred, then focused on a man to the right. He wore a white robe trimmed with a blue-and-gold knot pattern, the uniform of office of an archdruid.

Archdruids achieved the highest rank in a druid grove. They advised kings and queens, and their knowledge could turn war into victory or defeat. I had been taken down by a druid-triad, three people working together whose combined abilities were more than the sum of their parts.

"How long have I been out?" I asked.

He didn't answer, his eyes half-closed as he maintained the vestige of the sleeping spell on me. The sound of a door opening broke the silence. A gust of essence rolled over

me, a female Danann fairy whose signature was more pro-
nounced than anything I had ever sensed. The archdruid
glanced over my head, nodded, and excused himself. The
woman didn't move or speak, and I assumed she was one
of the Fianna taking over guard duty.

When I had reached the point where I wasn't thinking
about her anymore, she moved, striding across the room to
the empty chair. The sleep spell deadened my full reaction,
but I'm sure she saw it in my face.

"I am Maeve," she said, as if she needed an introduction.

The freaking High Queen of the Seelie Court at Tara
was sitting four feet away from me. Dressed in black
leather battle armor with silver filigree shaped in ancient
Celtic swirls designs, the woman who ruled all the Celtic
fey, who challenged the Elven King and changed the political landscape of an entire hemisphere by existing, reclined in the chair like she was taking afternoon tea with
friends. Her wings rippled and undulated to either side,
layer upon layer of gossamer membranes lifting and lowering in a mesmerizing display of color. She didn't have her
helm on, allowing her long black hair to fall and pool at her
waist. I couldn't look away from that face—expressionless
yet sharp-featured, and pale, almost pearlescent. Hypnotiz-
ing was the word. Even at a glance, it was easy to see how
she had captivated the world. In her right hand, she held the
spear.

I flexed my wrists in their bindings. "I'd shake, but I'm
a little indisposed."

She flicked her fingers. A ball of essence puffed through
the air, and the bindings vanished. I rubbed my wrists and
stretched my legs. Both my daggers were gone. I nodded at
the spear. "I believe that's mine."

Maeve looked at the spear as if she had only then realized she held it. "This? Take it."

The streak of essence that registered my access to the
spear glowed in my mind. I summoned the spear with a
mental command. It glided upright across the room and
into my hand. The dark mass jumped in my head as if jos-

tled awake. A small smile creased Maeve's lips, and the sleep spell amplified. She clenched her fingers, and the spear jumped back to her. I didn't feel it leave my hand. "Before you held the spear, it was Ceridwen underQueen's. Before her, it was mine. No one owns the spear, and anyone it chooses remains chosen."

I stood, unsteady on my feet. "Thanks for the info. I'll be going now."

She thrust her hand at me. "Sit."

My knees obliged and bent. The faith stone flared in my head but calmed as soon as it started. "So what's the game, Maeve? The Elven King's death wasn't enough? You want a scorched earth?"

"The fate of the world is no game, Connor Grey," she said.

I laughed. "Right. Of course. And only you can save it by destroying a city."

She leaned back in the chair and lightly held its arms. "This city's misfortune was fated a century ago with Convergence. Events merely unfold to their inevitable conclusion."

"Convergence doomed Boston? Seems like the trouble it has is that you neglected your people here," I said.

She tilted her head. "I am surprised you think that. Do you know nothing of history?"

"I know you let the Guildhouses rot from within. I know you use defense against the Consortium as an excuse for war. And now that Donor's out of the way, you think destroying the Elven kingdom will make you the sole fey ruler," I said.

Her face remained intent, but curious. "And to what purpose have I done all these things, Connor Grey?"

I shrugged. "Good question. Most times I think it's because you're a power-hungry asshole."

"Everyone is driven by power. Without power, kingdoms fall. Realms vanish. Without power, the Wheel of the World does not turn. Of course I'm driven by power, Connor Grey, just like you."

"Yeah, I don't think we're much alike," I said.

She smirked. A High Queen smirking at me felt more condescending than even I was used to. "The first thing you asked for when you awakened was a weapon," she said.

That stung a little. "I thought defending myself might be prudent," I said.

"You sound like Donor." Her tone indicated that wasn't a compliment.

I grunted, unflattered. "Was he wrong?"

She pursed her lips and shook her head, amused again. "No, actually, but misguided. He never understood that I acted in both our interests. He was selfish that way."

I tried to process what she was saying, but the sleep spell made my thinking sluggish. "I don't understand."

"There seems to be much you don't understand," she said.

"You had Donor on the defensive," I said.

That sly smile was back. "That tends to happen when you declare war on someone."

"You never declared . . . wait, you're not talking about here, are you? You're talking about Faerie," I said.

She narrowed her eyes at me, avid with listening, as if she needed me to say something she was waiting for. "Go on."

"You remember. You remember Faerie before Convergence," I said.

"Is that supposition or knowledge?" she asked.

"Are you saying you attacked Alfheim and started the war that caused Convergence?"

"Am I?"

The haze lay across my mind. I tried to shake it off, tried to piece together what she was saying. "You think I know something. That's why I'm here."

She waved a dismissive hand. "But you do know something. With every word, you confirm it. When I touched you through the gate in TirNaNog, I suspected as much. Remember what you know, Connor Grey."

My head refused to clear. "I can't think with this spell on me. Take it off."

She murmured a chuckle. "Do you think playing naïve will make me so? Think, sir. Why are you here?"

"Because I know you are responsible for Ceridwen underQueen's death. I can expose you to the Seelie Court," I said.

A slight crease formed between her eyebrows. She seemed as confused as I was. "Perhaps once that would have been inconvenient, but no longer. Victory is within my grasp. The chattering of the underKings and -Queens are nothing to me now."

"Then what the hell are you doing here?"

She leaned her head back, watching me from half-closed eyes. "I am disappointed. I thought that when we met, the situation would become evident to you. I thought you would understand."

"Understand what? War? Destruction? You're killing people out there," I said.

She leaned forward as if trying to press her words into my mind. "Think, Connor. Why am I here? In the place? Why are any of us? It's a backwater on the world stage, yet here we are. Why are Briallen and Gillen here? And Nigel and Eorla and the rest? Why are the most powerful people in the world gathered here of all places?"

"Because of you," I said.

Like a mother proud of her child, she lifted her fingers toward me as if trying to coax me to perform. "Close. Very close. Your memory is damaged," she said.

That was something I knew already. "You're here to destroy everything," I said.

"Destruction is the process of creation. Faerie was dying. I was trying to save it for all of us, and Donor refused to help. He would have let all of the Celts perish. I stole Audhumla to save us all."

Confused, I tucked my chin, trying to make sense of what she was saying. Audhumla was part of the Teutonic creation myth. In the beginning of time, so the story goes, a cow sprang up from the primordial void and provided nourishment to the first beings to come to life.

I stared at Maeve in disbelief. "You stole their cow?"

She shrugged. "I thought everyone knew I like cows." My jaw dropped, and she laughed. "I am not without humor, sir. Audhumla manifests as a cow because that's how the simple Teutonic mind works. She's not a cow. She's a metaphor of power—of creation, Connor. I was trying to save Faerie. I couldn't let it die. I needed Audhumla to revitalize the realm of Faerie."

I still couldn't get around the manifestation part. "You stole a cow," I said.

She scoffed at my feeble attempt to understand her. "I stole creation. I stole destiny. I stole the spark of all things so that all things could exist. It's not a cow, you fool. It's a metaphor for the power of the Wheel of the World," she said.

"And all those people you listed—you—you're all here, now, because, uh, the cow's here?"

Satisfied, she leaned back again. I took her for mad, but she seemed much too calm and confident for the crazy talk. "Now you see. I have spent over a century diverting attention elsewhere, so that none would suspect the power hidden in this city. I kept Donor off-balance, concerned about his petty kingdom abroad while I sought the tools to access the power here. You were gifted the sword against my wishes. In my surprise, the spear claimed you. The faith stone has fallen into your hands. I have them all now, save the bowl. I know the bowl is here. I felt it when I arrived. I know you must have it. You've drawn the others to you. The bowl is no different. Give it to me so that Faerie may live."

I shook my head. "Give you the power to destroy everything I know in the name of creating everything you want? I won't have that blood on my hands."

She stood and placed the tip of the spear against my chest. "I have no problem with your blood on my hands."

I smirked up at her. "Then you'll never know where the bowl is."

She pressed the spear forward. "It matters not. I have the

spear and the sword. I can pull the faith stone from your mind. They will bring the bowl into my hands. They are all a piece of the Wheel of the World. They call to each other. With the three together, the bowl will arrive. I would have you at my side again when that happens, but a Faerie without you is better than no Faerie at all."

"What the hell is that supposed to mean?" I asked.

She gripped me by the head, her palm resting against my forehead as her fingers clutched my scalp. Her hand glowed with essence, and she brought her face close to mine. "You must remember who you are. It's true I started the war, but I didn't cause Convergence. You did."

I screamed as her fingers bored into my skull and

everything

went

black

40

Black.

I drifted in a sea of black, a thick sluggish current that neither warmed nor cooled, a neutral texture that clung to my skin. I moved, my sense of balance registering a slow tumble through the black. It was black, then black, then black.

I didn't know how long I drifted before I realized I was painless. I had lived with pain for so long, I no longer felt like it. It felt like me. Numbness had replaced feeling; indifference to pain had replaced reaction to it.

Dazed, I tumbled, my mind blank, my thoughts disconnected. Black was black. It was a thing, confronting me with a nothingness of nothingness, relentless and infinite. I tumbled, and it was black, then black, then black.

"Focus."

The word cut across the black like the thrum of the deep. A curiosity surged through me at the break of the monotony, but only for a moment. The black returned, black and silent. Even as I considered I had imagined it, I lost the sense of it and faded away into the black.

"Grey."

The word cut across the black like the thrum of the deep. I had heard a sound that formed a word that formed a meaning. I was the sound that was the word that was the meaning. I was Grey. I knew this and remembered this and held on to this as the idea faded away into the black.

I remembered then the other word. I had a memory of another word. My name was not the first word, the first sound. It had been another word with a sound and a meaning, and I knew that, too.

"Focus, Grey."

I heard the words, pausing as I heard them, wondering whether I heard the words in my memory or heard them again in the black. It mattered not in the black. It felt the same. I heard the words and the memory and held them in my mind and remembered who I was.

A pinpoint of light stirred in the black. I saw it, then black, then black. I was tumbling again. I saw it, then saw it, then black. I saw it. The pinpoint of light stayed in my vision. It stayed, no longer shifting to black. I was still. The pinpoint of light in the dark moved, and I saw it and knew it for what it was: essence in the black.

There was light.

Light floated in the distance, essence light that soared toward me. Bursts of color flared, fireworks against the black, fading to darkness. I wondered if the colors were essence or simply a physiological reaction to the enveloping darkness. I wondered if they were the afterimages of essence I had seen, memory images of the colors of essence or levels of essence I couldn't normally sense with light. The colors flashed and flared, then faded, and always the darkness returned, except the pinpoint of light remained, growing in the black

The pinpoint changed, became shape, first a circle, then an oval, then a line. The light became what it was: essence in the black, essence moving toward me, essence I recognized, the shape of a body signature, shifting from white to blue to evergreen. The body signature arrived at last or in an instant. I wasn't sure which. I was sure of the body signature, though, and of the face that belonged to that signature and floated in front of me.

"Am I dead?" I asked Bergin Vize.

I had spent years as a Guild agent chasing Vize, elf terrorist and chronic adversary. I remembered that now. I had lost my abilities because of him—and he had lost his. He returned to Boston again and again, and each time I faced him and lost, until the last time. The last time he showed his face, he died in the destruction of a building. I watched him fall. I did not see him rise. No one found him. He was buried under tons of concrete and stone, the building he helped destroy, his tomb.

The face before me—Bergin Vize's face—did not smile. "Not quite. Not yet."

"I watched you die," I said.

"It's not important," he said.

My mind cleared, a lifting of fog and confusion. I was floating in darkness with Bergin Vize. "I think it is. If you are dead, I'm hallucinating. If you're alive, I need to kill you."

He did smile then. "After all this time, you still see only two alternatives? This has always been about us but never between you and me."

"Here we go again, Vize. Tell me how you want to save the world by destroying it," I said.

He shook his head. "Not me. Maeve."

Maeve. Of course, Maeve. She wanted to destroy the world. Vize did, too. Everybody wanted to destroy the world to make it something else. "I think she killed me. I think I'm dead. TirNaNog is gone, and I'm left with looking at you in the dark for eternity," I said.

Vize stared, serene and patient. In the black, his body shimmering, essence forming the shape of him except his right side. Where his arm should have been was nothingness, the stain of the same darkness in my head manifesting itself on his arm. Something glittered in the darkness, though, down where his hand should have been. Something familiar.

"Maeve has made a fatal error, Grey. She does not know I am here. She doesn't know about this place. Even better, she does not believe it exists. There lies my final chance."

"All right. I'll play, Vize. Where am I then?" I asked.

His face shifted, the essence of him flickering and reforming. "You know where we are. It's a place and a thing and an idea. It is the same thing that's been consuming us for the last three years. We are in the Gap. We are in the darkness that is nothing. We are here and not here."

I reached up and grabbed him by the neck, felt his pulse beneath my grip. "How about this? Does this feel here? Want to rethink that nothing and not-here crap?"

He smiled, his face fading in and out of darkness. "Like to like, Grey. You are essence here, as am I. It matters not whether we are physical or ethereal. How many times have you tried to kill me, Grey? How many times have I tried to kill you?"

I shoved him. He drifted a few feet away. "What the hell are you talking about?"

Vize lifted his dark hand, the hand that wore the gold ring that had ended our fight and caused us to lose our abilities. His hand and arm had been consumed with the dark mass like my mind had been. The ring burned in the darkness that was his hand, a mote that glowed bright with life in the black. "Do you remember?" he asked.

"I remember enough. I lost my abilities because of that ring," I said.

"Focus, Grey. Remember," he said.

I had been trying to remember for three years what had happened the night I fought Vize. I had tracked him down to a nuclear power plant he was planning to blow up. We fought. He lost control of his ring, and we lost our abilities. "Stop saying that."

"Do you know what a soul stone is?" he asked.

People made soul stones as safety measures. Split a piece of your body essence—or even a significant amount— bond it to a static object to create an essence ward, and, well, don't die. Without the destruction of someone's life force—what some called the soul—and its container—a body or a ward—a person could receive a fatal wound and live. All that needed to be done to save them was the uniting of the soul stone with the body. "Of course I do."

"We made a soul stone, Grey. We made a soul stone together. We saved the world," he said.

I frowned. "You and me? We made a soul stone? Not likely."

Vize held his hand out, a glitter of essence in the darkness. "The ring, Grey. We remade the ring with a piece of our souls. It was the only way to stop her from killing us because we are the only ones who can stop her from killing everyone."

I closed my eyes, but it didn't matter. Vize registered in my sensing ability, his body signature adrift in the dark. If I was dead and the Christian hell existed, this would be it. I was going to pay for everything I had done by being taunted by Vize forever. That was what I got for destroying Tir-NaNog.

"TirNaNog is not gone. It is here, and it is not here," he said.

I opened my eyes. "You can read minds. Great."

"Focus, Grey. You can do the same with me," he said.

I sighed, or at least thought I did, alone there in the dark with my nemesis gnawing at my mind. I didn't want to focus. I didn't want to think or remember. I wanted to be left alone. Drifting was a decent option for a change, especially if I was dead.

"You won't die. You can't yet," Vize said.

"Well, you certainly won't," I said.

"Listen to me" he said.

"You're not here," I said.

"She will condemn you as Donor condemned me. You will drift here with me on the edge of death in an ever-present now because our soul stone lies buried beneath the Guildhouse. We will drift here because we are tainted with the darkness. The two people Maeve cannot destroy, lost in the one place she cannot reach," he said.

"I knew this was hell," I said.

"Hell is a state of mind here, brother."

We drifted, not speaking. It might have been a moment or an eternity. We drifted.

"She has the sword and the spear, Grey. She is reaching for the stone. Her hand burns down through your mind as we speak. She will hunt down the bowl. She will destroy whoever touches it," he said.

"Why would she destroy everything?" I asked.

"Because she reaches beyond her reach. She thinks she can control what cannot be controlled. She thinks she can turn the Wheel of the World, but the Wheel of the World turns as It will," he said.

I didn't answer him. I didn't care anymore. I closed my eyes and let my body tumble through the darkness.

"Meryl will die," he said.

I opened my eyes and grabbed him, my hands burying themselves not in clothes, but his body signature. "What did you say?"

No satisfaction showed on his face, no mocking. "She will die, and you will never get to tell her you're sorry."

I shoved him. He didn't drift away. "She knows," I said.

"And I know you. I see it in your mind. You need to say good-bye. You need to face her. Call the bowl," he said.

"I can't call it. It's not like the spear," I said.

"But it is. Look inside yourself, see what the Wheel of the World has granted you to see. The bowl is the physical representation of bounty. It exists in the Wheel of the World beyond its physical form. We are beyond ourselves here. Call the bowl, Grey, and I will show you truth."

A suspicion had been growing within me the more he talked. Maeve had abilities I could only guess at. I wasn't drifting in the darkness with Vize. Maeve wanted me to believe that. If Vize said anything true, it was that Maeve had everything but the bowl. Calling it—and I did understand now that I could—would be handing her the thing she sought most. She had failed, though, by giving me more information than she intended. If I could call the bowl like I could call the spear, then I could call anything the Wheel of the World allowed me.

If I called the spear, Maeve would take it away from me. I could call something she hadn't possessed, something she could not touch because it had never claimed her. In the depths of my mind, an essence signature registered. It had always been there. I had never thought to look because I didn't understand I could. I summoned the essence to me, there in the dark, not the bowl and not the spear. In a flash of brilliant white, the sword appeared in my hand. I pointed it at Vize's chest. "You told me too much, Maeve. Game over."

Unfazed, Vize held out his hand. "Give me the sword."

I lifted the point from his chest and smiled. "Thought I was stupid, Maeve? Didn't think I would suspect a mind trick?"

"The sword, Grey."

The blade shimmered white in the dark, dark shadows swirling around it without touching it. "Take it from me," I said.

"It will be easier if you give it to me of your own free will," he said.

"Of course, it would. You never held the sword, Maeve. You only touched it as the dagger. You can't take it from me because you can't take it."

"This is your choice, Grey," he said.

I presented the hilt, feeling pretty smug. "Take it, Maeve. Go on. I dare you."

Vize grasped the sword and pulled it from my hand, pain stabbing my mind as my connection to the sword snapped. I gaped, fear creeping up my spine. I was wrong. I had given her yet another weapon. "I don't understand. You never held the sword."

"I am not Maeve," Vize said. "I held the sword in Tir-NaNog. It called to me then, and I call to it now."

"It's really you, Vize?" I asked.

"I was and am. Now take my hand," he said.

On his left hand, the ring smoldered with golden essence. It washed across my face with unsettling familiarity. It was me. It burned with my own living essence. Curious, I took his hand. The ring began to slip off his finger.

"I knew you wouldn't call the bowl, Grey. You aren't stupid. Your suspicious nature might save everything yet," he said.

The ring was sliding into my palm. "What do you mean?"

"Tell Eorla thank you for everything. Tell her I died with hope."

Still puzzled, I looked from my hand to his face. Smiling, Vize drove the point of the sword into my forehead. I convulsed in a shower of pain and essence. The darkness constricted like an iris and a burning cold swept over me as

everything

went

white

41

White.

Whiteness filled my vision with nothing to break the relentlessness of it. Above me, the white simply was, as if the air itself was color. Or no color. As if nothing else existed except the white. I hung limp in the air, as if there were no air, no gravity. My head burned, like a cold fire in my mind, blazing against a blanket of night.

Everything is white. I have been here before. This is where it started. Or ended. I don't remember which. Everything around me is white. I stared into a nothingness of white. I am here again. Around me, I see shadows of light flickering in the depths of the white. They spin and whirl, roll and stop, taunting me with patterns that disintegrate as they take shape.

Bursts of color flare in my vision, fireworks against the white, fading to darkness. More, then more, the darkness is closing on me, like the slow closing of my eyes. My mind, like my eyes, is closing, like my eyes are blinking. Like my mind is blinking.

My mind blinks.

The air begins to haze with white ambient essence, like a fog. Vize has taken out the security and is making his way toward the area where the spent fuel rods are stored. Emergency lights flash bright yellow as I follow him down a long corridor. People in hazmat suits stand frozen along the walls, like statues randomly arranged. They're not dead, but suspended, caught in an elven binding spell.

The corridor ends at a locked door, a sign flashes the evacuation order and warns of radiation. A keypad beside the door has lights that glow steady red. I don't have a code. I backtrack to the nearest person in a hazmat suit. The binding spell is not as sophisticated as I assumed. It will degrade within an hour if Vize doesn't kill us all. I hesitate, expecting a trap, but see none. I hold my breath and call up some essence, hoping it will not trigger something and kill us. I hit the binding spell with a counterspell. The man sways, startled to be aware and alert again.

I steady him and point to the door. "I need to get through. I need you to open that door."

His glasses behind the mask are crooked on his face. He looks like a family man, maybe fifty years old, not someone who expected to find himself in the middle of a terrorist attack. He straightens his shoulders. "No."

I wish his family could see him at that moment. The world is crashing down around him, he's got powerful fey throwing spells around, and he says "no" to me. The defiant glint in his eye is admirable but not convenient. "Look, I'm one of the good guys. Honest. I need to get in there and stop the guy who's doing this."

"You don't have a suit," he said.

"I'm a druid. I have a body shield that should work the same way," I said. I'm not sure how long my body shield will work on the other side of the door. It doesn't matter. Vize matters. Killing him matters more.

He shakes his head, the large hood moving from side to side. "I'm not worried about you. I'm worried that a guy with no suit is on a suicide mission."

I grin. I like this guy. I wish we were meeting under different circumstances, and I want to hit him for slowing me down. But I like him. "Sir, I can destroy that door with my abilities. If I wanted to hurt anyone but myself, we wouldn't be talking. You would be waking up to find a gaping hole in the wall. I'm trying to reduce risk, but if I have to sacrifice myself and everyone in this hall to try and stop Vize, I will. Please open the door."

I can't see his face as he looks down the hall at the other people bound in the spell. "Can you wake them up?"

I raise my arm and shoot a stream of essence down the center of the hall, tuning its resonance so that it disrupts the binding spells. One by one, people shift and sway on their feet. A few fall. "Satisfied?"

He walks to the door and punches in an access code. The system cycles. "You're gonna die in the there, you know that, right?"

I pat him on the shoulder. "Not if I can help it. Make sure the door closes behind me and get everyone out."

The door opens, and I don't wait for a response from the guy. I'm in the containment area. The air is thick with essence, a cloud I can't see through. An elven signature runs through, so it's Vize, but there's also a high-level resonance I've never seen. Vize is tapping into the reactor at a pure essence level. That's bad.

Uncertain in the fog, my body shield shudders around me like nothing I've ever experienced. It's a response to the radiation, a bombardment of neutrinos or some such I had no clear conception of. The air is humid, and beneath the sound of the emergency sirens and the hum of machinery, I hear a low rumble, like water boiling. My sensing ability registers multiple essence signatures and a fierce white light in front of me. It's the spent-fuel rod pool.

I reach a metal railing and watch rising essence warp and twist around it. It's water, a fine mist rising in the air. The surface of the containment is low—too low according to warning signs painted on the inner surface of the pool. I jog along the edge, sifting through the signatures for Vize. My senses are all screwed up, and I slam into a wall of solid air. Beyond it, powerful essence shimmers evergreen. It moves closer, resolving into the shape of a man. Vize appears in the mist.

"We need to talk," he says.

"You can do all your talking in a jail cell," I say.

He shifts his attention to the pool. "We don't have much time. You need to speak to Nigel Martin. Maeve is going to try to kill us. We have to stop her."

Ignoring him, I test the barrier with essence-infused hands, searching for weak points. There are always weak spots, no matter how good you are. "Looks like you're the one that's going to kill us if you expose those fuel rods," I say.

"I need the radiation. No matter what I say, you aren't going to believe me because you've been lied to. I am not going to let Maeve kill me this time."

Of course, I don't believe him. The man has killed people in his war against the Seelie Court. I have no idea what he's saying about Maeve's killing him. I decide to keep him talking to distract him while I break the barrier. "Maeve isn't going to kill you. I might, though. Reverse the spell and cover the rods."

"There's no one like us in the world, Grey. Only we can stop her if we join together," he said.

Okay, now he is getting loony. Die-hard anarchists never make sense. "Sure, Vize. Come closer so we can talk."

He stands before me, a look of fevered hope on his face. His youth surprises me, his almost black hair worn long for an elf, fanning out as though filled with static. I had thought him older. He holds his hands about a foot apart in front of him. A gold ring hovers between them, pulsing with essence, revolving around a shaft of light. "This is how we do it," he said.

"Do what?" I ask. I find a thin spot in the barrier, a space where radiation from the pool rubs against it, wearing it down.

"Stop Convergence. I need you to drop your body shield," he says.

I chuckle and return my attention to the weak spot. A few well-placed bursts of essence should propagate through the barrier and destabilize the shield spell. "And why would I do that?"

"Because this will be more painful otherwise," he says.

I debate whether to humor him and drop the shield. I'd have plenty of time to reengage my shield if he dropped the barrier to attack. I decide against it. I probably wouldn't like being bombarded with radiation from the pool just to play with his mind. "I guess we'll have to go the pain route."

I hit the weak spot with a blast of essence. Vize curses under his breath as he redirects his spell to deflect the hit. It doesn't work. His ring falls to the floor at his feet. The barrier crumbles, and I leap at him. His eyes lock with mine, and he smiles. "One door opens; another closes," he says.

I reach for the ring. He anticipates my attack. Even as my feet leave the floor, he is down on one knee, arm raised, and lets fly a bolt of elf-shot. It pierces my shield and slams into my head. Something tears inside me as I fall to the floor. I have never experienced such pain, never imagined it.

Vize grabs the ring and puts it on a finger of his left hand. He holds it up. The essence in my head refuses to dissipate, ricocheting against the inside of my skull. Vize clenches his fist and withdraws the elf-shot from my head. I twist in pain, watching in horror as the green essence jumps free with a brilliant shard of gold essence—my essence. He's pulled a piece of my body signature, my living essence, my utter soul. Vize grabs the mote of my essence in his ringed hand and fuses his essence into mine.

The floor vibrates with the shock of a concussive force. Vize stumbles back, surprise on his face as he looks up. I turn as a sheet of flaming essence sweeps the air. Great wings swirl with red and golden fire. They descend, and I recognize the body signature. Manus ap Eagan alights on the far side of the pool.

"It's too soon. You aren't strong enough," he shouts. He releases a volley of essence, white strikes of lightning burning with power. The essence tangles in the radiation vapor, splinters, and hits Vize. It leaps along his arm like wild static and burns out through the ring.

Vize and I scream as something blossoms in the white haze, something dark and hot, something wrong. The darkness flares out like a claw, knocking me on my back, throwing Vize off his feet, tossing Eagan away into the mist. Vize thrusts his hand in the air, into the darkness, and releases another burst of elf-shot. The darkness swallows it in silence, then descends onto Vize's hand. A piece of it fractures and hits me in the face. Darkness descends across my vision, then across my mind, like the slow descent of a falling curtain, like the closing of my eye, like my mind blinking.

My mind blinked.

Everything is white. I am running. Everything is white. He looks over his shoulder at me. He looks determined . . . or crazed . . . I can't tell. Everything is white. One minute we were facing each other, and now everything is white. He stops. He looks surprised. There is someone lying on the ground. Something about him is familiar. Everything is white, and there is no ground. There is someone lying in the white. Everything . . .

My mind blinked.

I stand on a plain, white grass waving against a white sky. It's not winter, pray, what is this new madness? Where have I come? I turn in place, searching, searching across the plain, searching about the standing stones, but Maeve is not there. Was she? What is this place?

The stones shimmer and glow with essence. It is more than Maeve expected, more than she could have suspected. It is too much. She has overstepped.

"Stand aside," she says.

I face her in the stone circle. Its radiance grows as the essence of the source is released. "It's too much, Maeve. We can't do this. It will destroy everything," I say.

"Everything but Faerie—*our* Faerie, m'love—the rest matters not," she says, and raises her arms.

"It matters, my queen. All the realms matter. The Wheel of the World cannot turn without all its creation. You will destroy what you seek to save," I said.

The stone circle becomes light. Maeve becomes light. "I will not fail my people," she said.

I raise my own arms, feel the power begin to course through me. "Nor shall I," I say.

She sings in a high, clear voice. I answer in my own.

My mind blinked.

I burn and fall, tearing through the Wheel of the World, bodiless but not broken. I stopped her, stopped Maeve, but fear I started something more.

I burn with essence, my true essence, my soul. I burn across the Ways, doors flashing by, places and times in the Wheel of the World.

I burn and fall through one of the Ways, caught up in the wake of the Wheel of the World. I burn across the landscape of a new place, a new world beyond the old.

I burn and pull things in my wake, people and places, fragments of minds and realms.

I burn upon the earth, my passage burning through a forest of cold. I burn and the trees lie down and the sky goes white.

I am not in Faerie.

I burn with exhaustion and pain and cannot become myself. I am my own essence, burning white without a body in the dark forest. I pause and rest and prepare to return, to being, to a body.

I burn and they approach, men burning with power, burning with their own essence. I feel their hunger, two men hungry for power. I see their faces and know them. I see their faces and remember them, one a druid, one a shaman. They strive over me, strive for my essence, strive for my power, my soul.

I am weak, too weak, borne along the tide of their struggle, tossed to first one, then the other. They tear at each other, tear at me. They are matched and cannot overcome. They are tearing me apart; they are pulling apart my soul.

I tear and am undone. I feel myself tear away from my self, one part to the druid, one part to the shaman. I am no longer whole.

The druid takes me away, takes his portion of me away with him. I am fading without the missing part of me; part of my soul has gone. I feel it out there, feel it receding in the shaman's hands.

I reach out for my missing half, feel my missing half reach out for me. We drift apart, the druid and the shaman take us away, away from being whole. The shaman is gone. I am gone.

I am losing myself, losing myself, losing myself. My memory slips away, my mind with it, myself. I am becoming not myself, a blank slate, an empty vessel.

I feel my thoughts fade to nothing, to something new, to something with no memory. Changed.

Like a newborn. And

everything

goes

white

42

I convulsed in the chair, astounded at the pain of five streams of molten essence boring into my head. Maeve's hand seared into my face. She stared down at me, her expression suffused with concentration. Anger swept over her face, and she yanked her hand away. I gasped in relief at the sudden absence of pain.

She glared, her wings whirling in the air, deep red flickering among the veining. "What have you done?"

My head fell forward as I caught my breath. The pain was gone. That was all I cared about, the relentless pain of her attack had stopped. I heard her question. I heard it and laughed. What had I done, indeed.

"I survived." I laughed and heard the edge of madness in the sound. I had survived, that was what I did. She tried to take the stone and . . . awareness dawned on me.

I didn't have the stone.

The cold burn of the faith stone in my head was gone. My mind felt free, the pressure gone, delicious silence filled the space between my ears for the first time in . . . I raised my head. I had no pain. The chronic pressure had stopped. The constant drumbeat of sound pounding across my temples had vanished. Silence filled my head, glorious silence.

The dark mass was gone, too.

A flutter rolled through my stomach, a steady building of emotion that rose and spread across my chest. It bubbled up my throat and out in a slowly building sound of laughter. I was myself again. I was free.

Maeve grabbed me by the neck, thrusting me out of the chair and against the wall behind me. "What . . . have . . . you . . . *done*?"

I laughed in her face. Her angry confusion was priceless. In disgust, she threw me aside. I steadied myself against the floor and activated my body shield. "You blew it, Maeve. The stone's beyond your reach now."

Maeve's wings flared, essence spinning through the membranes in blues and reds. Pressure built against my face, and an electric static prickled against my shield. Maeve's face sharpening with clarity as all else fell away in a haze. My shield was no defense against her probe, her face swimming closer. She slipped inside my mind like a manic thief, rummaging through my thoughts with abandon. Images and memories flashed, people I had known and loved and hated. The stream of memory tossed me about.

I retreated before her onslaught, fled to the inner regions of my mind. I touched a spark of essence within me, a brilliant core of light and power. The darkness was gone, no longer barring me from my inner self, no longer hiding the core of my being from my reach. I found my soul. I wrapped my will around it, bound my mind to it like a mighty fist, and thrust Maeve out.

Essence surged through me, an electric thrill as every nerve ending in my body fired at once. My body ignited, brilliant flows of golden light and power coursing through pathways long lost. Connections joined, strengthened, and merged, building within me. Tears sprang to my eyes. I was free of pain. I was free of the darkness and the pain. I was free. My abilities churned inside me with renewed life. I was whole again. I was a druid again.

Maeve crouched against the far wall, utter shock on her face.

"Game's over, Maeve," I said. This time, I knew it with a clarity beyond doubt. She couldn't touch me anymore.

She recovered, the haughty pinch of condescension slipping back onto her face. "You're not half the druid you once were."

Bergin Vize's face arose in my mind, his face in the darkness as he made his ultimate sacrifice. He gave up his life to me, so that our soul would heal as one, two halves rejoining after a century of separation. "Is that supposed to be a bad joke?"

A harsh sound of derision slipped from her. "How coarse you have become, how disappointing."

Memories fluttered through my mind, still fragments, unsorted vestiges of the past. I wasn't quite sure who I was once, but I doubted I was any more patient than whoever I used to be. I stood. "I'll be going now."

"No, you won't. I will have what I demand," she said.

I created a sending in my mind, marveling at the ease of something so simple after so long. I cast it out, calling to Eorla for help. Maeve tilted her head, no doubt sensing it, then smiled as the sending shredded in the air. I shot a burst of essence from my hand into the ceiling. The masonry cracked and shed to the floor, exposing glass sheathing.

"The room is shielded," she said. "No one will hear you. Now, let's sit and discuss the matter."

I needed to draw essence from something organic, but the sterile room offered nothing. "Now you want to talk? My how your tune changes. So civil now that you need cooperation instead of coercion."

Maeve resumed her seat and leaned on her hand as if bored. "Sit."

I snorted. "Shall I beg, too? Roll over?"

The spear glittered in my mind, its spark warm against

my body signature. Its power seemed unlimited, a sliver of the Wheel of the World itself. Meryl had said to me once that she didn't think anything could prevent the spear from going where it desired. But Maeve had shown she could pull it away from me without effort. She knew how to use it better than I did. That didn't mean she had complete control of it.

"Sit," said Maeve. She was calm, used to her orders being followed.

I stepped toward the empty chair facing her, acting as if I was going to comply. With the snap of mental command, I called the spear. It blazed in my hand, there and not there, a thing of solid light and essence. Startled, Maeve thrust out her hand, a moment too late, as I threw the spear. It punctured the glass even as it vanished and appeared in her hand.

She leaned back, clutching the spear with her own power. I wasn't going to get it back anytime soon. "It matters not. This compound is well guarded. I have no fear of whatever rabble you summon if they even live. The area from which you were taken has been neutralized. There is no one left."

I sat facing her, my mind racing for options. "And you're proud of that? For that alone, you convince me not to cooperate at all."

"Then I will flay you alive and keep you alive until you give me what I seek," she said.

A vibration shuddered through the room, subtle at first, then steady. I cocked my head, listening to the tension of essence in the air. "I think some rabble has arrived."

She flicked her hand. "It is being dealt with."

The vibrations increased. Maeve glanced at the ceiling as cracks formed in the glass. Her eyebrows drew together as she built an added layer of protection above us. I had no idea what was going on, but neither did she. "You're not looking so confident there, Maeve. Why don't we go see what's going on?"

She flexed her fingers, tossed a binding spell on me. As

it draped over me, I shifted my shield and flung the spell away. Flexing old ability muscles felt good. Maeve ignored me, focusing on the fracturing glass overhead.

The room trembled, the glass ceiling creaking and cracking into smaller and smaller pieces. Fragments dusted down, settling on the barrier spell, drifting through it in slow motion. They hit the floor with a sharp patter, like crystallized raindrops.

The ceiling split with a concussive force of air. Maeve stood, still calm, still holding the spear as the crack widened. The masonry curled upward like a lid being peeled off a can. Dust rained down, obscuring our sight, but I glimpsed patches of night sky and flashes of white light.

With a resounding boom, the ceiling shattered and flew upward, exposing the room to the outside. A brilliant sphere of essence hovered overhead, the shape of a Danann fairy inside it burning bright.

Manus ap Eagan lowered to the height of the room, his muscled frame no longer frail. His face—sunken and worn for three years—had regained its hawklike sharpness, his dark eyes smoldering with red heat. He hovered outside Maeve's barrier with a wolfish grin on his face.

Nice to see you, Guildmaster, I sent.

And you, Grey. Prepare to flee. This is an extraction only, he replied.

"Release your prisoner, Maeve, and submit to my authority," Eagan said.

"This is treason, Manus. I shall post your head on my gate," she said.

"The Seelie Court will know the full weight of your transgressions against me and all our people," he said.

Maeve reared back to throw the spear. I grabbed it by the end, feeling it slick and electric in my hand. Maeve whirled to face me, and the spear slid toward her. "Do you think you can best me?" she asked.

I tightened my grip, using my body essence. "Not really."

I was tempted to jump away, but she would come with me. I wasn't strong enough to fight her alone, and wherever

I jumped, I would be alone with her. I raised my hand and let my body become a conduit for the essence from the spear. I shot a bolt of essence at the barrier above us. Eagan matched my bolt with another from above. The barrier rippled and shredded.

Maeve yanked the spear out of my hand and pointed it at me. "Don't think I won't kill you. I've waited a hundred years for this moment."

I reached into my mind and saw the sword, burning bright with essence. The air crackled with ozone as I materialized it in my hand. The blade had changed. No longer pure metal, it glistened with essence, the runes illuminated with light. At the base of the blade, the faith stone formed part of the cross guard, the blade itself passing through the heart-shaped blue crystal.

Green elf-shot blasted a gaping hole in the floor between us. Eorla descended through Eagan's protective shield, her evergreen coat flaring around her. She landed beside me, her skin aglow with emerald light. "You have much to answer for, High Queen," she said.

Maeve smiled. "I didn't answer to Donor. I won't to you."

"We shall see." Eorla wrapped her arm around me and swept me off my feet. Maeve fired as we rose through the roof, her shot rocking against our shields. She fired again, and we skittered sideways as Eagan returned fire.

We flew above the roofline, rising into a sky lit with battle. Boston City Hall sprawled below us, its massive concrete structure defended by Danann fairies. Archers from the Consortium ringed the brick plaza around the building, raining elf-shot into the confused whirl of Dananns.

Eagan spun around us, his massive wings primed with essence. It was thrilling to see him back in peak form. He hovered above the hole in the roof, staring down at Maeve. *This isn't over, Maeve.*

He released a spherical burst of essence that knocked away the Dananns above, and we soared into the night sky, followed by Maeve's scream of rage.

43

From the roof of a brownstone building on D Street, I watched thick smoke roll into the night sky toward the east. True to her word, Maeve's troops had rampaged through the Weird, destroying whatever fell in their path. From Fort Point Channel to Blackhawk Terminal, the air burned an angry orange. Fire-engine lights flickered in a few spots, but not many. The city was protecting vital service locations like the power and sewer plants. It had no choice. The destruction was too widespread. The wind shifted, bringing an acrid stench with it.

The sword had shrunk back to its dagger shape. I held it flat against my palm, staring at it, wondering at the path it had taken to arrive in my possession. The faith stone encased the base of the blade, a cold light burning in the heart-shaped stone. It lit the runes inscribed on the blade, soft blue glimmers that resonated with power and memory.

Despite its beauty, it made me feel shame. The sword and the stone belonged together. Together, they were something greater than their individual parts. Together, they formed the image of the document Meryl found in the Guildhouse archives. Meryl hadn't been trying to kill me. On some unconscious level, she had understood that the two wards needed to be joined, and Nigel's compulsion had tried to force her to do it.

I focused my thoughts on a mote of essence in my mind. I visualized Meryl's body signature, wrapped the sense of it around my thoughts, and pushed them out.

I didn't understand, I sent. I colored the sending with earnestness and apology.

She answered immediately. *We both screwed up. If you can forgive me for almost stabbing you in the head, I guess I can forgive you for your anger about it.*

A door opened and closed behind me, a brief flash of light sweeping across the roof. Eorla came up beside me, taking in the view. "I'm surprised to see you smile while looking at this."

"Not that. Just the way life happens," I said.

Eorla surveyed the burning skyline. "She shows no mercy."

"Like any true fanatic," I said.

"Her forces are massing. They're going after the consulate soon," she said.

"He saved my life," I said.

She peered at me, curious and expectant.

I held up my left hand so she could see the gold band. It was Vize's ring—our ring. When he died in the Gap, his essence transferred into it and bound itself to my flesh. "Bergin saved my life."

Eorla hugged herself, looking away from me. "Where is he?"

I took her elbow and made her face me. "Under the Guildhouse. He saved my life, Eorla. He said to tell you thank you for everything and that he died with hope."

Tears welled in her eyes. "He once said to me that if he had to die for his cause, he would rather die in hope than despair."

For the second time, I took her in my arms to comfort

her over the loss of someone she loved. Vize's death was without grief for me, yet I didn't have the satisfaction I thought I would. He went and screwed that up for me by saving my life. He was dead, but he was part of me. I was satisfied in a detached way but not glad.

The blare of a siren startled us apart. The sky overhead had become a smear of black and gray rippling in the wind. A vague sensation draped over me, an essence of a profound nature, wild and untamed, yet constrained by a force of will. Shapes were moving in the shadows of smoky clouds, enormous beings striding across the sky. "What the hell is that?"

Eorla pointed toward the Weird, her hand trembling. "There. Over there."

The siren blast was coming from the top of the warehouse that housed Yggy's bar. The old civil-defense horns were going off. I didn't think they worked anymore, but that wasn't what made me shiver. Heydan stood beside the siren tower, his head reaching almost to the top, almost thirty feet tall. He glowed white with power, facing the city. He leaned on the tower with his right hand and held a sword in his left, pointing toward the center of the city. The figures in the sky above him gathered together and moved toward downtown.

"What does it mean?" I asked.

"He calls the Old Ones to battle," she said.

"That's good. We can use the help," I said.

Eorla turned toward the door. "You mistake me, Connor. It's the end of the world."

44

I waited in a room with no windows but two doors, both closed. I wasn't in the mood to see outside anyway. When Eagan had ferried me across the city, I had seen the extent of the destruction. We had flown along the edge of it, dipping and diving among downtown city streets to elude our pursuers. More than once, we had flown through smoke and fire. The room stank of it because we all stank of it.

Eorla entered with a glamoured Dylan. They placed documents on the table and sorted through several vials of glow bees as reports flowed in from across the city. Dylan looked a little the worse for wear, his uniform torn and covered with dirt and soot.

Keeva arrived next. I hadn't seen her since she let me escape the safe house. I had doubted her, but she stood with me in the end. I resisted the urge to smile as our eyes met because there was nothing to smile about after her sacrifice. She placed a brown binder envelope on the table. Stone-faced, she unwound the string holding the binder closed and removed a sheaf of documents. She pushed them toward me. "Callin won't be coming."

I pulled the papers toward me. "Is he all right?"

"He's still in AvMem, but he's weak. We didn't want to risk his coming here."

"Risk? What risk?" I asked.

"Look at the documents, Connor," she said.

The top sheets were index forms, categorizing the rest of the paperwork. Reports were organized like Guild case files, but without any official markings. They referred to people whose names I didn't recognize. My name jumped off the page on the first case. It was a record almost a decade old, an elf arrested for attempted kidnapping—*my* attempted kidnapping. I remembered some of the outlined events, but I had no recollection of someone's trying to kidnap me. The next case was similar, this time an Inverni fairy charged with attempted murder—*my* attempted murder. Case after case showed more of the same: attempted murder or kidnapping; stalking; conspiracy to commit murder. All of them listed me as the target. The problem was, I had no idea about the history described, as if a parallel series of events occurred that I knew nothing about. They were all filed by the same Guild agent over the ten-year period.

"Who is Shadow?" I asked.

"Callin," Keeva said.

"He's Shadow? But he was . . ." Cold realization swept over me. Callin had been kicked out of the Guild for insubordination and failure to perform over a decade ago. His firing had coincided with my return to Boston and the break in our relationship. I cleared my throat. "What was his assignment?"

Joe popped into the air. He hovered over the table, holding the stone ward bowl like a host trying to decide where to put food on a crowded table. He winked, placed the bowl in front of me, and sat next to it. Essence shimmered in it, a soft swirl of blue and white that swelled in reaction to the people in the room.

Keeva frowned. "You. I was his handler. He was personally responsible for stopping seventeen assassination attempts."

"Well, I helped on three of those," Joe said.

"I don't understand," I said.

Keeva glanced at the other closed door with annoyed hesitation. "You needed protection. We provided it."

"Protection from whom?"

Eorla and Rand had stopped talking to listen to us.

"Maeve. Donor. Anyone you ever pissed off, which is pretty much everyone," she said.

I shook my head. "I am so lost."

The other door opened, and Eagan entered, the Eagan of my youth, strong, healthy, and fully in command. He took a seat at the table and gestured at the binder. "You are the linchpin in a long-term strategy, Grey. The dwarf Brokke had a vision. He foresaw another war for dominance among the fey. He predicted that certain people might be able to avert the war. You are one of those people. We took it as our duty to keep you alive."

"We?"

Eagan glanced at Keeva. "Your partners were informed. We've had someone guarding you at all times."

"Why wasn't I told?"

"Because Brokke said your knowledge would turn events for the worse. It's what ruined Bergin Vize. He became obsessed with the vision," Eorla said.

"Vize tried to start the war," I said.

Eorla nodded. "He thought if he challenged Maeve to act before she was ready, he would undermine her ability to succeed."

I looked at Eagan. "You stopped me from killing him at the nuke plant. You could have prevented all this bloodshed."

Eagan shook his head. "I had to stop you. Vize hadn't made his full turn for the worse then. We didn't know which one of you to pin our hopes on. One of you could have died. Neither of you was ready."

"Why not?" I asked.

Eagan nodded his head. "Brokke said success would come from humility. Neither of you had that then."

And Vize never learned it until too late, I thought. "Who else knows about this? Briallen? Nigel?"

Eagan shook his head sharply. "We could not risk it. Brokke saw what the knowledge did to Vize. He said we had to be more careful than he was with Donor's people. Briallen's loyalties are too often obscure. Nigel will always blindly follow Maeve. In fact, I am deeply concerned about his hand in these current events."

"I wouldn't worry about that. He's out of the picture," I said.

"Dead?" asked Eagan.

"No, but just as good," I said.

Eagan looked about to question me further, but he let it pass. "Trust in this has been paramount."

I glanced across the table at Dylan. "He shouldn't be here."

"He has access to Maeve's black ops network. We need him," Eagan said.

"He's a loyal Guildsman who lied to Eorla, and now you want me to believe he can be trusted?" I asked.

"He has been instrumental in these last few days. His intelligence gave us the location of your imprisonment," Eagan said.

"You have to trust me," Dylan said.

"Why? You didn't trust me," I said.

"You know it wasn't that simple," he said.

"It never is with you, Dylan," I said. He had the decency to look away.

"What happened to you? You've . . . changed," Eorla asked.

I caressed the bowl. The essence glittered inside it as I trailed my fingers along the surface. "This, actually. Maeve wanted this bowl."

"Why?" Eagan asked.

I glanced at him. "Why don't you start with telling me about the faith stone."

Eagan arched an eyebrow. "What's to tell? I used it to protect the Guildhouse."

"You didn't tell Maeve about it" I said.

"Brokke said not to. With good reason, it seems," he said.

"An underKing of the Seelie Court acted on the orders of an advisor to the Elven King?" I asked.

Eagan grinned. "I'm not going to revisit a hundred years of decisions, Grey. Brokke made a convincing case. He knew things. He never steered me wrong."

I looked at Keeva. "What was in it for you?"

She stared down at the table, her face cold and hard. "My choices are none of your business. I've sacrificed enough without answering to you."

"MacGoren had to die. Brokke predicted it," Eagan said.

She glared at him. "You could have told me sooner."

Eagan showed no sympathy. "You made the right decision, Keeva. MacGoren would have killed Connor or exposed you and our operation. He had to be removed, and you knew that when you walked into that room. If you had known he had to die, would you have followed through? Ask Eorla about knowledge of the future. Ask her how easy it is to stand aside and watch someone you love die."

Keeva met his gaze. "I did what needed doing. I would have liked a choice."

"You had one. You made the hard one, so that we can all live," Eagan said.

I looked at Eorla. "You knew your husband would be killed?"

She nodded. "Brokke said a druid would kill him, and a druid did. I told Alvud the vision. It made him reckless. He didn't suspect the druid would be glamoured as a troll. And, yes, Manus, as you imply, it was hard knowing what was to come."

"What does she want with the bowl?" Eagan asked.

"It's part of a package. She said she had the stone, the sword, and the spear, and only needed the bowl," I said.

"I no longer sense any of those things about you," Eagan said.

"I can call them to me. What do they mean in all this?" I said.

"Brokke said to tell you: The Ways seal and unseal. A needle binds as it pierces." Eorla said.

"He told me to tell you: The bones of the earth are steadfast and eternal," Eagan said.

"He told me to tell you: Tell me what to do," said Dylan.

Joe laughed. "No one owns the cow."

Everyone looked down at him. Joe turned his head this way and that, annoyed and embarrassed at the same time. "What? Brokke said it, not me."

Their words shifted in my mind. I recognized them, remembered them from somewhere else, somewhere stark and white and dangerous. And beautiful beyond words. I never saw Brokke there, but he heard the same things I did. Something beyond powerful had reached out and touched us both. More doors opened in my mind—memories of the past, decisions made and efforts failed. Convergence wasn't an event. It was a process, one that had been leading to this moment for over a century.

I bit back a laugh and a sob. "I know what I have to do."

45

Meryl leaned off the side of the bed and rummaged around on the floor. We were in a room in the safe house. Several floors above us, the others worked out the final details of their battle plans, deciding who would do what and the risks involved. Eorla and Eagan had known for a long time that they would have to defend the city. They had plans and contingency plans, and contingency plans for their contingency plans. It was fascinating to watch them work together. They had been secret allies for years, yet protecting their own positions in case . . . well, in case I died or Vize died or the world went to hell. After I saw the shape of their strategy, I didn't need to hang around. In the final analysis, what they did was a distraction—for me and for Maeve. The endgame would be decided by two people, no matter the plans.

Meryl propped herself on the pillows and lit a clove cigarette. As the sweet smell filled the air, I curled on my side next to her. While she smoked, I used one finger to trace small circles in the damp skin of her cleavage. "Thank you for coming," I said.

"Is that a pun?" she asked.

I poked her in the side, and she chuckled. "My poor taste in humor is finally rubbing off on you," I said.

"I have to ask you something," she said.

I propped my head up on my hand. "What?"

She flicked ashes on the floor. "We just had farewell sex, didn't we?"

I forced myself to grin. "I hope not."

She glanced at me through half-closed eyes. "Tell me something more wasn't going on. Tell me you're not planning on dying."

"I'm not planning on dying," I said.

She sighed, staring at the ceiling. "Gods, I know that tone."

"You've heard it before," I said. I wasn't asking.

"You're not planning on it, but it's likely," she said.

I stretched out my arm and laid my head on her shoulder. "You remember everything, don't you? About Faerie. You remember it."

"It sucks," she said.

"Did you know who I was when we met here?" I asked.

"No. You don't look the same. I had planned on avoiding you like the plague this time," she said.

"Why?"

She stared at the burning ember of her cigarette. "Because I was tired of serving the Wheel of the World. I thought Convergence was an opportunity to be left alone and do what I liked this time. Whenever I've gotten involved with you, one of us dies. I was hoping to avoid that this time."

I trailed my hand down her body. I remembered her from Faerie. She didn't call herself Meryl then. We weren't friends. Not enemies, exactly, but she had a knack for screwing up my life. This time had been different.

"The Wheel of the World turns, and we turn with It," I said.

She snorted. "You don't believe that anymore."

No, I didn't. Maeve was right about one thing. The Wheel of the World turned as It willed, but sometimes we could nudge it in different directions. "I need you to do me a favor—two, actually."

She smirked. "Do I have a choice?"

"Absolutely."

"Shoot."

"I need to you to get my parents out of the city and as far away as possible," I said.

She quirked an eyebrow at me. "Okay. And?"

"I want to send you away, too. You'll be a fail-safe in case I fail. When you get to where you're going, you can decide whether to come back or not," I said.

"What if I decide not to?" she asked.

"I'm sending someone else, too. He's already agreed," I said.

"Okay," she said.

"Okay? That's it? You're not going to argue and ask details?" I asked.

She put the cigarette out against the wall. "Nope. I've spent lifetimes letting the Wheel of the World dictate my choices, and each time, I've helped fuck it up. This time, I want to be in it for the ride. I'm going to trust you. I've never done that before."

I rolled on top of her and kissed her. "Don't die on me, okay?"

"You either," she said.

I don't think either of us believed we would have a choice. It was nice to think we would, though. Maybe this time we would. I slipped off the bed and pulled my jeans on. "Bathroom break. I'll be back," I said.

She stared at me, bemused. "I know."

I glanced at her, curious at her tone, but she was checking her nails. As I left the room, a door opened down the hall, and Murdock stepped out. We both stopped short, glancing back and forth as if looking for an escape. "What the hell are you doing here?" I asked.

He closed the door behind him and slipped his hands in his pockets. "I know people on the force who aren't happy with the side we're on."

"Were you one of my secret bodyguards all this time?" I asked.

He frowned. "If there's one thing that never changes about you, Connor, it is the crazy that comes out of your mouth."

"Seriously, Leo. Eagan said all my partners knew," I said.

He shook his head. "I have no idea what you're talking about."

A strange sense of relief settled over me. "So, all this time we've been friends, it's been because we're friends?"

"I'm still not getting what you're talking about, but I'll say, yeah, we were friends," he said.

"Were?" I asked.

He studied his feet. "Why are you doing this?"

"Because I've been wondering if everyone who's saved my life did it because some vision told them it was necessary," I said.

He narrowed his eyes at me, a little confusion and a little annoyed. "I'm not even going to respond to that."

I grinned. "Actually, that's the perfect response. Thanks. Are you okay?"

"It is what it is."

"I'm sorry," I said.

Murdock tilted his head. "I know. I still don't blame you. That doesn't mean being around you is easy."

"I get that. I'm glad you're here, though," I said.

"And I'm glad you're alive," he said.

I held my hand out, and he shook it.

"Let's go take down a fairy queen," I said.

46

Dawn came according to the clock, but a darkness lay over the city. The sky rippled with curtains of essence, dark indigos and maroons shifting and swirling like a painting by a madman. Ceridwen and I stood on top of the Hancock Tower, sixty stories above the city. The building was the tallest in New England and gave us a view unlike any other. To the east, the ruined Celtic fleet filled the inner harbor, hundreds of broken ships rising and falling on the water's whitecapped surface. The Weird smoked with fire, dozens of plumes that obscured the horizon. Amid the gloom, essence burned with dazzling brilliance over City Hall Plaza, where Maeve had made her joint headquarters with the human civilian forces.

"Well, this is a bit daunting," I said.

Joe popped in and circled, trying to control his flight in the buffeting winds. He gave up and settled himself among some utility conduits. "Did I ever tell you about the time I was at a party up here, and we accidentally blew out a bunch of windows in the building?"

"I remember seeing pictures of that when I was a kid," I said.

He grinned. "Good times."

From our vantage point, subtle changes rippled through the streets, a shifting of essence signatures. Eorla was moving some of her people around as a distraction while her main force gathered in the tunnels beneath the city. Out by the Tangle, the Dead made their own strategic feints toward downtown. Maeve no doubt had her own sentries in place, but I hoped the key movements would be lost in the mix.

"Everyone's in place," Ceridwen said.

"Remember what I said: Don't be tempted to stay in any one spot. As soon as you use the spear, she will sense it," I said.

Her smile was grim. "I am not a novice at this business, Grey."

I grinned at her. "It's nerves, Ceridwen. Trust me. I know what you're capable of. I've been on the business end of the spear when you've had it."

She pulled her helm on, and the Hunter glamour settled over her. If nothing else, she was going to scare the hell out of whoever saw her. She held out her hand. *"Ithbar,"* she said.

The essence image of the spear in my mind flashed. The spear appeared in her hand and an instant later, Ceridwen was gone. In the distance to the southeast, a brilliant burst lit the sky over Castle Island in Southie. A thunderclap rolled through the air, and the sky above the old fort rippled with an explosion of light. Dark figures dropped through the air, huge unshapely bodies that landed on the island and in the water.

"Ick. Was that supposed to happen?" Joe asked.

"It's a gamble. If we stop Maeve, we'll have to deal with the Fomorians running loose. If we don't stop her, there's not going to be much left around here anyway," I said.

On cue, explosions rocked the nearby Thomson Park, the ancient oaks that formed the Boston druid grove went up in flames. Despite the sacred nature of the grove, it could be used as a power source for Maeve's archdruids. The damage was regrettable—especially for druids—but necessary for the city's defense.

"Callin always liked setting things on fire," Joe said.

I glanced down at him. "You're strolling down memory lane today."

"Am I? It's all the same. Yesterday is today is tomorrow. One war is the same as another a hundred years later," he said.

The passions of the day meant little to the survivors of tomorrow. We fought over land and power. Win or lose, the grievances remained and festered. Today, Maeve was losing her mind, but I wondered if I was any different. What I intended to do had a smaller chance of success than Maeve's goal, but a higher chance of saving lives. After the smoke cleared and the bodies were counted, I doubted anyone would care who'd had the better motive.

As hoped, Maeve's forces reacted to the distractions. A wave of Dananns swept up from the harbor ships and made for Castle Island. A smaller force went south toward the fort. They were not going to like what they found. The Fomorians had decimated the Dananns long ago. They weren't going to be in a forgiving mood for being locked in their prison for centuries.

From the west side of the roof, another wave of essence blew out in Forest Hills. The vast cemetery there had been the site of another battle. Igniting essence over it would destabilize the area and force Maeve's forces to the ground. With a blast of wind, Ceridwen appeared back at my side. "As predicted, she retrieved the spear."

A host of Dananns rose from the Park Plaza Hotel. They gathered in a V-formation, speeding over our heads across the sky. "And there goes the second wave to Forest Hills. Eorla should be in position. Shall we proceed?" Ceridwen asked.

"I still don't know what you're planning, Ceridwen. I can't plan for contingencies if you don't tell me," I said.

The glamour obscured her face, but I could hear the

amusement in her voice. "Success at chess is difficult with only a queen, Connor Grey."

I grinned. I bet myself that Ceridwen could do it. "It's time then," I said.

She rose and slipped her hands into the loops on the back of my jumpsuit. With no effort, we soared into the sky, then dropped toward the Common. Ceridwen coasted low, bringing me in from the western side of the park. Maeve had people there, but they were few. Her main forces were in Park Square and heading north toward the Consortium consulate. A few potshots of essence sparkled in the air as we passed, but they seemed to come from people more startled than intent on murder. If only Maeve weren't so intent.

Ceridwen dropped me next to the pillar on the hill in the Common. Joe swirled in around us, his sword out, his face set.

"You are sure I should leave you?" Ceridwen asked.

"I'm sure. You'll know when to come back," I said.

She held her hand out. "May the gods speak favor when you die."

I shook. "May the Ways open to all your paths."

Ceridwen glided off through the air toward the Weird. I looked up at Joe. "I need you to leave, Joe. I want to have as few variables as possible for this part."

"I don't know what variables are, but if they're anything like marbles, I think you don't have enough," he said.

I pointed into the sky, smiling to soften my request. "Go."

He pulled a long face, like a chastised child. "You always send me away."

"And you always come back," I said. He tapped the flat of his sword against his forehead and winked before vanishing.

I trailed around the pillar, letting my hand rub against the cold granite. The essence that burned in the stone flared at my touch. When I sealed the Way into TirNaNog, the pillar had appeared, the last remnant of the Land of the

Dead. I thought it was only that, a stone pillar testament to my destruction. And it was. But it was something I hadn't realized or anticipated then. I couldn't have because I didn't remember until now.

It was the pillar of TirNaNog, but over time, as the gargoyles gathered around it, as the energies of the blocked Ways built within it, it became something more, something vital. It wasn't just a stone pillar anymore or the pillar of TirNaNog. It was also the Irminsul of the Teutonic tribes, and the standing stones of Carnac and Salisbury Plain, and all the stone pillars that marked the way to all the realms. It was the ash of the Alfheim, the oak of the Aes Sidhe. The pillar had become a metaphor like so many other things in my life, a metaphor for something that mere words could not contain, a connection to the Wheel of the World unlike any other. The gargoyles knew and had waited, drawn to the promise and threat of its power.

Meryl trudged up the slope. She had two cups in her hands and her giant bag over her shoulder. Our eyes met when she glanced up, and we both smiled. She wore knee-high boots with thick silver buckles and a black body stocking under her leather jacket. She had dyed her hair gray.

She handed me one of the cups. "I brought you coffee. I've got Guinness in my bag for later."

We tapped cups. "Thanks," I said.

She blew at the hot steam rising from her cup. "There is going to be a later, right? I mean, I paid for the beers this time."

I arched my eyebrows. "You know the answer to that."

"Heh, thought I'd ask in case you had any revelations," she said.

Heydan was standing next to us. One moment he wasn't there, the next he was. He wasn't thirty feet tall any longer like he had been on the roof of Yggy's earlier, but his normal eight. He seemed the most logical choice to go with Meryl. I liked the symmetry of it—male and female, Celt and Teut. Their personalities balanced each other, too. Plus, they liked each other. "Well met," he said.

I looked at Meryl. "You don't have to do this."

She took my cup, placed it next to hers on the ground, and wrapped her arms around me. "How often does a girl maybe, possibly, sorta, kinda get the chance to start the universe over if her boyfriend screws up?"

"We don't know it will work. You might die," I said.

"You don't know if what you're about to do will work either, but you're still going to try it. You might die," she said.

I gazed down at her face. "How the hell did this happen to us of all people?"

She grinned. "Thank the fucking Wheel of the World, babe."

I kissed her on the top of the head. "I love you, Meryl Dian."

She took my head in her hands and kissed me long and hard on the lips. "I love you, Connor Grey."

She stepped back and held her hand out to Heydan. "Ready, big guy?"

His massive hand closed over hers. Heydan stared down at me, his eyes aglow with white light. He nodded once, then faced the stone. As one, they stepped toward the pillar and vanished. I felt them for a moment as their body signatures danced across the surface of the granite, then they slipped away toward a place I hoped existed, a place the pillar touched, deep inside the Gap.

The place of the beginning that was the end of all things.

47

I was alone.

My stomach clenched with doubt as I rested my forehead against the pillar. I hoped I was doing the right thing and I had not sent the woman I loved to her death. That she vanished gave me hope that I was right. The pillar reached deep into the Wheel of the World. Maeve hadn't lied. The source was here. The pillar touched it. I sensed it.

I lifted my head and searched among the gargoyles. My gaze settled on a little one, a short man, proudly displaying his oversized nakedness. A single horn grew from his forehead. He stared at me with sightless stone eyes. I knew he'd be there.

"Hey, Virgil," I said.

His voice rasped across my mind like sandpaper. *Home,* he said.

I placed my hand on the pillar and closed my eyes. Maeve would sense what I was about to do. With luck, she would be delayed as she regrouped her forces. If I timed it right, at least some of this would end well, and I could repay a debt.

I gasped as essence from the stone coursed through my body like liquid fire. I held out my other hand and released waves of white lightning that danced among the gargoyles, jumping from one to the next. The light merged, became layered streams that revolved around the pillar. Faster and faster they spun, forming a swirling vortex with the pillar at the center

The gargoyles shuddered, stone coming alive with movement, stone flowing across the ground amid rivers of faint blue light. The blue light blossomed from the gargoyles like flower petals and danced in counterpoint to the white essence. Voices rose, cheers of joy and cries of anguish, as the gargoyles slumped and lost their shapes. The river of stone curved with the heat of the passage of light, lapping the pillar in a solid circle. The essence light revolved, blue and white, until the stone that was the gargoyles became a flat ring on the ground

I lifted my hand palm upward, chanting the ancient hymn I had invoked so long ago. The ground shook as the stone rose, a massive ring borne on yet more massive columns. A great wind came up as lightning filled the sky. I dropped my hands to my sides, breathing air crisp with the spark of electricity. The white essence light settled onto the stone, became one with it, infused it with a power that I had feared had been lost to the World. The stone ring stood around the pillar, its megalithic arches framing the swirling of the blue essence outside the circle.

Unbound from the gargoyles, the blue essence fragmented into orbs that stretched and touched the ground. I sang a song of unity, of earth and air that formed living shape. Earth swirled upward, first in a few places, then dozens, then hundreds, maybe thousands of columns of fecund earth. It wasn't creation, but re-creation, a binding of souls to the material world, to become what they once were.

The columns of earth coalesced, sprouting limbs and heads. Bodies formed, sunburned skins tattooed with lines and circles of blue woad. Clear-eyed men and strong-faced women stared at me through the arches, the blue essence settling within them. They raised their arms, raised high shields and spears and swords, and let out a great shout that echoed with a resounding roar. The humans of Faerie stood restored, alive and unbowed.

A man entered the ring, stout with a drape of cloth over his shoulder belted at the waist. He planted his spear on the ground between us, his deep eyes wary beneath a wide brow pitted with blue swirls.

"My lord has magicked his face, but I still see his nature," he said.

"Good to see you, too, Virgil," I said.

He cocked his head. "Does my lord not recognize me?"

"I am no one's lord now, Cruth. Call me Connor," I said.

His gaze went to my sword, considering, probably wondering how someone holding such a weapon could not be a lord in his world. We weren't in his world anymore, though. I was Connor now.

"We have waited as you asked," he said.

My memory flashed back a century, to a wide plain filled with men and women marching. I remembered fearing that the humans would be helpless in the face of what was to come, powerless against the onslaught of Maeve's madness, armed with little more than their courage. I remembered thinking I did not want to see them die for a madwoman's lust for power. I remembered thinking I could save them, protect them from her gaze, hiding their life force in gargoyle-shaped stone. I was wrong. I delayed their fate. The Wheel of the World turns as It will, no matter the hopes of men and women.

"The battle is to be joined, Cruth. I don't know if I can stop the High Queen's slaughter. I cannot save anyone, but I can give you a chance to save yourself," I said.

"The People of the Way have never doubted your heart," he said.

"You are in a place other than you knew. The humans here are confused. They have great power, but I do not think they will use it against the People of the Way. I need you to keep them from this henge until the matter is settled.

I will try to save as many as I can. Will the People of the Way lend me their courage?"

He clenched his fist. "We shall be as bones, bones of the earth, steadfast and eternal," he said.

"I promise I will try," I said.

"We hear and hope," he said.

Cruth withdrew from the henge, shouting to his people. They picked up his call, their voices rising in answer, beating spears against rough shields. The call spread out from the henge, and as one the humans of Faerie marched, their faces set with determination and wonder as National Guard tanks appeared in the surrounding streets. They set their backs to me and their spears to the ground, chanting a war cry of protection. I hoped too many of them didn't get shot.

As they receded down the hill, a gap among them traveled up through the crowd, like a ship cutting a wave through turbulent seas. Three people appeared in the path, walking side by side. I smiled with gratitude and regret as Dylan, Callin, and Murdock entered the stone circle.

"You didn't have to come, Dylan," I said.

He shrugged, no longer wearing the Rand glamour but still in his uniform. "I didn't have to do a lot of things, Con, but I always had your back."

Callin looked tired but not weak. His left arm was bound across his chest with bandages, but his head was bare. A thick scar ran across his forehead. "What are you doing out of the hospital, Cal?" I asked.

He grinned, that shit-eating grin that charmed and infuriated. "I heard my little bro picked himself a fight. You didn't think I'd sit that out, did you?"

"I hoped you would," I said.

He scratched at his head. "Yeah, well, I never did live up to your expectations."

A bubble of emotion formed in my chest. I didn't want to let it break free. With two long strides, I had my arms wrapped around my brother. Even with his one arm, he had a grip like a steel vise. He smelled of wood soot and essence-fire. I kissed him on the side of his neck and whispered in his ear. "You're the greatest druid in the whole world, big bro."

He pushed me away, his eyes glassy as he surveyed the Common. "A drink would come in handy about now."

Murdock and I stared at each other. I didn't know what to say. After all this time, after everything that had happened, this man stood by my side. He didn't do it because some crazy dwarf convinced him. He didn't do it because he was using me as part of some crazy scheme. He did it because he thought it was right. When I was at the worst point in my life, he saw something in me that no one else did, something that made him my friend. I couldn't explain it. I doubted he could. All I knew was that I had never met anyone who deserved my gratitude more than he did. I held my hand out, and he took it.

A light formed in the sky over downtown, a glow that flickered with rage and omen. A deep rumble rolled through the air. The essence light downtown rippled and brightened, moving toward the Common. Pink essence flashed in front of me, and Joe somersaulted out of it, naked as the day he was born.

"Did I miss the party?" he asked.

"It's about to start," I said.

48

The sky burst across the eastern horizon, a radiant glow that trembled against my skin. Rank upon rank of Dananns filled the air, row upon row of vibrant wings humming with power. A streak of white at their head marked the vanguard of the High Queen's Fianna and, at their center, the fierce silver star of Maeve herself.

They swept into the sky, higher and higher, an astounding host of fey. Maeve had emptied Tara—and Germany and France and everywhere else—and brought all her forces here, to this place, for her final victory.

Joe laughed nervously beside me. "I don't think we have enough cups for all these guests."

"We'll have to manage," I said.

The earth trembled. In the empty space between the stone circle and ranks of the People of the Way, the ground heaved like waves. Cracks appeared, dirt spewing upward as the vibrations radiated outward. A crevasse opened, deep and lit with green light. Something large moved within it, swelling up from the depths. A misshapen head appeared, wide and grim, on a long neck. The troll planted his enormous hands on the ground and hauled himself up beneath the dark sky.

Behind him, the crevasse boiled with more essence, a strange stew of colors that pulsed with a regular rhythm. More figures scrambled out of the hidden tunnels beneath the Common. A cloud of green light blossomed, and Eorla rose from the earth, a shining emerald star. The solitaries gathered beneath her, then spread along the field with fire in their eyes.

"She does know how to make an entrance," Dylan said.

"So does Bastian," I said.

On buildings around the Common, elven archers appeared, on hotels and apartments and the towering high-rises in the Back Bay. The rooflines blazed with the green of ready elf-shot pointed at the sky. I didn't think he'd come. I thought he'd wait it out, let the Celts destroy each other and pick over the leftovers. Instead, he had gathered the Alfheim in the city and joined the stand against Maeve.

It wasn't enough. Maeve had us outnumbered and outgunned. We were a slaughter waiting to happen. I had nothing more than a hope and a prayer that I would be able to stop it.

The front edge of the Dananns dipped as the lead warriors descended. The Fianna and archdruids landed, Brion Mal at their head, and formed a loose arc facing me. Behind him, Keeva brought down the Boston Guildhouse troops. Her stoic look told me she knew her coming betrayal would do little to stop the carnage.

With her court in full array, Maeve descended, her wings rippling with swirls of gold and silver. She wore her helm, black leather and silver filigree, and held her scepter of office. She landed several feet away, confident and calm. She pointed the scepter at the ground. "Submit," she said.

I tilted my head and gave her a lopsided smile. "A hundred years ago, I refused that order, Maeve. Nothing's changed."

"Your memory has returned?" she asked.

I met her eyes, knowing she would see the depth of

knowledge there, the glitter of an Old One. "And I remember telling you how certain treasures could accomplish your goal if they could be found."

"You didn't have the power to stop me then. You don't have it now," she said.

I tightened my grip on the sword, the faith stone burning on the blade. I held my other hand out, and the spear materialized. "I didn't have these then," I said.

With a dismissive gesture, she thrust her hand out. The spear shuddered in my hand but stayed. The four treasures together in my hands gave me the power to resist hers. The confidence on Maeve's face faltered. "I have only to give the word, and my forces will decimate your collection of traitors. If you keep the spear, their blood will be on your hands, not mine."

I shook my head. "You're going to kill them all anyway, Maeve. Do you think I've learned nothing about you? Why do you think I hid the humans from you? When they abandoned you in Faerie, you were going to kill them all. I remember now. Slaughter is your only solution to opposition."

Her attention lifted over my head. I hesitated, feeling a little silly that she might be pulling the look-behind-you trick, then turned to follow her gaze. Out of the west, the sky burned blue, blue like indigo, like the deepest well of the ocean. Like the Dead. At their head, Ceridwen rode the dream mare on its cloud of smoke and embers. Her red cape flared in the wind of her passage, her great antlered helm warning everyone from the path of the Hunter of the Dead. And the Dead followed after her, the Dead of the ages, elf and fairy, dwarf and druid, all adversaries in life, now united in death.

The People of the Way withdrew, opening their formation as the Hunter came through. Ceridwen and her followers took up position, their smaller numbers in the face of the Danann host made up for by the fear they instilled in the people around them.

Ceridwen reined in the dream mare next to me. Maeve narrowed her eyes, a sensing pulse emanating from her face. Ceridwen surprised her by thrusting the scan back with her hand.

"I have met the King of the Dead. You are not the true Hunter," Maeve said.

"No, I am not he, but I am a hunter who has found her prey," Ceridwen said. She removed her helm, letting her thick red braids fall to her waist, as she dismounted. The Dananns behind Maeve shifted in place, surprised to see one of their own come back from the Dead.

I felt a tug as Ceridwen called the spear with a mental command. Curious, I let it go. The spear hovered through the air and into her grasp. She thrust her arm up. "I hold the Spear of Truth. I am Ceridwen, underQueen of the Seelie Court. I was betrayed into my death at the order of the High Queen."

Brion Mal stepped forward, anger sending flashes of red swirling through his wings. "What druid trick is this?"

Lift up your sword, macGrey. Show them the stone, Ceridwen sent. Still unsure as to her plan, I lifted the sword. The faith stone pulsed, a radiant haze that wafted into the sky and gave strength to her words.

Ceridwen approached Mal. My breath caught as the two faced each other, the same resolute brow, keen gaze, and royal bearing. "This is no trick, my liege. My blessing is upon this man. Avenge your daughter for the Seelie Court. Show the High Queen the same mercy she showed me," Ceridwen said. As she spoke, the carnelian ring she had given me flashed on my sword hand.

Mal looked like he was about to explode. "Ceridwen? Is it truly your shade, daughter?" Mal said.

"Aye, Father," she said.

An astonished murmur ran through the assembled Dananns. The air rippled with sendings as Mal stalked toward Maeve. She didn't retreat before him but held her scepter higher for all to see. "We are the High Queen. We are the Seelie Court. Do not believe this traitor's trickery. Ceridwen underQueen died at his hand."

Mal raised the hilt of his sword to his face, pointing the blade upward. A red burst of essence flashed on his own hand, revealing a ring. The ring on my finger responded by flaring brighter. They were matched. "You lie, Maeve," he said. "This man holds the blessing of Clan Mal in his hand. You have broken faith with your own people. You have denied yourself the right to our arms at your side."

He lifted his sword straight up and rose in the air. Sendings vibrated in the air as Mal sent orders out to his followers. The Fianna lifted into the air after him. Bank after bank of Dananns disengaged from formation and flew off toward the sea.

Keeva brought down the Guildhouse contingent and arrayed them behind me. In a flash of white light, Manus ap Eagan appeared next to Keeva. He didn't appear triumphant, but saddened. "It pains me that you lost your way, Maeve. Abdicate, and this is over."

Maeve held her hand toward him, palm outward. "I name you traitor to the crown, Manus ap Eagan, and strip you of all your rights, titles, and privileges."

"The crown is no longer yours," he replied.

Confusion broke out among the remaining Dananns as more joined the departing fey. Many of them. Not all. Maeve still controlled considerable forces of her own.

Ceridwen held the High Queen in a cold, steady gaze. "How does it feel to be abandoned in your time of need, Maeve? You shall suffer what I have suffered."

Maeve pursed her lips. "So be it, Ceridwen. I do not fear the consequences. Death has not stopped your revenge. It will not stop mine."

Ceridwen moved closer, smiling now. She pointed the spear at Maeve. "Do not be so sure, betrayer. TirNaNog is no more. Guard your life well. The Land beyond the gate no longer waits for you."

Ceridwen mounted the dream mare and tossed me the spear. "Your move," she said. With one more look at Maeve, she snapped the reins and rejoined the Dead.

Unmoved, Maeve returned her attention to me. "The power of Audhumla will be mine regardless. Once released, you will be lost in the maelstrom, and I will pluck the tools from your corpse."

"I guess that's what's you're going to have to do, Maeve. I will fight you to my dying breath," I said.

"Then you will die," she said.

Dylan and Callin moved in front of me, their shields shimmering as they wove a protection wall around me. I hadn't seen Cal in action in years. I had forgotten how good he was. How I could have believed all this time that he had failed his calling humbled me.

"You cannot stop me," she said.

Murdock raised his gun. "A bullet will stop a lot of things."

"Leo . . ." I said.

"She killed my father and my mother. My brother is dead because of her," he said.

"Leo, don't. You can't kill her in cold blood," I said. Dylan and Callin shifted to either side of me, uncertain as they maintained the shield.

"One bullet. I can end this with one bullet," he said.

"It won't end for you. You know you will have to live with it," I said.

"Kill the man behind you, human," Maeve said. "He's the one for you to blame. He made your father bitter. He made your brother go mad. He made your mother a whore, child. End him, and you will end this. I promise you rich reward if you stand by me."

Leo's gun wavered in his hand. He inhaled deeply, then found his resolve again, tightening his grip on the cold steel of his weapon. "Do you know what the Devil is, lady? The master of lies. He makes lies seem like truth. And you know what faith is? The way to see through lies."

Leo lowered his weapon. "I will defend him against you. I will kill you if I have to, but you won't make me a murderer."

I gripped his shoulder, more proud of him than I thought I'd ever been of anyone. I flattered myself thinking Murdock stood by me. His faith made him stand by truth. I happened to be on the same path and was glad of it.

Maeve tilted her head, a strong sending permeating the

air. A shout went up from the Dananns who had not abandoned her, and they descended. An answering cry went up from the ground, and essence raged as the battle was joined. With her hands spread wide, Maeve released a bolt of essence. When it struck the pillar, the granite burned white with power. The ground trembled as the pillar rose, stretching taller. "I have touched the source and set it free at last. You cannot stop it," she said.

The spear flared, burning in my hand, a molten sliver of the Wheel of the World. An odd sensation of joy mixed with sorrow came over me. "I never said I wanted to."

I sheathed my sword and took the stone bowl out of my jacket. It had come alive with light, static dancing in the recess. I glanced at Maeve, then slammed the base of the bowl against the pillar, holding it against the stone. Lifting the spear, I shoved it into the recess of the bowl. It bored into the granite as if it were clay. I convulsed as essence coursed into me through the conduit I had made, the purity of essence that nurtured all things, the source, Audhumla, the sacred being that gave life. I stretched out my hand. Surprised, Maeve backed away.

"Moo, bitch."

Essence exploded out of me and hit her in flames of white. It flung her into the sky, and she soared upward, a rag doll flailing in a tangle of smoke and tattered wings. She burned across the sky, trailing smoke and essence. And

everything

went

white

49

White.

I remember this place. I tumble through the white, living and dying with the fall. There is no up here or down, no east or west, north or south. All of it is one. I focus my thoughts, calm the initial panic of arriving, and the falling slows.

Everything is white. It always is here. White is everything.

I stop falling. Whiteness fills my vision with nothing to break the relentlessness of it. Above me, the white simply is, as if the air itself is color. Or no color. As if nothing else exists except the white. I hang limp in the air, as if there is no air, no gravity.

I stare into a nothingness of white. I am here again. Around me, I see shadows of light flickering in the depths of the white, white-on-white shadows that spin and whirl, roll and stop, taunting me with patterns that disintegrate as they take shape.

And then they take shape.

Two vast shadows resolve out of the white. They move toward me, or I toward them. One is a man, taller, barrel-chested, his hair flows in waves, his beard a cascade. The other is a woman, curved, her hair black as a raven's wing, and her face—Danu's blood, her face—Danu's . . .

I shudder. I do not believe in gods and goddesses. I do not seek the supernatural to explain the unexplained. And yet . . . my body goes weak with understanding. I do not know if they are what they seem, but I know who she is, and I tremble with her presence.

"You are here and here and here," she says.

"Lady, tell me what to do," I say.

The man laughs a bass tone that fills me with awe and joy. "Tell him, Mother. Tell us."

She looks at him. I cannot see her face for the radiance of it. "The Wheel of the World turns as It will."

He laughs and laughs. "You've interfered, Mother. I saw it. I remember this man."

"I acted. I did not guide," she said.

"Who is this man, Mother? I see him and see him and see him."

"You see the Ways, my son. You walk the Ways and see all."

The joy slips on his face, a troubled crease to his massive brow. "The Ways have closed, Mother. I see him, but I do not see all."

"Not all of them, my son. Not all. As long as one Way remains, the Wheel turns," she says.

He cocks his head as he looks at me, the colors in his eyes shifting like the sea in a storm. "Have you ever met someone and felt like you've known him forever?" he asks.

"No," I say.

He laughs, with a deep rumble in his wide chest.

"Liar," he says. "Liar."

"I have met several who are all the same. I think they're you," I say.

"True," he says. "True."

"Have I died?" I ask.

"Have you lived?" he asks, and roars with laughter like the sound of time out of time.

She reaches out to me, her hands aglow. She reaches out to me and holds my face. "You live and die, and the Wheel turns. You strive and toil, and the Wheel turns. You elect and decline, and the Wheel turns."

"Tell me what to do. Please. Tell me what to do," I say.

She kisses me, her lips like light. "Choose," she says.

"Change," he says.

And they are gone. They are there and not there.

I am alone.

I fall into the white. I fall and fall, and I see shadows of white-on-white. The white grows white. A shape takes shape. A circle forms and a spire. The spire begins in the white and ends in it. The circle contains it yet cannot hold it.

I see the shape, and the shape is a circle. It grows dark white. Still white. White stone. Granite. It is a stone ring of infinite doors, a circle of many Ways. It is a stone circle with a standing center stone.

I made that. I made it with my mind and my heart. It holds the power of all, all is one, like a wheel, and I laugh. Like the Wheel of the World.

I reach out and gather it in my hand, feel its power, its joy, and its sorrow. I can fix this. I can change this. I can make it right. I can make it all, and everything in it will be mine. I can make it right. The power surges into me, surges and flows and does not stop. It is more than everything. I can become one with it and make it mine. It surges and flows, and it is infinite. And . . .

It is too much.

I pause. The power pauses. I feel it waiting, ready to surge through me with no end. It is too much. Too much for me. Too much for anyone. That is its strength and its flaw. It cannot be contained. It cannot be free. It is too much for anyone. It needs everyone. I cannot hold it. I do not want it. I want a choice. I want change. To turn, the Wheel of the World must have choice and change, and everything in It—everyone—must choose and change as they will so that It may turn.

I gather what is in me and thrust it back, let the power

surge and flow into the ring of stone. It surges and flows. It opens the Ways. All the Ways open, and the Wheel turns.

And I fall in ecstasy and sorrow for what is and always is. Change is change. It is not Light. It is not Dark.

It is Grey.

50

I woke up on the ground, facing the sky and smelling burning flesh. Smoke tumbled across the Common, thick, acrid billows flickering with essence and fire and death. Bodies surrounded me, dozens, maybe hundreds. I pulled myself up and leaned against the pillar.

My sword lay on the ground, scorched black on the blade. The faith stone was gone. I no longer sensed it anywhere. The sword shifted in my hand when I picked it up and went cold.

I heard sobbing. I searched through the stone ring, going from opening to opening, bodies spread across scorched grass. Here and there, essence signatures glimmered. They weren't all dead, some, but not all. The sobbing grew louder. I went through a gate in the stone ring and stopped in my tracks.

Kevin Murdock knelt on the ground. He rocked in place, his eyes squeezed shut as sobs wracked his body. Leo lay next to him on the ground, soot-stained and bloodied. I staggered forward, my heart pounding in my chest.

"Kevin . . ." I said.

He jerked his head up at the sound of my voice. His eyes blazed with essence when he saw me. "Get away from him," he screamed.

My shield kicked on, but the force of Kevin's blast hurtled me backwards. I slammed into the stone ring, screaming as the force of it cracked ribs and broke my leg. I fell to the ground, writhing.

Dazed, I lifted my face from the dirt. My sensing ability flickered on and off. I saw something behind Kevin, a subtle glow of a body signature in Leo's chest. "Not dead," I slurred.

Kevin came toward me, tears streaming down his face, essence smoking off his hands. "Not dead? Not dead? Look around you. *They're all dead.*"

He fired. My body shield rattled around me, and I flopped onto my back. "Kevin, listen . . ."

He thrust his hand out. "You did this. You killed them. You killed everyone."

I dragged myself backwards as he fired again. My shield absorbed the shock but crushed me against the stone ring. I tried to tap essence from the ground, but my body was spent. I laughed in futility at the irony. I had my abilities back but no more strength to use them than if I had none at all.

"You think this is *funny*?" Kevin screamed.

He was almost on top of me when he fired again. My head snapped to the side, my shield crushing my cheekbone. My vision swam as the shield failed. I clutched the ground, trying to pull strength from the raw earth, but I was too weak.

Kevin reared back and punched me. I held my arm up to block the blow too late, spots flashing in my left eye. I dropped my hands to my sides, staring up at him. "You don't understand," I mumbled.

"I don't," he said.

He held his palm up to my face. I watched the essence coalesce, loops and swirls of white growing on his palm. I closed my eyes, trying to push away, pushing against the ground, but I was against a stone gate of the henge, with no room to maneuver. My hand fell on something cold and hard. I closed my fist around it, felt the heft of the blade as I gripped my sword. With the last of my strength, I thrust it up.

Kevin's jaw fell open in shock as he hunched forward. His head shuddered as he fought the pain, his hands clawing the air in front of him. Blood gushed over my hand as Kevin stared down in disbelief at the sword buried in his abdomen. He lifted his face, and his expression crumbled into rage. Essence ignited in his hands. I pushed the sword in deeper, and he collapsed over me, his last bolt of essence searing into my chest. Something tore inside, something important that pulled away, and my legs went numb.

I wrapped my arms around him, burying my face in his chest, and wept until I passed out.

Cold woke me. I stared across the remains of the Common. People roamed among the bodies, their faces slack with horror. The westering sun cast the field red with light that threw long dark shadows. Kevin lay on his back beside me, my sword rising from his body like a cross. As I pulled it free, Joe fluttered up from my side. I didn't even know he was there.

"I came too late," he said.

The sword shivered and shrank in my hand. The essence drained out of it, and it went cold. I struggled to smile. "You came, Joe. That's all that matters."

He settled on the ground. "I can't find anyone. The world keeps changing."

"It's okay. It'll settle down," I said. I held the dagger out. "Do me a favor and take this to Briallen."

He took the dagger. It was almost as long as he was tall. "I shouldn't leave you. I'll keep calling for someone."

"Do this for me first, Joe. I promised her," I said.

His lip trembled. He nodded and winked out. I closed my eyes.

I opened my eyes. Joe sat on my thigh, the dagger across his lap. The setting sun lit his vacant stare with a harsh light.

"What happened?" I asked.

He didn't look at me. "She shielded her house and wouldn't answer my call."

"Bring it back, Joe. You have to do it for me before it's too late," I said.

He looked at me with a world of hurt. "Do I have to?"

"Yeah, Joe, you do," I said.

He bowed his head and disappeared. I closed my eyes.

I opened my eyes. Joe lay curled against my chest, his wings folded flat, his essence light dimmed.

"What happened?" I asked.

He spoke without moving. "I called her again, but she didn't answer. I flew over the house and looked in the backyard. It was empty. Water was flowing in the fountain. I dropped the dagger, and it pierced the shield barrier and landed in the water. A mist rose, and I thought I saw someone moving in it. I heard a wail of grief that keened higher and higher, until it broke my heart. The mist disappeared, and the fountain was empty."

I rested my hand on him and closed my eyes.

"Thanks, buddy. You're the best."

Epilogue

The wind blew bitter cold off the ocean as Briallen verch Gwyll ab Gwyll followed the porters. She cinched the rope on her black alb and gathered her cloak around her. The porters walked the dirt path, worn hard with age and use, as it sloped downward to the beach. Briallen studied the ground in front of her, the wooden bier in the upper edge of her sight. She thought of nothing in particular—the sound of the wind through the grass, the cry of the seabirds. She had walked the path before.

The porters reached the beach, and their gait slowed against the heavy sand. They took care to keep the bier level and not jostle the body. Briallen did look up then, staring into the distance ahead. The sky was flat white around her as it always was on the beach.

They walked beneath a sunless sky down the endless beach. There was no telling how far to walk. It was different every time. The strand of the shore wound off into the haze. It might never end, she thought. Places like the beach were like that.

A dark spot appeared on the sand ahead, beside the path

the porters took. That was different. Briallen had never seen it before and was more surprised as they drew closer. The spot resolved into a figure bundled in black, sitting on the sand. The porters did not pause as they passed. They knew their place and kept walking.

Briallen paused. The huddled shape lifted its head and threw back a hood. Meryl Dian stared after the bier. Tears streamed down her face as the porters meandered above the foam of the tide.

"I loved him," she said. "I didn't mean to, but I loved him this time."

Briallen held her hand out, and Meryl took it. Like a mother, she gathered the smaller woman into her arms and held her to her breast. "Do not lament love. It has a power beyond even the Wheel of the World."

They stood together as the porters walked on. There was world enough and time on the beach. Meryl's tears subsided, and Briallen released her. They followed after the bier, first Briallen, then Meryl. Though they made no effort, they reached the porters without speed.

Ahead three figures appeared, three woman in black albs. They stood in a row along the beach, barring the way. The porters did not vary their pace, did not quicken with the end of their journey in sight, but walked until they reached a barge in the surf. With care, they lowered the bier and stepped away. Meryl hung back as the three women joined Briallen on the barge, two to each side of the body.

Briallen looked up as a bird cried in the wind, a crow, lost in the flat white of the sky. She looked at the woman across from her and nodded. The woman lifted her hood and settled it back on her shoulders, her expression blank. Briallen exhaled, a coil of essence rolling from her lips, settling over the woman's face.

Keeva macNeve lifted her head, startled. She stared at Briallen, then down at the body. She pressed her lips together in regret and resignation. "I gave him Challenge," she said. "I gave him cause to thrive and rise above his ability. I gave him trial and tribulation. I failed him."

Briallen looked at the woman beside her and nodded. She pushed back her hood. Briallen exhaled, and awareness came into Maeve's gaze. Expressionless, she stared at the body, showing no emotion. "I gave him Ambition," she said. "I gave him cause to challenge himself and rise above the world. I gave him reason for being. I failed him."

Briallen looked at the third woman and hesitated, then nodded. She exhaled as the woman released her hood. Ceridwen gasped as she stared at the body. "I gave him . . ." Uncertain, she looked up at Briallen. Briallen arched her eyebrow and nodded again. Ceridwen released a shuddering breath, collecting her thoughts, then smiled with sadness. "I gave him Love . . . Love Unrequited. I gave him cause to . . . to find his heart's desire. I gave him strength to hold on to something more precious than I had to offer. I failed him."

Briallen exhaled slowly. "I gave him Wisdom," she said. "I gave him knowledge and hope. I gave him curiosity to seek what he needed to find. I failed him."

Silence fell over them, broken by the shush of the sea and sigh of the wind. The porters approached the barge, leaving Meryl alone on the sand. Briallen held out a hand to her. "You've earned a place here," she said.

Meryl swallowed hard as she walked down the beach. A porter helped her onto the barge. Ceridwen slipped an arm around her waist and pulled her close.

Meryl stared at the body, clenching her fists, fighting back tears. "I gave him Love. I gave him desire and dreams and . . . I gave him my heart and my soul." She lifted a defiant chin, staring Briallen in the eye. "I did not fail him. He did not fail me."

Briallen's lips parted in surprise, but she did not speak. The world had changed. The Wheel of the World had turned. Change was not to be denied. She looked into the distance, to the horizon lost in the mist. "We go now to Avalon, the Isle of Apples, the Isle of Healing. Pray rest, good man, and, perhaps, heal."

The porters pushed the barge into the surf. It drifted

along the beach until a current caught it, and it pulled away from shore. The beach receded. A spot of pink essence flashed in the air above the barge, circled once, and vanished.

The barge faded into the mist of the sea.

Leonard Murdock knelt at the communion rail of St. Brigid's Church. He found what solace he could in the silent room. The resident priest had already heard his confession. He had made his penance. The empty pews behind him gave mute witness to his prayers. He paused with his eyes closed, listening for something that would give meaning to his faith. Sometimes he thought he heard something. Sometimes he thought he only wished it. Either way, he believed it made no difference.

He crossed himself, a faint light lingering on his hands, and exited the church. Janey smiled as he got in the car.

"Let's go get some sushi," he said.

"Sushi? You? What brought that on?" she asked.

He smiled and started the car. "I was thinking change would do me good."

Robin crept along the verge of the forest, arrow notched as he peered from the underbrush. The great trees loomed over him, casting shadows of green gloom. Ahead, the plain of flowered meadow spread, rolling miles of green toward a distant wood. Nothing moved, the Dead quiet or off in some other pocket of TirNaNog.

He relaxed his bow and strolled into the meadow. The flowers let out a sweet perfume as he passed, rising up from the crush of his foot. He hiked to the top of a low rise and took in the view.

Near the horizon, something dark moved in the grass. Robin chewed on his lip, debating whether to retreat to the forest or continue on. He didn't feel like fighting today or getting killed again. The dark spot drew closer, running low to the ground. It became an animal shape, not a person, but no less worrisome. Robin was about to retreat when he recognized the animal.

The black dog bounded and leaped in the grass, making straight for him. Robin had nothing to fear from it—he was already dead—but the Cu Sith still liked to kill for sport in the Land of the Dead. Robin notched his arrow, more to threaten than anything else. Sometimes the Cu Sith didn't want to die that day either and moved on.

The black dog reached the rise. Robin sighted down the length of his arrow, then relaxed. Not all Cu Sith were the same, and this one had taken a liking to him. "Hey, Uno," he called.

The black dog trotted up the hill and stopped. Robin tilted his head, curious as the dog hunched its back, then flowed up on its hind legs. As if a great wind blew over it, its fur drifted away like smoke.

"Hey, stranger," Shay said.

Tears shocked from Robin's eyes. He ran down the hill into Shay's arms.

The woman awoke to the sounds of chickens. She eased into a sitting position, wincing. She was naked and filthy, covered in dirt and shit. Her back screamed with pain as she stood. She twisted her arm, feeling along the skin, touching scabs. Her hand came away speckled with dried blood.

The chickens became agitated, gathering along the fence. She heard the sound of footfalls and huddled against a wall daubed with mud. A large woman appeared, her face beaten red with sun and wind. She wore homespun, poorly done, and was barefoot. She threw some feed over the fence, turned away, then paused. Placing her hands on the rough fence, she leaned over the rail, her suspicious face becoming angry. "You there! What're you doin'?"

The woman cowered on the ground, struggling to find her voice. "N-n-noth . . ."

The larger woman stared, taking in the bare flesh and the dirt, and her face softened somewhat. "What're you called?"

The woman searched the ground as if to find the answer there. Her mind was a jumble. She didn't remember how she had arrived in such a place, didn't understand what had happened to her. A name floated up in her mind, a sound teasing at her memory.

"Mae . . ." She paused. A sound like that. She thought there might be more, but the idea faded away.

The large woman laughed. "May, is it? Now there's a bit of luck. Whether for me or thee remains to be seen. Come along then. I could use a girl. I'll show you were the water ditch is."

Awkwardly, the woman climbed the low fence.

May, she thought. It felt right, but . . . off somehow. She hobbled behind the woman. It was a name as good as any for a girl found in a midden.

Meryl opened her eyes and stared at a night sky. The stars glimmered overhead, placid in their place. She got to her feet, brushing grass off her knees. She twisted a leg, noticing one of her boot buckles had bent. She leaned down and fixed it, stomping her foot to reposition the leather.

When she straightened, the full moon revealed a long field of new grass. Miles in the distance, an electric light glowed on the horizon. She frowned, trying to place a city surrounded by grass but came up empty. She sighed and adjusted her boots again. They weren't for hiking, but she didn't have much choice.

The moon flashed off something in the corner of her eye, and she turned. Puzzled, her eyebrows drew down as she stared at her MINI Cooper sitting on the grass. Then she shrugged and got in.

The radio came on in a roar of static when she started the engine. She played with the tuner, but couldn't find a station. Opening the console, she popped in a CD and turned it up full blast. As she wheeled the car around, something dangled from the rearview mirror. She stopped and hit the dome light. A silver acorn hung on a chain. She grinned and pulled it on over her head.

Hitting the gas again, she bumped over the grass, driving into the night.

I hear voices, soft voices, whispering words in sorrow. I hear the lapping of waves, the soft caress of the deep. I feel the kiss of sea on my skin, the rock of a barge beneath me.

I am who I always am. I am myself. I am here, again, here on my journey. It begins and ends this way. Someday it will not begin again. Someday it will not end again. Not today.

I reflect on my life as I must, sorting through things done well and things not, and things not at all. Deeds of valor and of fear, of strength and weakness, love and hatred. All the deeds of my life parade before me. Undone deeds mock me. Deeds undone mock me more.

The Wheel of the World turns. It widens as It turns, gathering up speed and urgency, filling with life and love, death and sorrow. It fills until It fails, and collapses again, falling into Itself like a gyre. It turns, the Wheel of the World, and we turn with It. *Turning and turning in the widening gyre The falcon cannot hear the falconer; Things fall apart; the centre cannot hold; Mere anarchy is loosed upon the world, The blood-dimmed tide is loosed, and everywhere The ceremony of innocence is drowned; The best lack all conviction, while the worst are full of passionate intensity . . .*

Apple blossoms. I smell apples blossoms.

From *New York Times* Bestselling Author
SIMON R. GREEN

THE BRIDE
WORE BLACK LEATHER

A Novel of the Nightside

Meet John Taylor: Nightside resident, Walker—the new
representative of the Authorities—and soon-to-be husband of one of the Nightside's most feared bounty hunt-
ers. But before he can say, "I do," he has one more case
to solve as a private eye . . . which would be a lot easier
to accomplish if he weren't on the run, from friends and
enemies alike.

And if his bride-to-be weren't out to collect the bounty
on his head . . .

penguin.com

Explore the outer reaches
of imagination—don't miss these authors
of dark fantasy and urban noir who take you
to the edge and beyond . . .

Patricia Briggs	Anne Bishop
Simon R. Green	Marjorie M. Liu
Jim Butcher	Jeanne C. Stein
Kat Richardson	Christopher Golden
Karen Chance	Ilona Andrews
Rachel Caine	Anton Strout

M15G0610